Emmanuel Guibert

ARIOL

Just a Donkey Like You and Me

PAPERCUTZ™

ARIOL Graphic Novels available from PAPERCUTZ™

ARIOL graphic novels are also available digitally wherever e-books are sold.

Emmanuel Guibert
Marc Boutavant
ARIOL
Just a Donkey Like You and Me
PAPERCUTZ

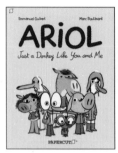

Graphic Novel #1
"Just a Donkey Like You and Me"

Emmanuel Guibert
Marc Boutavant
ARIOL
Thunder Horse
PAPERCUTZ

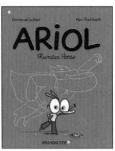

Graphic Novel #2
"Thunder Horse"

Emmanuel Guibert
Marc Boutavant
ARIOL
Happy as a Pig...
PAPERCUTZ

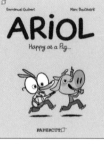

Graphic Novel #3
"Happy as a Pig..."

Emmanuel Guibert
Marc Boutavant
ARIOL
A Beautiful Cow
PAPERCUTZ

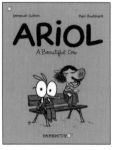

Graphic Novel #4
"A Beautiful Cow"

Emmanuel Guibert
Marc Boutavant
ARIOL
Bizzbilla Hits the Bullseye
PAPERCUTZ

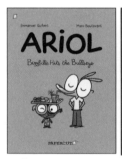

Graphic Novel #5
"Bizzbilla Hits the Bullseye"

Emmanuel Guibert
Marc Boutavant
ARIOL
A Nasty Cat
PAPERCUTZ

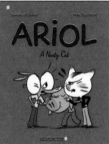

Graphic Novel #6
"A Nasty Cat"

Emmanuel Guibert
Marc Boutavant
ARIOL
Boxed Set of Graphic Novels #1-3
PAPERCUTZ

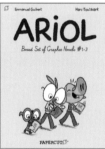

Boxed Set of Graphic Novels #1-3

Emmanuel Guibert
Marc Boutavant
ARIOL
Where's PETULA?
PAPERCUTZ

Coming Soon!
"Where's Petula?"

ARIOL graphic novels are available for $12.99 only in paperback, except for "Where's Petula?" which is $9.99. The ARIOL Boxed Set is $38.99. Available from booksellers everywhere. You can also order online from www.papercutz.com. Or call 1-800-886-1223, Monday through Friday, 9-5 EST. MC, Visa and AmEx accepted. To order by mail, please add $4.00 for postage and handling for first book ordered, $1.00 for each additional book and make check payable to NBM Publishing. Send to: Papercutz, 160 Broadway, Suite 700, East Wing, New York, NY 10038.

papercutz.com

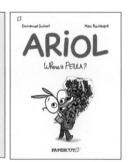

Just a Donkey Like You and Me

To Madame Paré,
– Emmanuel Guibert

ARIOL

#1 Just a Donkey Like You and Me

Emmanuel Guibert – Writer
Marc Boutavant – Artist
Joe Johnson – Translation
Michael Petranek – Lettering
Nelson Design Group, LLC – Production
Jeff Whitman – Production Coordinator
Michael Petranek – Associate Editor
Jim Salicrup
Editor-in-Chief

Volume 1: Ariol, un petite âne comme vous et moi ©Bayard Editions – 2008

ISBN: 978-1-59707-399-8

Printed in China
January 2015 by O.G. Printing Productions, LTD.
Units 2 & 3, 5/F, Lemmi Centre
50 Hoi Yuen Road
Kwon Tong, Kowloon

Papercutz books may be purchased for business or promotional use. For information on bulk purchases please
contact Macmillan Corporate and Premium Sales Department at (800) 221-7945 x5442.

Distributed by Macmillan
Fourth Papercutz Printing

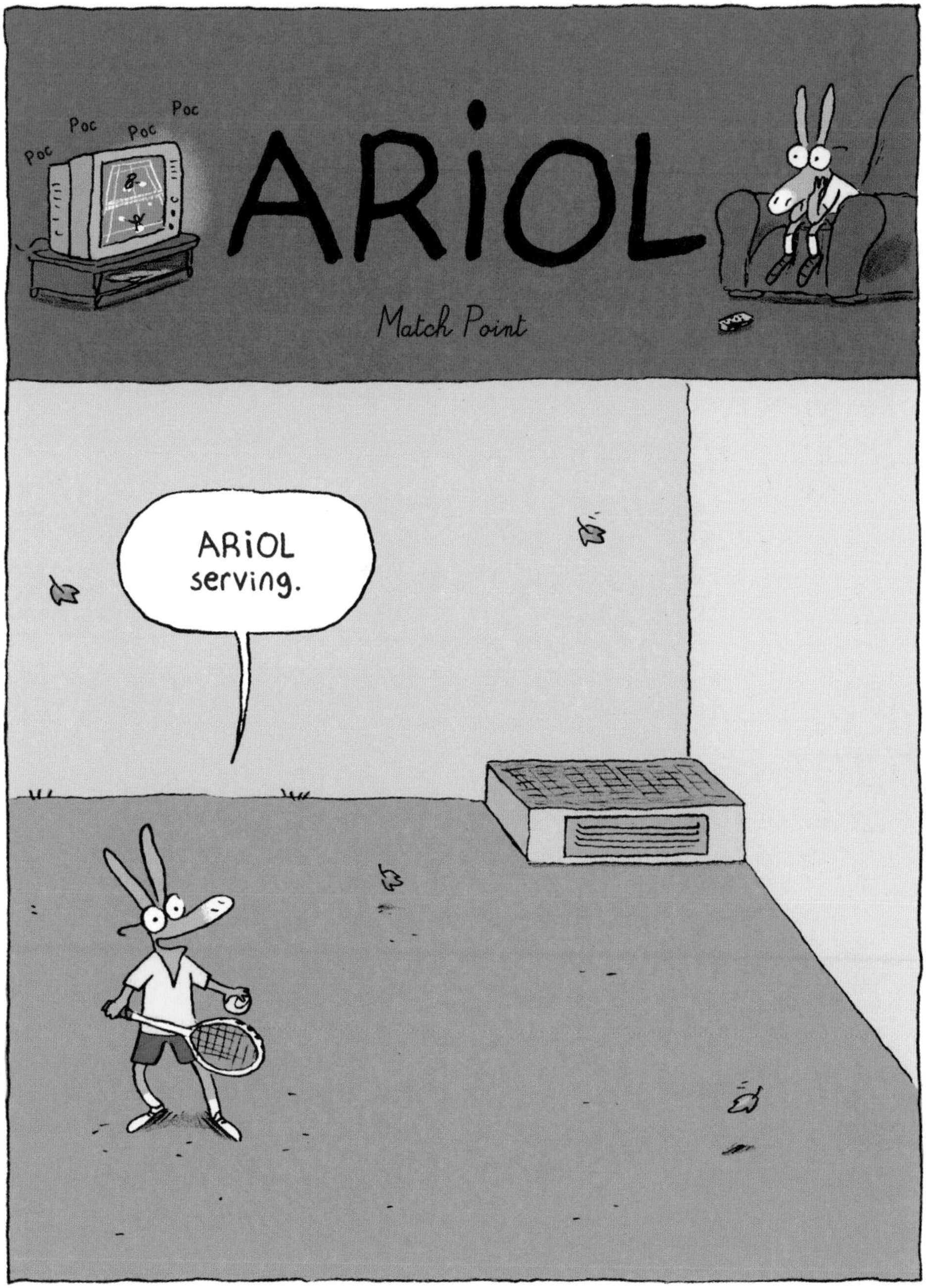
Poc
Poc
Poc
Poc
ARiOL
Match Point
ARiOL serving.

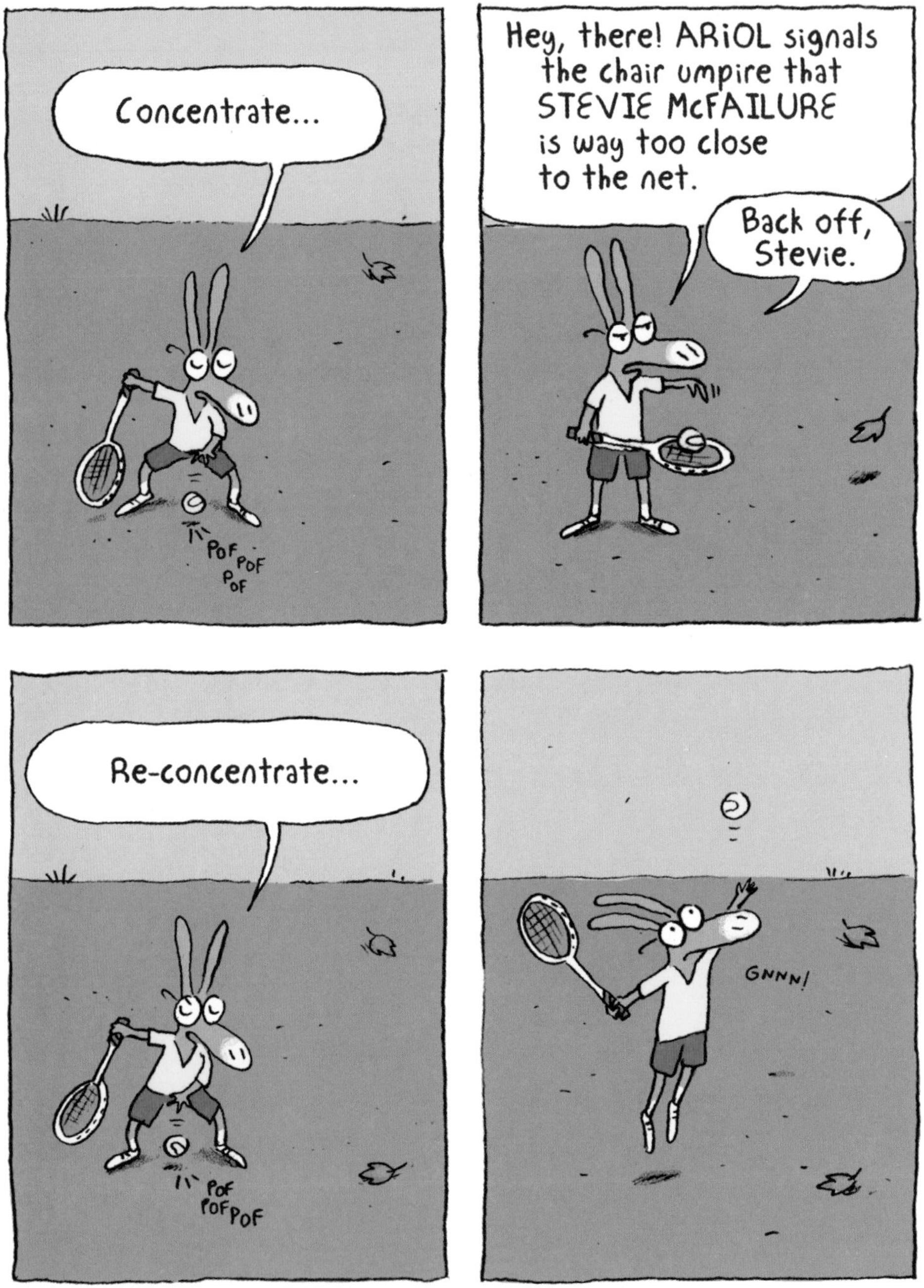
Concentrate...
POF POF POF
Hey, there! ARiOL signals the chair umpire that STEVIE McFAILURE is way too close to the net.
Back off, Stevie.
Re-concentrate...
POF POF POF
GNNN!

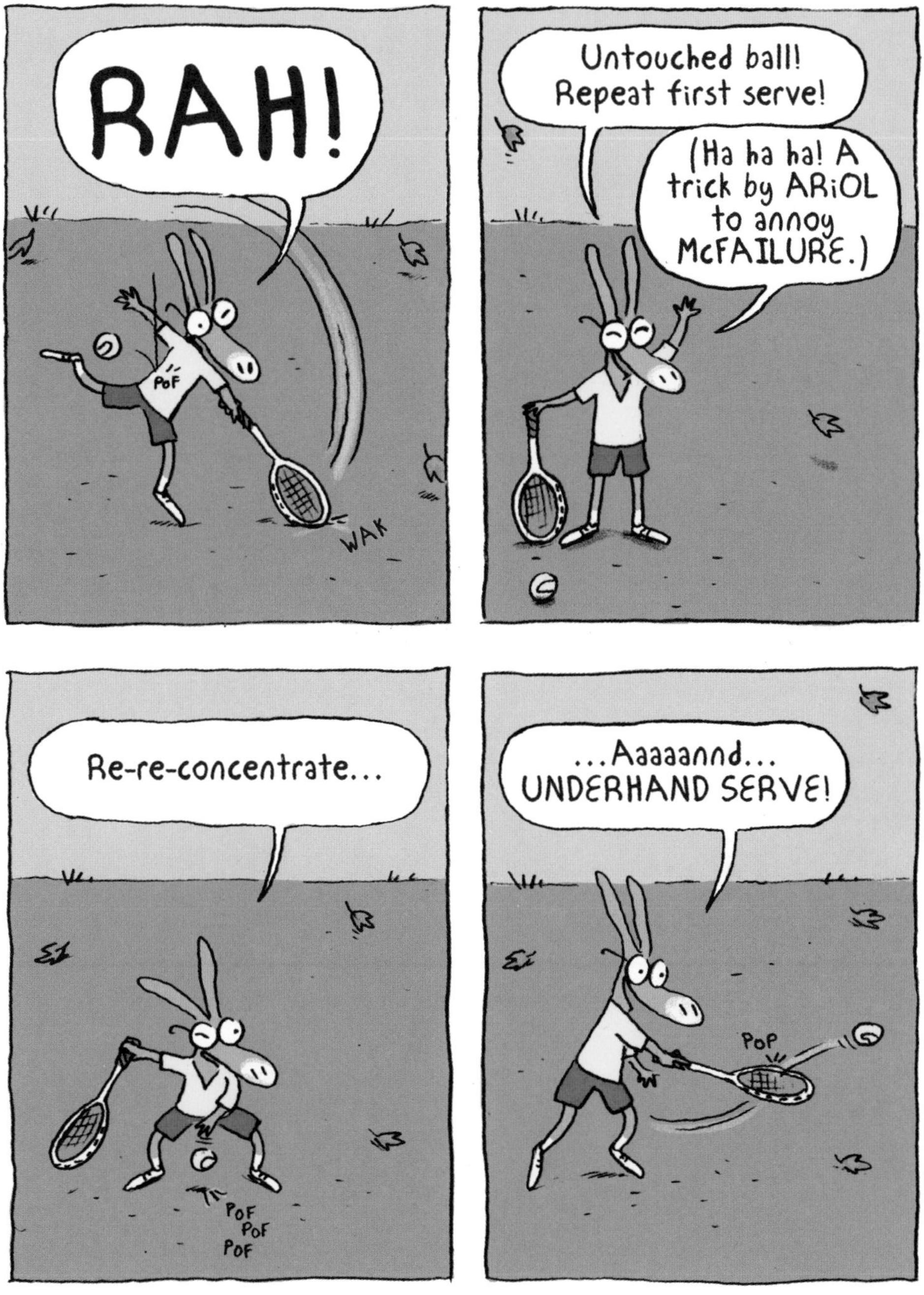
RAH!
PoF
WAK
Untouched ball! Repeat first serve!
(Ha ha ha! A trick by ARiOL to annoy McFAILURE.)
Re-re-concentrate...
PoF PoF PoF
...Aaaaannd... UNDERHAND SERVE!
POP

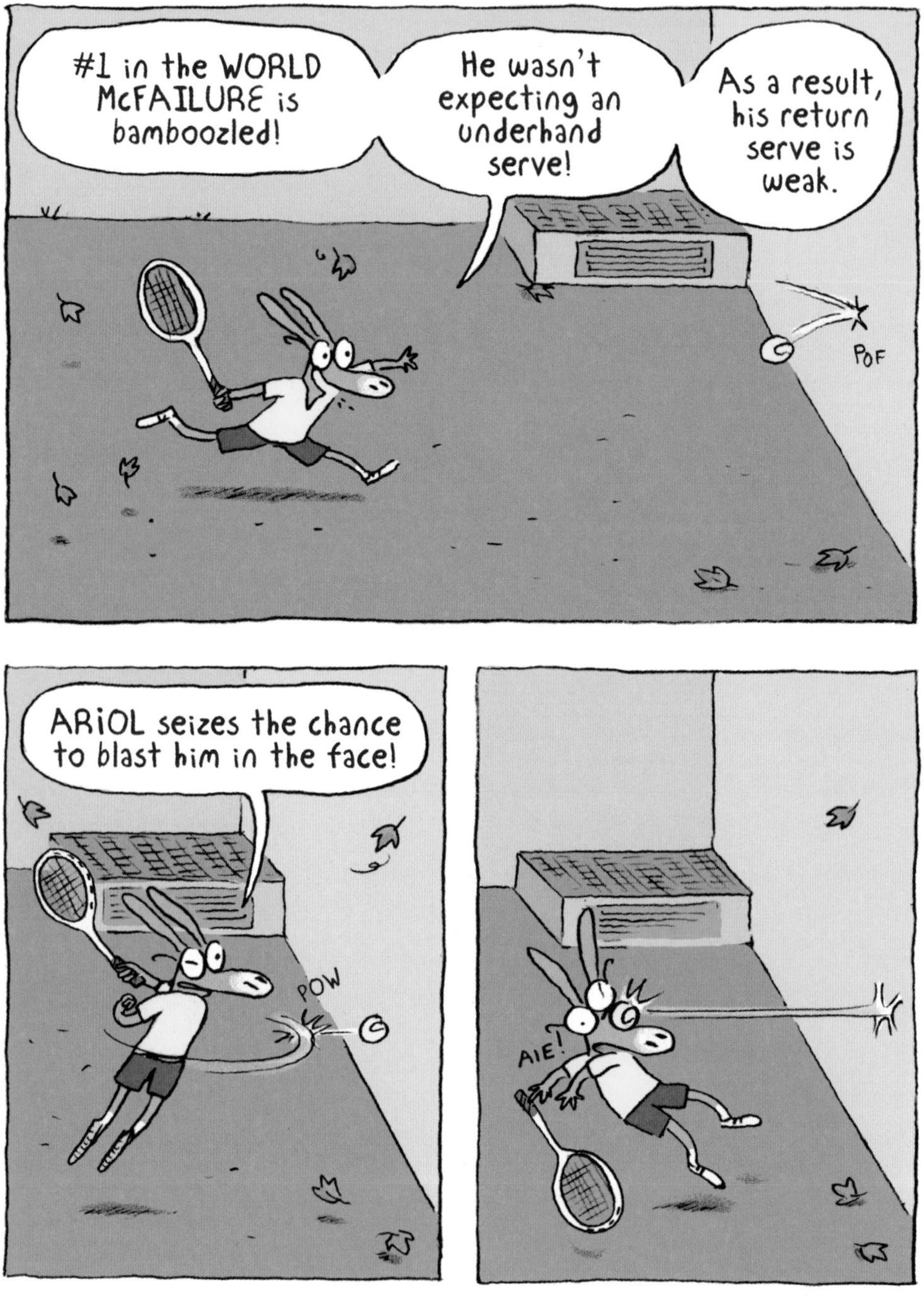

#1 in the WORLD McFAILURE is bamboozled!
He wasn't expecting an underhand serve!
As a result, his return serve is weak.
POF
ARIOL seizes the chance to blast him in the face!
POW
AIE!

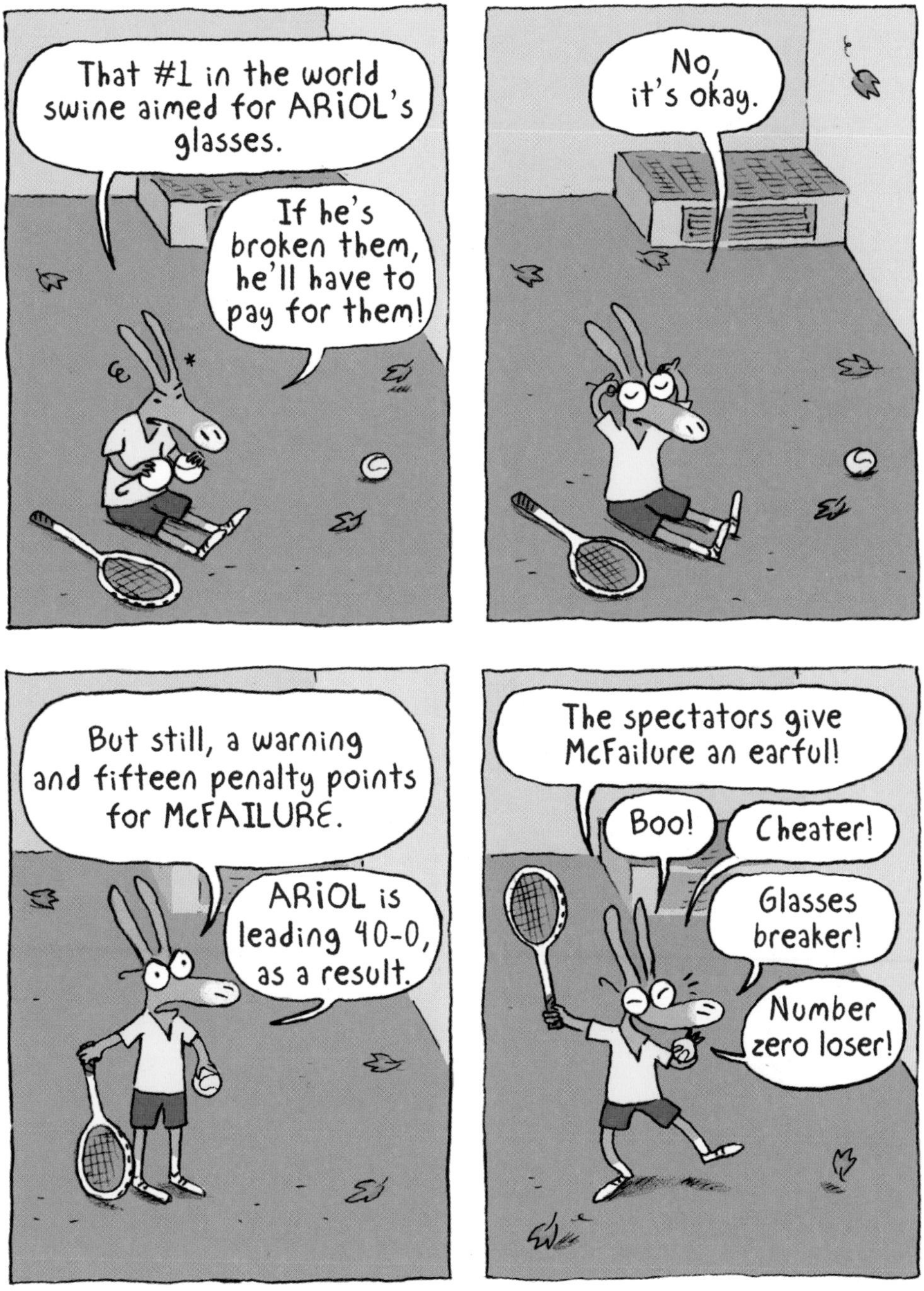
That #1 in the world swine aimed for ARIOL's glasses.
If he's broken them, he'll have to pay for them!
No, it's okay.
But still, a warning and fifteen penalty points for McFAILURE.
ARIOL is leading 40-0, as a result.
The spectators give McFailure an earful!
Boo!
Cheater!
Glasses breaker!
Number zero loser!

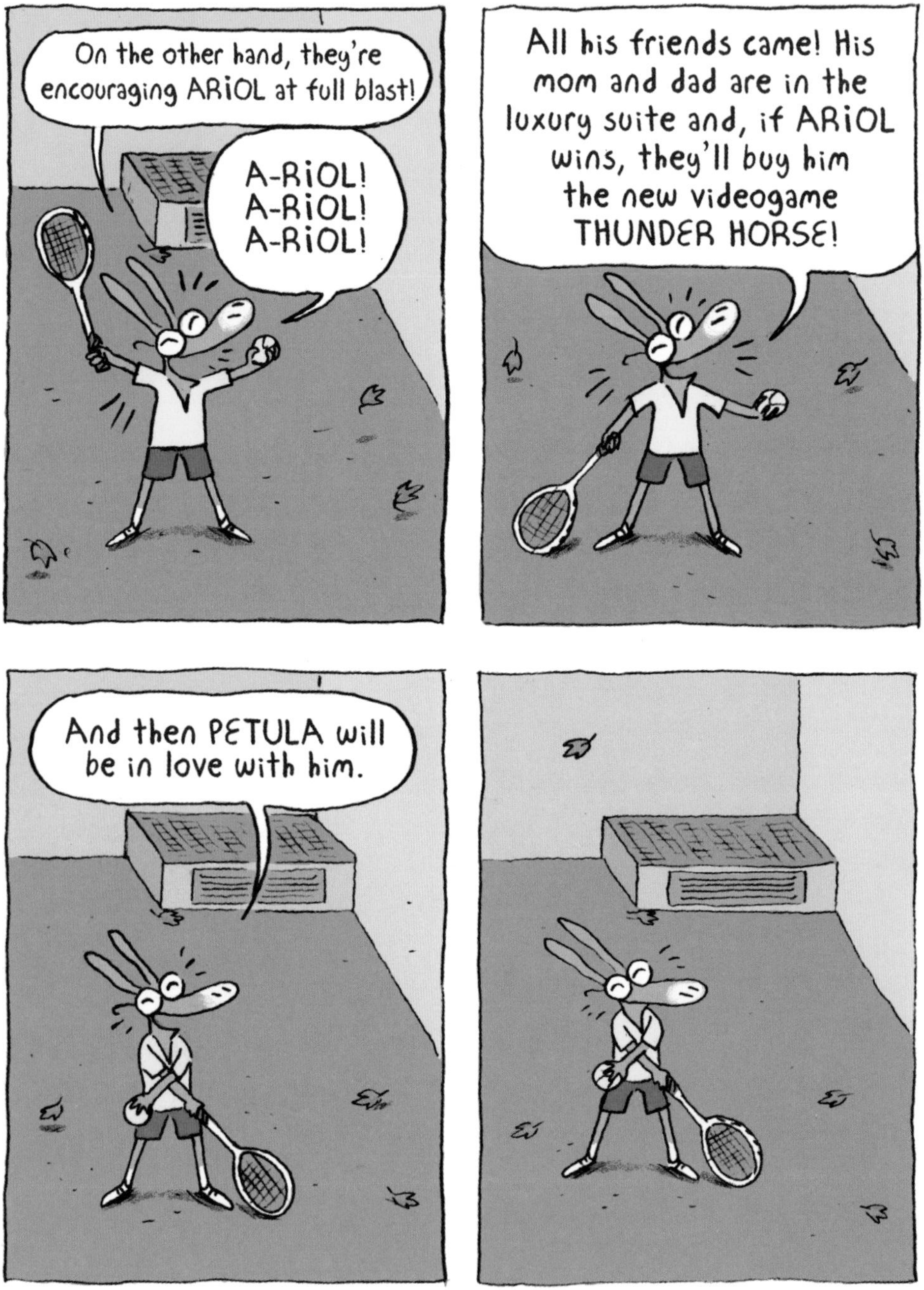
On the other hand, they're encouraging ARIOL at full blast!
A-RIOL! A-RIOL! A-RIOL!
All his friends came! His mom and dad are in the luxury suite and, if ARIOL wins, they'll buy him the new videogame THUNDER HORSE!
And then PETULA will be in love with him.

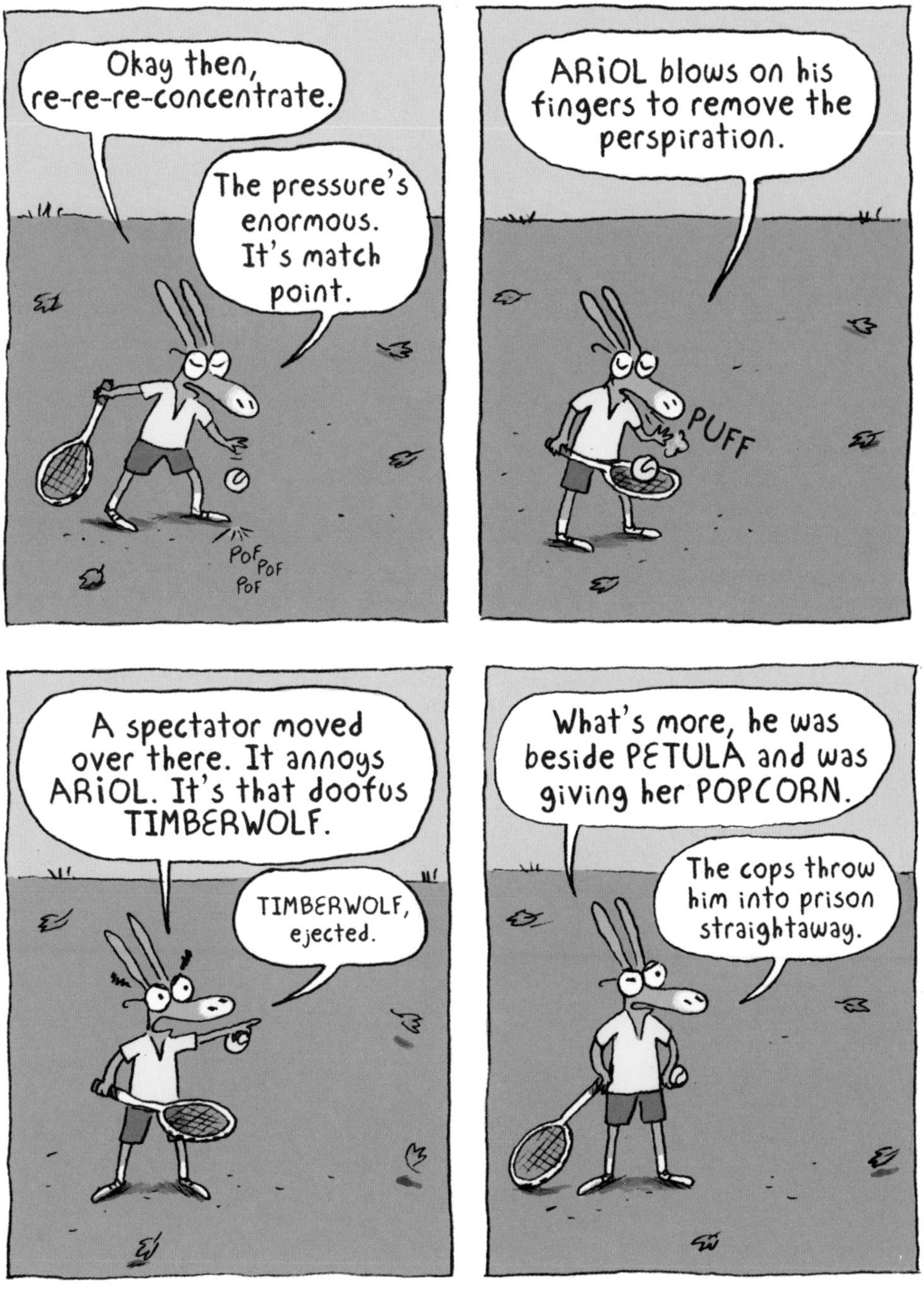
Okay then, re-re-re-concentrate.
The pressure's enormous. It's match point.
POF POF POF
ARiOL blows on his fingers to remove the perspiration.
PUFF
A spectator moved over there. It annoys ARiOL. It's that doofus TIMBERWOLF.
TIMBERWOLF, ejected.
What's more, he was beside PETULA and was giving her POPCORN.
The cops throw him into prison straightaway.

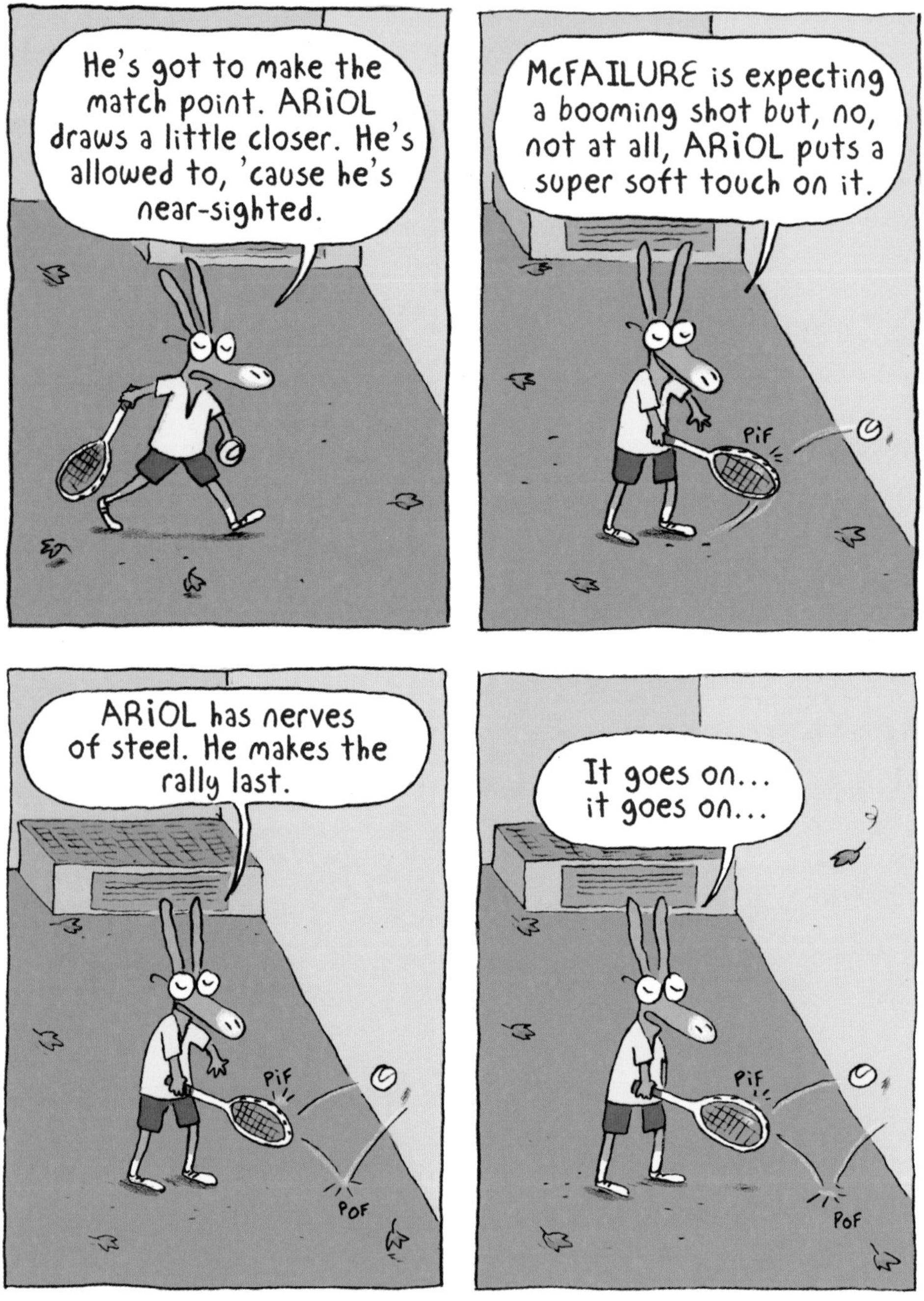
He's got to make the match point. ARIOL draws a little closer. He's allowed to, 'cause he's near-sighted.
MCFAILURE is expecting a booming shot but, no, not at all, ARIOL puts a super soft touch on it.
PIF
ARIOL has nerves of steel. He makes the rally last.
PIF
POF
It goes on... it goes on...
PIF
POF

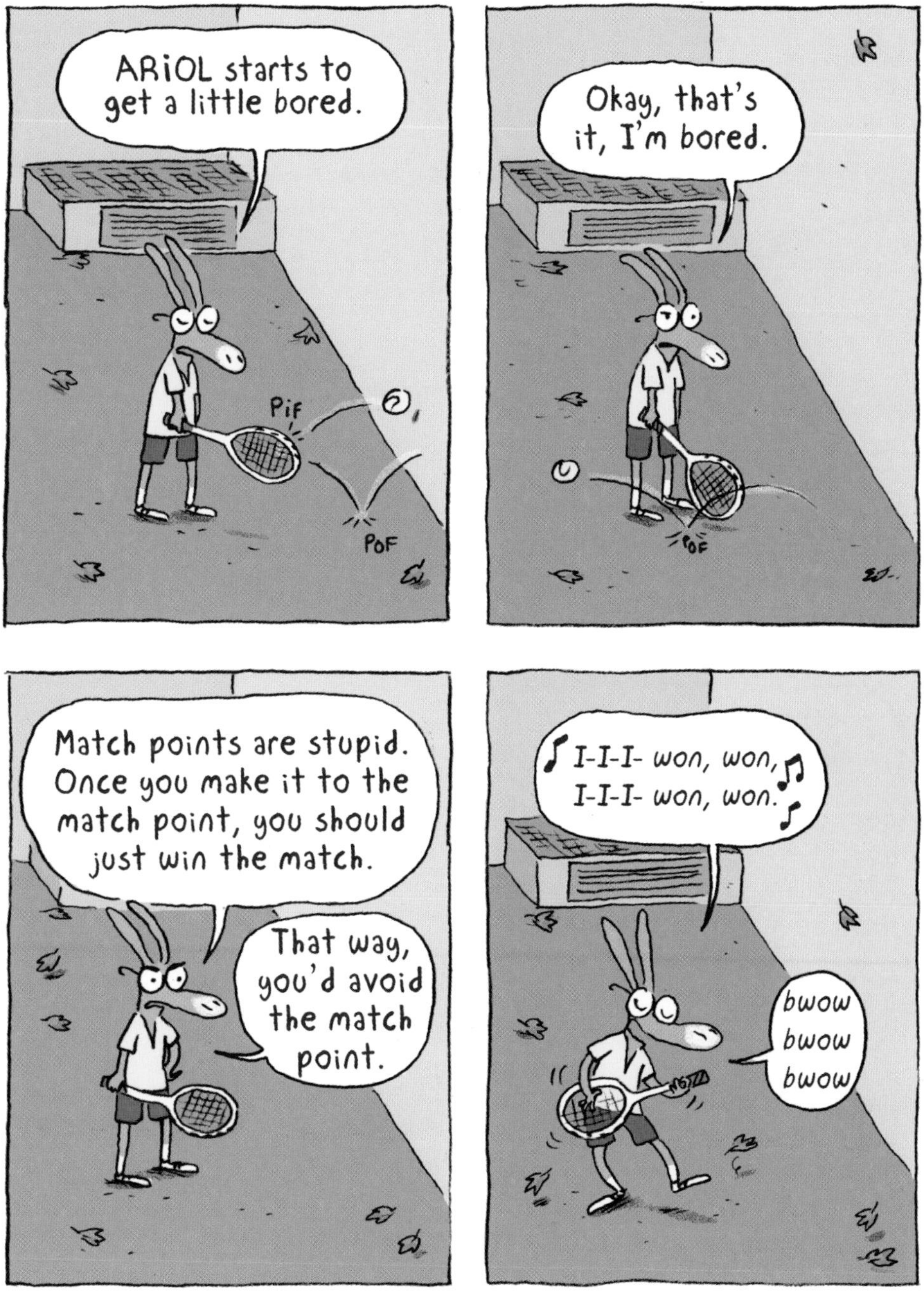
ARiOL starts to get a little bored.
PiF
POF
Okay, that's it, I'm bored.
POF
Match points are stupid. Once you make it to the match point, you should just win the match.
That way, you'd avoid the match point.
I-I-I- won, won, I-I-I- won, won.
bwow bwow bwow

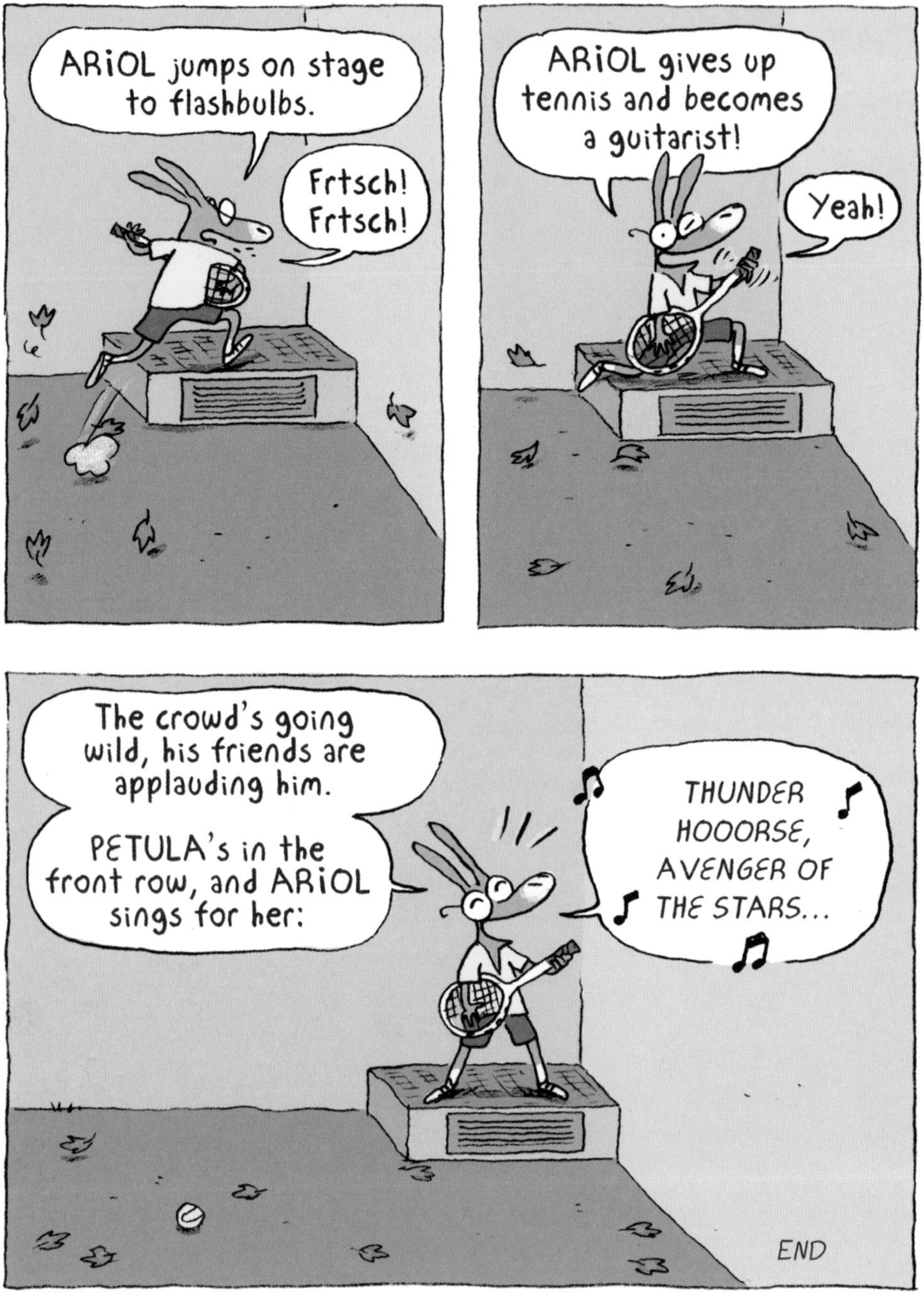
ARiOL jumps on stage to flashbulbs.
Frtsch! Frtsch!
ARiOL gives up tennis and becomes a guitarist!
Yeah!
The crowd's going wild, his friends are applauding him.
PETULA's in the front row, and ARiOL sings for her:
THUNDER HOOORSE, AVENGER OF THE STARS...
END

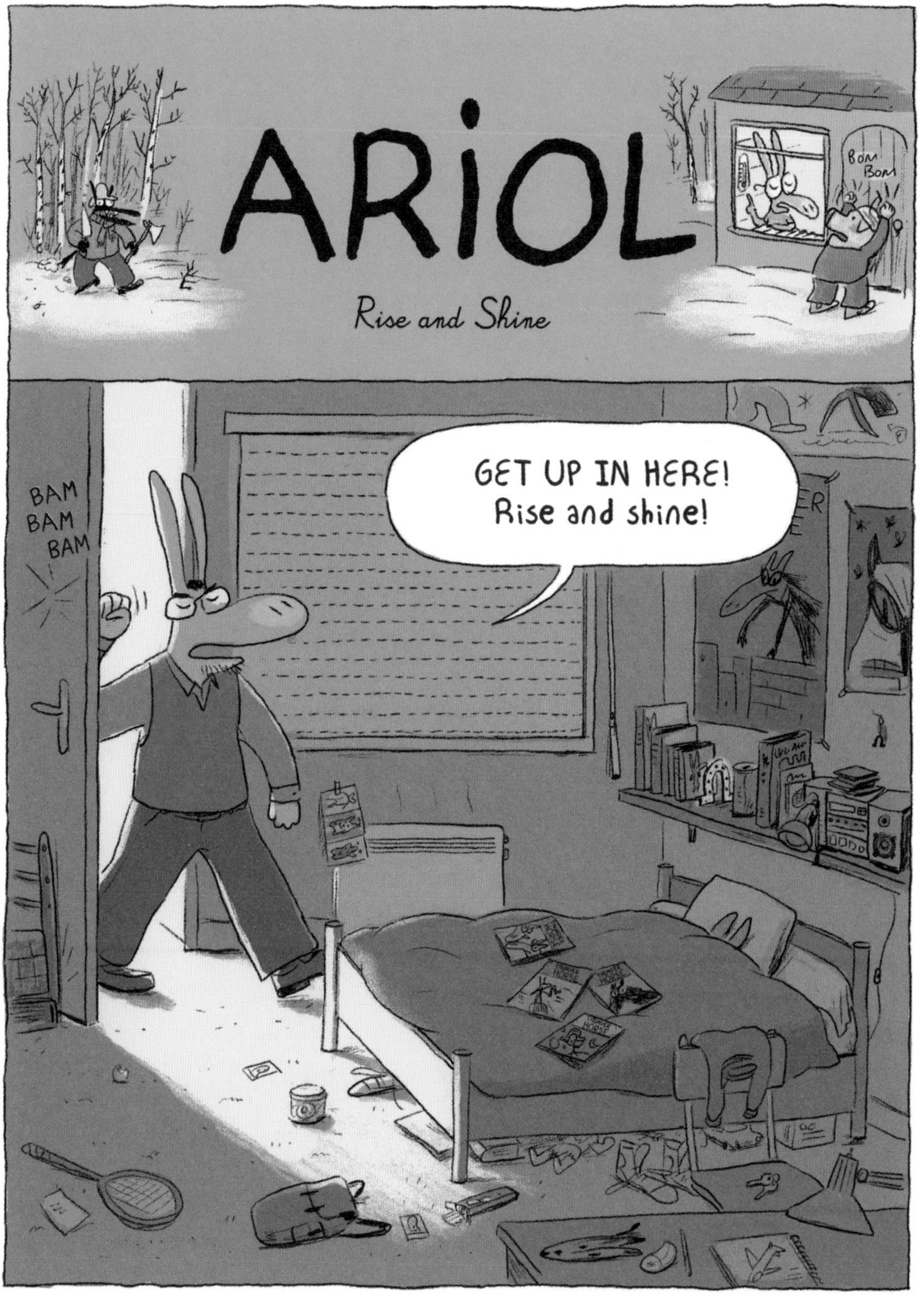
ARIOL
Rise and Shine
BOM BOM
BAM BAM BAM
GET UP IN HERE! Rise and shine!

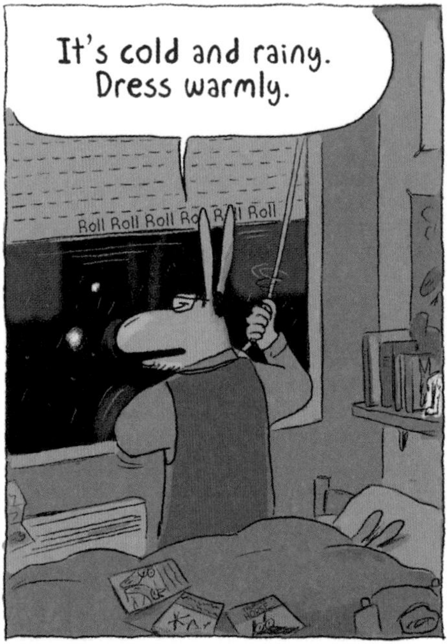
It's cold and rainy. Dress warmly.
Roll Roll Roll Roll Roll Roll

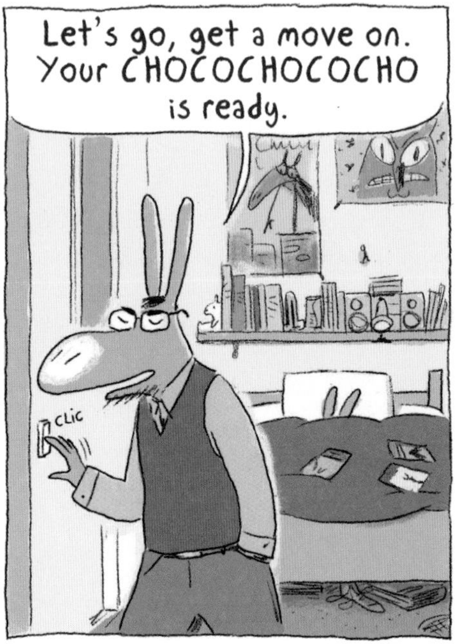
Let's go, get a move on. Your CHOCOCHOCOCHO is ready.
CLIC

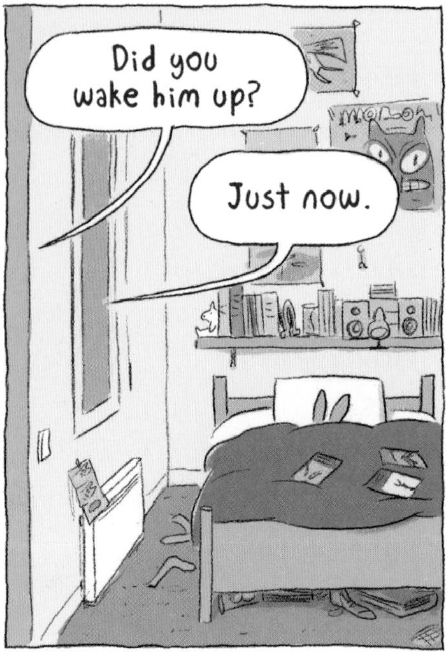
Did you wake him up?
Just now.

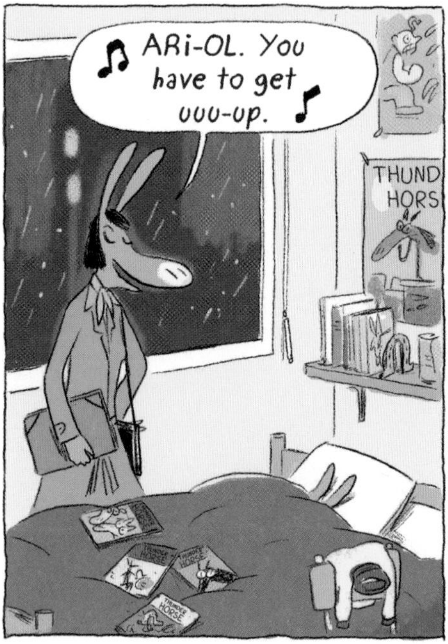
ARi-OL. You have to get uuu-up.
THUND
HORS

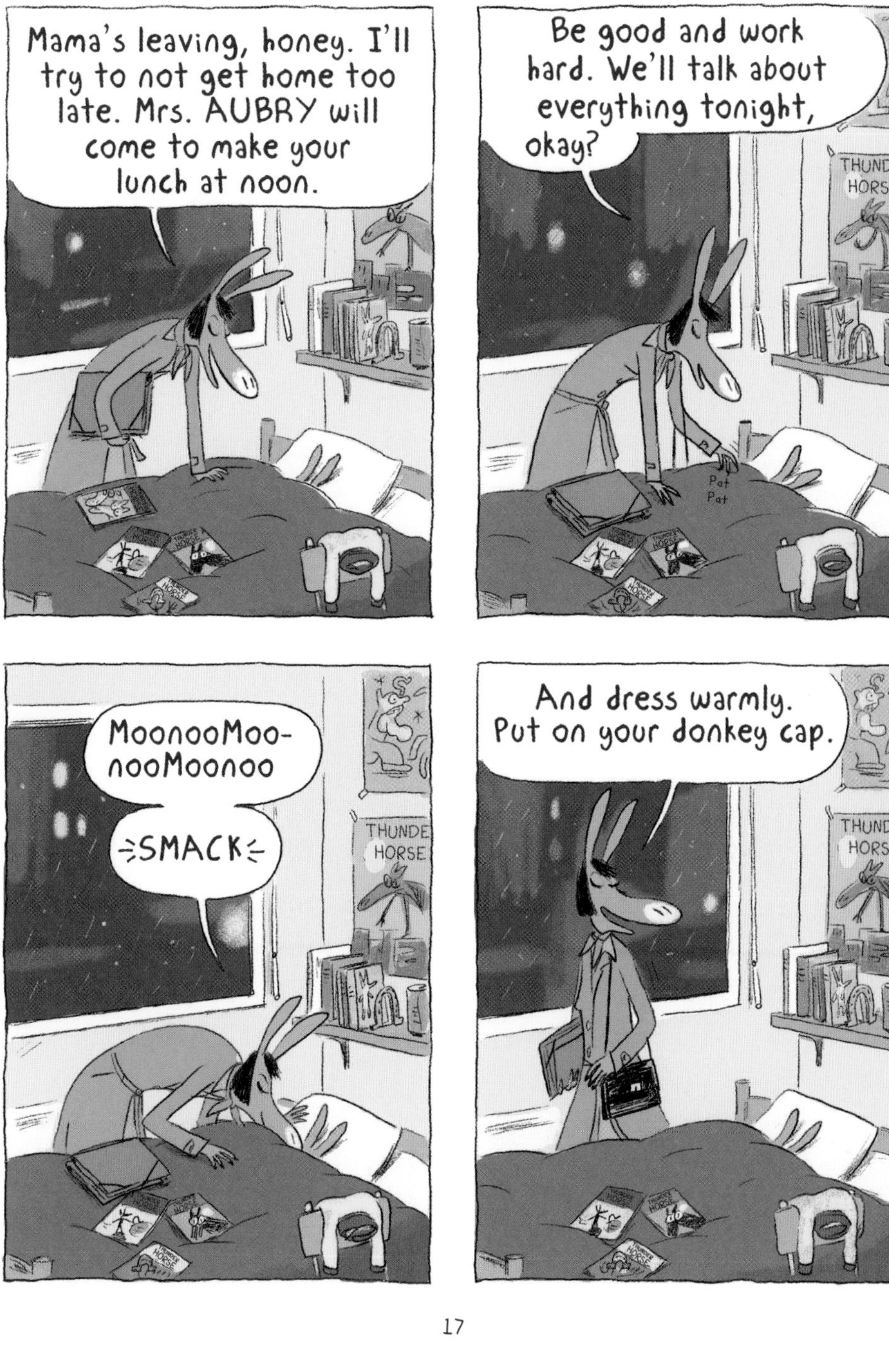
Mama's leaving, honey. I'll try to not get home too late. Mrs. AUBRY will come to make your lunch at noon.
Be good and work hard. We'll talk about everything tonight, okay?
Pat Pat
MoonooMoo-nooMoonoo
SMACK
And dress warmly. Put on your donkey cap.

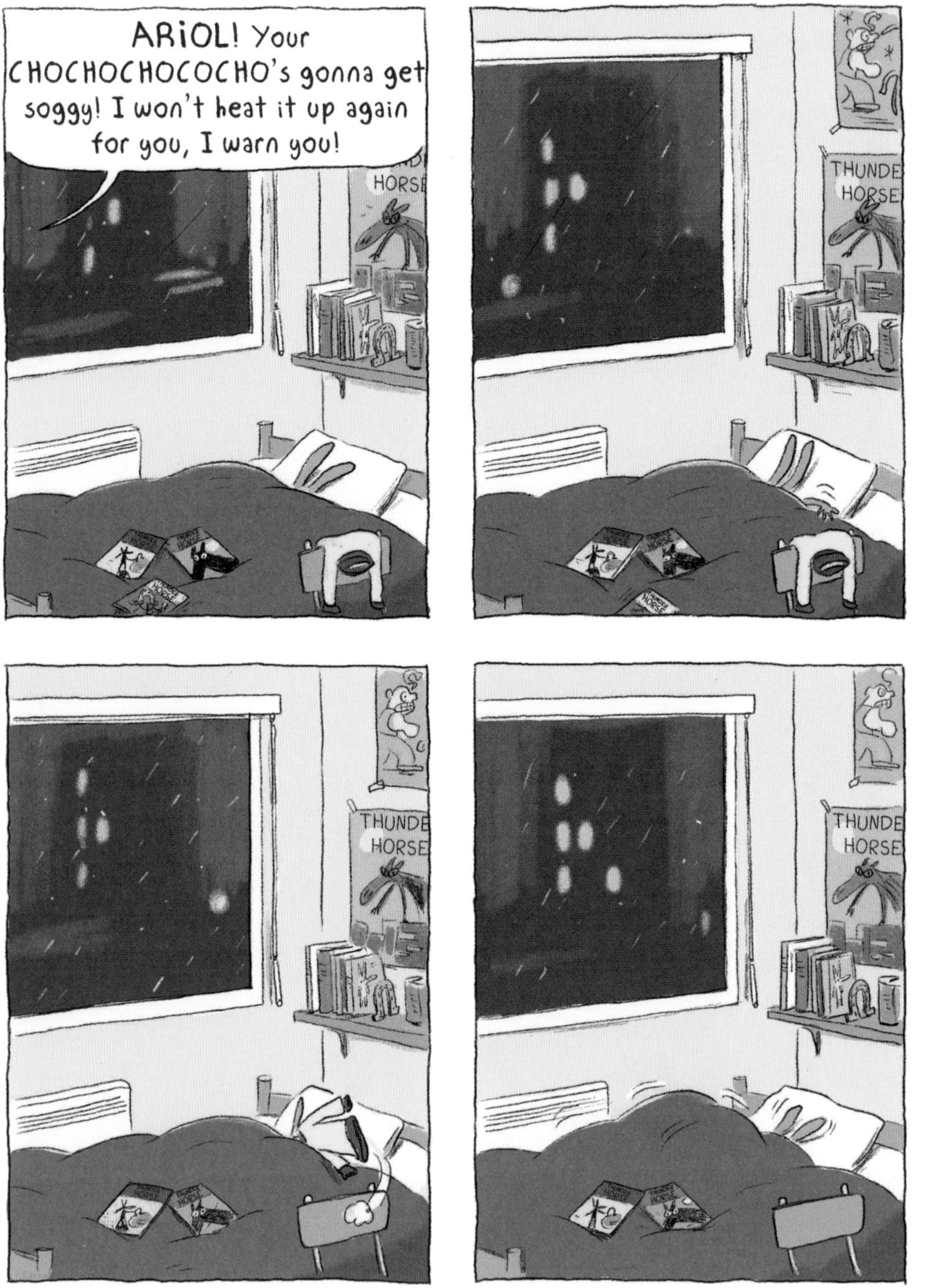
ARiOL! Your CHOCHOCHOCOCHO's gonna get soggy! I won't heat it up again for you, I warn you!
THUNDE
HORSE

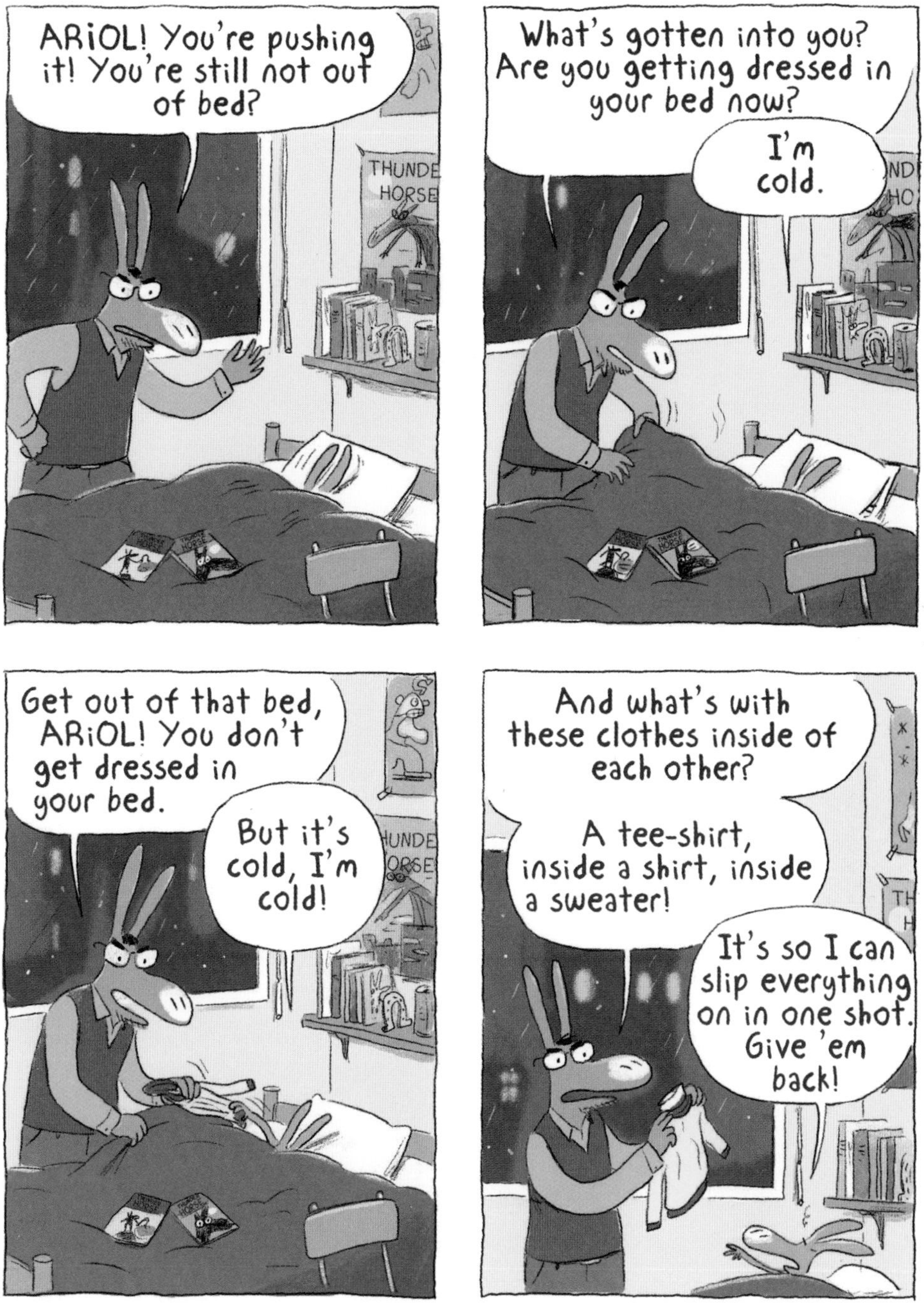
ARiOL! You're pushing it! You're still not out of bed?
What's gotten into you? Are you getting dressed in your bed now?
I'm cold.
Get out of that bed, ARiOL! You don't get dressed in your bed.
But it's cold, I'm cold!
And what's with these clothes inside of each other?
A tee-shirt, inside a shirt, inside a sweater!
It's so I can slip everything on in one shot. Give 'em back!

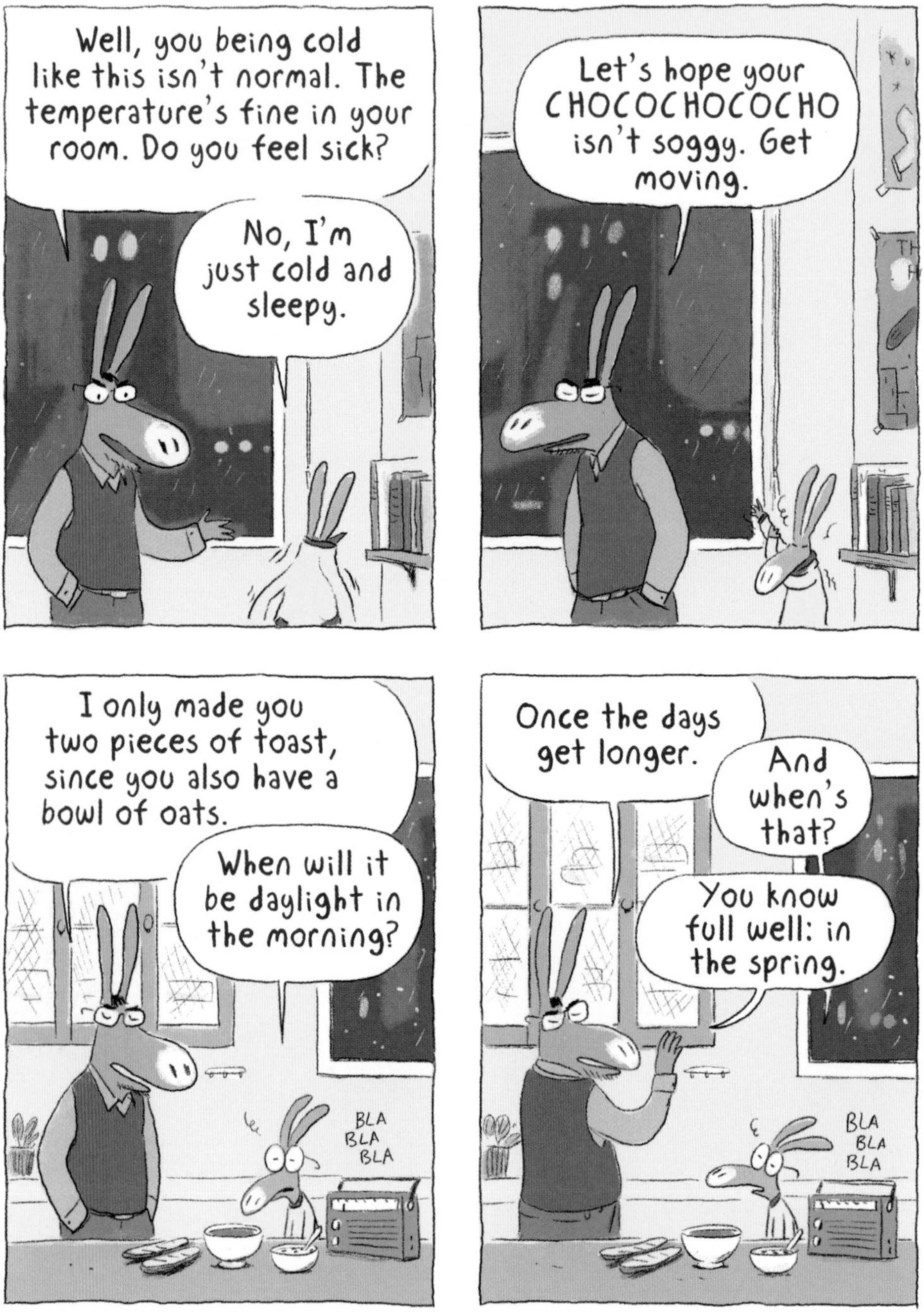
Well, you being cold like this isn't normal. The temperature's fine in your room. Do you feel sick?
No, I'm just cold and sleepy.
Let's hope your CHOCOCHOCOCHO isn't soggy. Get moving.
I only made you two pieces of toast, since you also have a bowl of oats.
When will it be daylight in the morning?
BLA BLA BLA
Once the days get longer.
And when's that?
You know full well: in the spring.
BLA BLA BLA

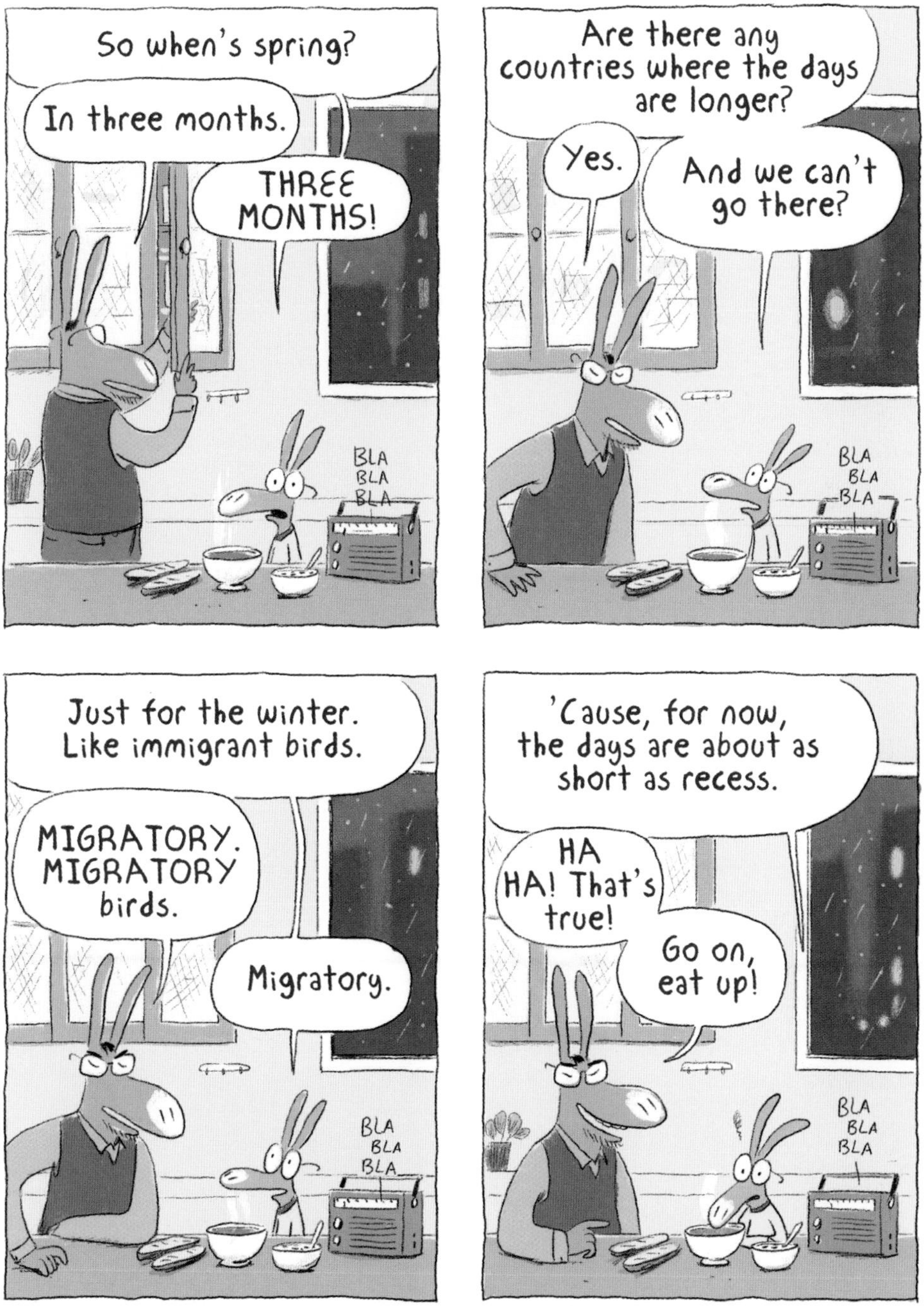
So when's spring?
In three months.
THREE MONTHS!
BLA BLA BLA
Are there any countries where the days are longer?
Yes.
And we can't go there?
BLA BLA BLA
Just for the winter. Like immigrant birds.
MIGRATORY. MIGRATORY birds.
Migratory.
BLA BLA BLA
'Cause, for now, the days are about as short as recess.
HA HA! That's true!
Go on, eat up!
BLA BLA BLA

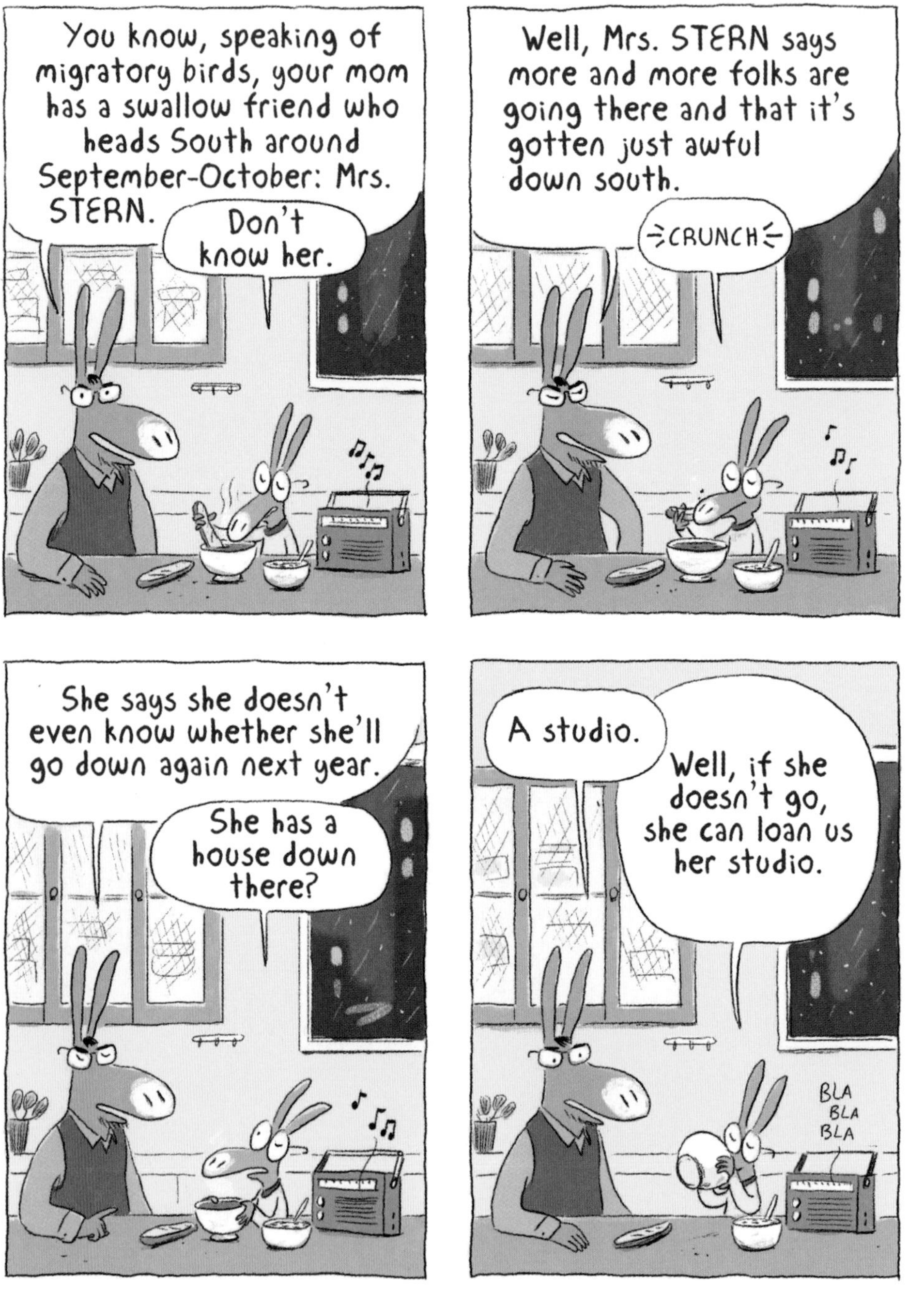
You know, speaking of migratory birds, your mom has a swallow friend who heads South around September-October: Mrs. STERN.
Don't know her.
Well, Mrs. STERN says more and more folks are going there and that it's gotten just awful down south.
CRUNCH
She says she doesn't even know whether she'll go down again next year.
She has a house down there?
A studio.
Well, if she doesn't go, she can loan us her studio.
BLA BLA BLA

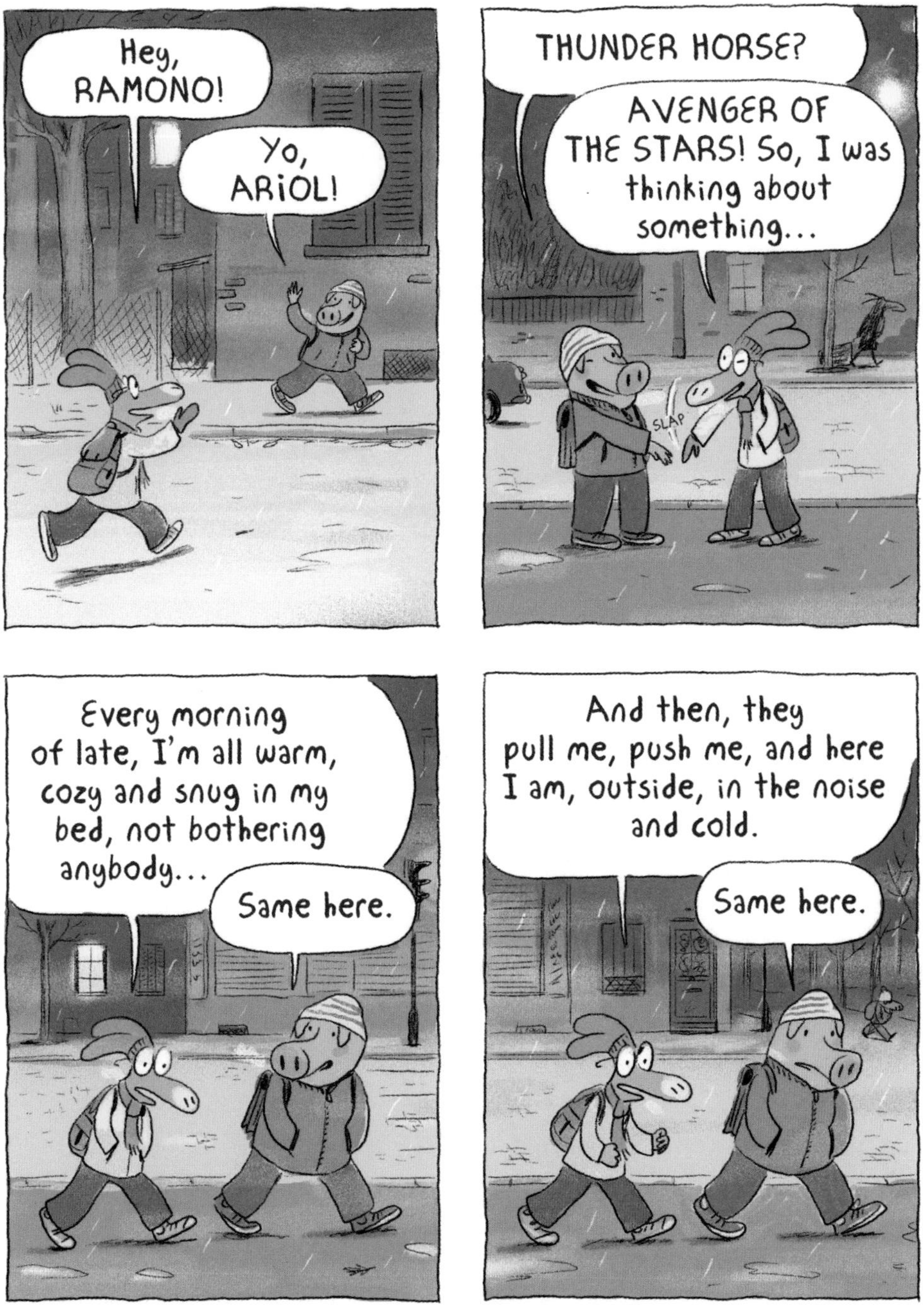
Hey, RAMONO!
Yo, ARIOL!
THUNDER HORSE?
AVENGER OF THE STARS! So, I was thinking about something...
SLAP
Every morning of late, I'm all warm, cozy and snug in my bed, not bothering anybody...
Same here.
And then, they pull me, push me, and here I am, outside, in the noise and cold.
Same here.

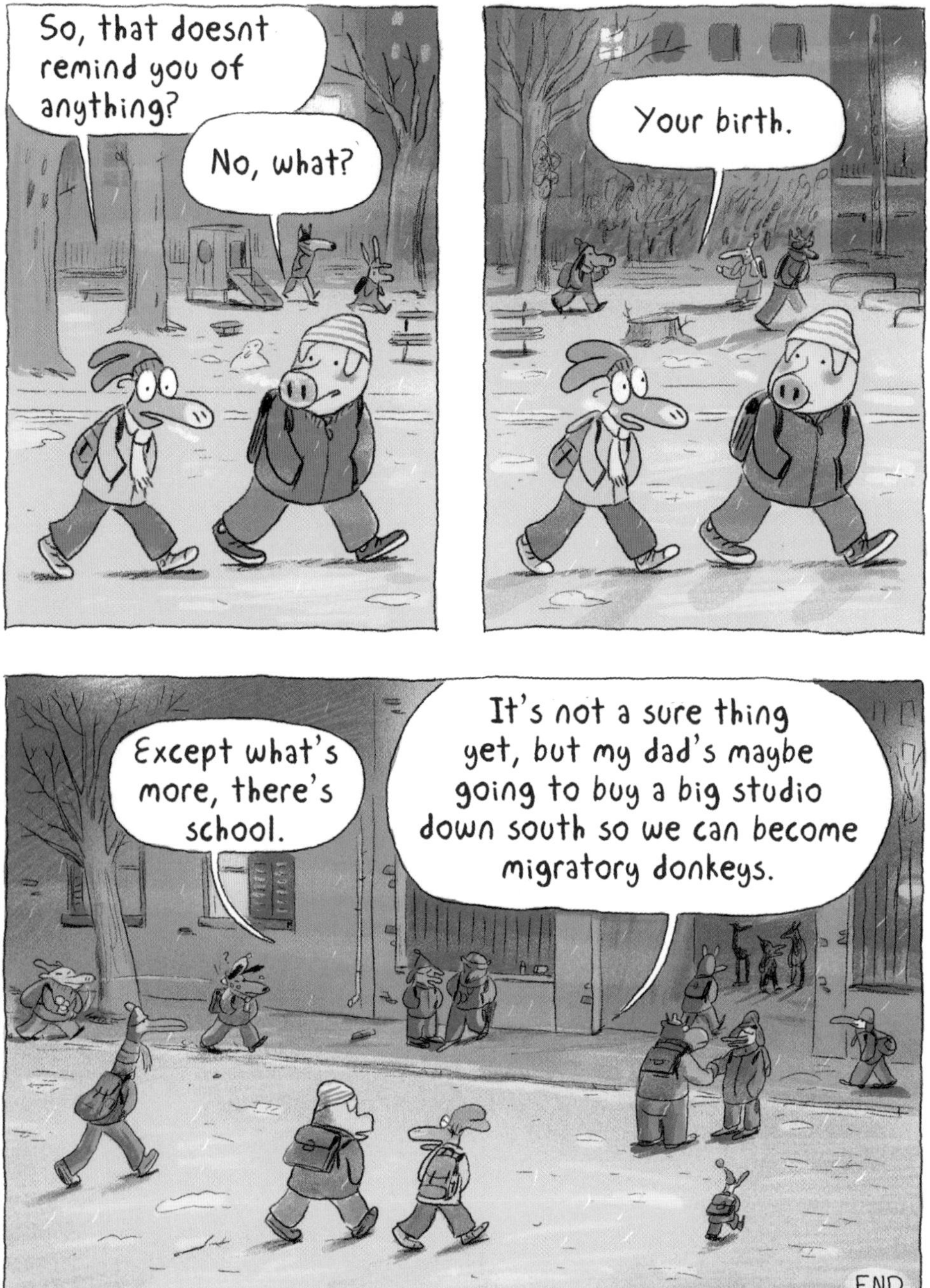
So, that doesnt remind you of anything?
No, what?
Your birth.
Except what's more, there's school.
It's not a sure thing yet, but my dad's maybe going to buy a big studio down south so we can become migratory donkeys.
END

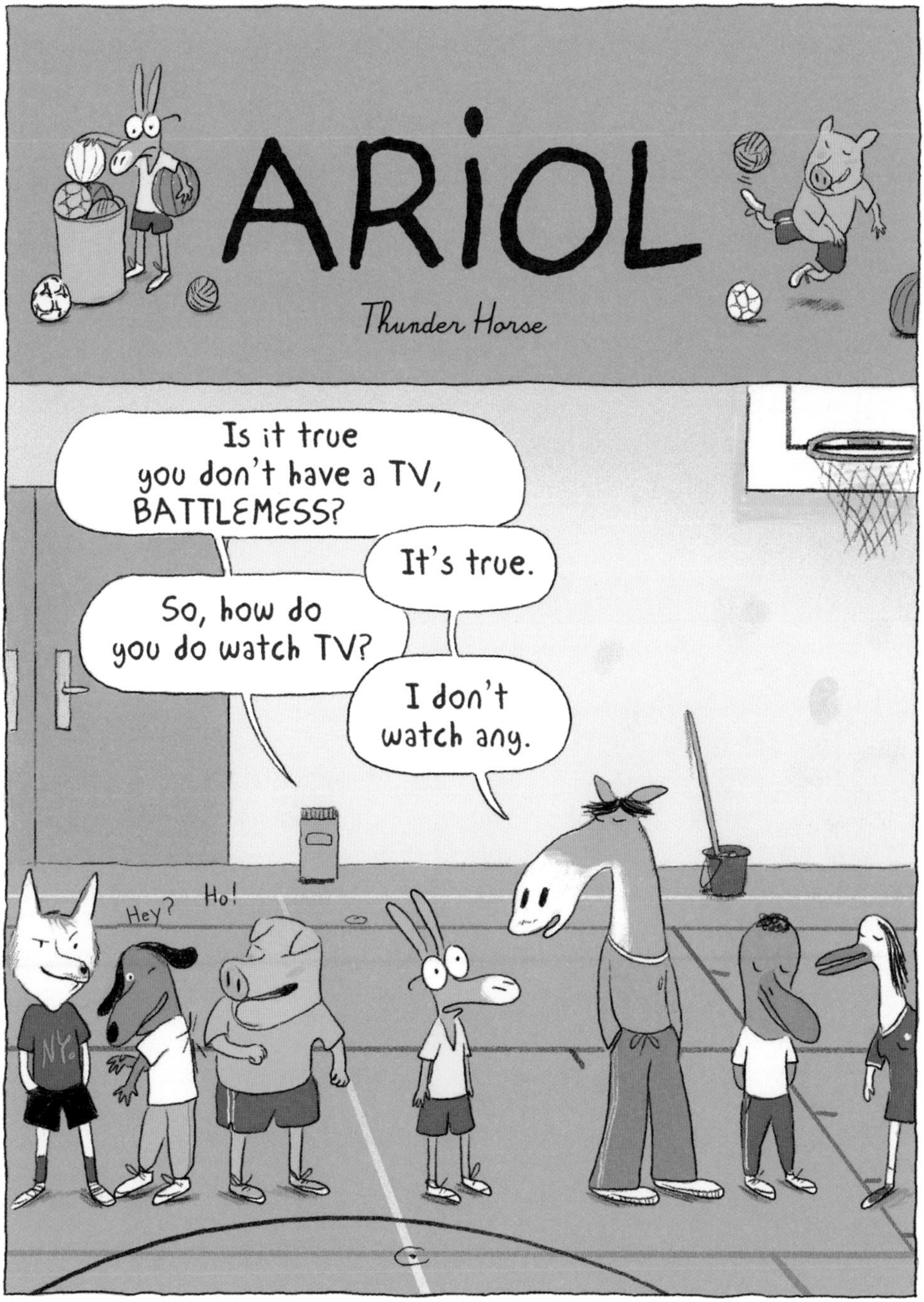
ARiOL
Thunder Horse
Is it true you don't have a TV, BATTLEMESS?
It's true.
So, how do you do watch TV?
I don't watch any.
Hey?
Ho!

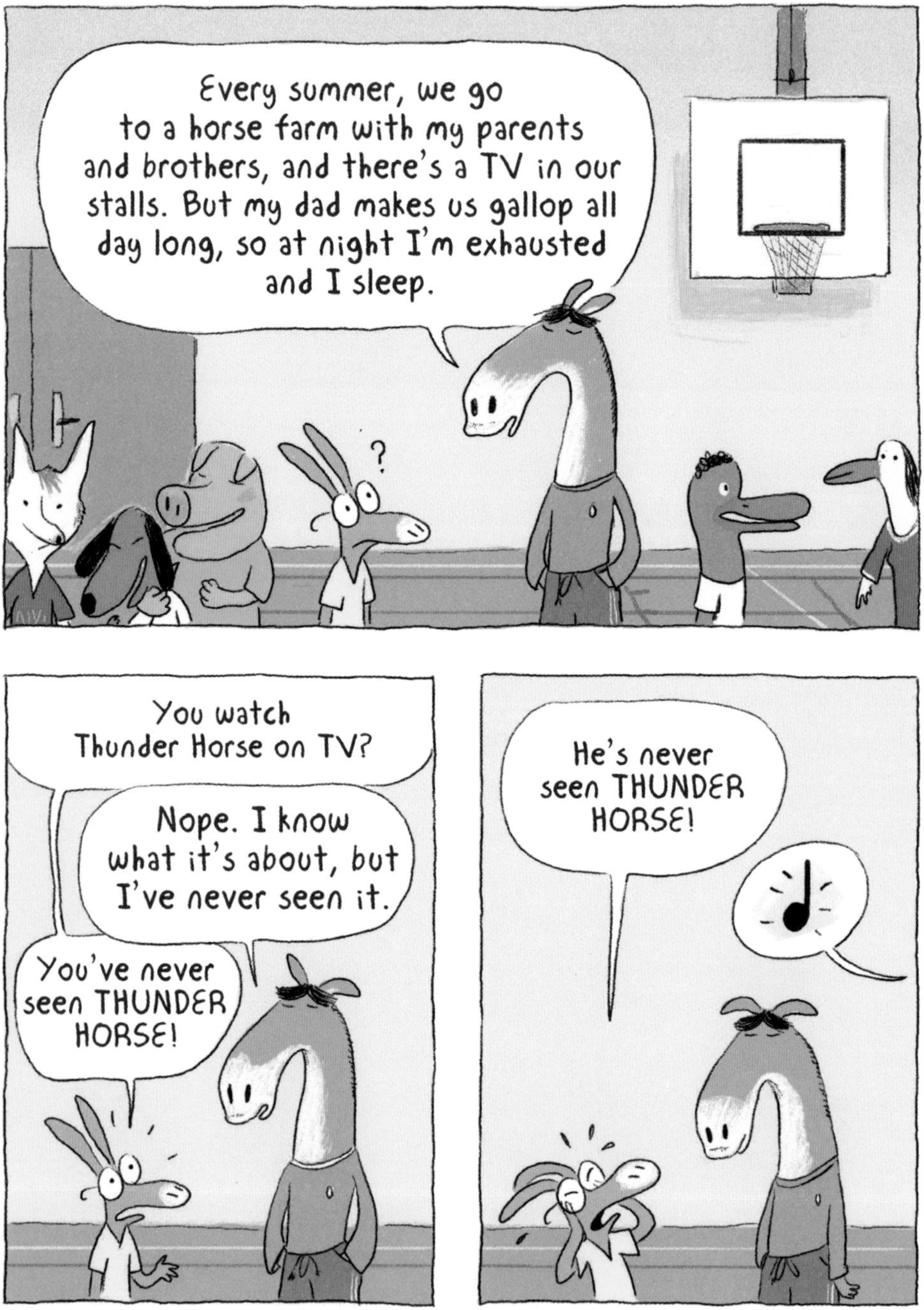
Every summer, we go to a horse farm with my parents and brothers, and there's a TV in our stalls. But my dad makes us gallop all day long, so at night I'm exhausted and I sleep.
?
You watch Thunder Horse on TV?
Nope. I know what it's about, but I've never seen it.
You've never seen THUNDER HORSE!
He's never seen THUNDER HORSE!

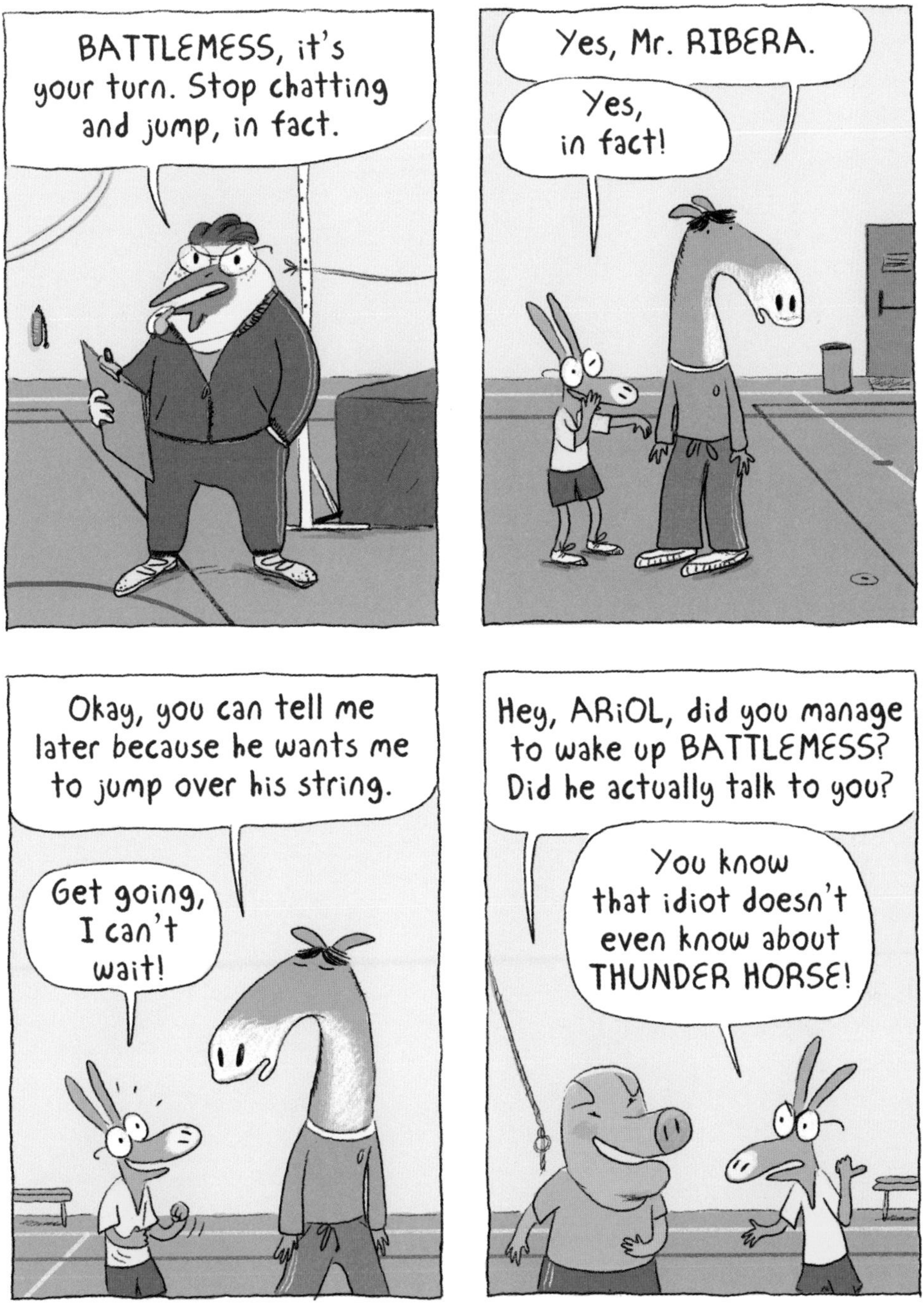
BATTLEMESS, it's your turn. Stop chatting and jump, in fact.
Yes, Mr. RIBERA.
Yes, in fact!
Okay, you can tell me later because he wants me to jump over his string.
Get going, I can't wait!
Hey, ARiOL, did you manage to wake up BATTLEMESS? Did he actually talk to you?
You know that idiot doesn't even know about THUNDER HORSE!

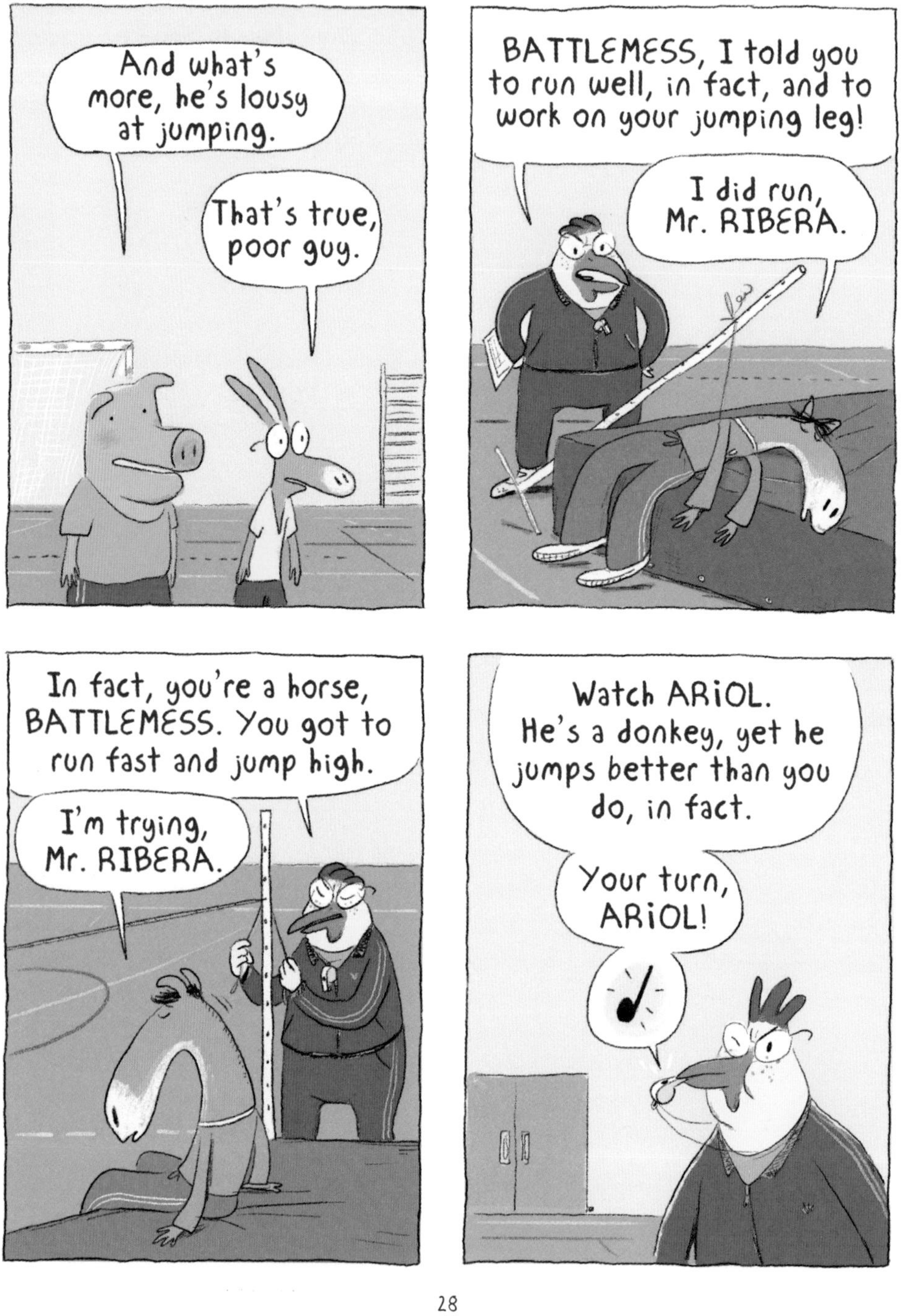
And what's more, he's lousy at jumping.
That's true, poor guy.
BATTLEMESS, I told you to run well, in fact, and to work on your jumping leg!
I did run, Mr. RIBERA.
In fact, you're a horse, BATTLEMESS. You got to run fast and jump high.
I'm trying, Mr. RIBERA.
Watch ARIOL. He's a donkey, yet he jumps better than you do, in fact.
Your turn, ARIOL!

Hold my glasses for me, RAMONO. And don't get the lenses dirty.
No worries.
You're THUNDER HORSE and PETULA's watching you... You're THUNDER HORSE and PETULA's watching you...
HOP
HA! HA! HA!
Look at ARIOL!
Teacher's pet!
Hey, ARIOL! Go home to your mommy!

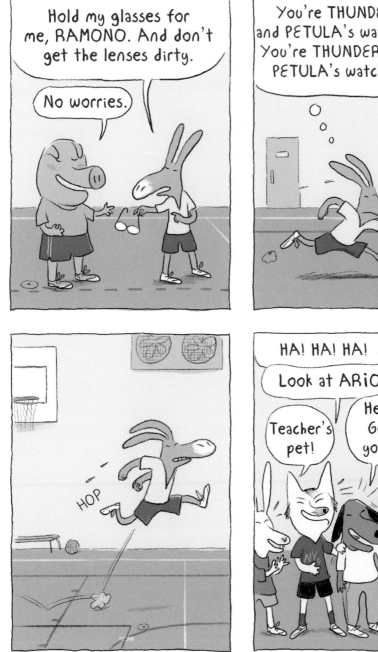

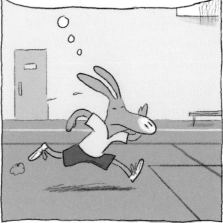

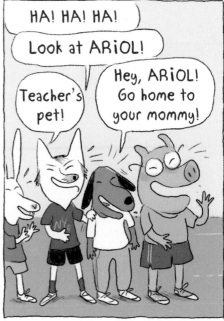

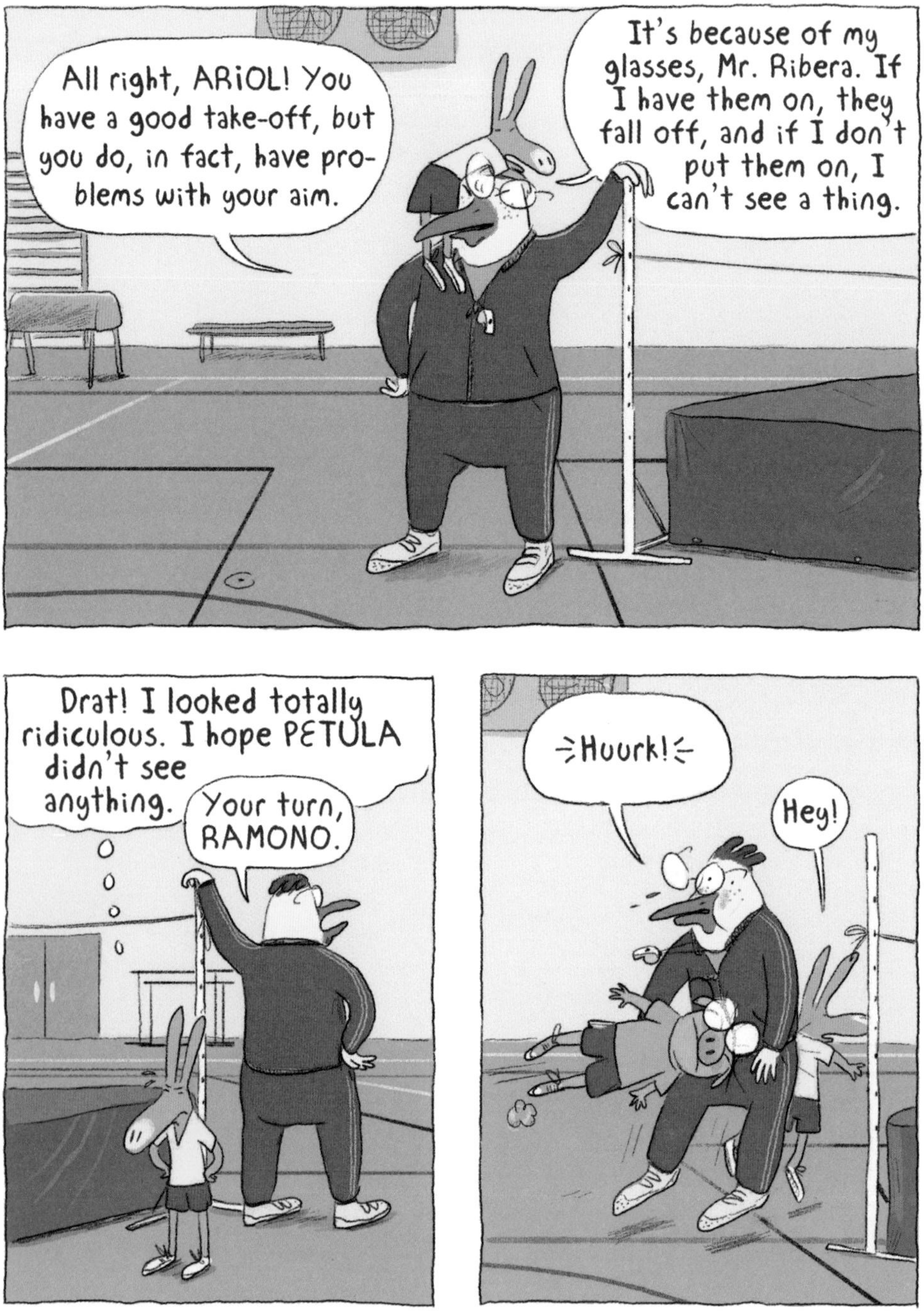
All right, ARiOL! You have a good take-off, but you do, in fact, have problems with your aim.
It's because of my glasses, Mr. Ribera. If I have them on, they fall off, and if I don't put them on, I can't see a thing.
Drat! I looked totally ridiculous. I hope PETULA didn't see anything.
Your turn, RAMONO.
Huurk!
Hey!

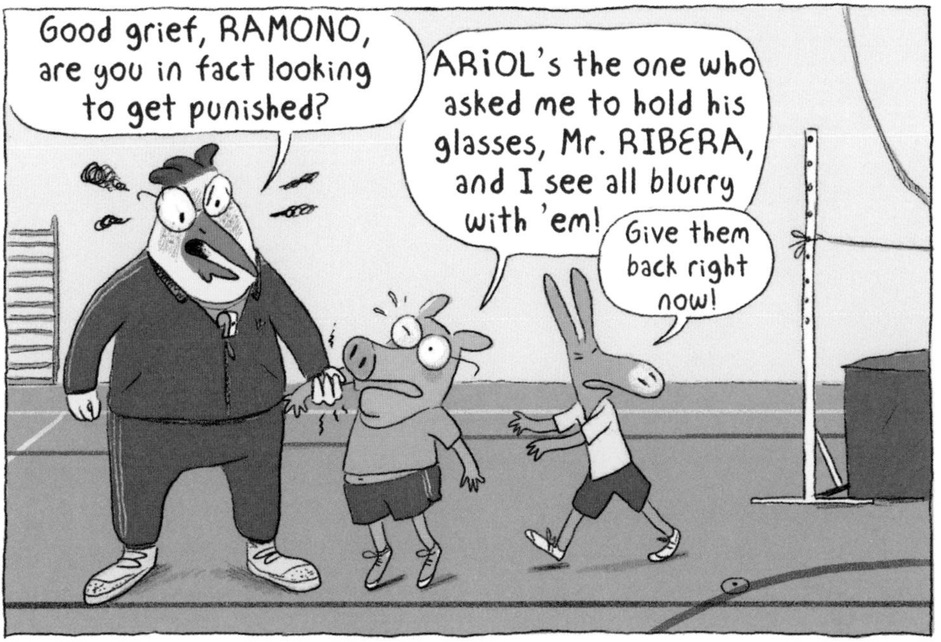
Good grief, RAMONO, are you in fact looking to get punished?
ARiOL's the one who asked me to hold his glasses, Mr. RIBERA, and I see all blurry with 'em!
Give them back right now!

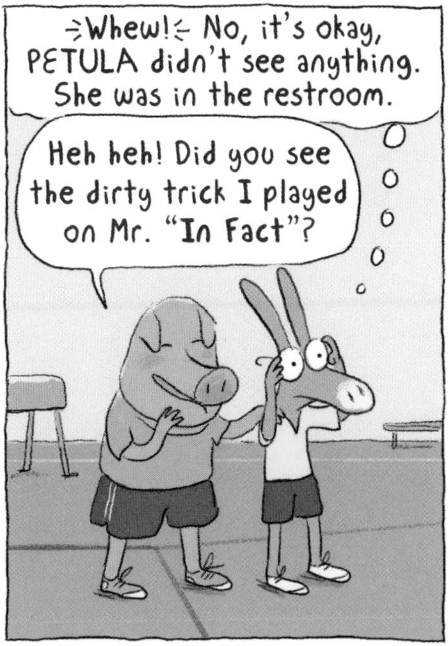
Whew! No, it's okay, PETULA didn't see anything. She was in the restroom.
Heh heh! Did you see the dirty trick I played on Mr. "In Fact"?

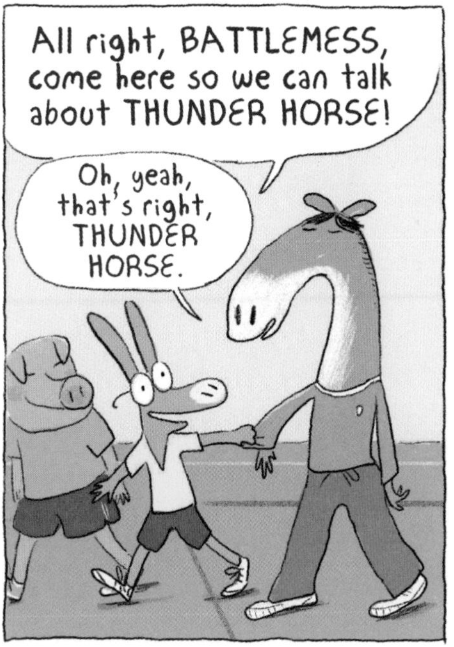
All right, BATTLEMESS, come here so we can talk about THUNDER HORSE!
Oh, yeah, that's right, THUNDER HORSE.

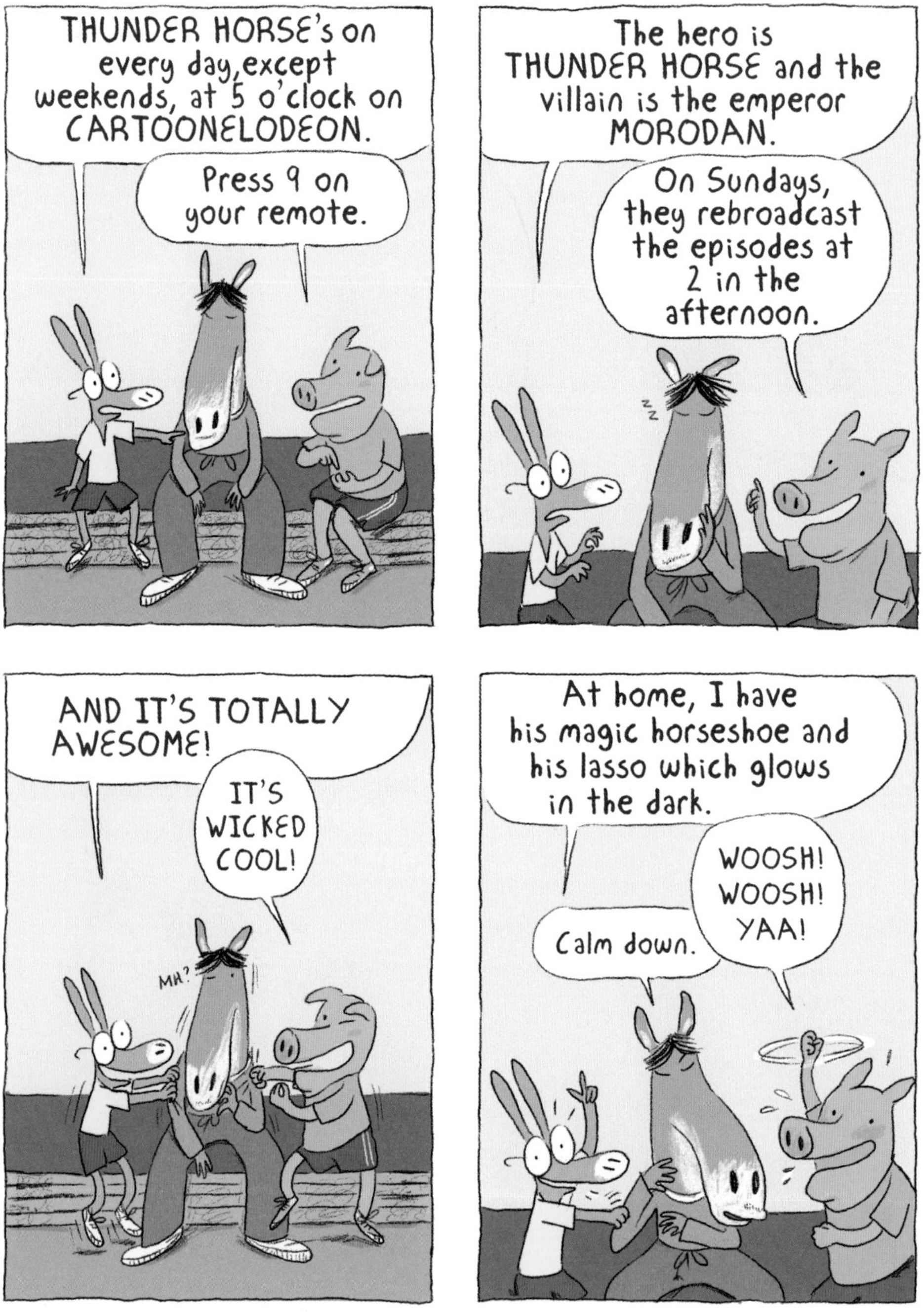
THUNDER HORSE's on every day, except weekends, at 5 o'clock on CARTOONELODEON.
Press 9 on your remote.
The hero is THUNDER HORSE and the villain is the emperor MORODAN.
On Sundays, they rebroadcast the episodes at 2 in the afternoon.
AND IT'S TOTALLY AWESOME!
IT'S WICKED COOL!
MH?
At home, I have his magic horseshoe and his lasso which glows in the dark.
Calm down.
WOOSH! WOOSH! YAA!

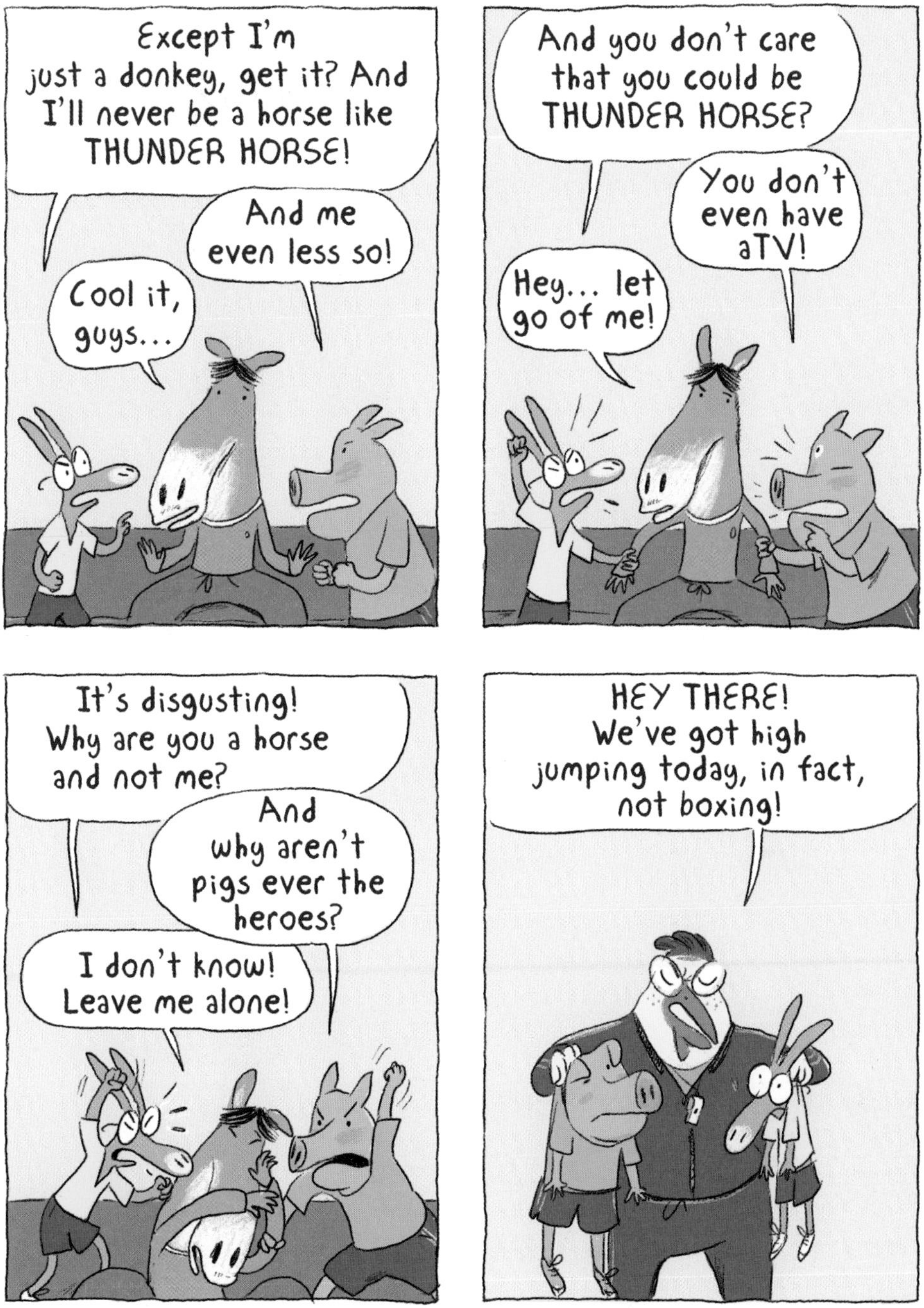
Except I'm just a donkey, get it? And I'll never be a horse like THUNDER HORSE!
And me even less so!
Cool it, guys...
And you don't care that you could be THUNDER HORSE?
You don't even have aTV!
Hey... let go of me!
It's disgusting! Why are you a horse and not me?
And why aren't pigs ever the heroes?
I don't know! Leave me alone!
HEY THERE! We've got high jumping today, in fact, not boxing!

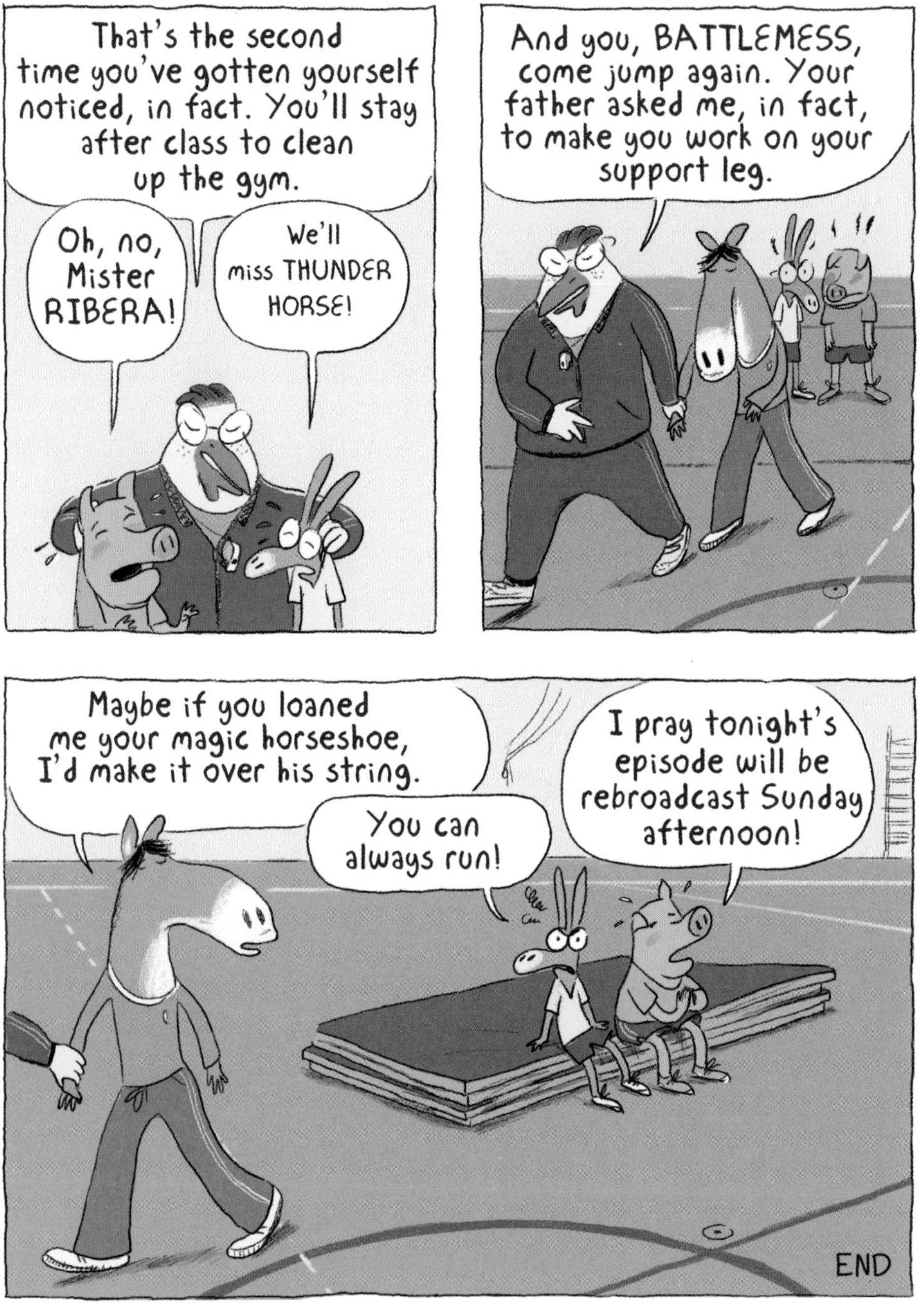
That's the second time you've gotten yourself noticed, in fact. You'll stay after class to clean up the gym.
Oh, no, Mister RIBERA!
We'll miss THUNDER HORSE!
And you, BATTLEMESS, come jump again. Your father asked me, in fact, to make you work on your support leg.
Maybe if you loaned me your magic horseshoe, I'd make it over his string.
You can always run!
I pray tonight's episode will be rebroadcast Sunday afternoon!
END

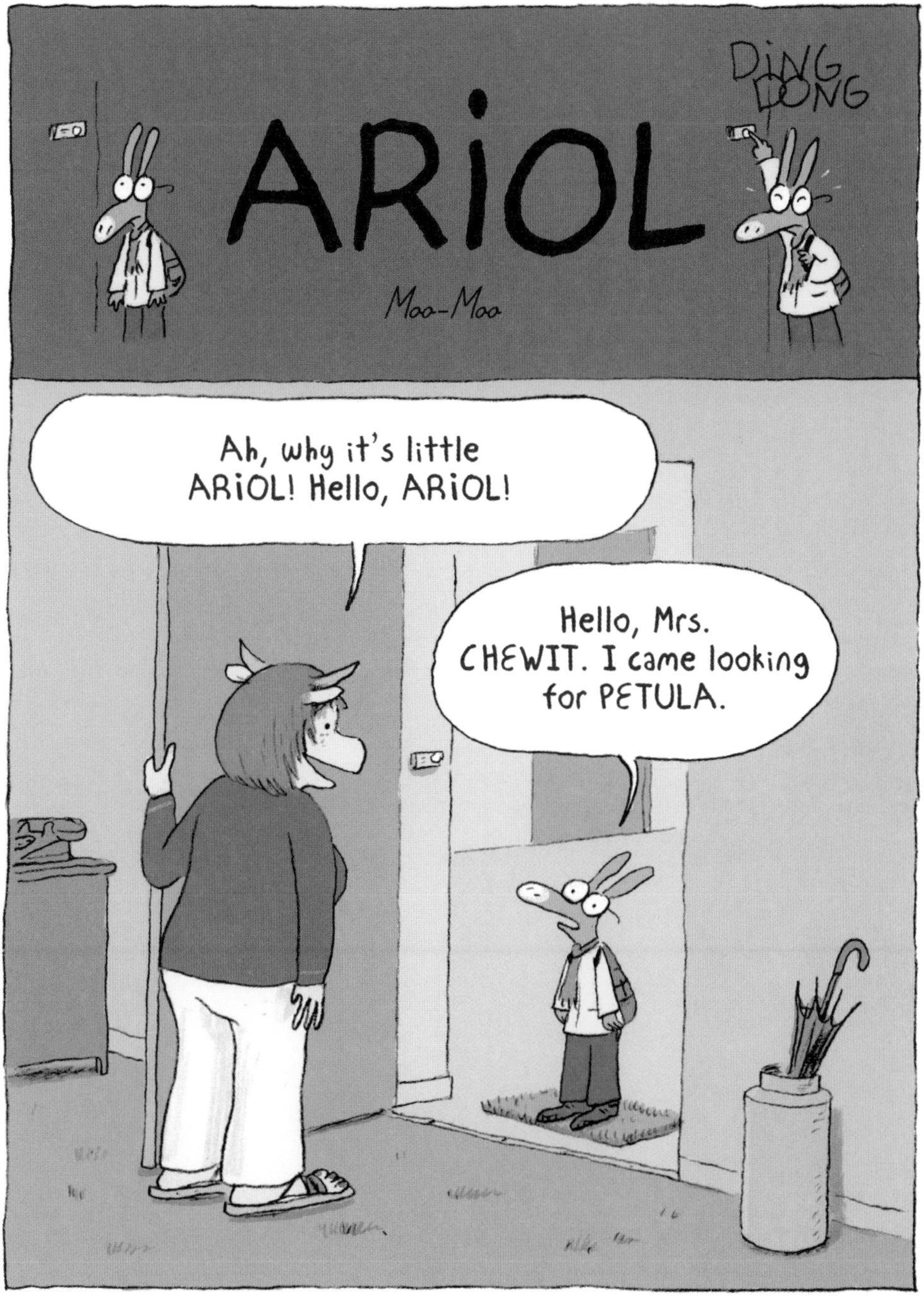
ARiOL
Moo-Moo
DiNG DONG
Ah, why it's little ARiOL! Hello, ARiOL!
Hello, Mrs. CHEWIT. I came looking for PETULA.

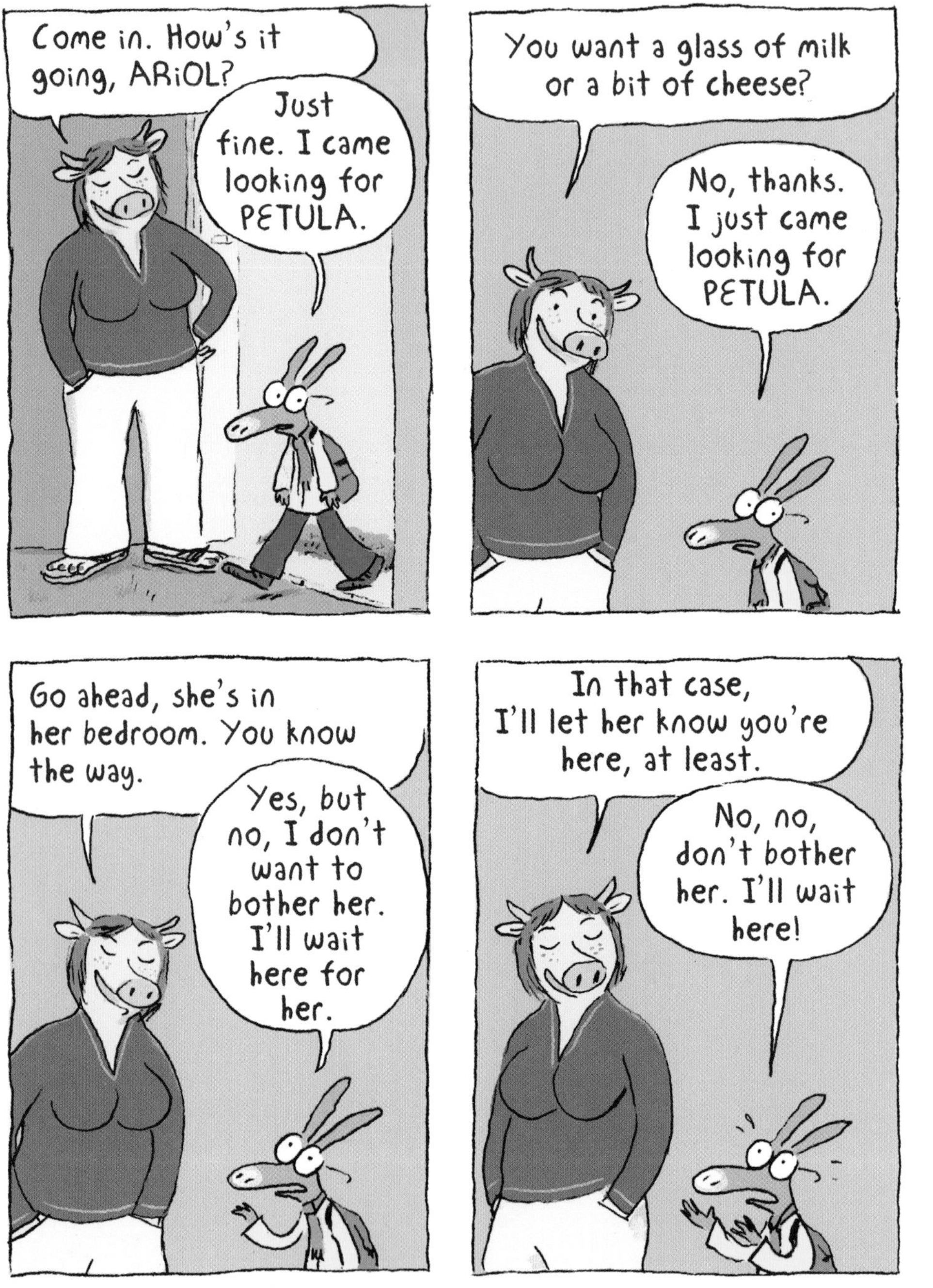
Come in. How's it going, ARiOL?
Just fine. I came looking for PETULA.
You want a glass of milk or a bit of cheese?
No, thanks. I just came looking for PETULA.
Go ahead, she's in her bedroom. You know the way.
Yes, but no, I don't want to bother her. I'll wait here for her.
In that case, I'll let her know you're here, at least.
No, no, don't bother her. I'll wait here!

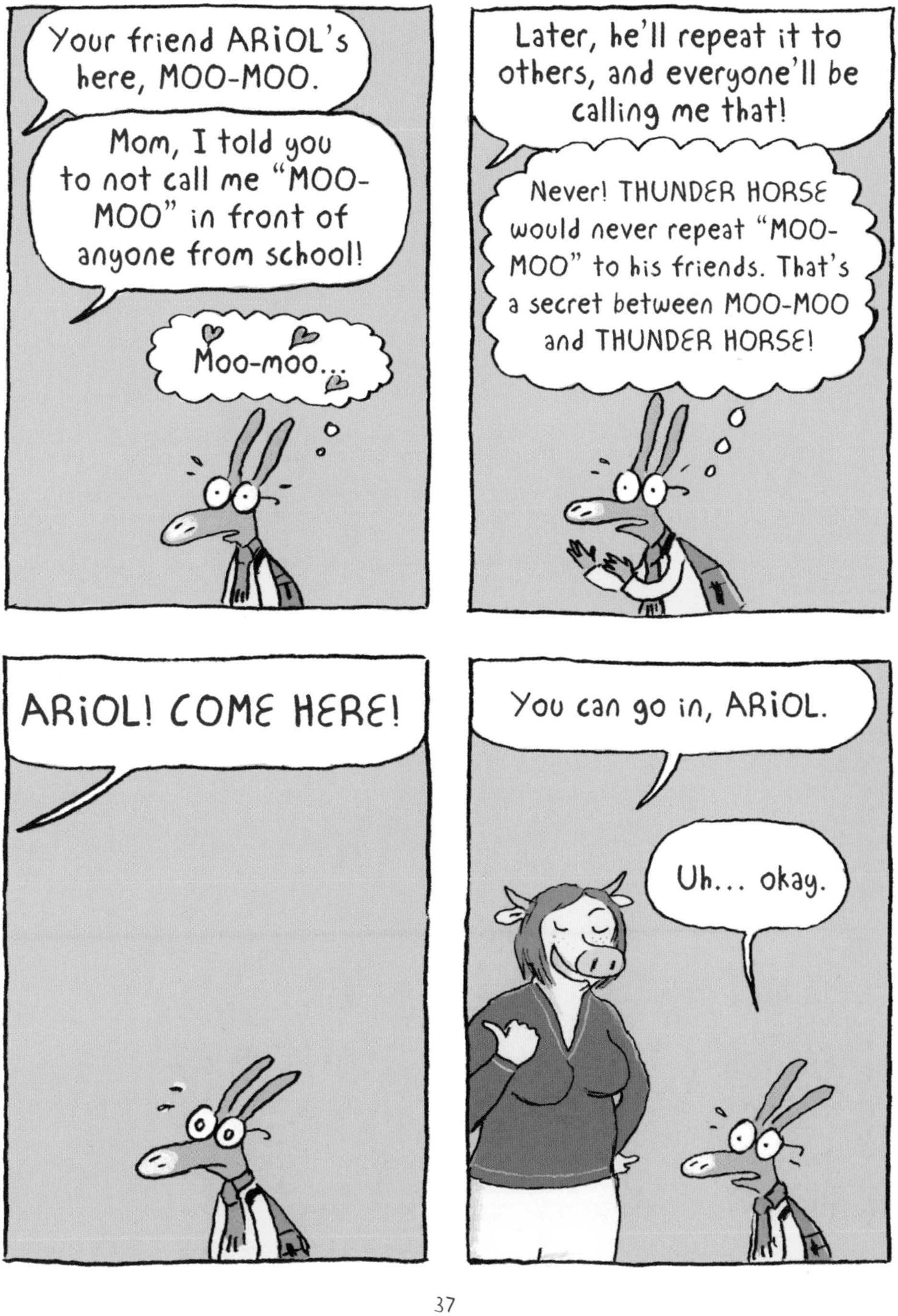
Your friend ARiOL's here, MOO-MOO.
Mom, I told you to not call me "MOO-MOO" in front of anyone from school!
Moo-moo...
Later, he'll repeat it to others, and everyone'll be calling me that!
Never! THUNDER HORSE would never repeat "MOO-MOO" to his friends. That's a secret between MOO-MOO and THUNDER HORSE!
ARiOL! COME HERE!
You can go in, ARiOL.
Uh... okay.

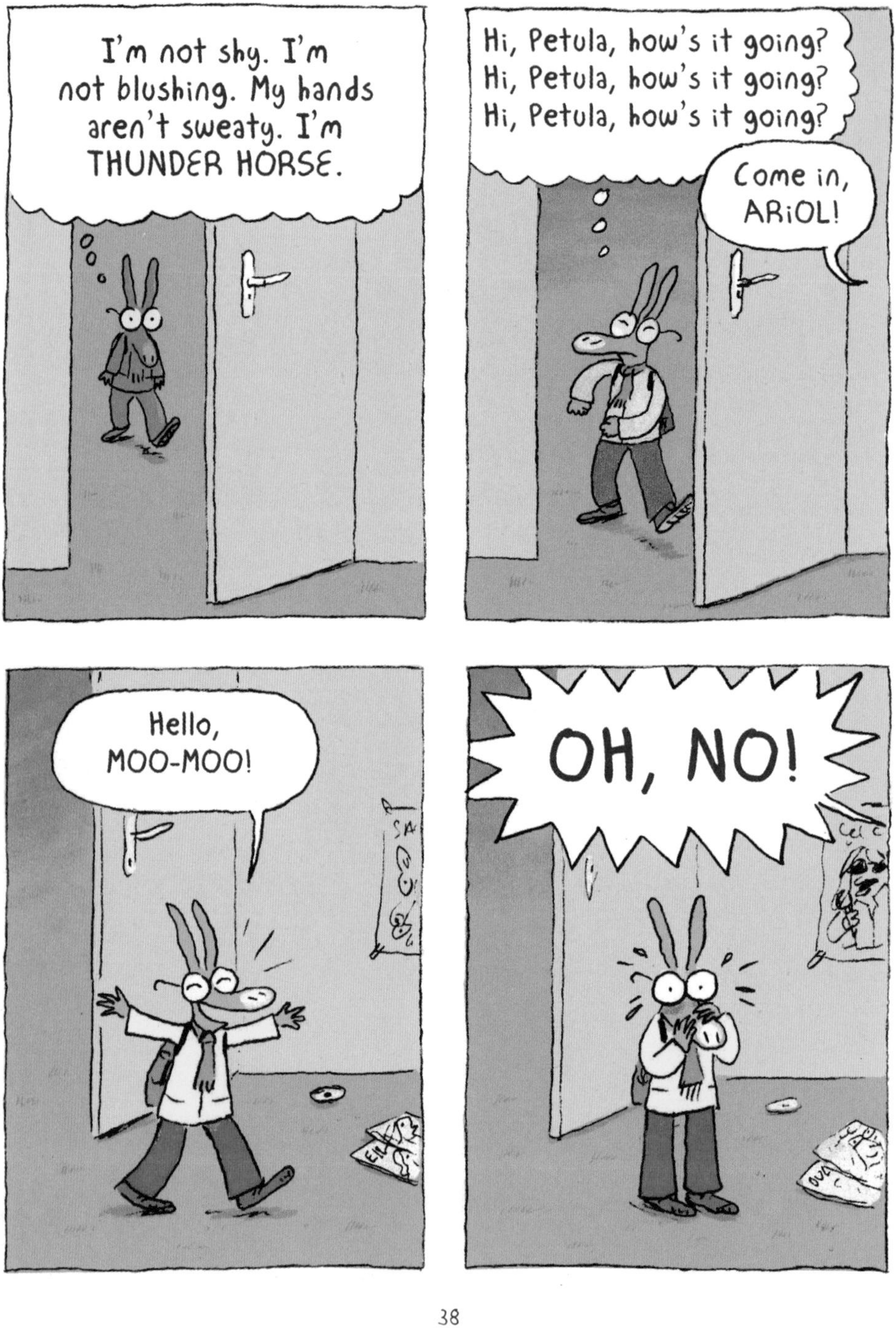
I'm not shy. I'm not blushing. My hands aren't sweaty. I'm THUNDER HORSE.
Hi, Petula, how's it going? Hi, Petula, how's it going? Hi, Petula, how's it going?
Come in, ARiOL!
Hello, MOO-MOO!
OH, NO!

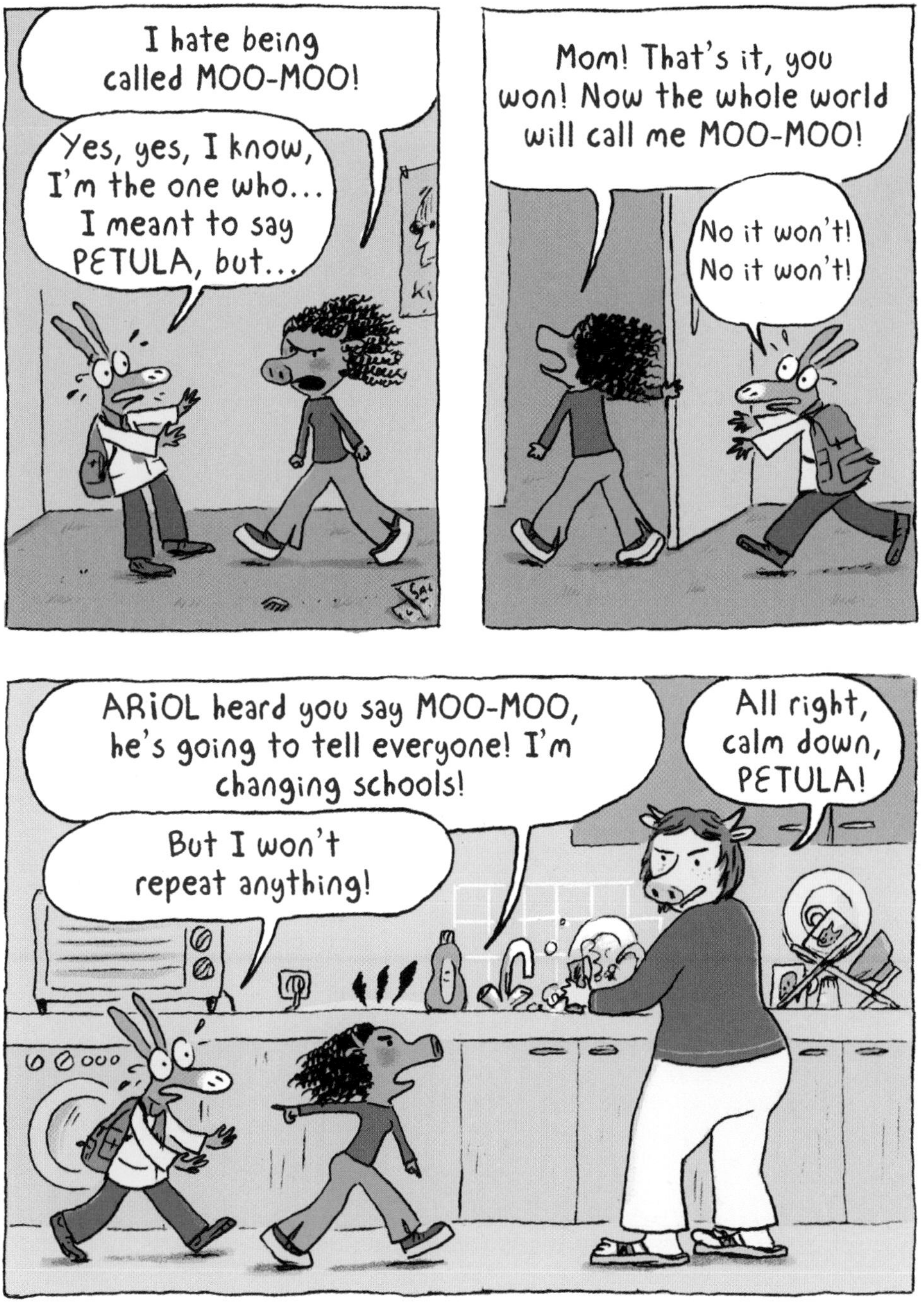
I hate being called MOO-MOO!
Yes, yes, I know, I'm the one who... I meant to say PETULA, but...
Mom! That's it, you won! Now the whole world will call me MOO-MOO!
No it won't! No it won't!
ARIOL heard you say MOO-MOO, he's going to tell everyone! I'm changing schools!
But I won't repeat anything!
All right, calm down, PETULA!

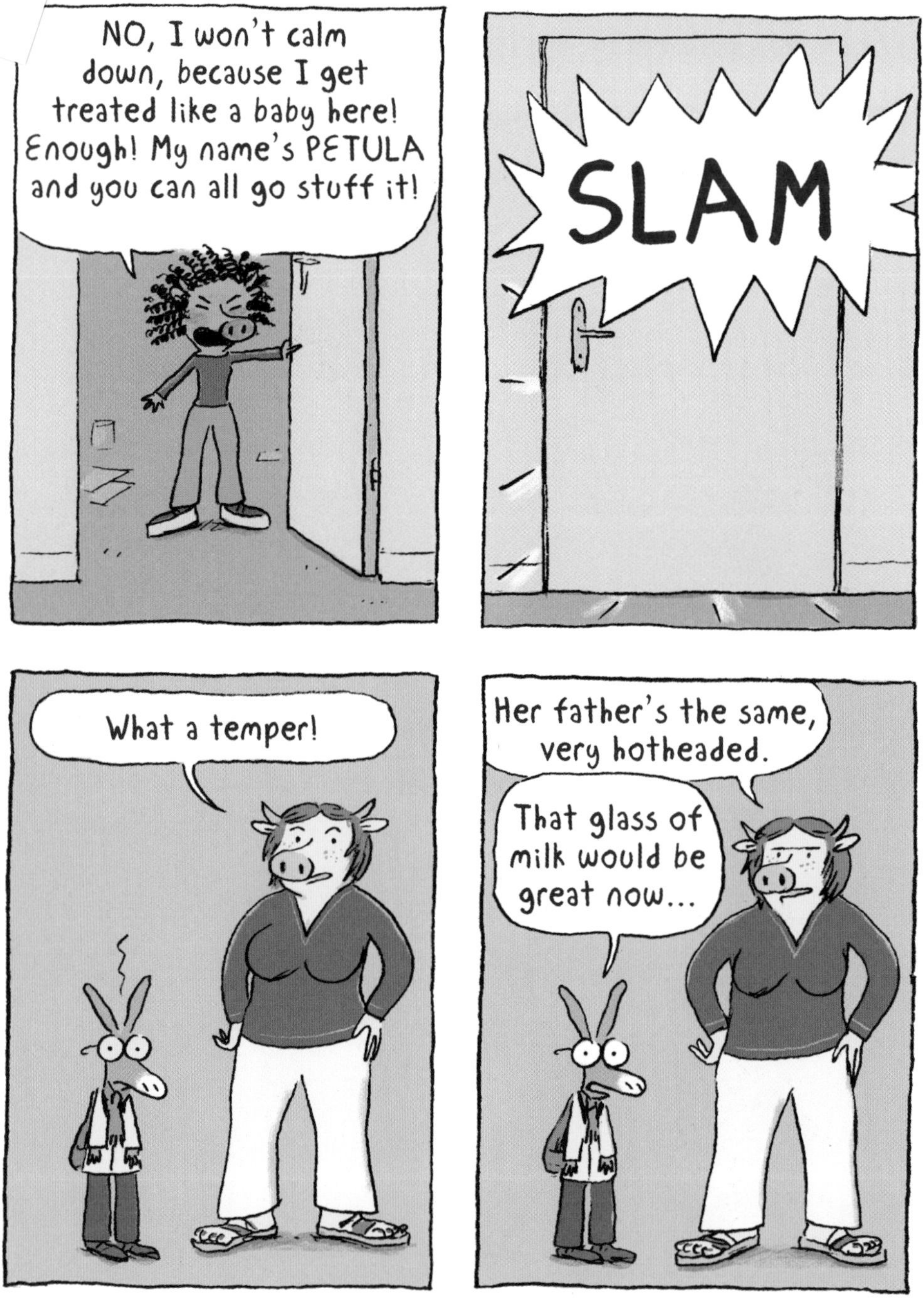
NO, I won't calm down, because I get treated like a baby here! Enough! My name's PETULA and you can all go stuff it!
SLAM
What a temper!
Her father's the same, very hotheaded.
That glass of milk would be great now...

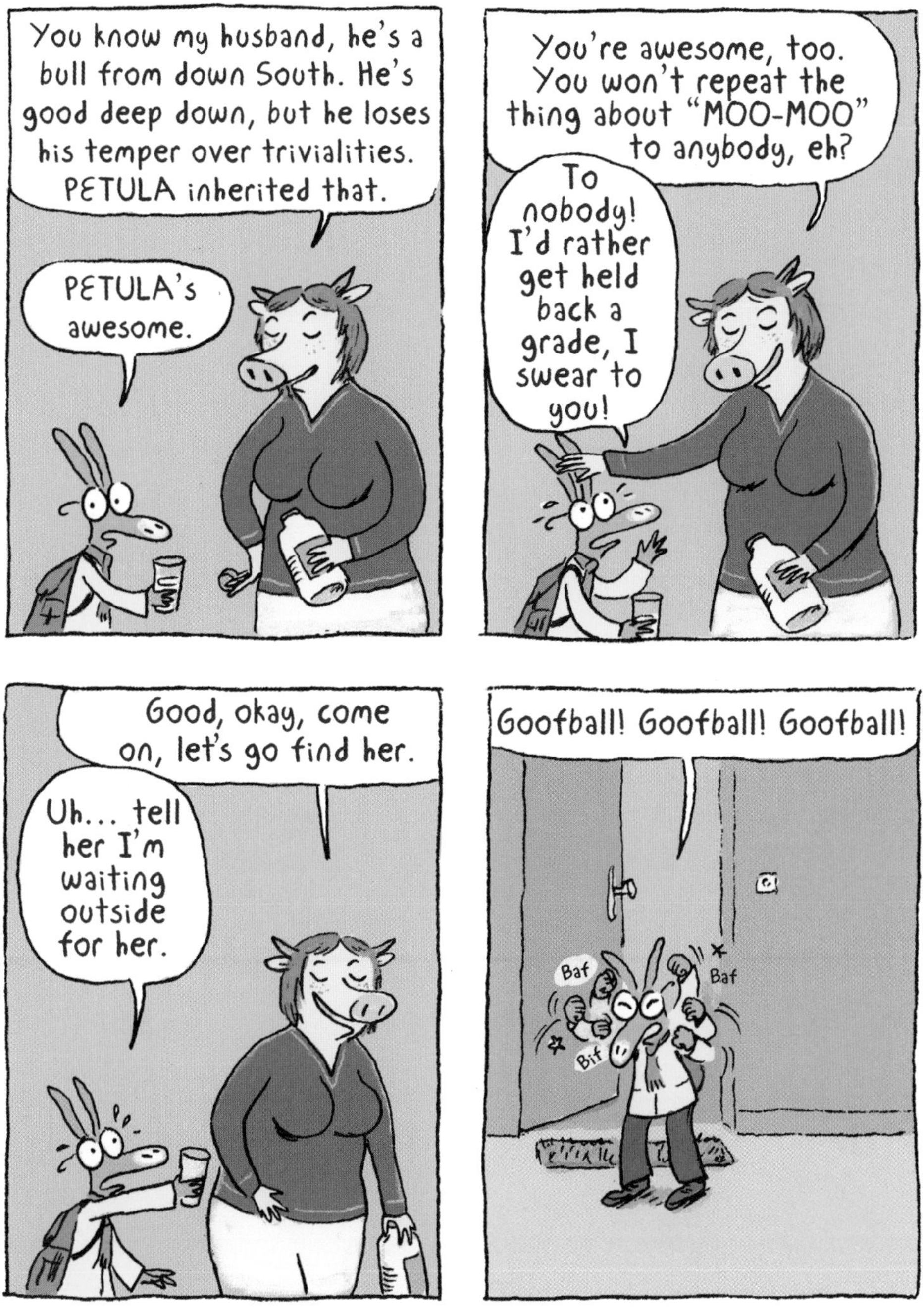
You know my husband, he's a bull from down South. He's good deep down, but he loses his temper over trivialities. PETULA inherited that.
PETULA's awesome.
You're awesome, too. You won't repeat the thing about "MOO-MOO" to anybody, eh?
To nobody! I'd rather get held back a grade, I swear to you!
Good, okay, come on, let's go find her.
Uh... tell her I'm waiting outside for her.
Goofball! Goofball! Goofball!
Baf
Baf
Bif

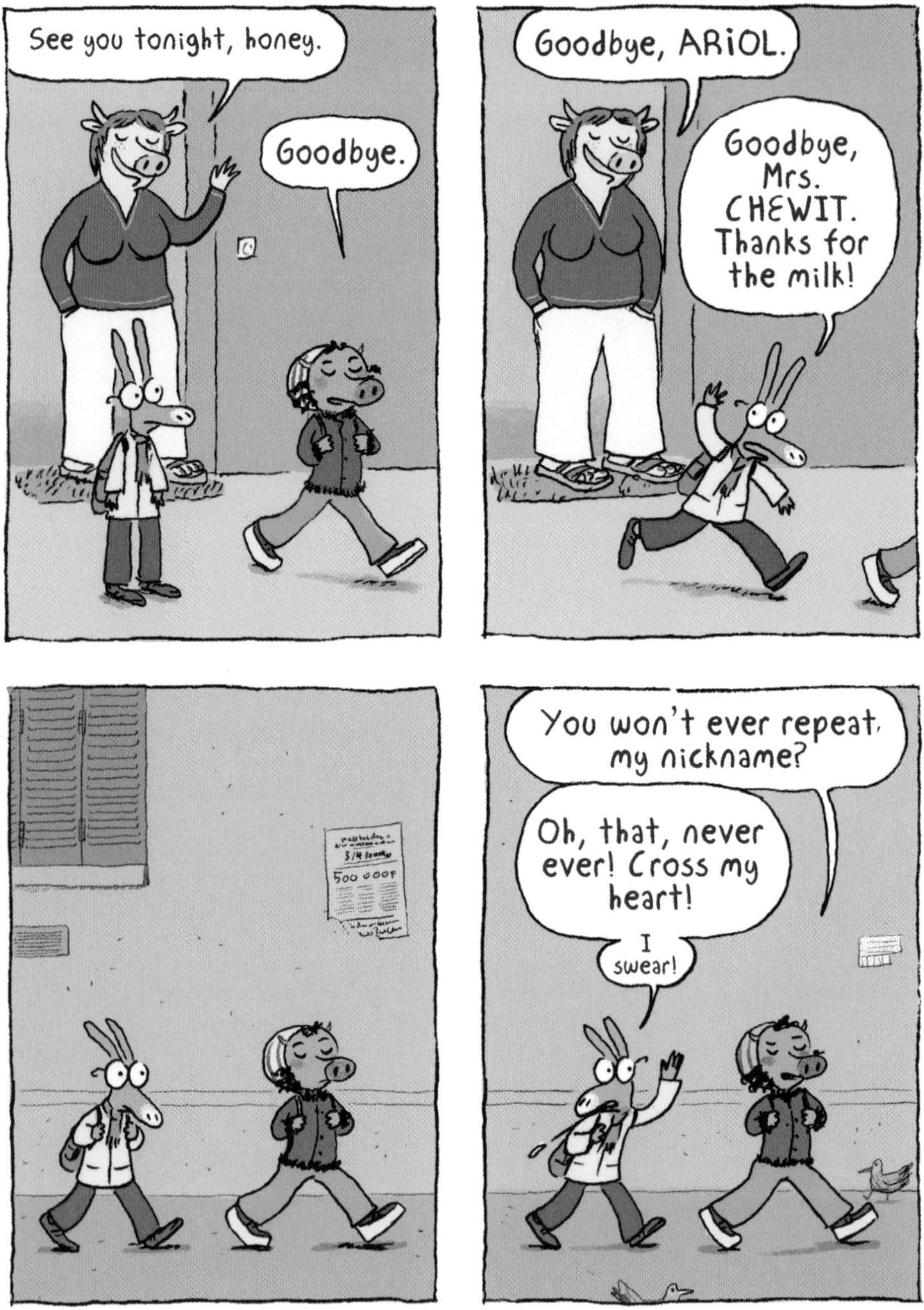
See you tonight, honey.
Goodbye.
Goodbye, ARIOL.
Goodbye, Mrs. CHEWIT. Thanks for the milk!
You won't ever repeat my nickname?
Oh, that, never ever! Cross my heart!
I swear!

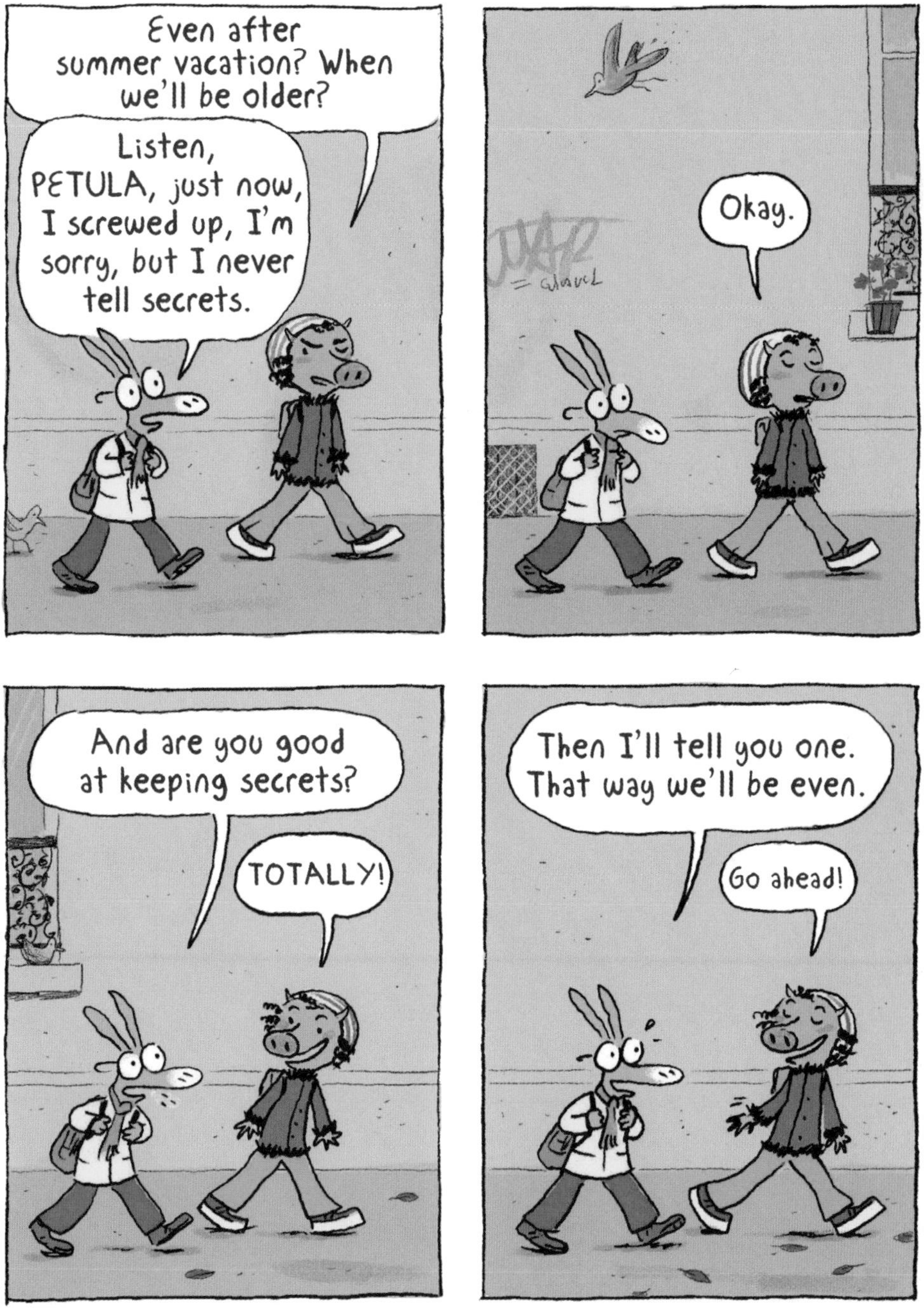
Even after summer vacation? When we'll be older?
Listen, PETULA, just now, I screwed up, I'm sorry, but I never tell secrets.
Okay.
And are you good at keeping secrets?
TOTALLY!
Then I'll tell you one. That way we'll be even.
Go ahead!

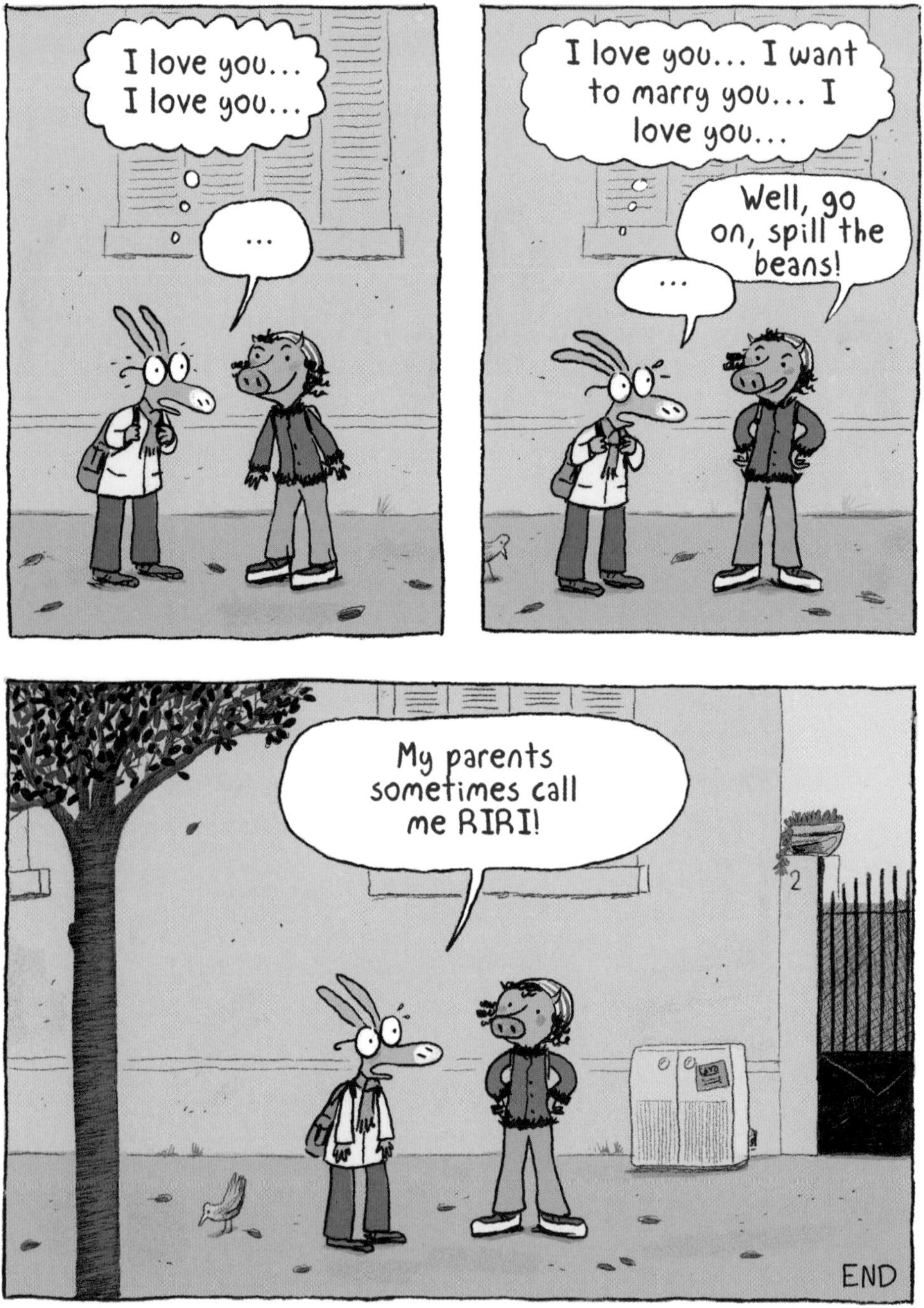
I love you...
I love you...
...
I love you... I want to marry you... I love you...
...
Well, go on, spill the beans!
My parents sometimes call me RIRI!
2
END

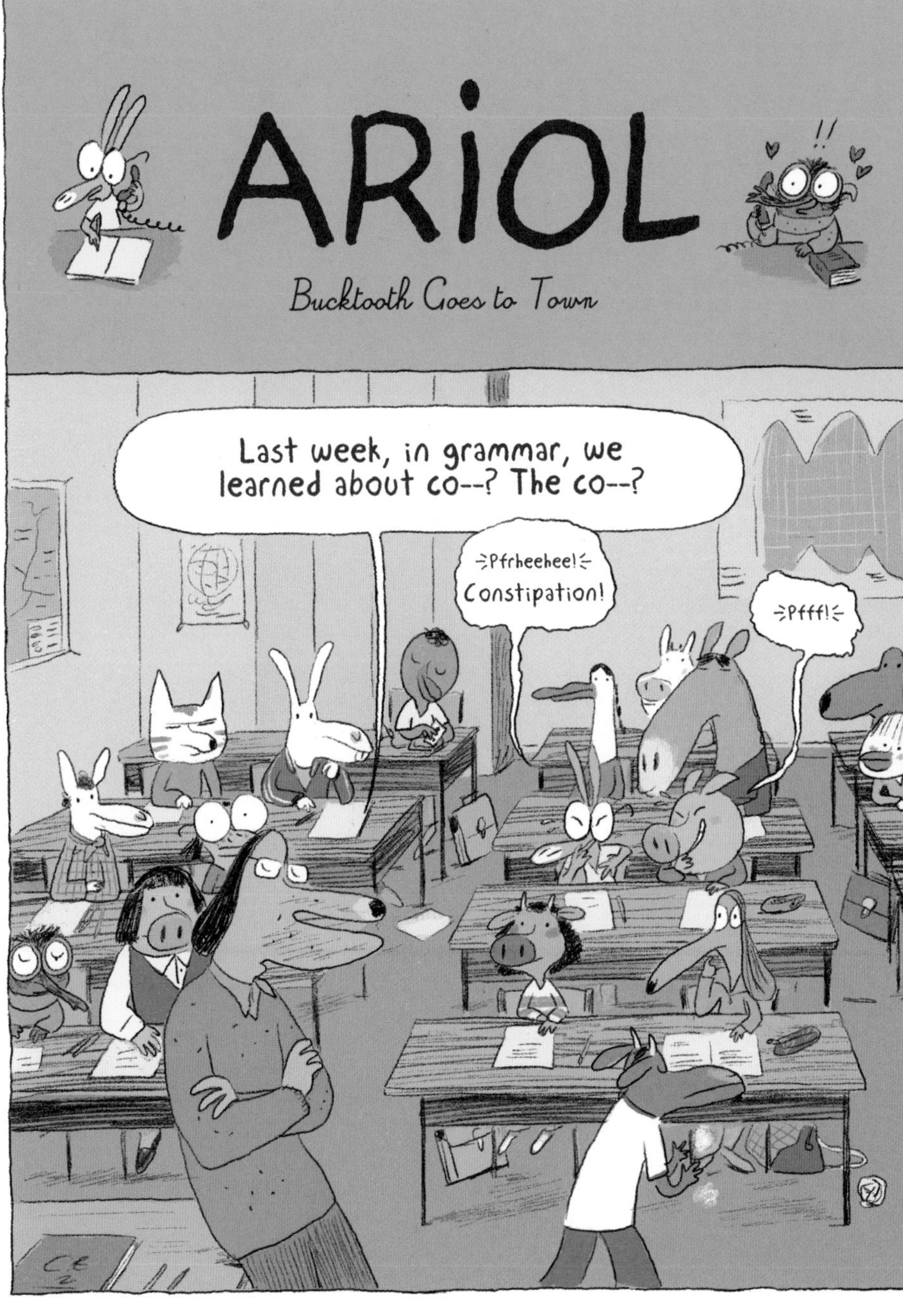

ARIOL
Bucktooth Goes to Town
Last week, in grammar, we learned about co--? The co--?
Pfrheehee!
Constipation!
Pffff!

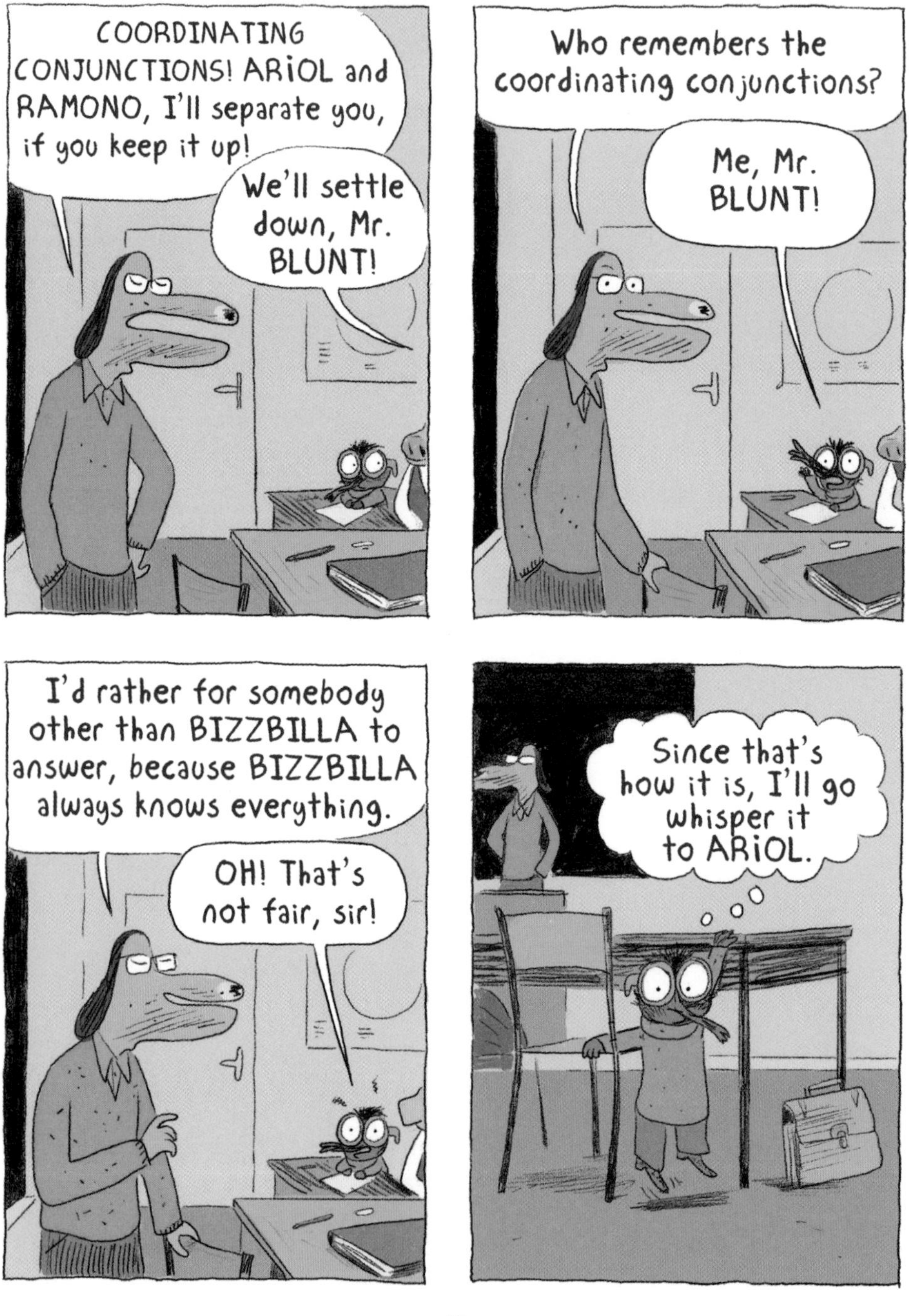
COORDINATING CONJUNCTIONS! ARIOL and RAMONO, I'll separate you, if you keep it up!
We'll settle down, Mr. BLUNT!
Who remembers the coordinating conjunctions?
Me, Mr. BLUNT!
I'd rather for somebody other than BIZZBILLA to answer, because BIZZBILLA always knows everything.
OH! That's not fair, sir!
Since that's how it is, I'll go whisper it to ARIOL.

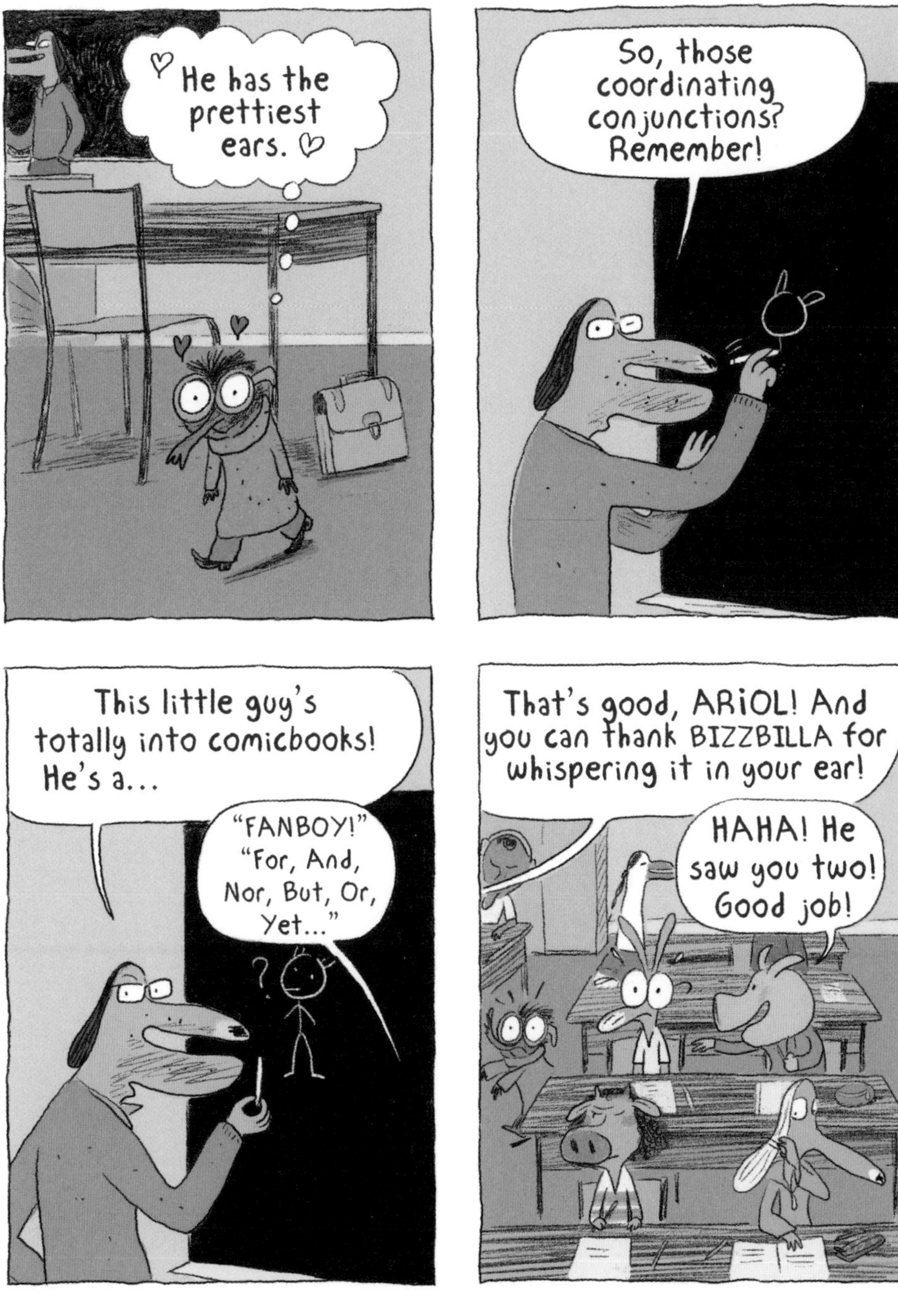
He has the prettiest ears.
So, those coordinating conjunctions? Remember!
This little guy's totally into comicbooks! He's a...
"FANBOY!" "For, And, Nor, But, Or, Yet..."
?
That's good, ARiOL! And you can thank BIZZBILLA for whispering it in your ear!
HAHA! He saw you two! Good job!

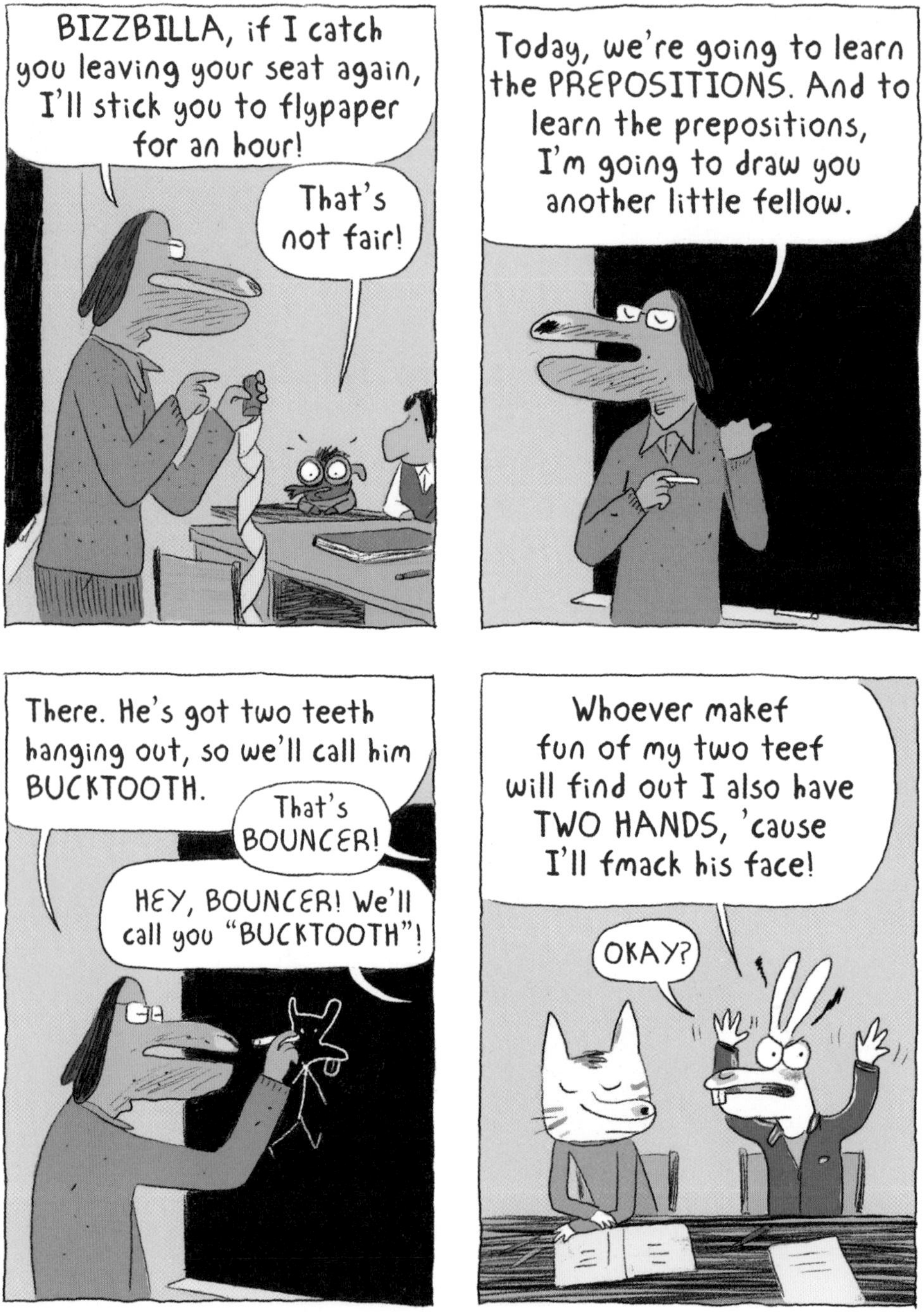
BIZZBILLA, if I catch you leaving your seat again, I'll stick you to flypaper for an hour!
That's not fair!
Today, we're going to learn the PREPOSITIONS. And to learn the prepositions, I'm going to draw you another little fellow.
There. He's got two teeth hanging out, so we'll call him BUCKTOOTH.
That's BOUNCER!
HEY, BOUNCER! We'll call you "BUCKTOOTH"!
Whoever makef fun of my two teef will find out I also have TWO HANDS, 'cause I'll fmack his face!
OKAY?

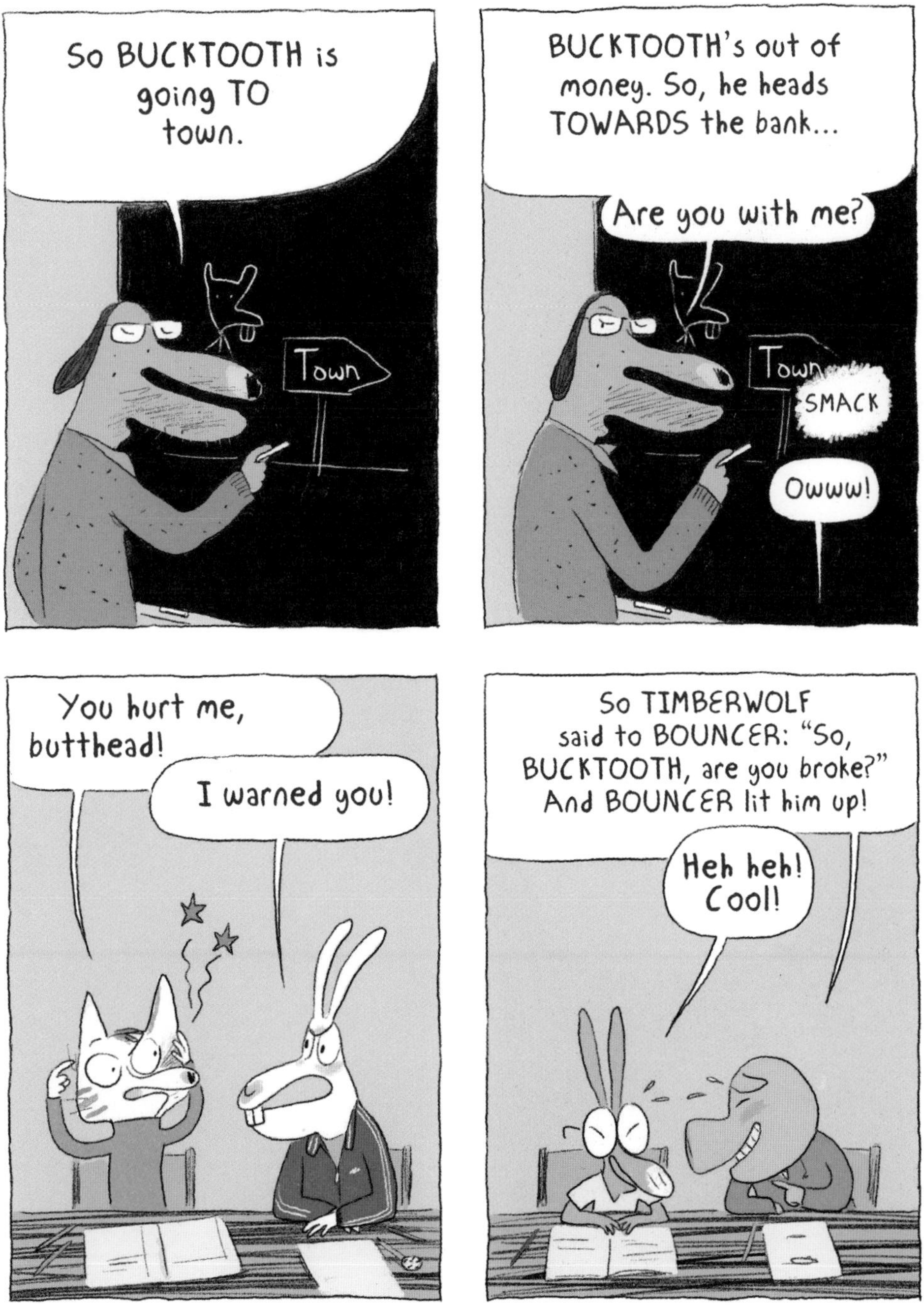
So BUCKTOOTH is going TO town.
Town
BUCKTOOTH's out of money. So, he heads TOWARDS the bank...
Are you with me?
Town
SMACK
Owww!
You hurt me, butthead!
I warned you!
So TIMBERWOLF said to BOUNCER: "So, BUCKTOOTH, are you broke?" And BOUNCER lit him up!
Heh heh! Cool!

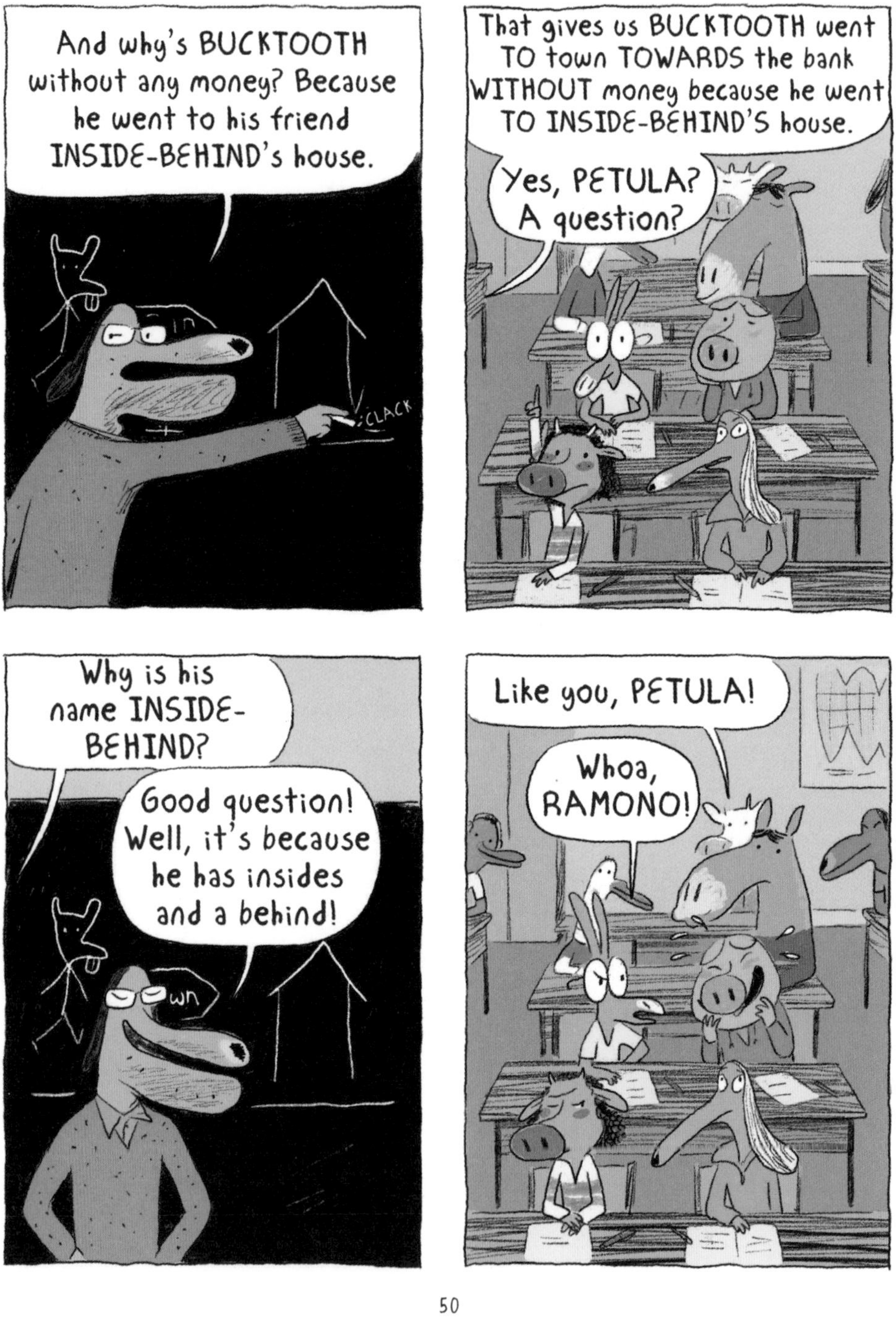
And why's BUCKTOOTH without any money? Because he went to his friend INSIDE-BEHIND's house.
in
CLACK
That gives us BUCKTOOTH went TO town TOWARDS the bank WITHOUT money because he went TO INSIDE-BEHIND'S house.
Yes, PETULA? A question?
Why is his name INSIDE-BEHIND?
Good question! Well, it's because he has insides and a behind!
wn
Like you, PETULA!
Whoa, RAMONO!

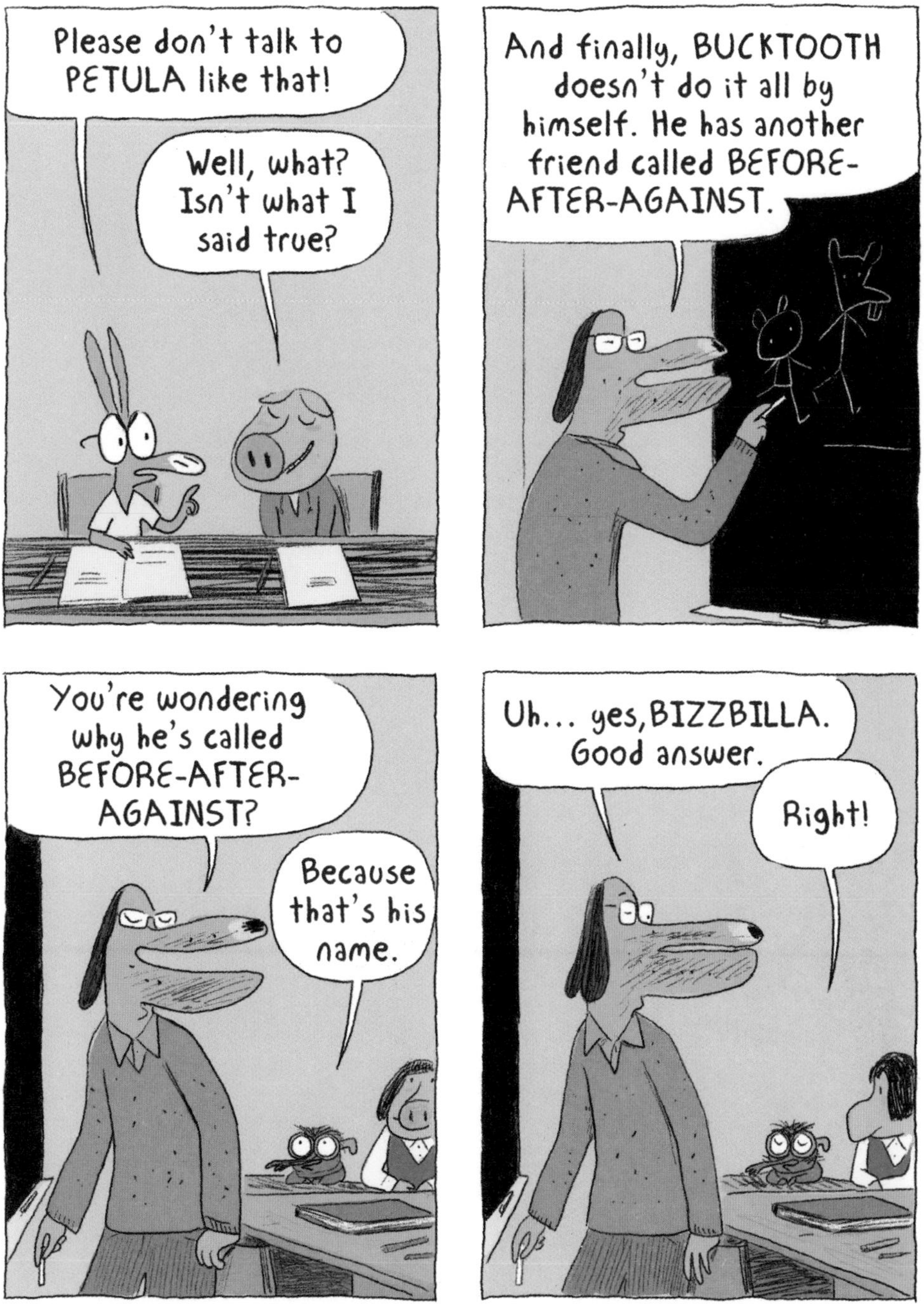
Please don't talk to PETULA like that!
Well, what? Isn't what I said true?
And finally, BUCKTOOTH doesn't do it all by himself. He has another friend called BEFORE-AFTER-AGAINST.
You're wondering why he's called BEFORE-AFTER-AGAINST?
Because that's his name.
Uh... yes, BIZZBILLA. Good answer.
Right!

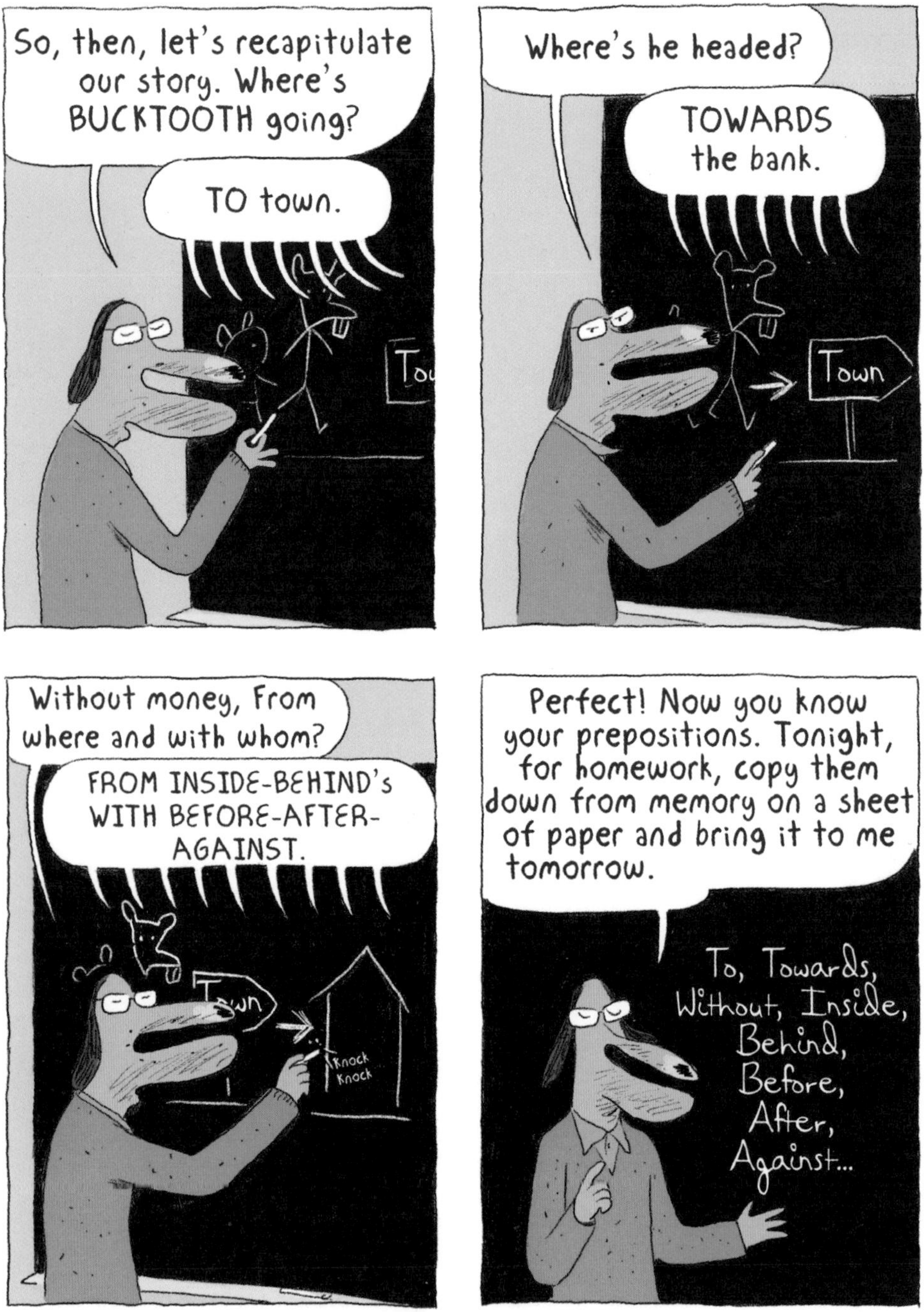
So, then, let's recapitulate our story. Where's BUCKTOOTH going?
TO town.
Where's he headed?
TOWARDS the bank.
Town
Without money, From where and with whom?
FROM INSIDE-BEHIND's WITH BEFORE-AFTER-AGAINST.
Knock Knock
Perfect! Now you know your prepositions. Tonight, for homework, copy them down from memory on a sheet of paper and bring it to me tomorrow.
To, Towards, Without, Inside, Behind, Before, After, Against...

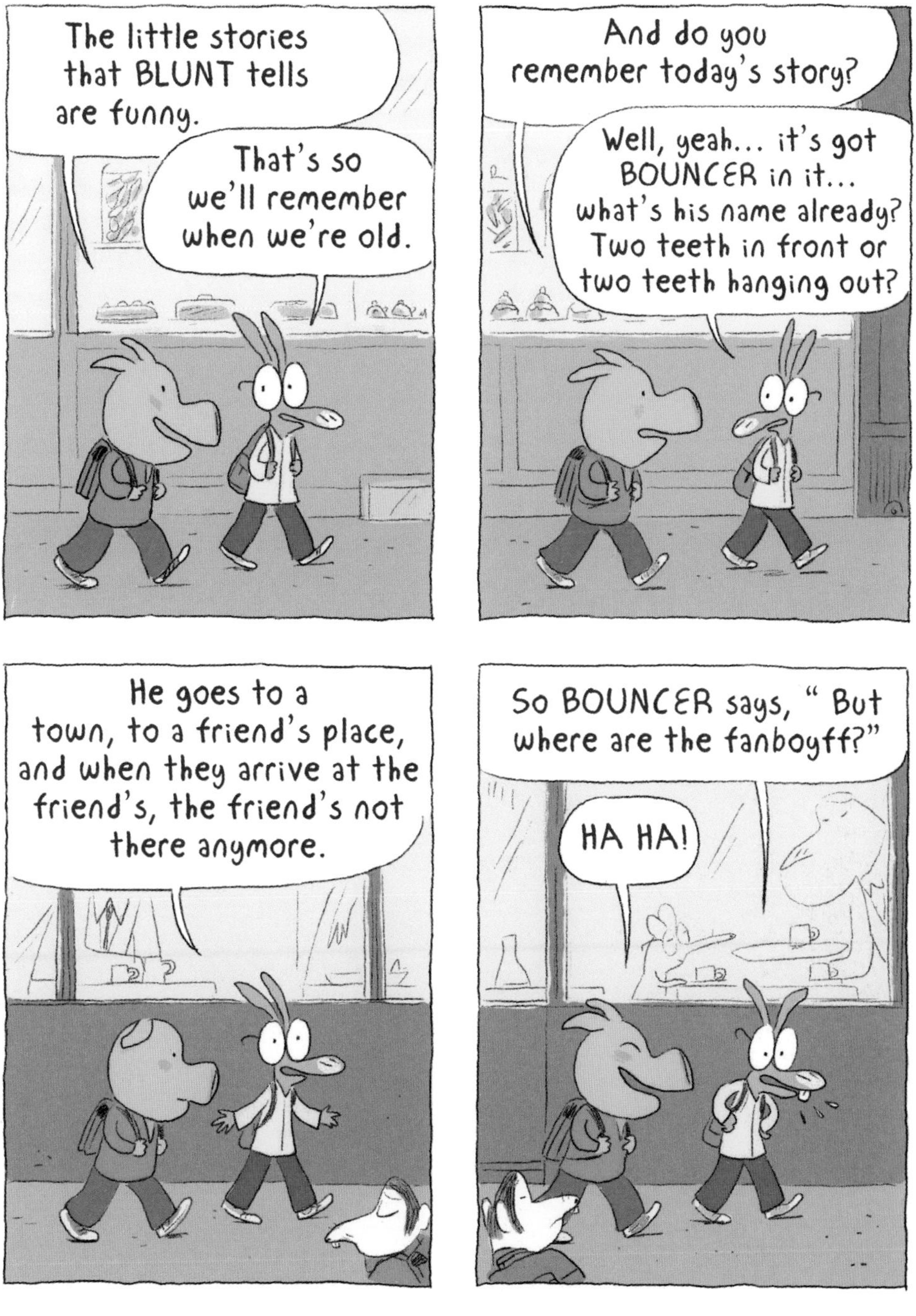
The little stories that BLUNT tells are funny.
That's so we'll remember when we're old.
And do you remember today's story?
Well, yeah... it's got BOUNCER in it... what's his name already? Two teeth in front or two teeth hanging out?
He goes to a town, to a friend's place, and when they arrive at the friend's, the friend's not there anymore.
So BOUNCER says, " But where are the fanboyff?"
HA HA!

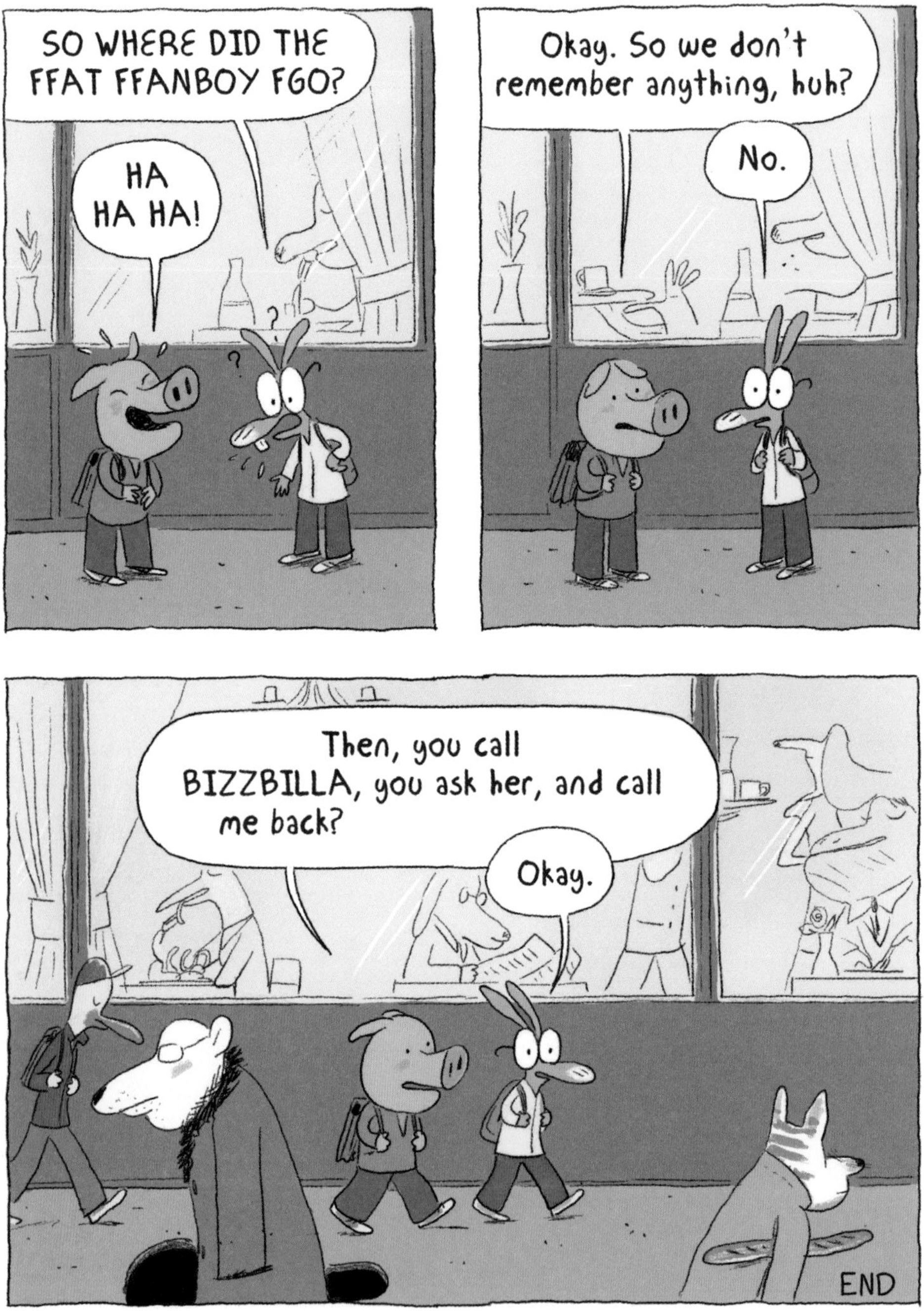
SO WHERE DID THE FFAT FFANBOY FGO?
HA HA HA!
?
?
Okay. So we don't remember anything, huh?
No.
Then, you call BIZZBILLA, you ask her, and call me back?
Okay.
END

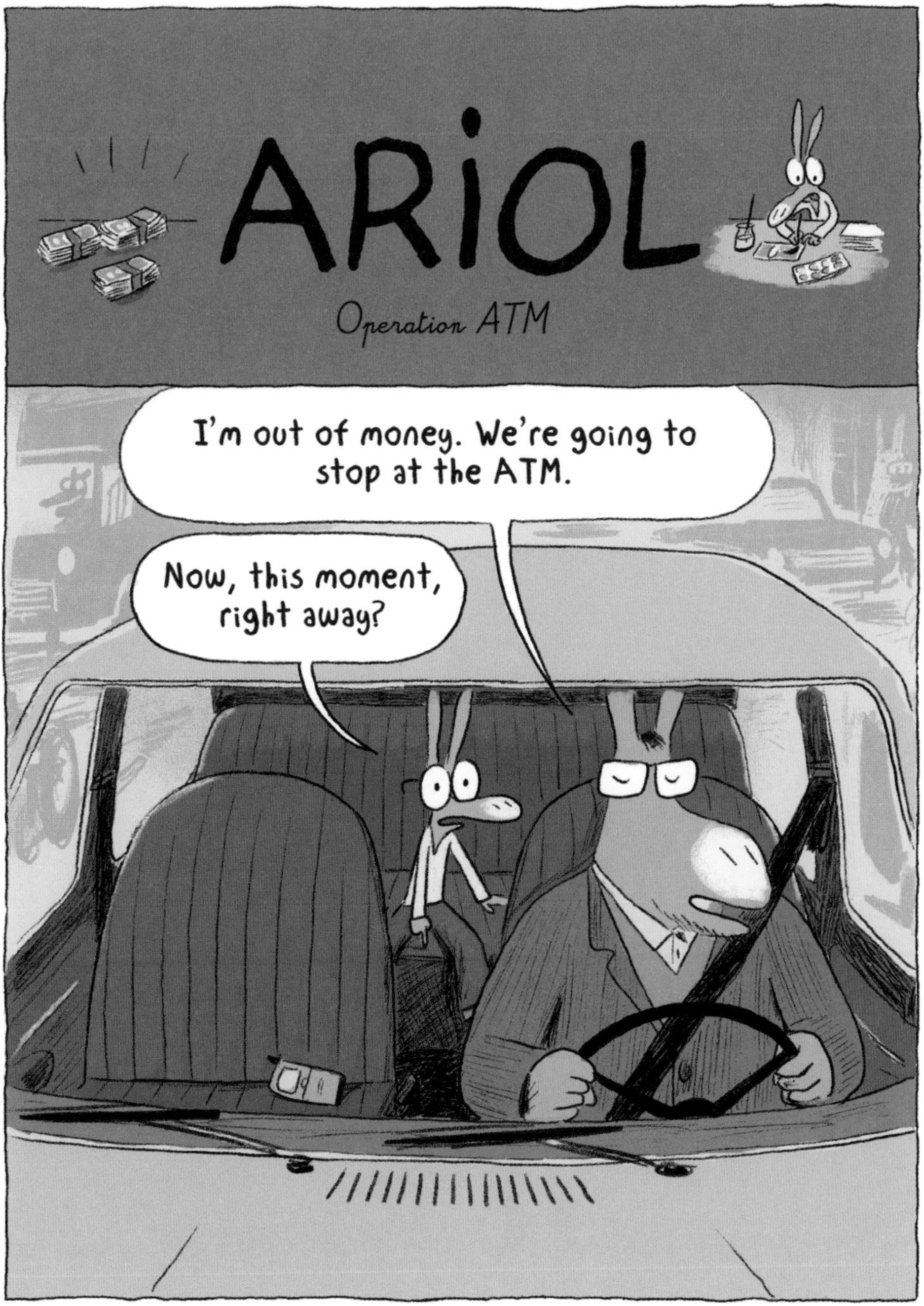
ARIOL
Operation ATM
I'm out of money. We're going to stop at the ATM.
Now, this moment, right away?

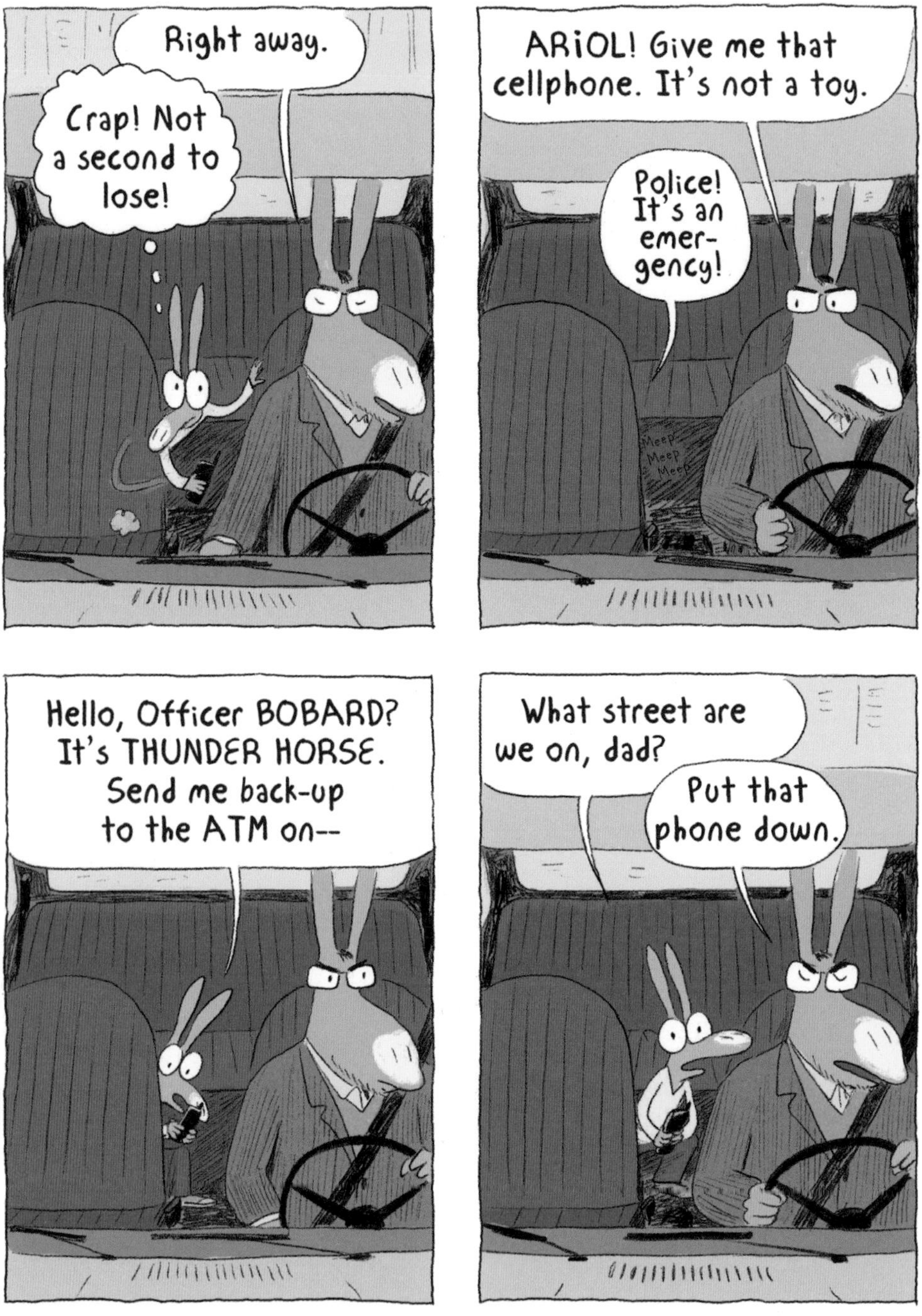
Right away.
Crap! Not a second to lose!
ARiOL! Give me that cellphone. It's not a toy.
Police! It's an emer-gency!
Meep Meep Meep
Hello, Officer BOBARD? It's THUNDER HORSE. Send me back-up to the ATM on--
What street are we on, dad?
Put that phone down.

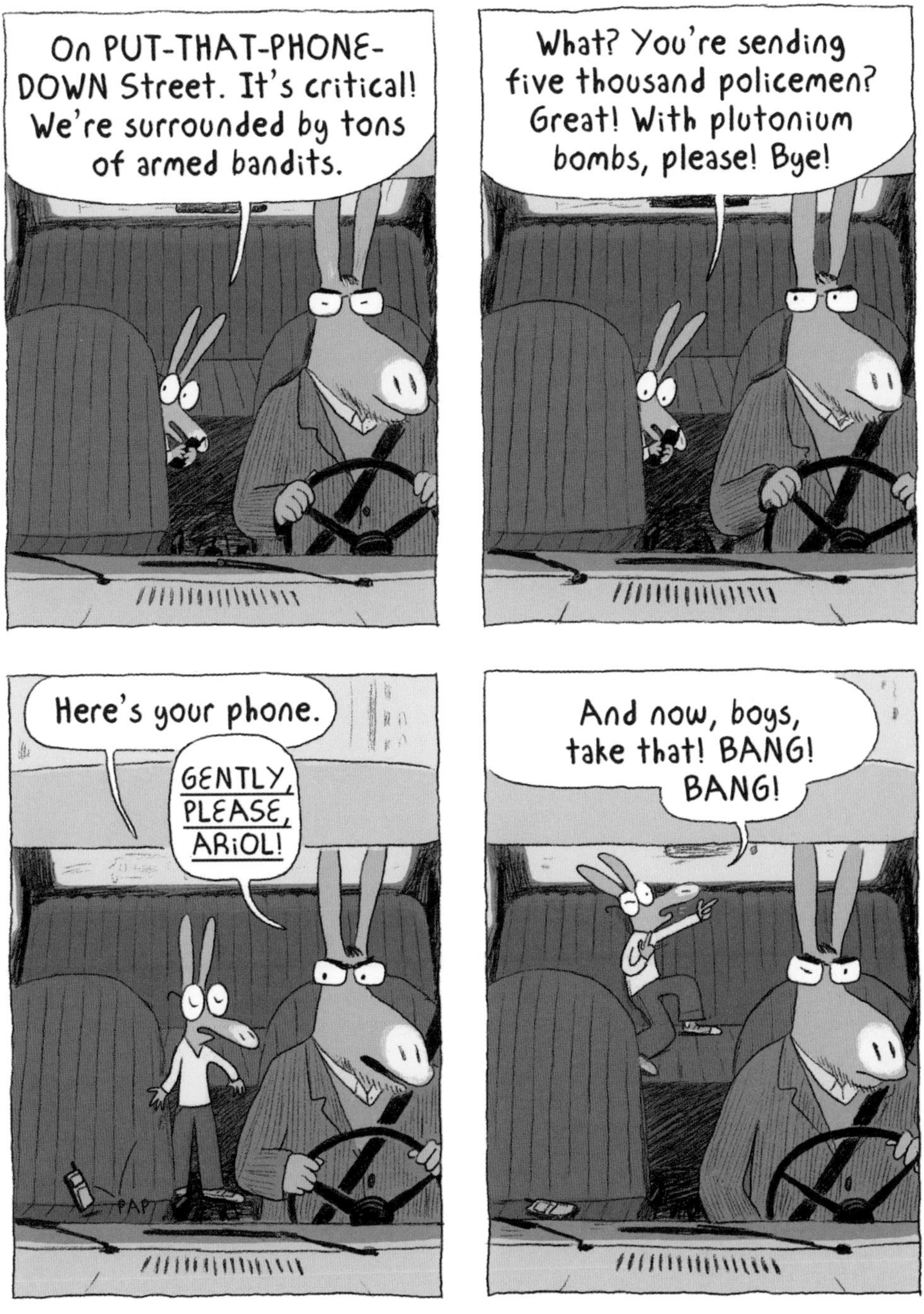
On PUT-THAT-PHONE-DOWN Street. It's critical! We're surrounded by tons of armed bandits.
What? You're sending five thousand policemen? Great! With plutonium bombs, please! Bye!
Here's your phone.
GENTLY, PLEASE, ARiOL!
PAP
And now, boys, take that! BANG! BANG!

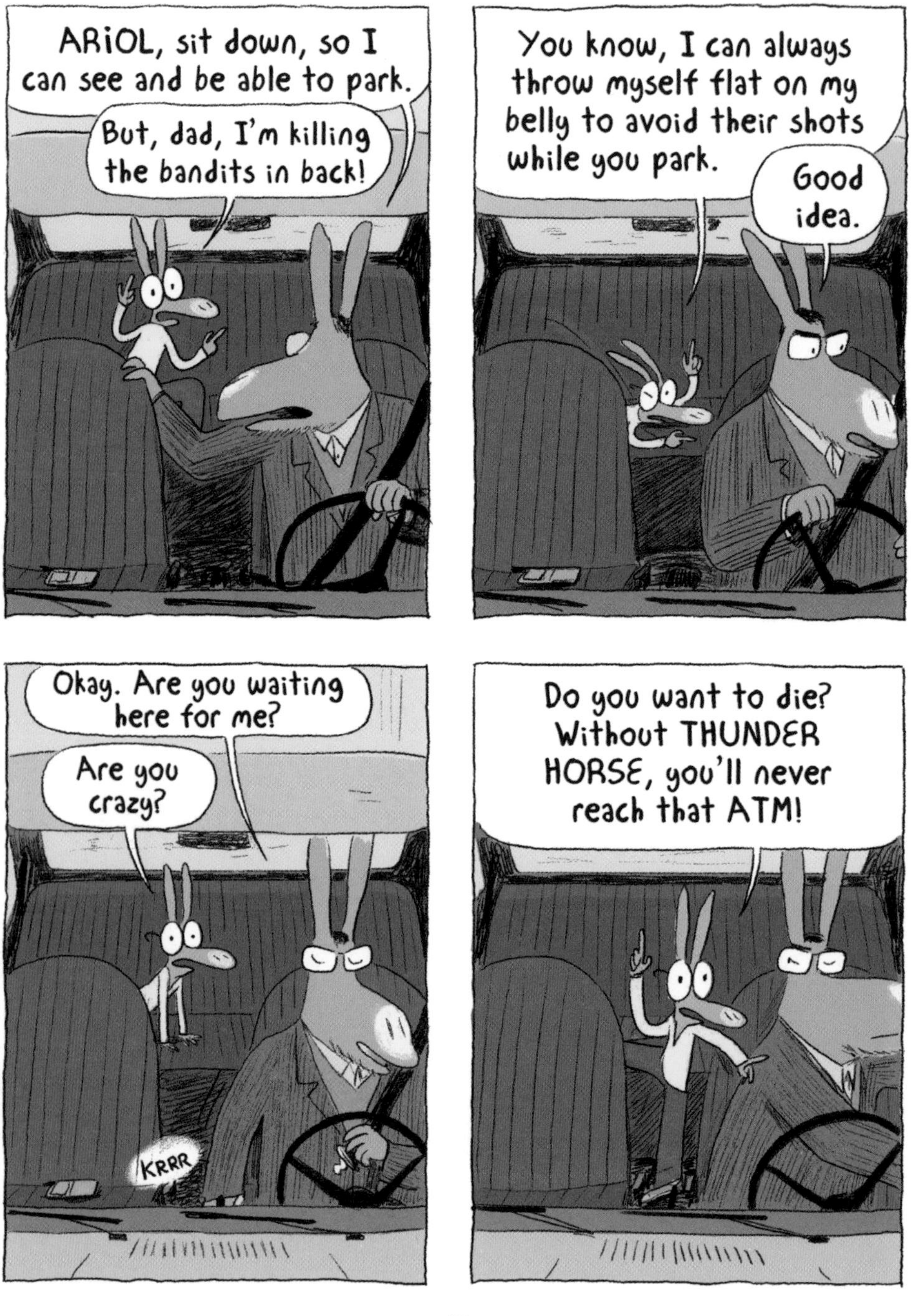
ARiOL, sit down, so I can see and be able to park.
But, dad, I'm killing the bandits in back!
You know, I can always throw myself flat on my belly to avoid their shots while you park.
Good idea.
Okay. Are you waiting here for me?
Are you crazy?
KRRR
Do you want to die? Without THUNDER HORSE, you'll never reach that ATM!

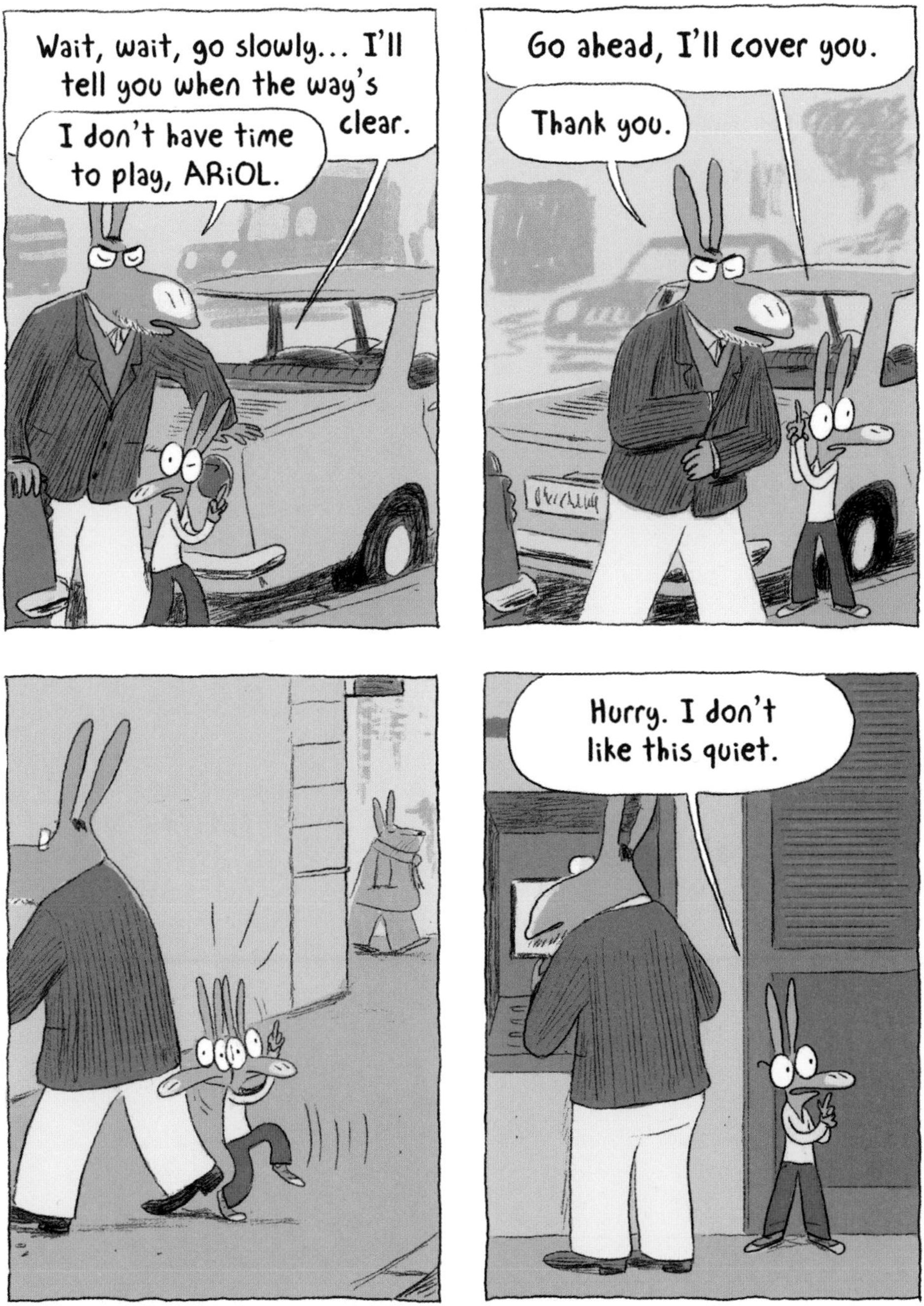
Wait, wait, go slowly... I'll tell you when the way's clear.
I don't have time to play, ARiOL.
Go ahead, I'll cover you.
Thank you.
Hurry. I don't like this quiet.

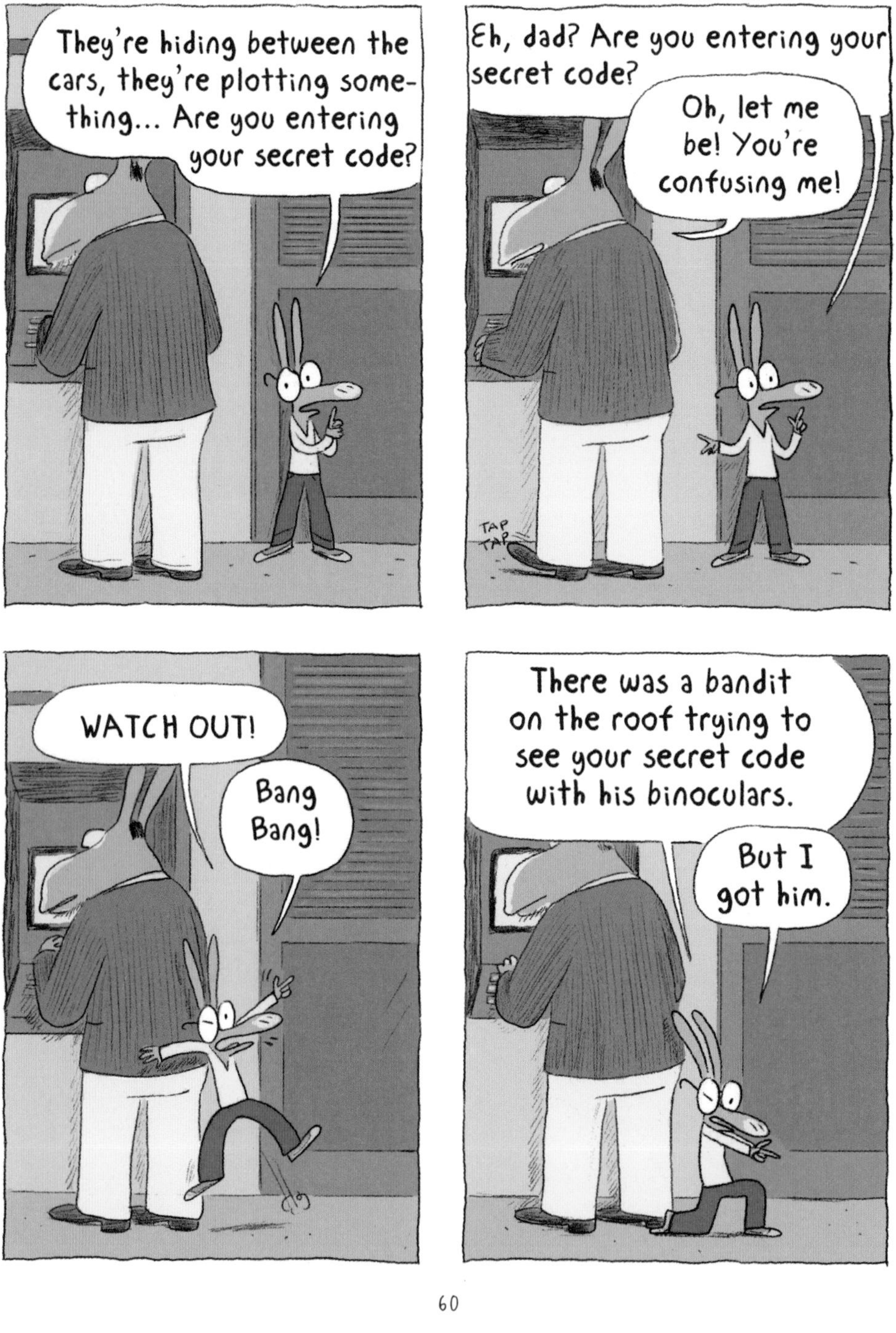
They're hiding between the cars, they're plotting something... Are you entering your secret code?
Eh, dad? Are you entering your secret code?
Oh, let me be! You're confusing me!
TAP TAP
WATCH OUT!
Bang Bang!
There was a bandit on the roof trying to see your secret code with his binoculars.
But I got him.

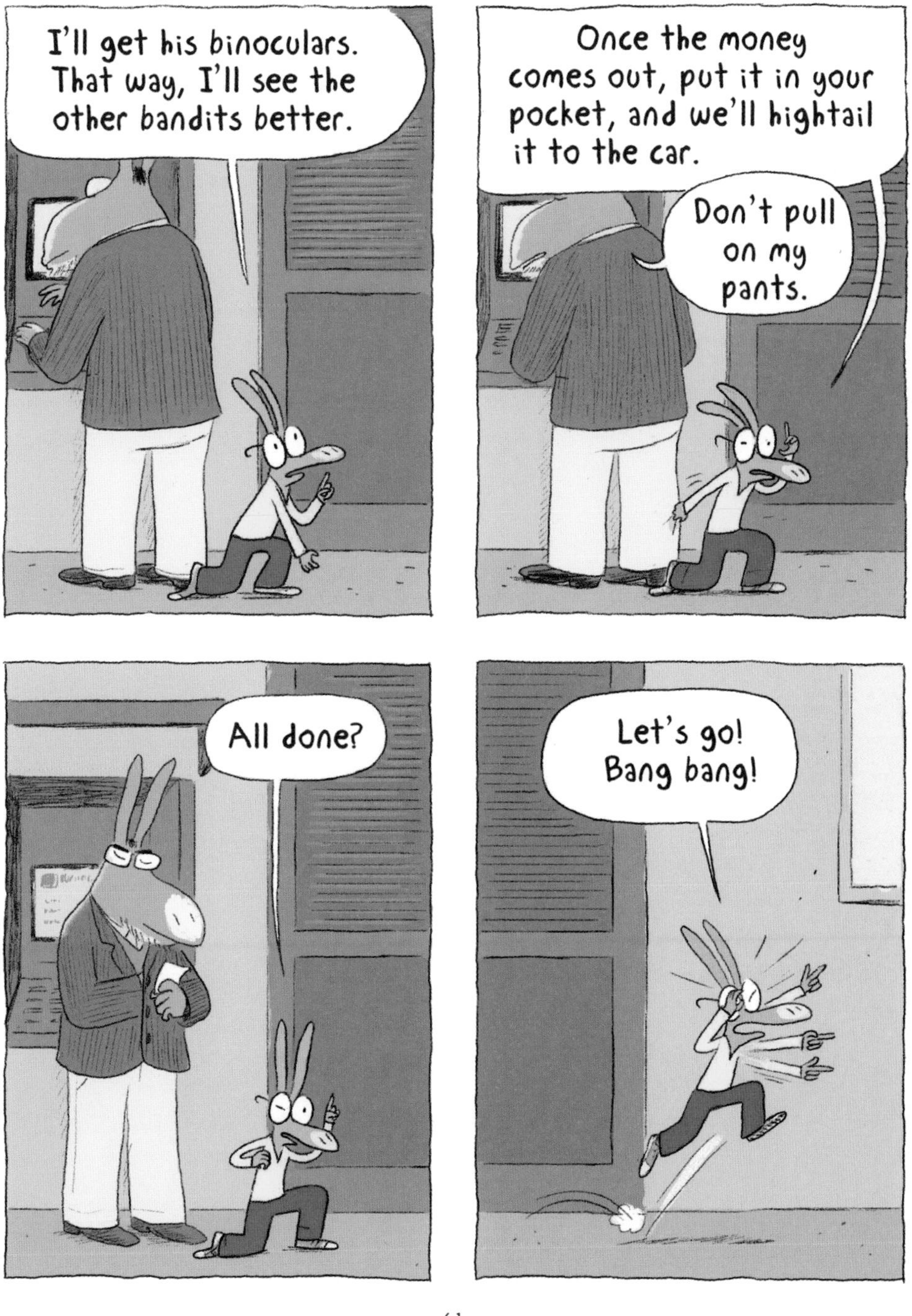
I'll get his binoculars. That way, I'll see the other bandits better.
Once the money comes out, put it in your pocket, and we'll hightail it to the car.
Don't pull on my pants.
All done?
Let's go! Bang bang!

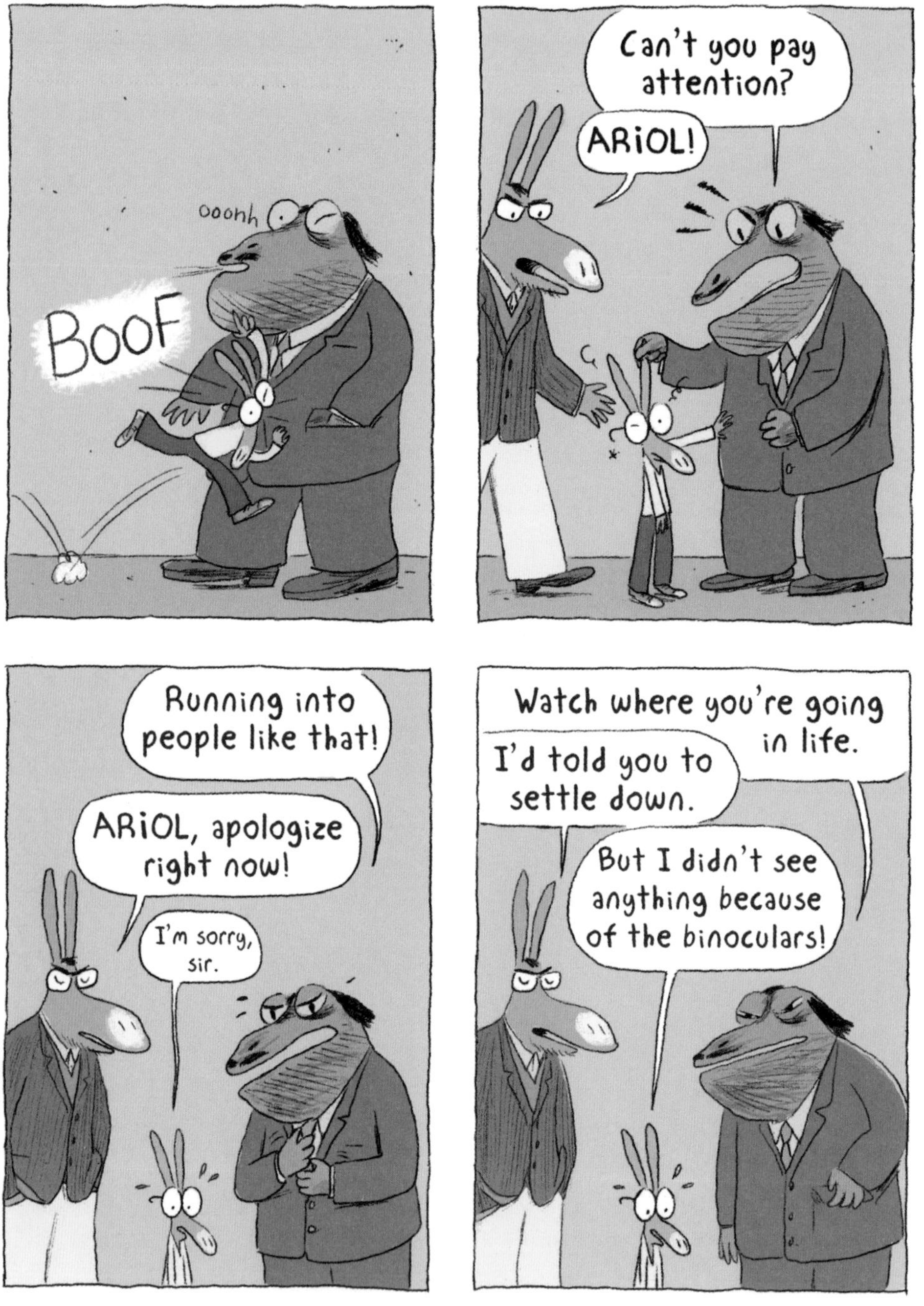
ooonh
BOOF
Can't you pay attention?
ARiOL!
Running into people like that!
ARiOL, apologize right now!
I'm sorry, sir.
Watch where you're going in life.
I'd told you to settle down.
But I didn't see anything because of the binoculars!

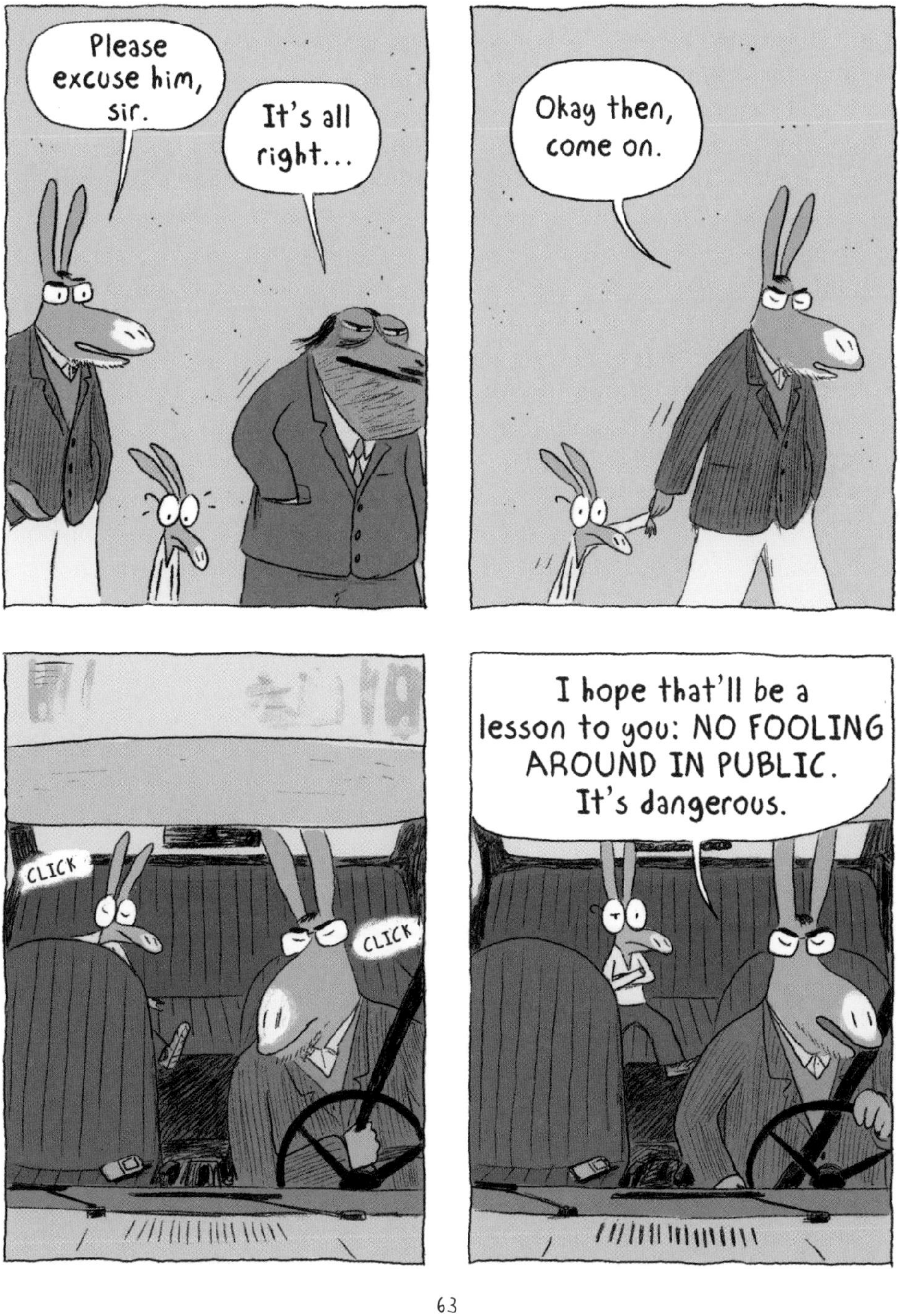
Please excuse him, sir.
It's all right...
Okay then, come on.
CLICK
CLICK
I hope that'll be a lesson to you: NO FOOLING AROUND IN PUBLIC. It's dangerous.

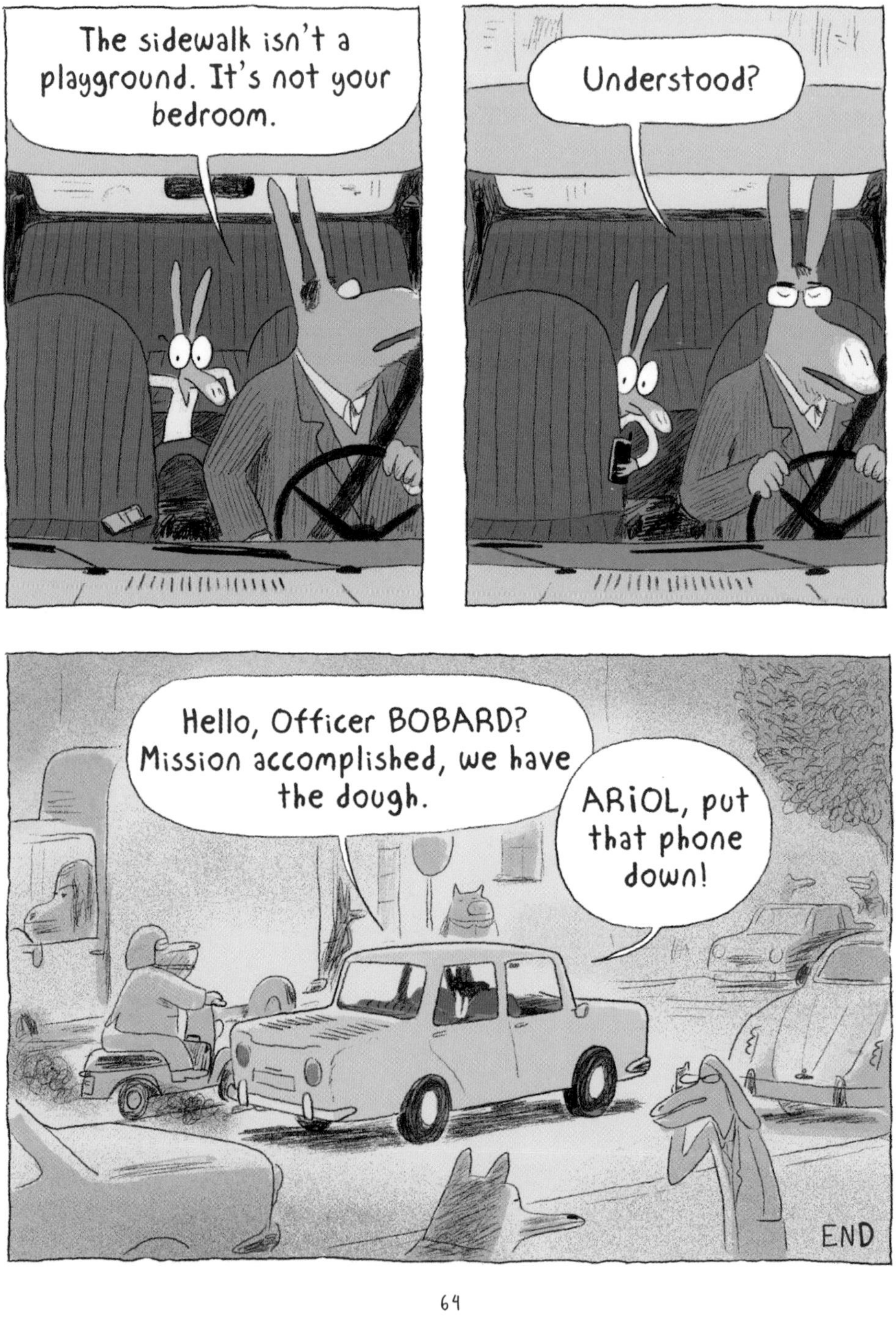
The sidewalk isn't a playground. It's not your bedroom.
Understood?
Hello, Officer BOBARD? Mission accomplished, we have the dough.
ARiOL, put that phone down!
END

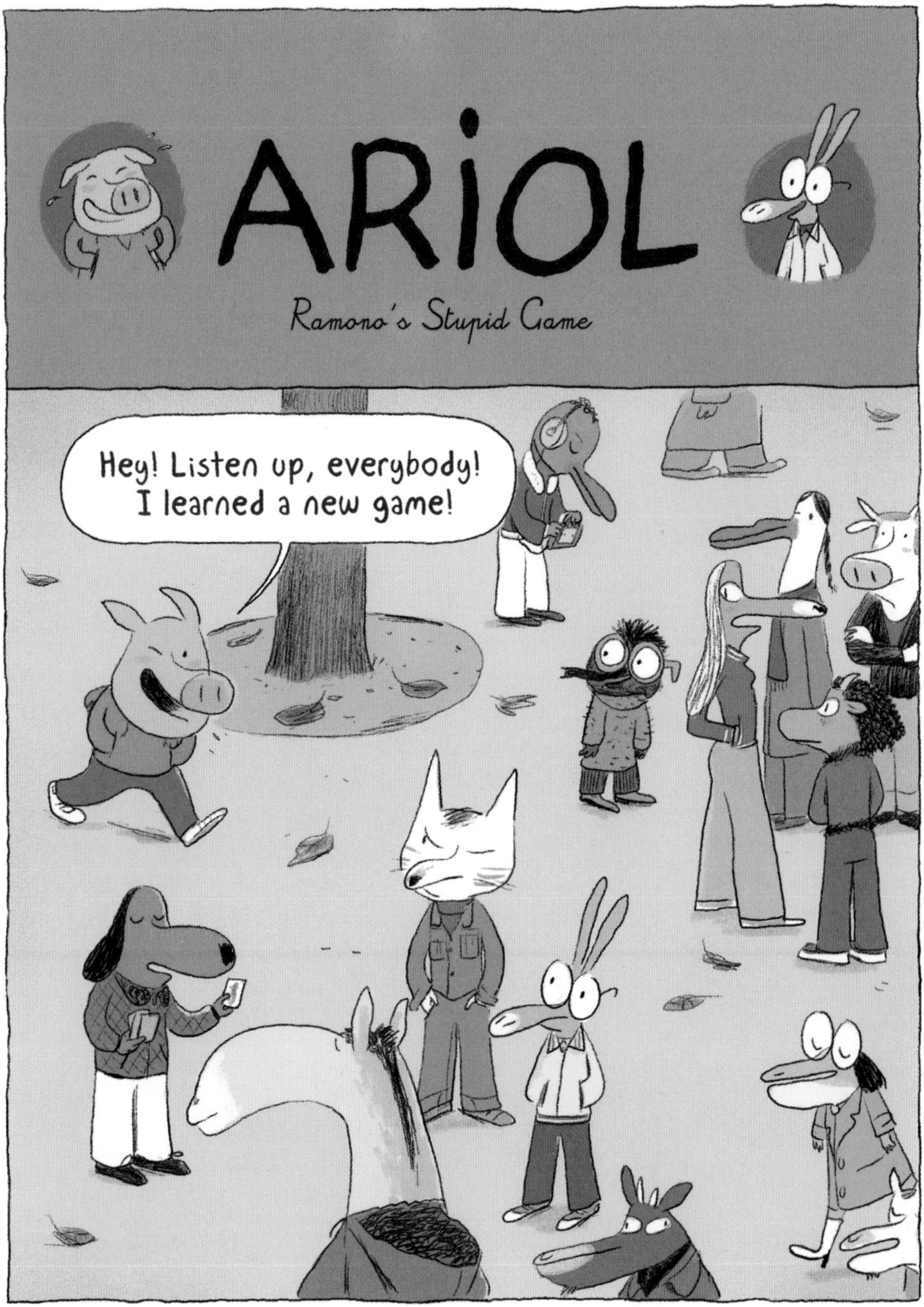
ARiOL
Ramono's Stupid Game
Hey! Listen up, everybody! I learned a new game!

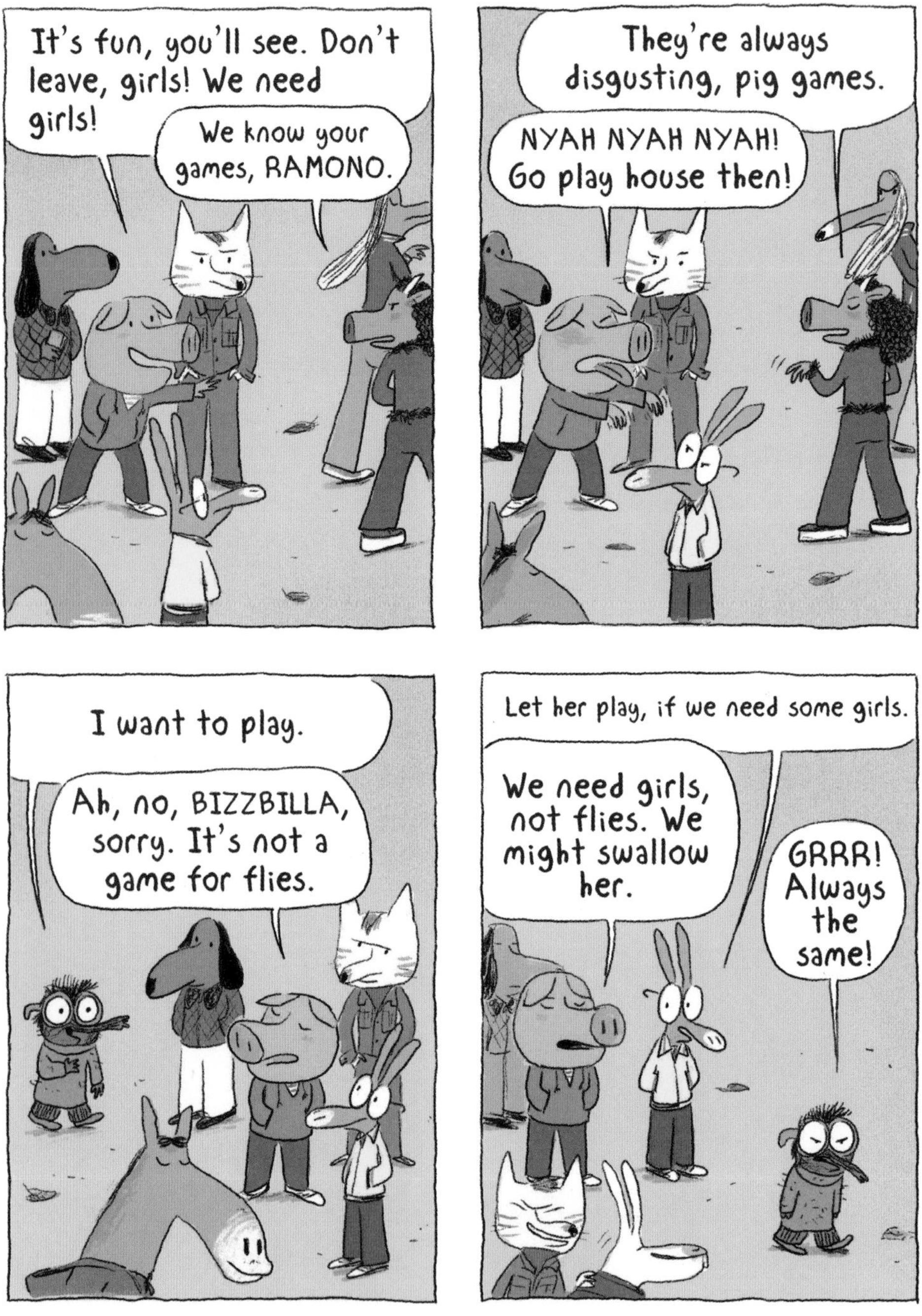
It's fun, you'll see. Don't leave, girls! We need girls!
We know your games, RAMONO.
They're always disgusting, pig games.
NYAH NYAH NYAH! Go play house then!
I want to play.
Ah, no, BIZZBILLA, sorry. It's not a game for flies.
Let her play, if we need some girls.
We need girls, not flies. We might swallow her.
GRRR! Always the same!

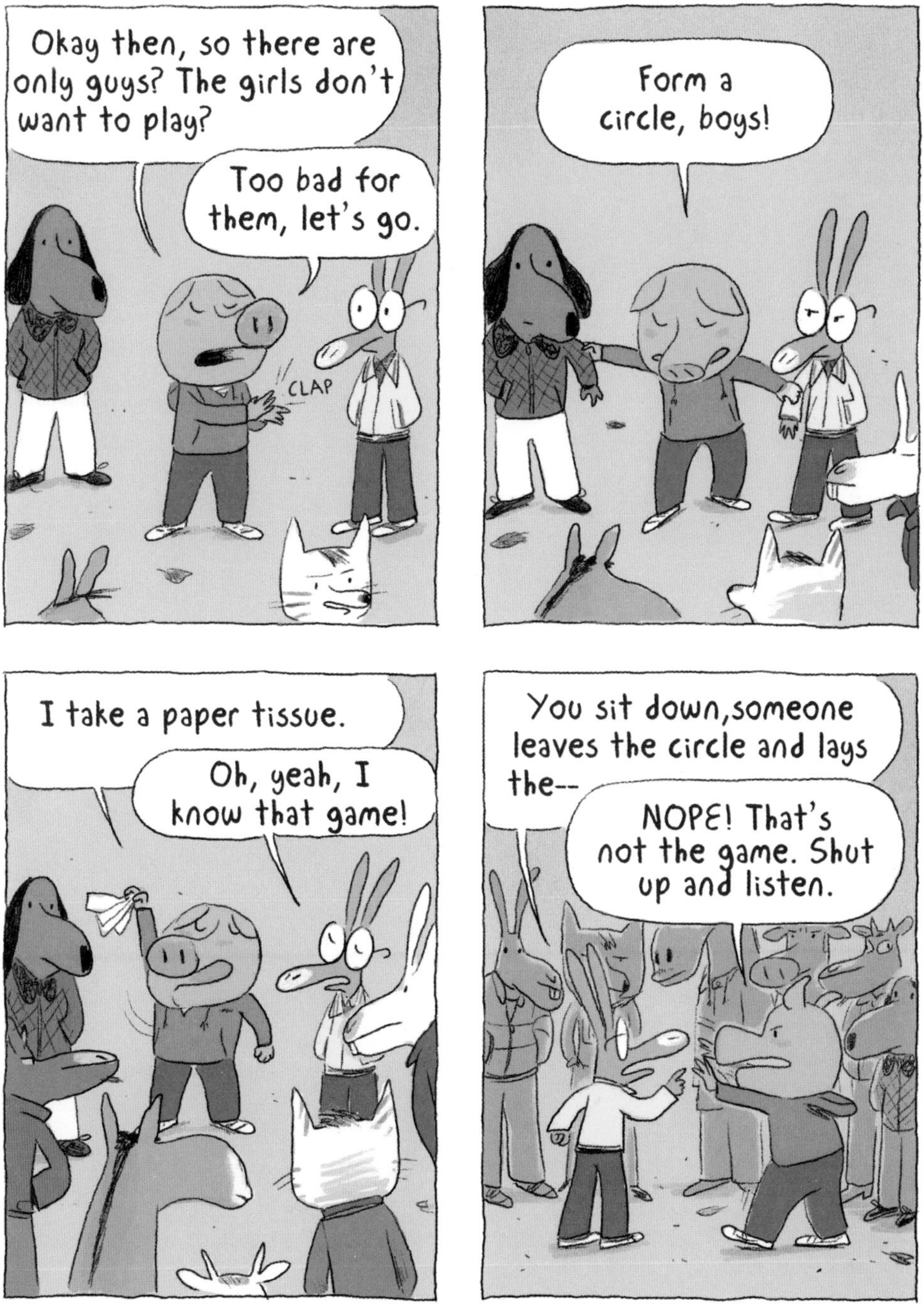
Okay then, so there are only guys? The girls don't want to play?
Too bad for them, let's go.
CLAP
Form a circle, boys!
I take a paper tissue.
Oh, yeah, I know that game!
You sit down, someone leaves the circle and lays the--
NOPE! That's not the game. Shut up and listen.

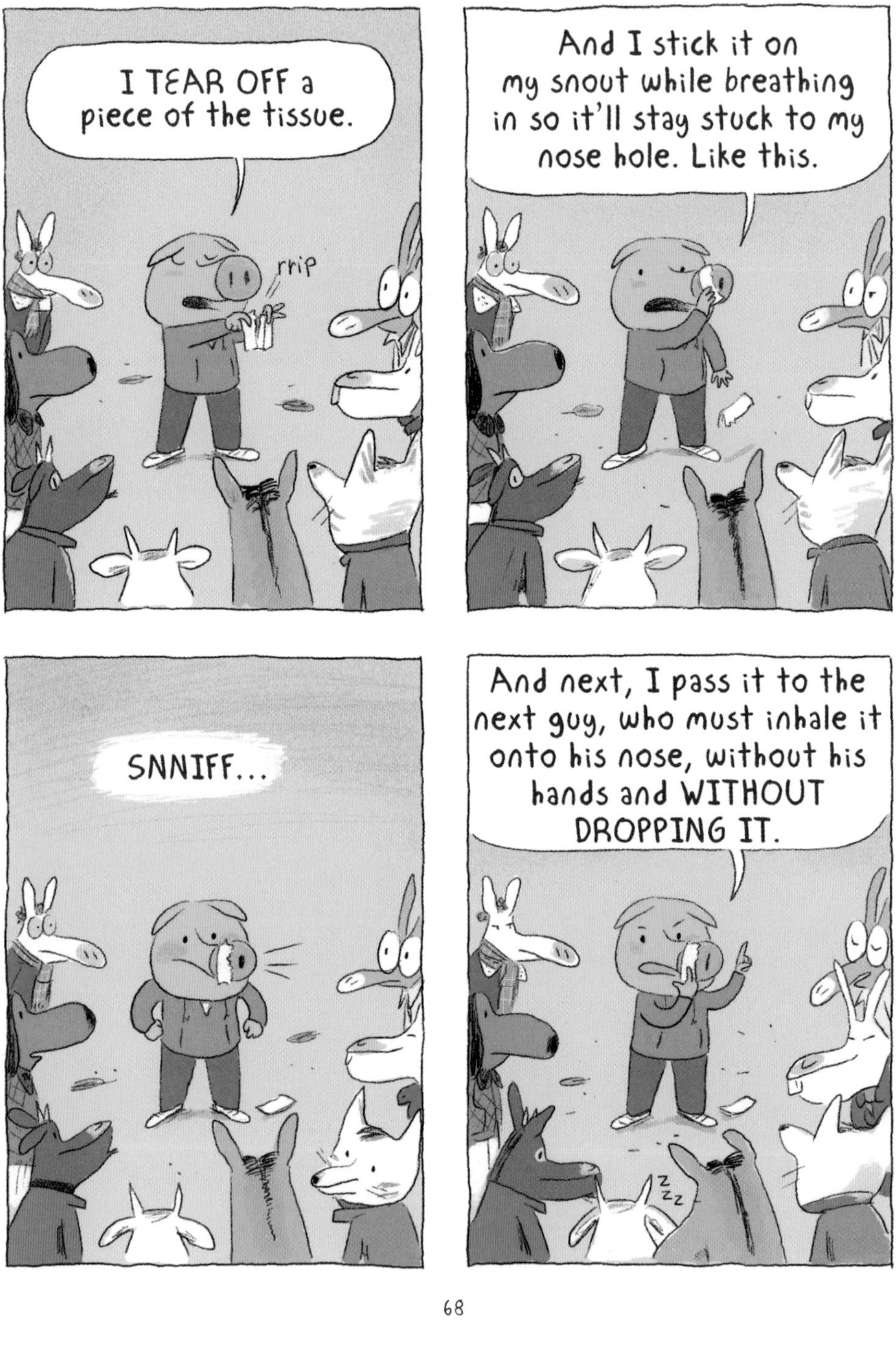
I TEAR OFF a piece of the tissue.
rrip
And I stick it on my snout while breathing in so it'll stay stuck to my nose hole. Like this.
SNNIFF...
And next, I pass it to the next guy, who must inhale it onto his nose, without his hands and WITHOUT DROPPING IT.
Z Z Z

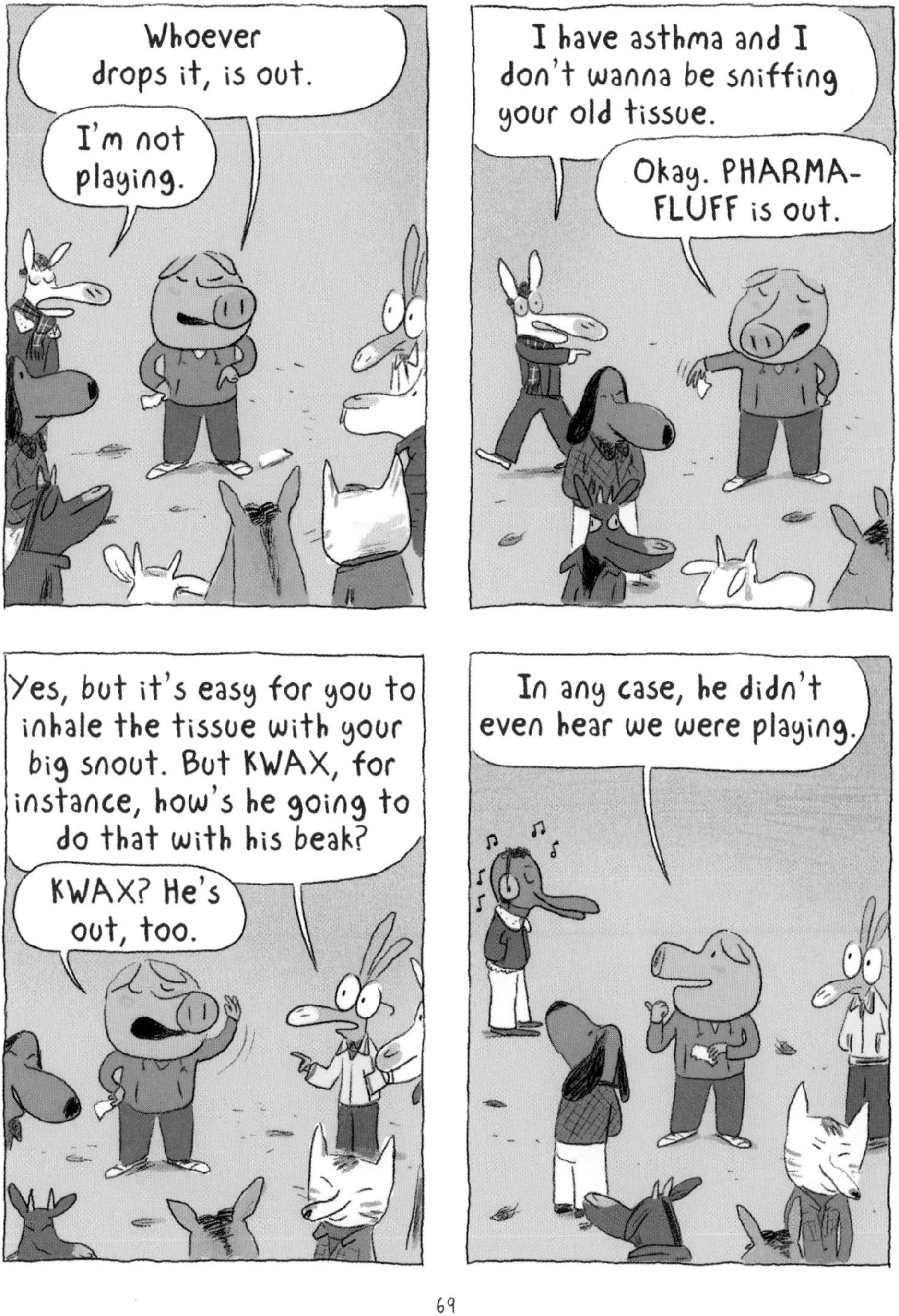
Whoever drops it, is out.
I'm not playing.
I have asthma and I don't wanna be sniffing your old tissue.
Okay. PHARMA-FLUFF is out.
Yes, but it's easy for you to inhale the tissue with your big snout. But KWAX, for instance, how's he going to do that with his beak?
KWAX? He's out, too.
In any case, he didn't even hear we were playing.

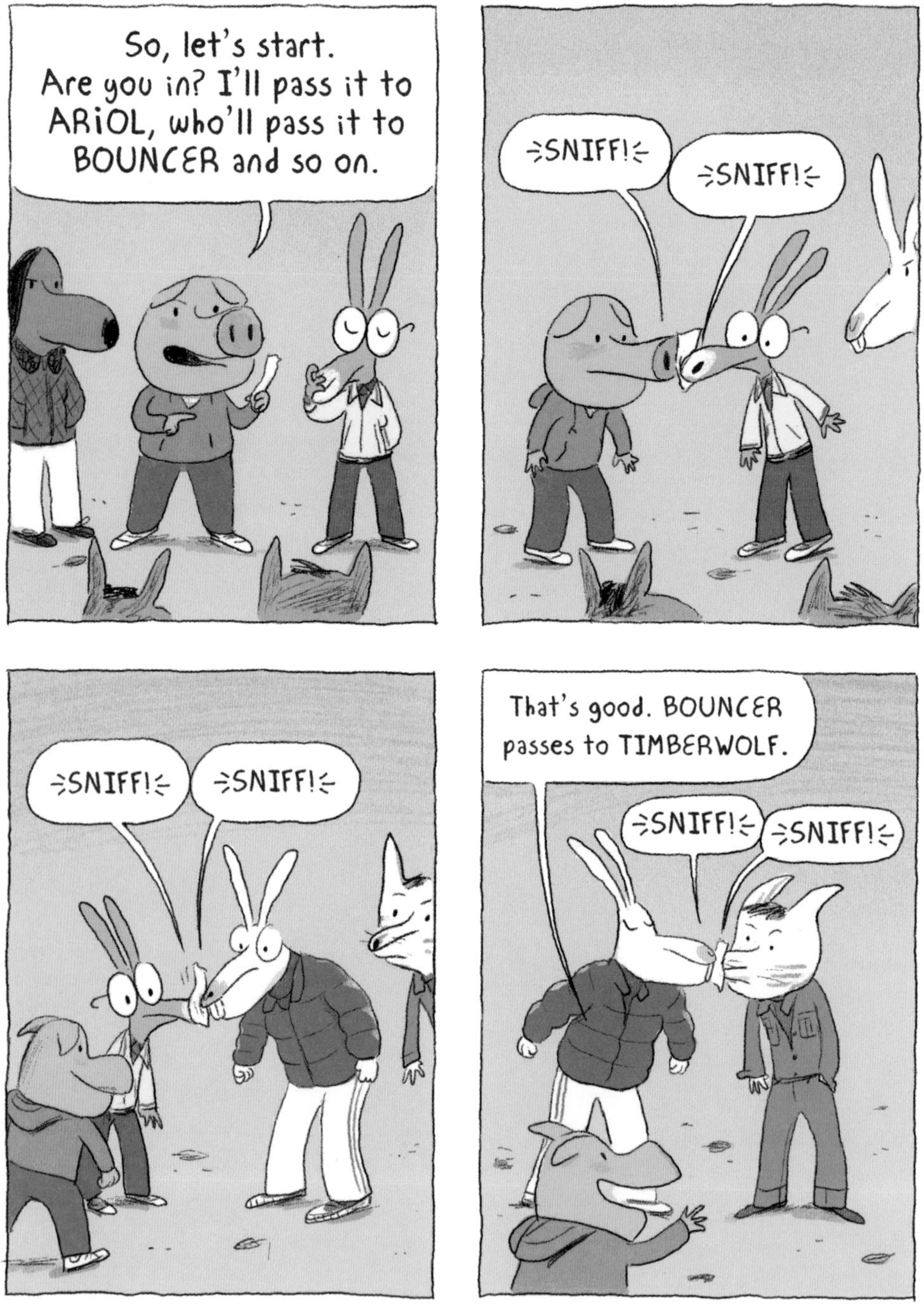
So, let's start. Are you in? I'll pass it to ARIOL, who'll pass it to BOUNCER and so on.
SNIFF!
SNIFF!
SNIFF!
SNIFF!
That's good. BOUNCER passes to TIMBERWOLF.
SNIFF!
SNIFF!

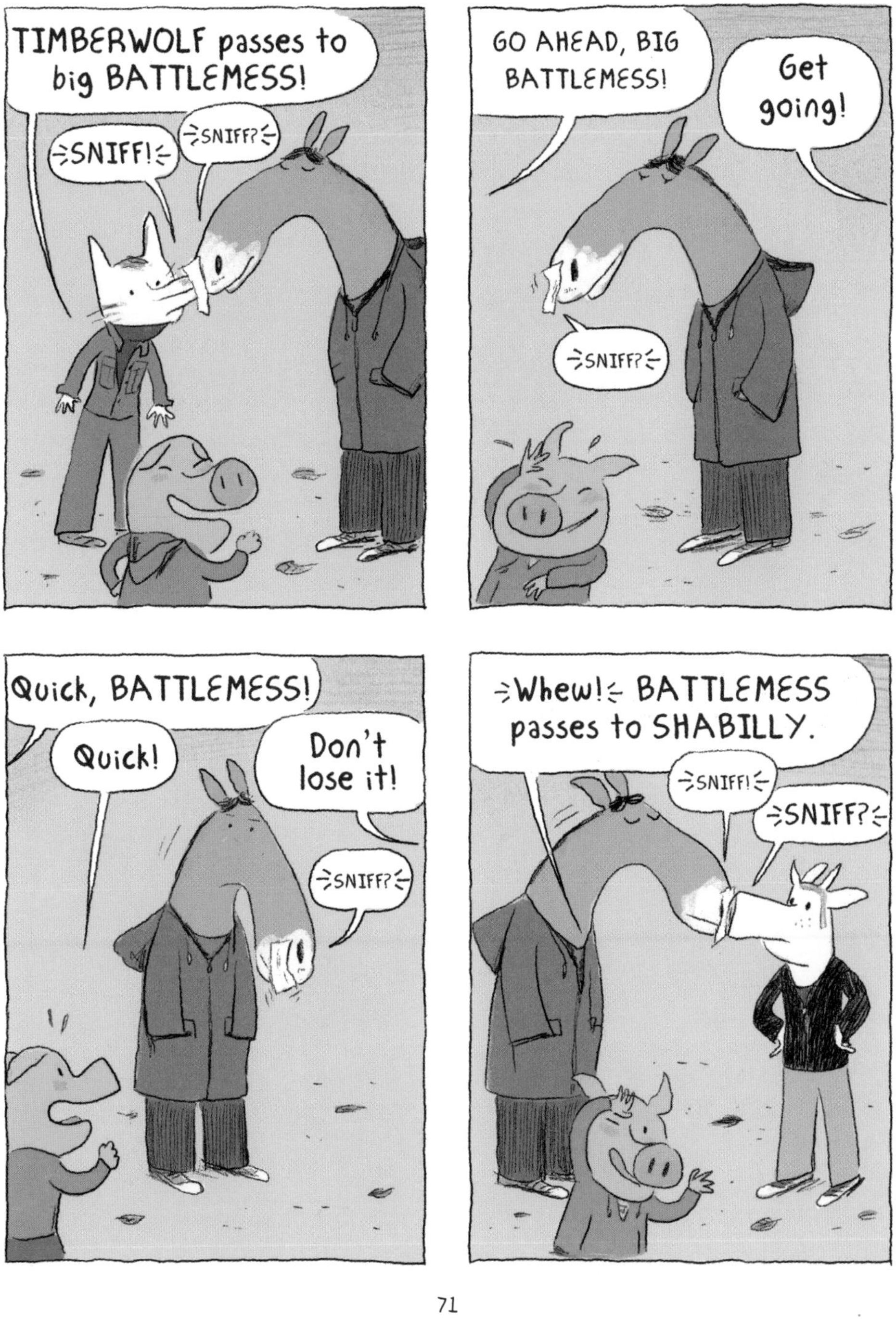
TIMBERWOLF passes to big BATTLEMESS!
SNIFF!
SNIFF?
GO AHEAD, BIG BATTLEMESS!
Get going!
SNIFF?
Quick, BATTLEMESS!
Quick!
Don't lose it!
SNIFF?
Whew! BATTLEMESS passes to SHABILLY.
SNIFF!
SNIFF?

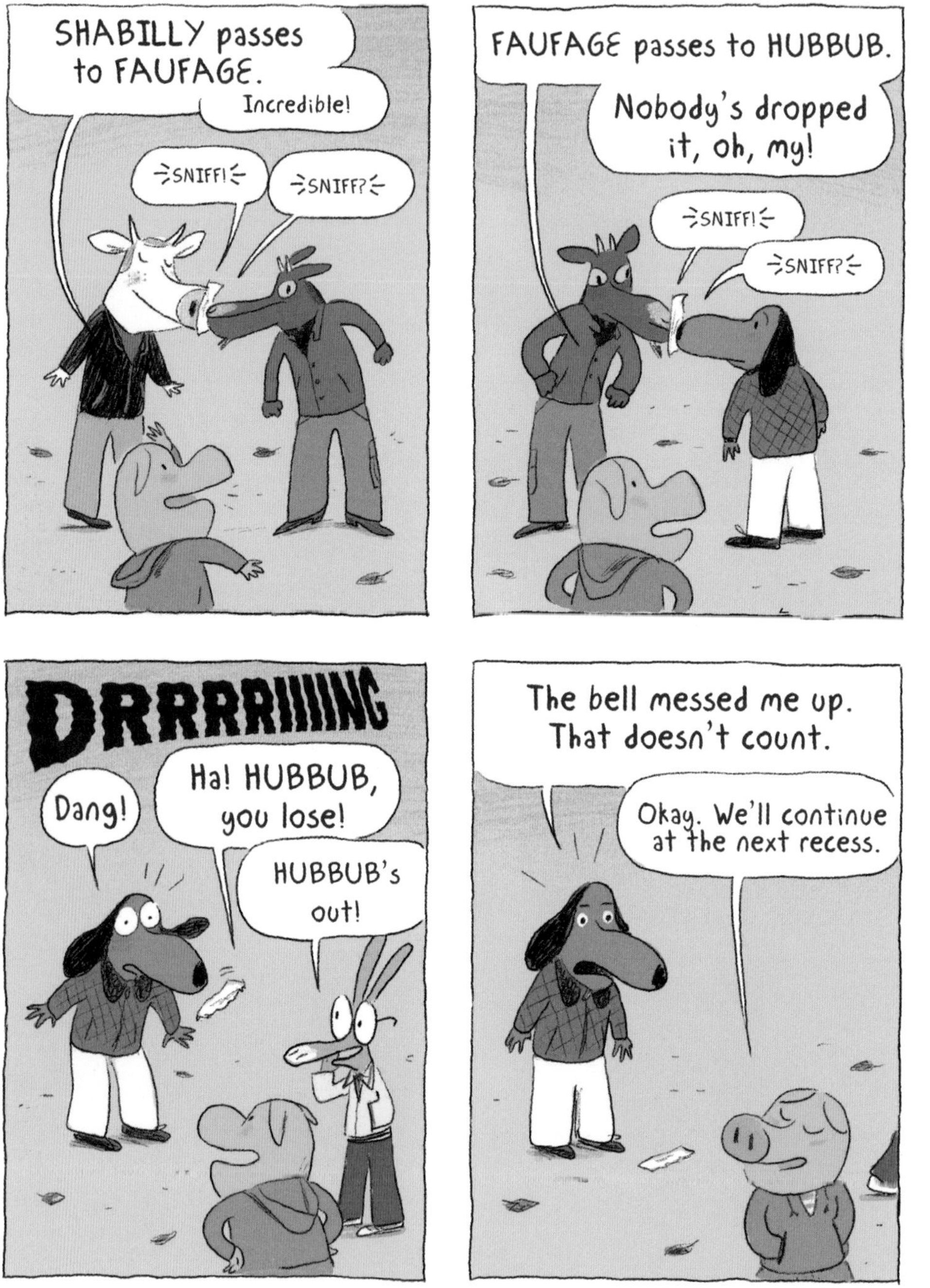
SHABILLY passes to FAUFAGE.
Incredible!
SNIFF!
SNIFF?
FAUFAGE passes to HUBBUB.
Nobody's dropped it, oh, my!
SNIFF!
SNIFF?
DRRRRIIIING
Dang!
Ha! HUBBUB, you lose!
HUBBUB's out!
The bell messed me up. That doesn't count.
Okay. We'll continue at the next recess.

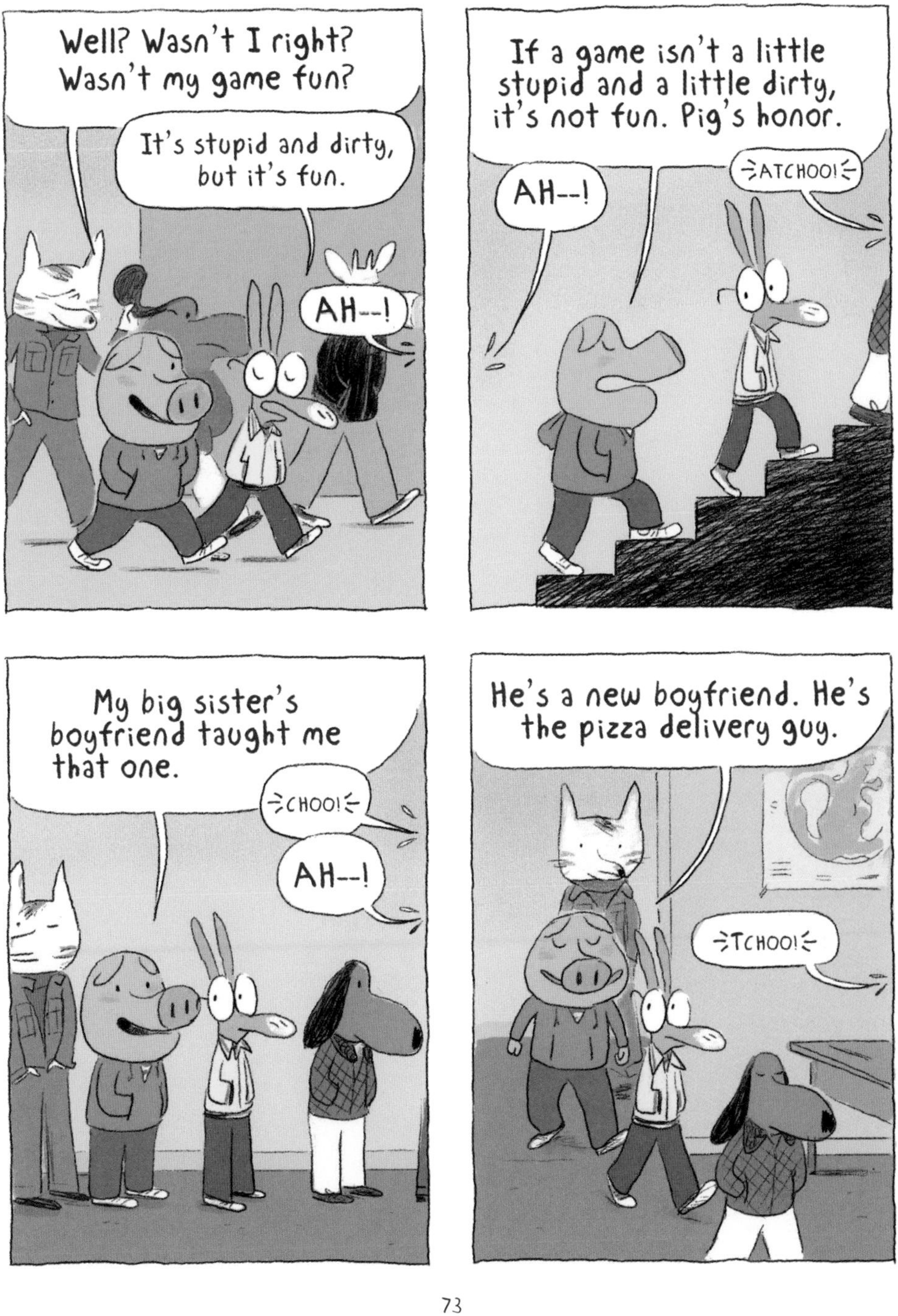
Well? Wasn't I right? Wasn't my game fun?
It's stupid and dirty, but it's fun.
AH--!
If a game isn't a little stupid and a little dirty, it's not fun. Pig's honor.
AH--!
ATCHOO!
My big sister's boyfriend taught me that one.
CHOO!
AH--!
He's a new boyfriend. He's the pizza delivery guy.
TCHOO!

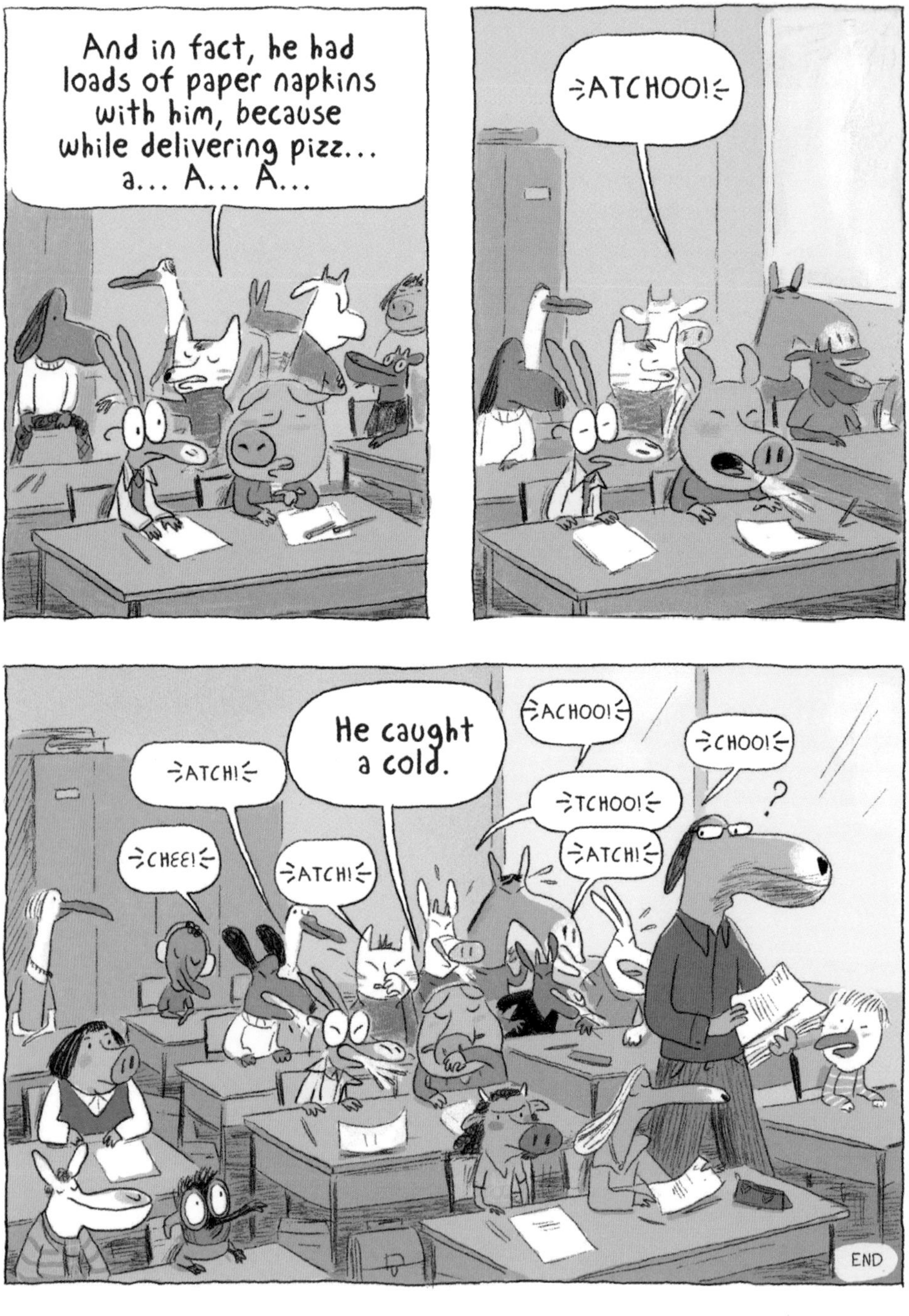
And in fact, he had loads of paper napkins with him, because while delivering pizz... a... A... A...
ATCHOO!
ATCH!
CHEE!
ATCH!
He caught a cold.
ACHOO!
TCHOO!
ATCH!
CHOO!
?
END

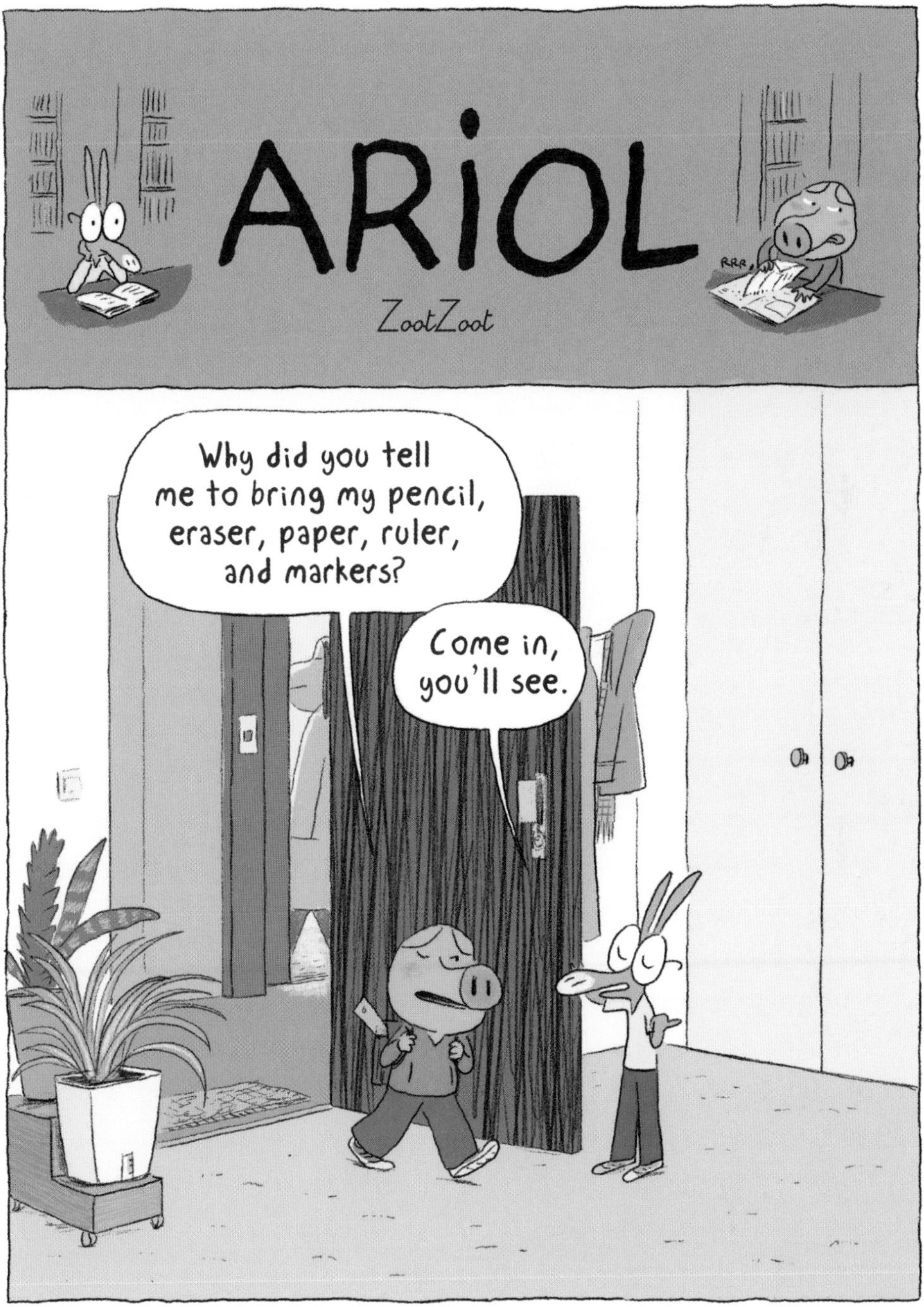
ARIOL
ZootZoot
Why did you tell me to bring my pencil, eraser, paper, ruler, and markers?
Come in, you'll see.

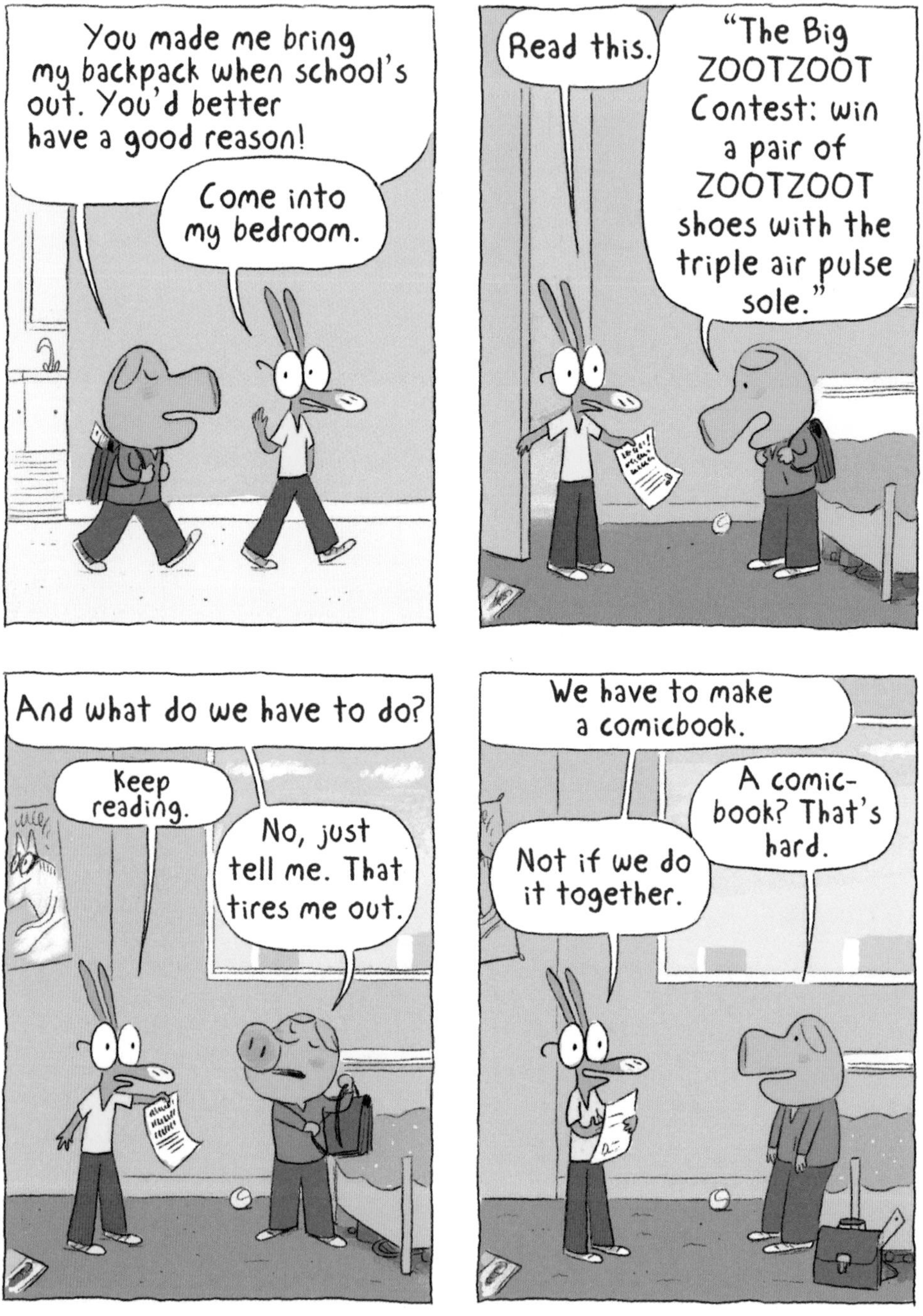
You made me bring my backpack when school's out. You'd better have a good reason!
Come into my bedroom.
Read this.
"The Big ZOOTZOOT Contest: win a pair of ZOOTZOOT shoes with the triple air pulse sole."
And what do we have to do?
Keep reading.
No, just tell me. That tires me out.
We have to make a comicbook.
A comic-book? That's hard.
Not if we do it together.

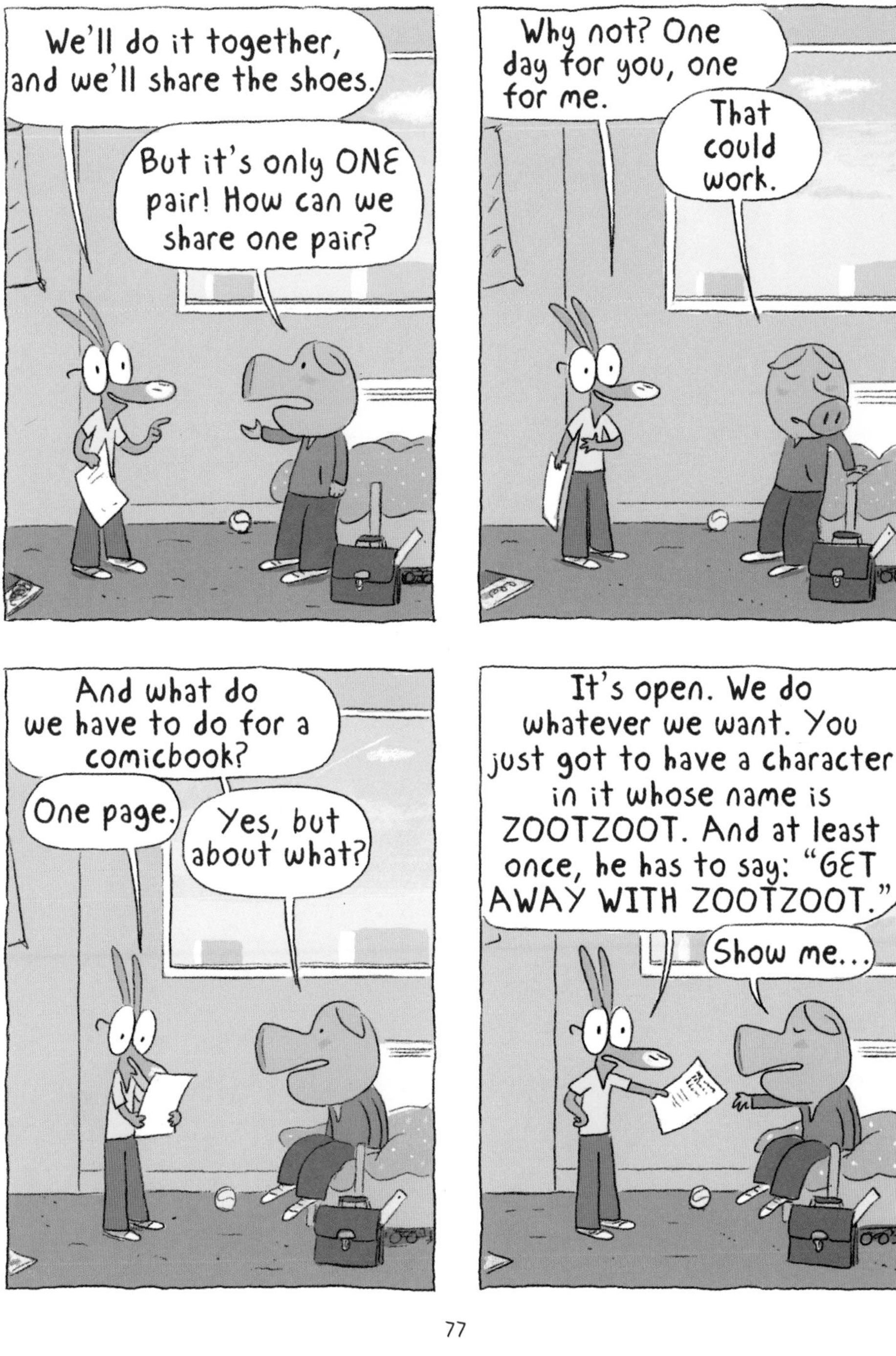
We'll do it together, and we'll share the shoes.
But it's only ONE pair! How can we share one pair?
Why not? One day for you, one for me.
That could work.
And what do we have to do for a comicbook?
One page.
Yes, but about what?
It's open. We do whatever we want. You just got to have a character in it whose name is ZOOTZOOT. And at least once, he has to say: "GET AWAY WITH ZOOTZOOT."
Show me...

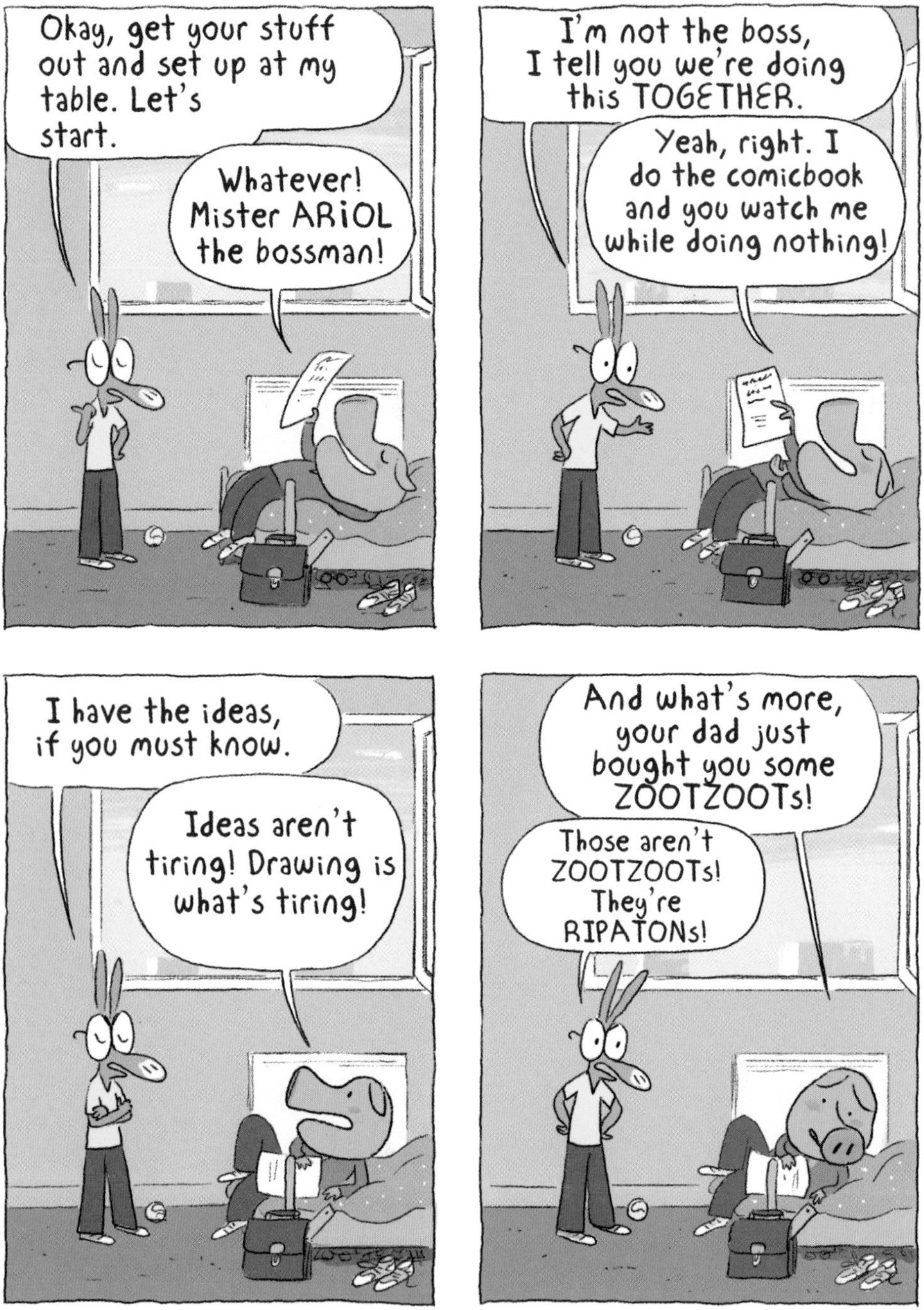
Okay, get your stuff out and set up at my table. Let's start.
Whatever! Mister ARIOL the bossman!
I'm not the boss, I tell you we're doing this TOGETHER.
Yeah, right. I do the comicbook and you watch me while doing nothing!
I have the ideas, if you must know.
Ideas aren't tiring! Drawing is what's tiring!
And what's more, your dad just bought you some ZOOTZOOTs!
Those aren't ZOOTZOOTs! They're RIPATONs!

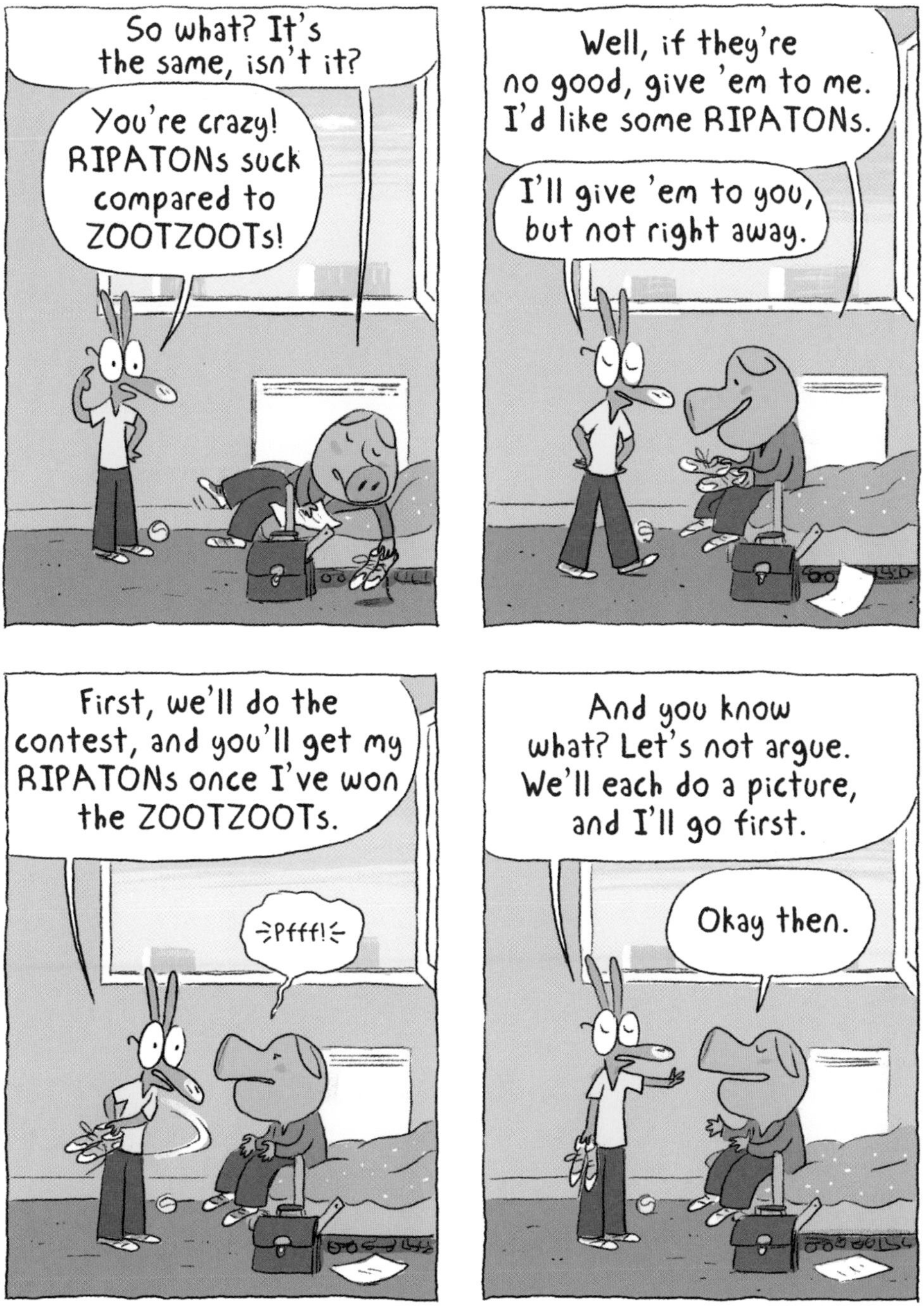
So what? It's the same, isn't it?
You're crazy! RIPATONs suck compared to ZOOTZOOTs!
Well, if they're no good, give 'em to me. I'd like some RIPATONs.
I'll give 'em to you, but not right away.
First, we'll do the contest, and you'll get my RIPATONs once I've won the ZOOTZOOTs.
Pfff!
And you know what? Let's not argue. We'll each do a picture, and I'll go first.
Okay then.

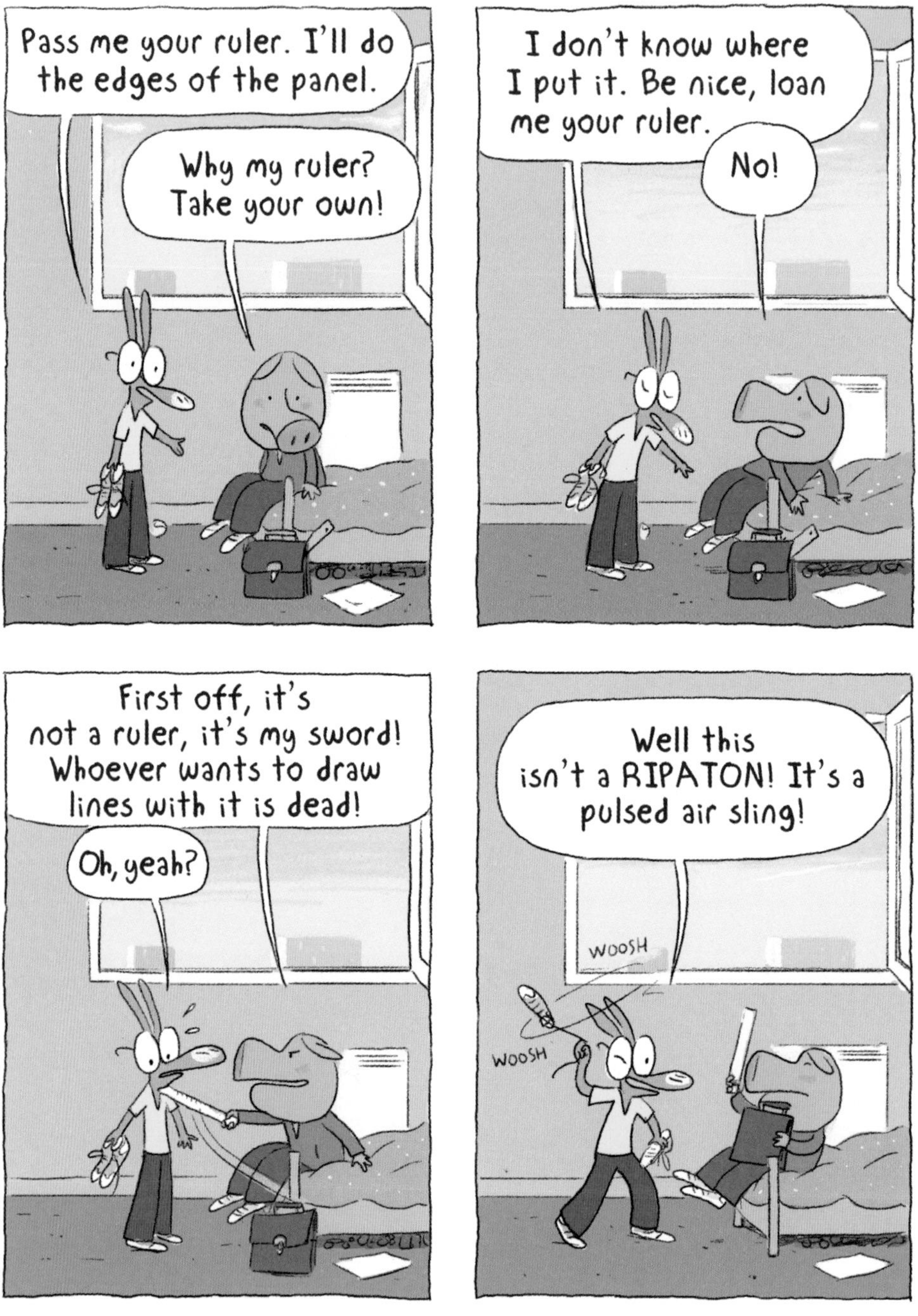
Pass me your ruler. I'll do the edges of the panel.
Why my ruler? Take your own!
I don't know where I put it. Be nice, loan me your ruler.
No!
First off, it's not a ruler, it's my sword! Whoever wants to draw lines with it is dead!
Oh, yeah?
Well this isn't a RIPATON! It's a pulsed air sling!
WOOSH
WOOSH

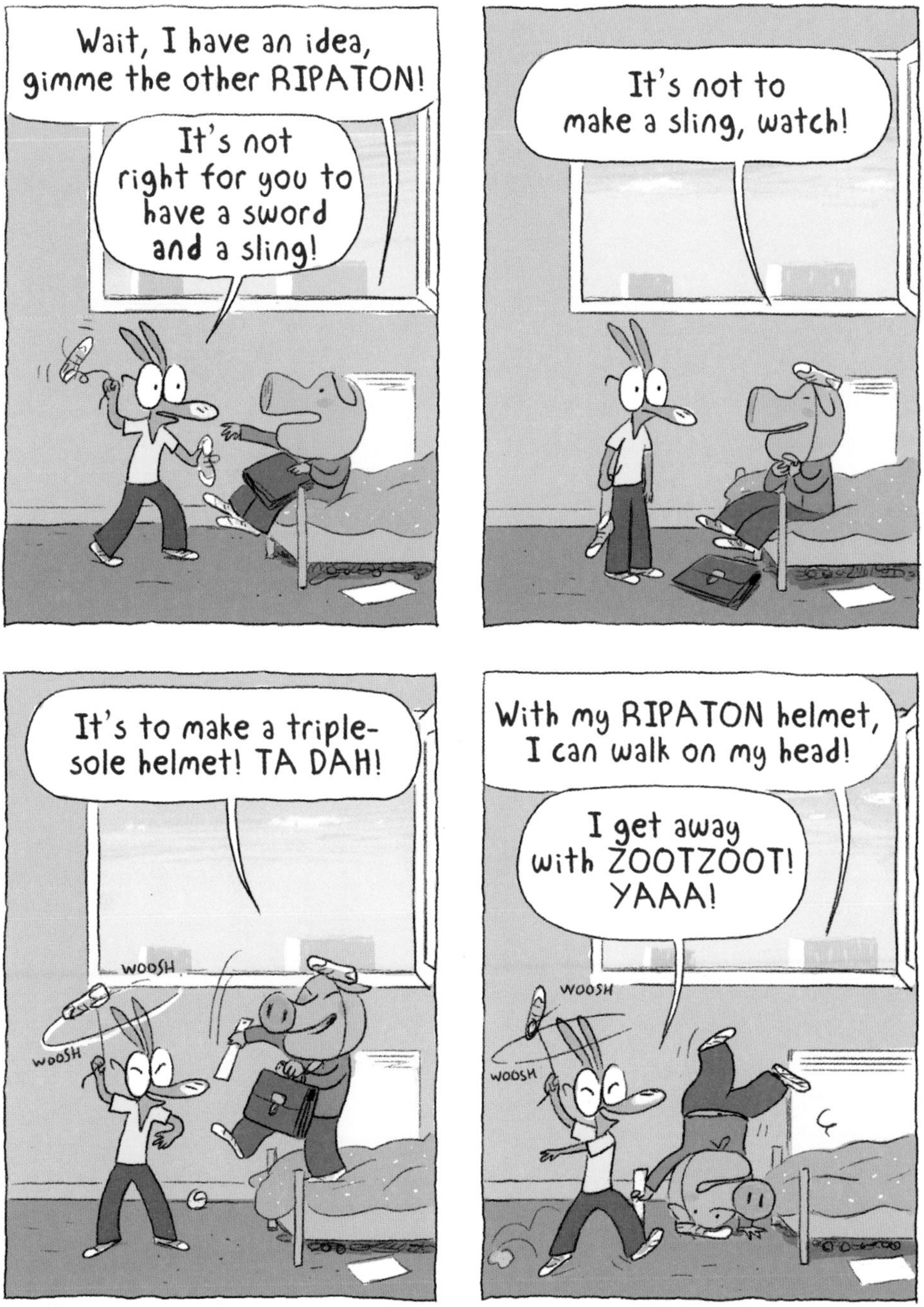
Wait, I have an idea, gimme the other RIPATON!
It's not right for you to have a sword and a sling!
It's not to make a sling, watch!
It's to make a triple-sole helmet! TA DAH!
WOOSH
WOOSH
With my RIPATON helmet, I can walk on my head!
I get away with ZOOTZOOT! YAAA!
WOOSH
WOOSH

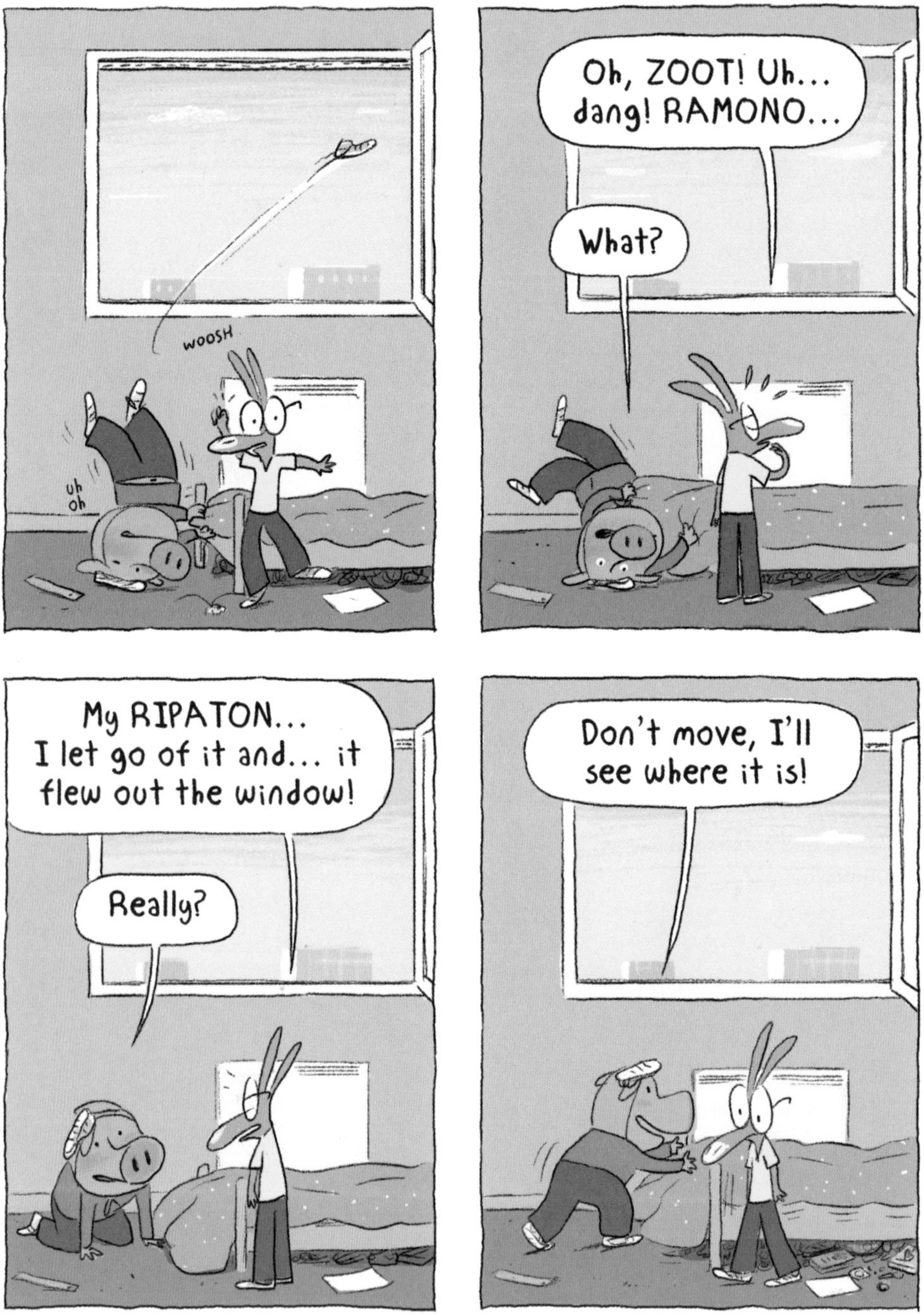
WOOSH
UH OH
Oh, ZOOT! Uh... dang! RAMONO...
What?
My RIPATON... I let go of it and... it flew out the window!
Really?
Don't move, I'll see where it is!

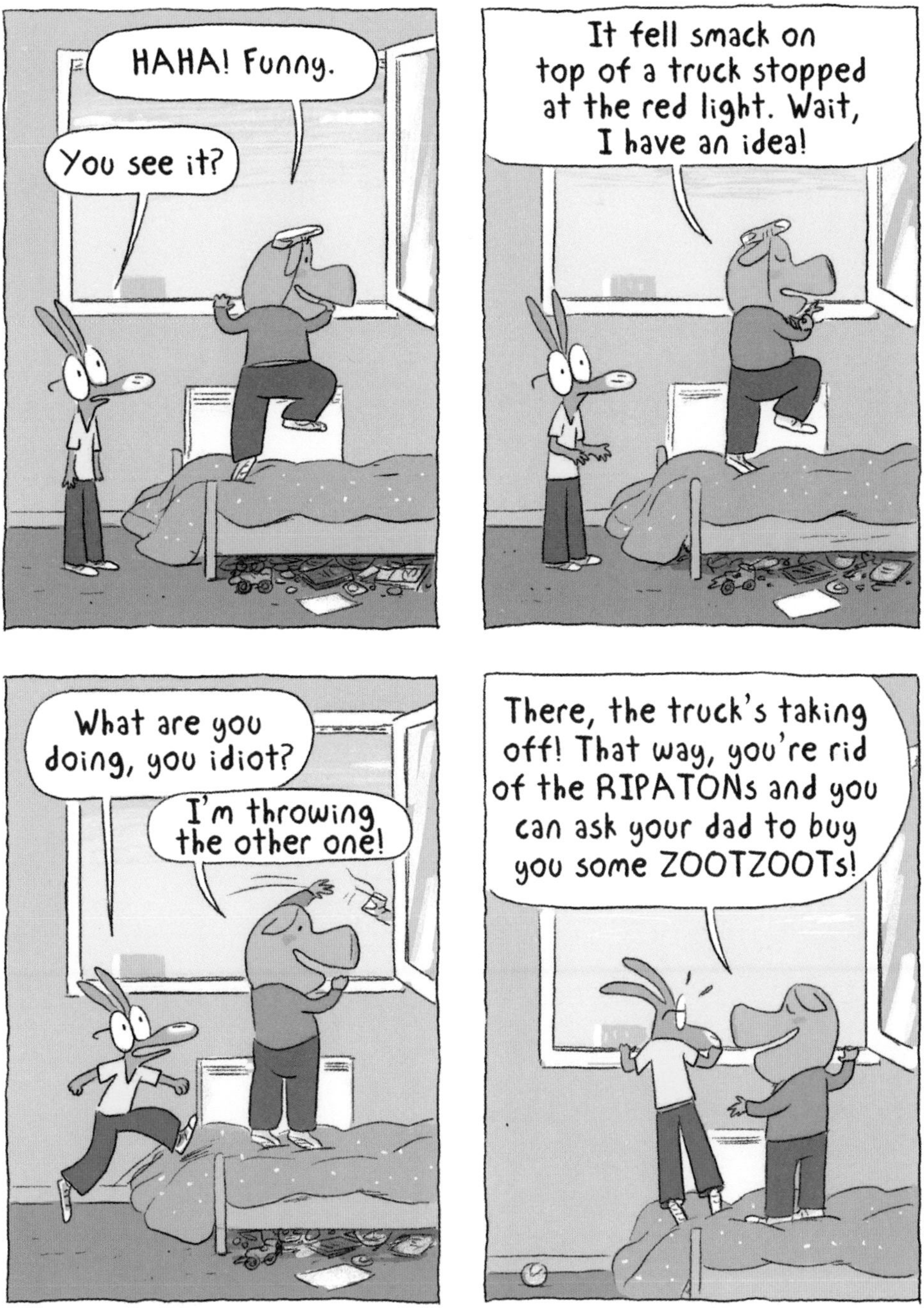
HAHA! Funny.
You see it?
It fell smack on top of a truck stopped at the red light. Wait, I have an idea!
What are you doing, you idiot?
I'm throwing the other one!
There, the truck's taking off! That way, you're rid of the RIPATONs and you can ask your dad to buy you some ZOOTZOOTs!

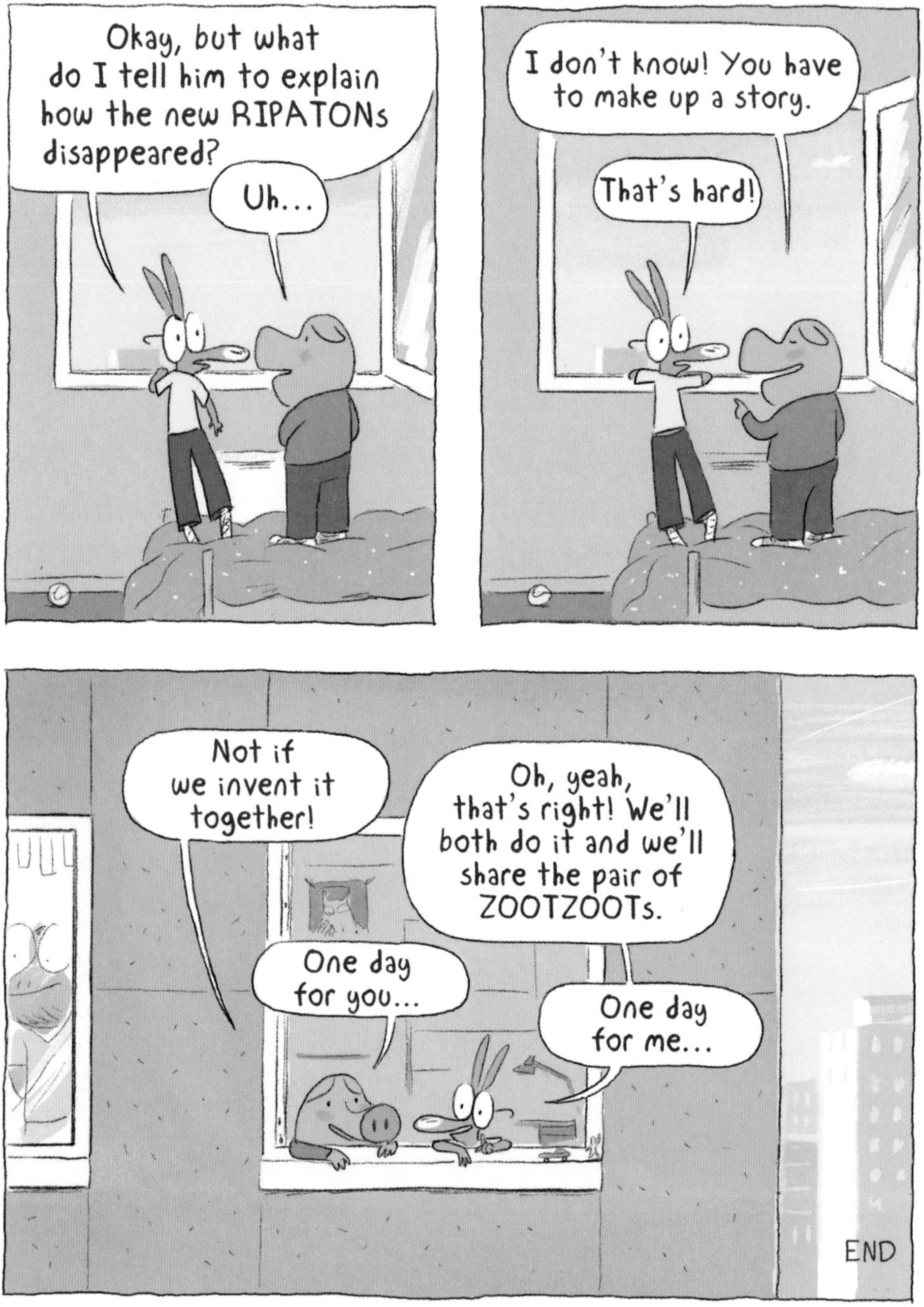
Okay, but what do I tell him to explain how the new RIPATONs disappeared?
Uh...
I don't know! You have to make up a story.
That's hard!
Not if we invent it together!
Oh, yeah, that's right! We'll both do it and we'll share the pair of ZOOTZOOTs.
One day for you...
One day for me...
END

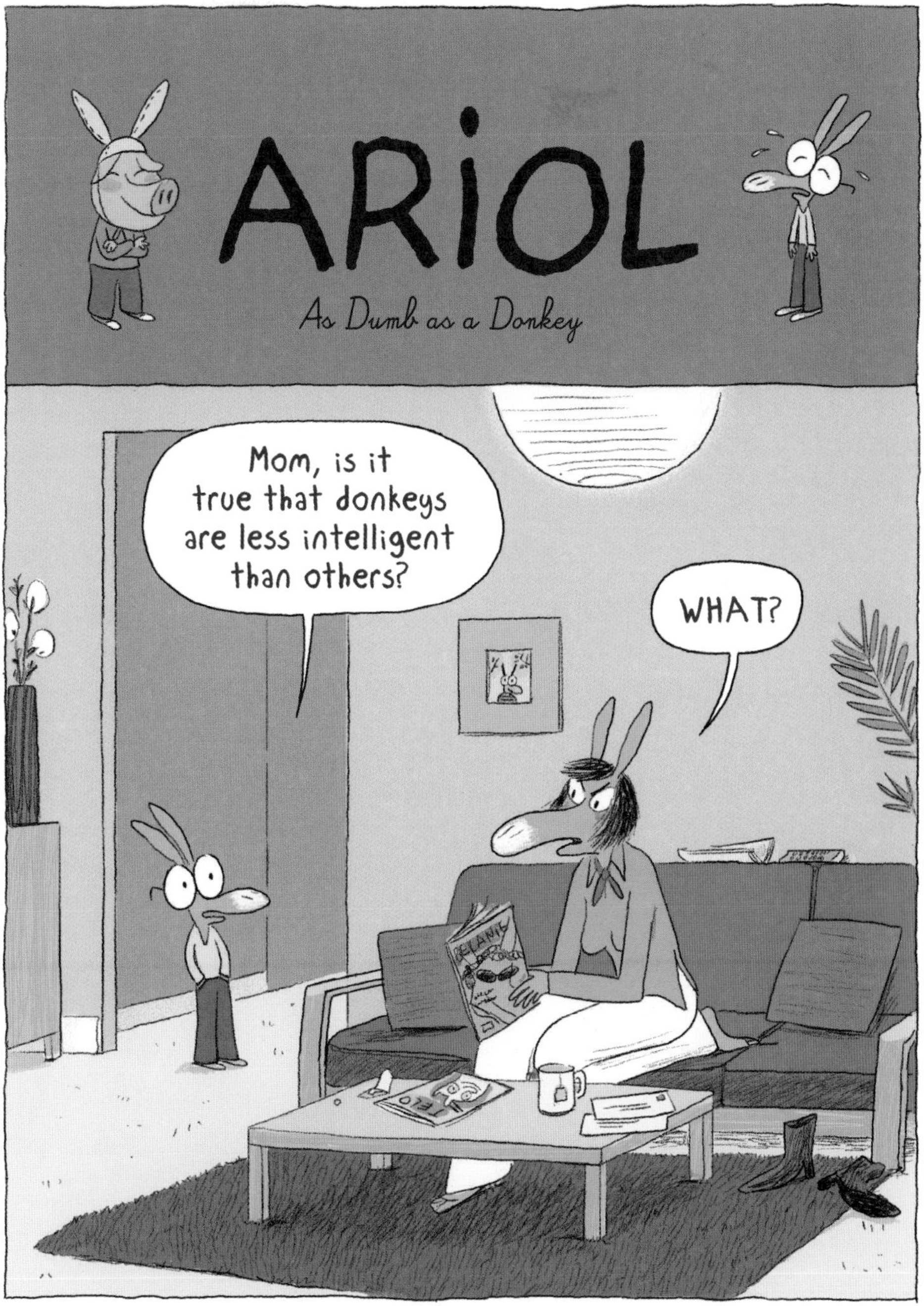
ARIOL
As Dumb as a Donkey
Mom, is it true that donkeys are less intelligent than others?
WHAT?

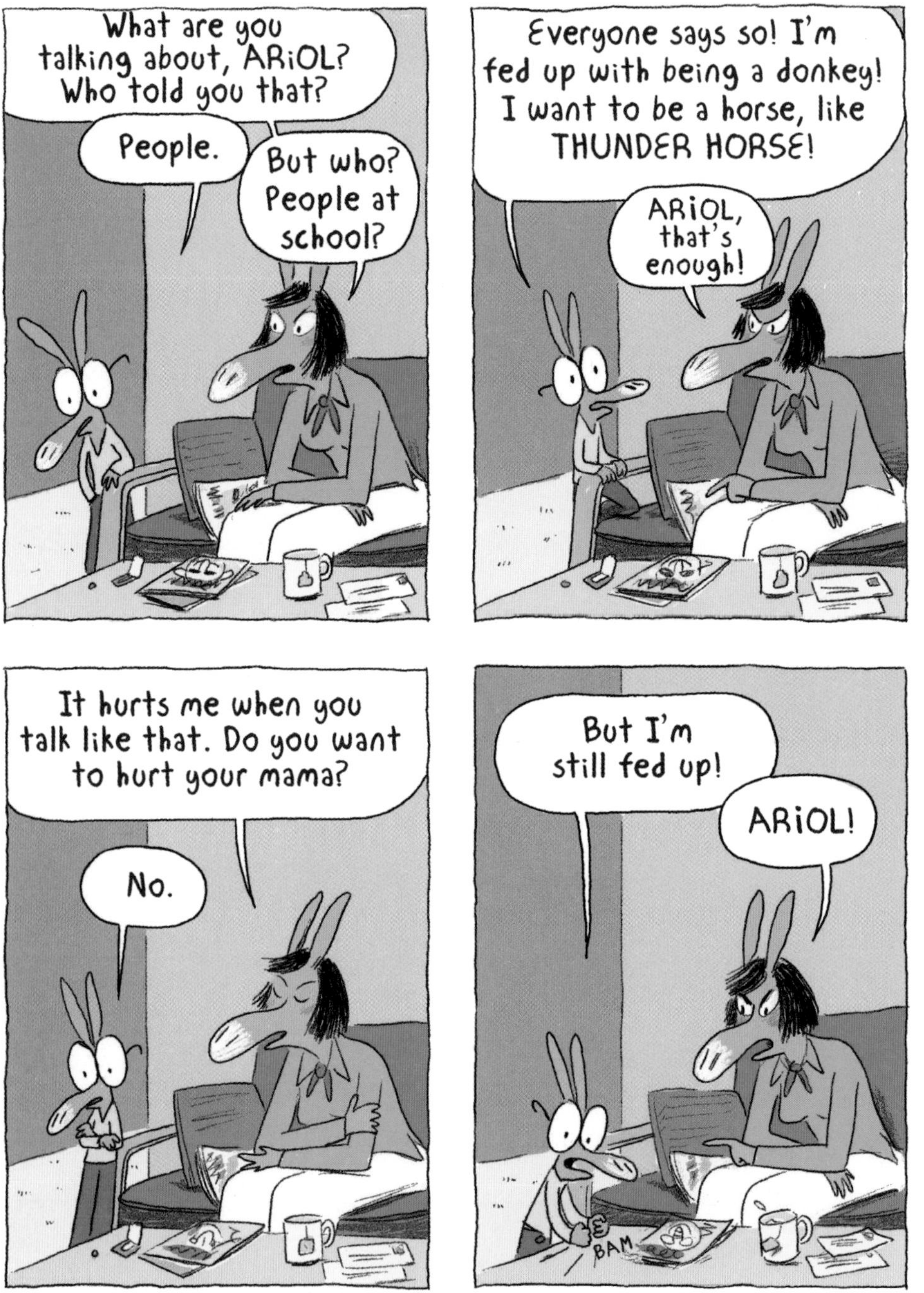
What are you talking about, ARiOL? Who told you that?
People.
But who? People at school?
Everyone says so! I'm fed up with being a donkey! I want to be a horse, like THUNDER HORSE!
ARiOL, that's enough!
It hurts me when you talk like that. Do you want to hurt your mama?
No.
But I'm still fed up!
ARiOL!
BAM

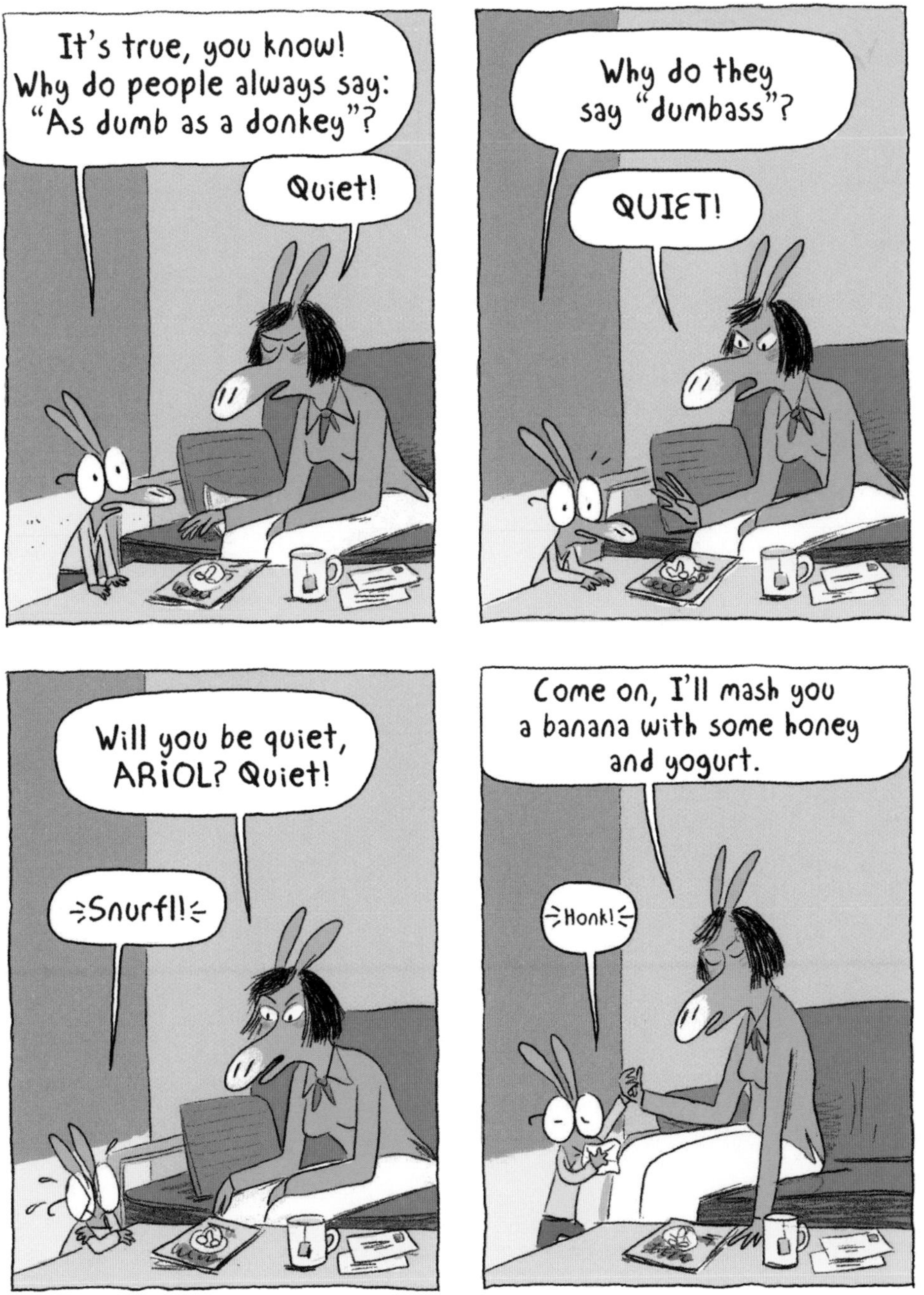
It's true, you know! Why do people always say: "As dumb as a donkey"?
Quiet!
Why do they say "dumbass"?
QUIET!
Will you be quiet, ARIOL? Quiet!
Snurfl!
Come on, I'll mash you a banana with some honey and yogurt.
Honk!

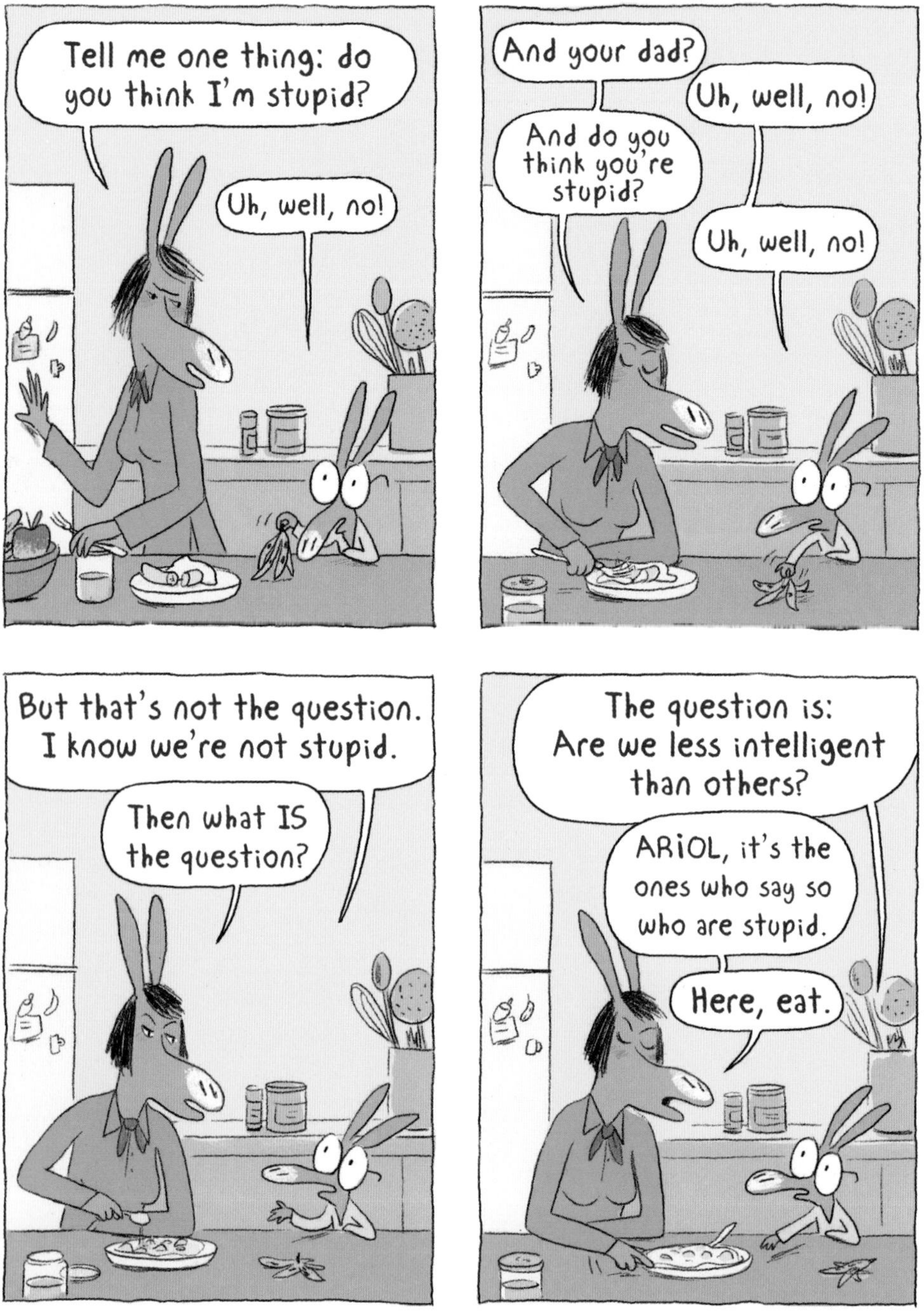
Tell me one thing: do you think I'm stupid?
Uh, well, no!
And your dad?
Uh, well, no!
And do you think you're stupid?
Uh, well, no!
But that's not the question. I know we're not stupid.
Then what IS the question?
The question is: Are we less intelligent than others?
ARIOL, it's the ones who say so who are stupid.
Here, eat.

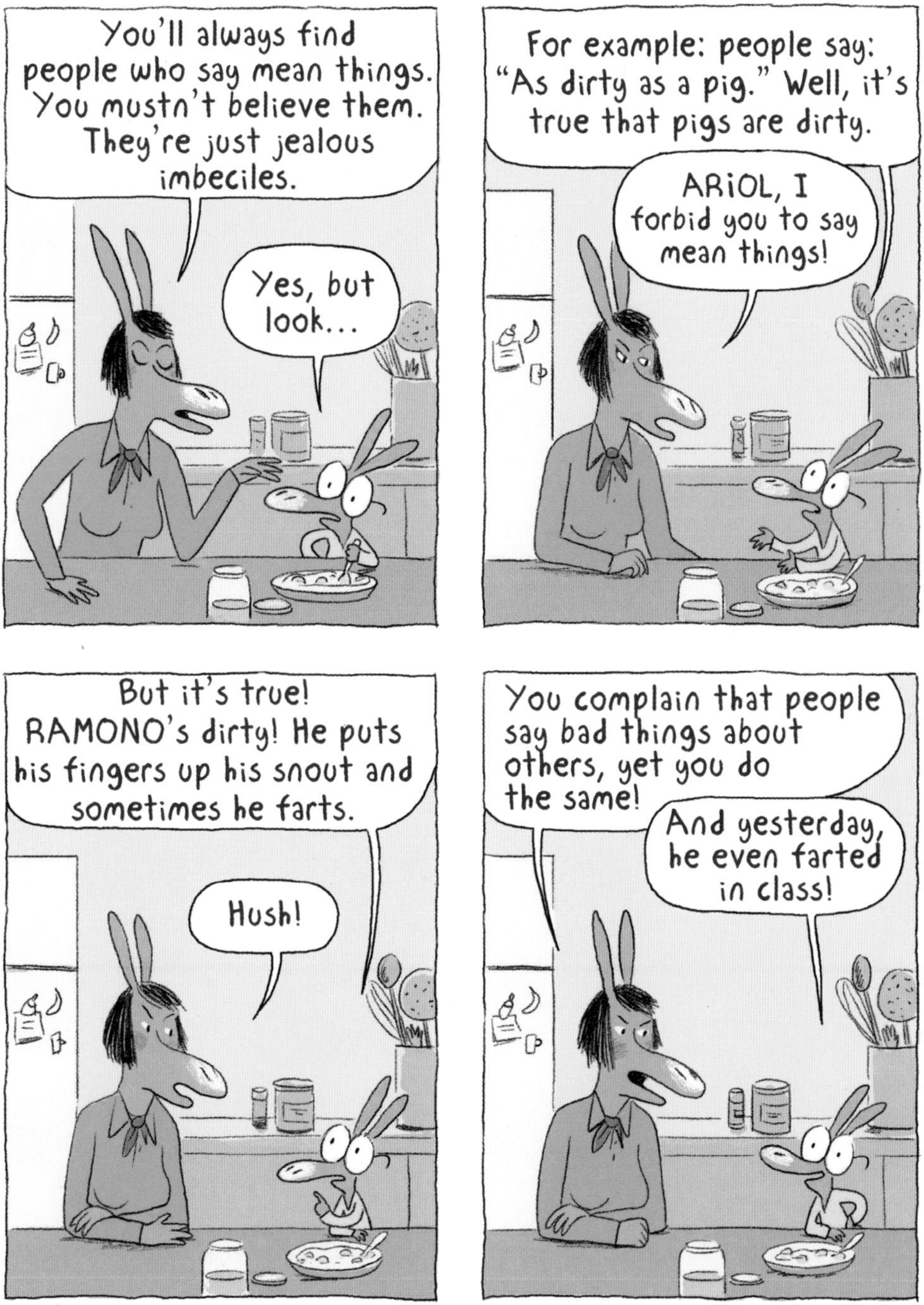
You'll always find people who say mean things. You mustn't believe them. They're just jealous imbeciles.
Yes, but look...
For example: people say: "As dirty as a pig." Well, it's true that pigs are dirty.
ARIOL, I forbid you to say mean things!
But it's true! RAMONO's dirty! He puts his fingers up his snout and sometimes he farts.
Hush!
You complain that people say bad things about others, yet you do the same!
And yesterday, he even farted in class!

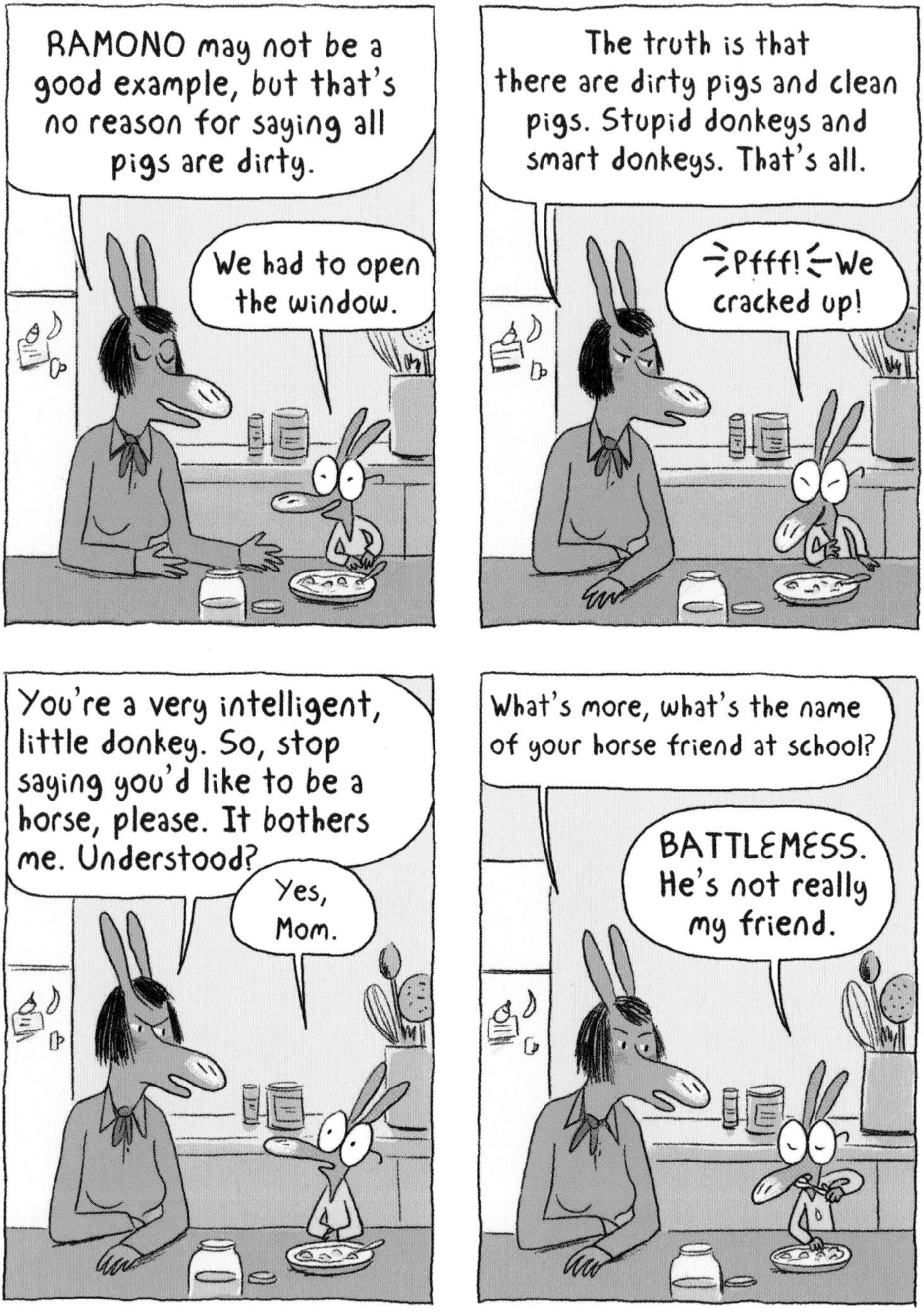
RAMONO may not be a good example, but that's no reason for saying all pigs are dirty.
We had to open the window.
The truth is that there are dirty pigs and clean pigs. Stupid donkeys and smart donkeys. That's all.
Pfff! We cracked up!
You're a very intelligent, little donkey. So, stop saying you'd like to be a horse, please. It bothers me. Understood?
Yes, Mom.
What's more, what's the name of your horse friend at school?
BATTLEMESS. He's not really my friend.

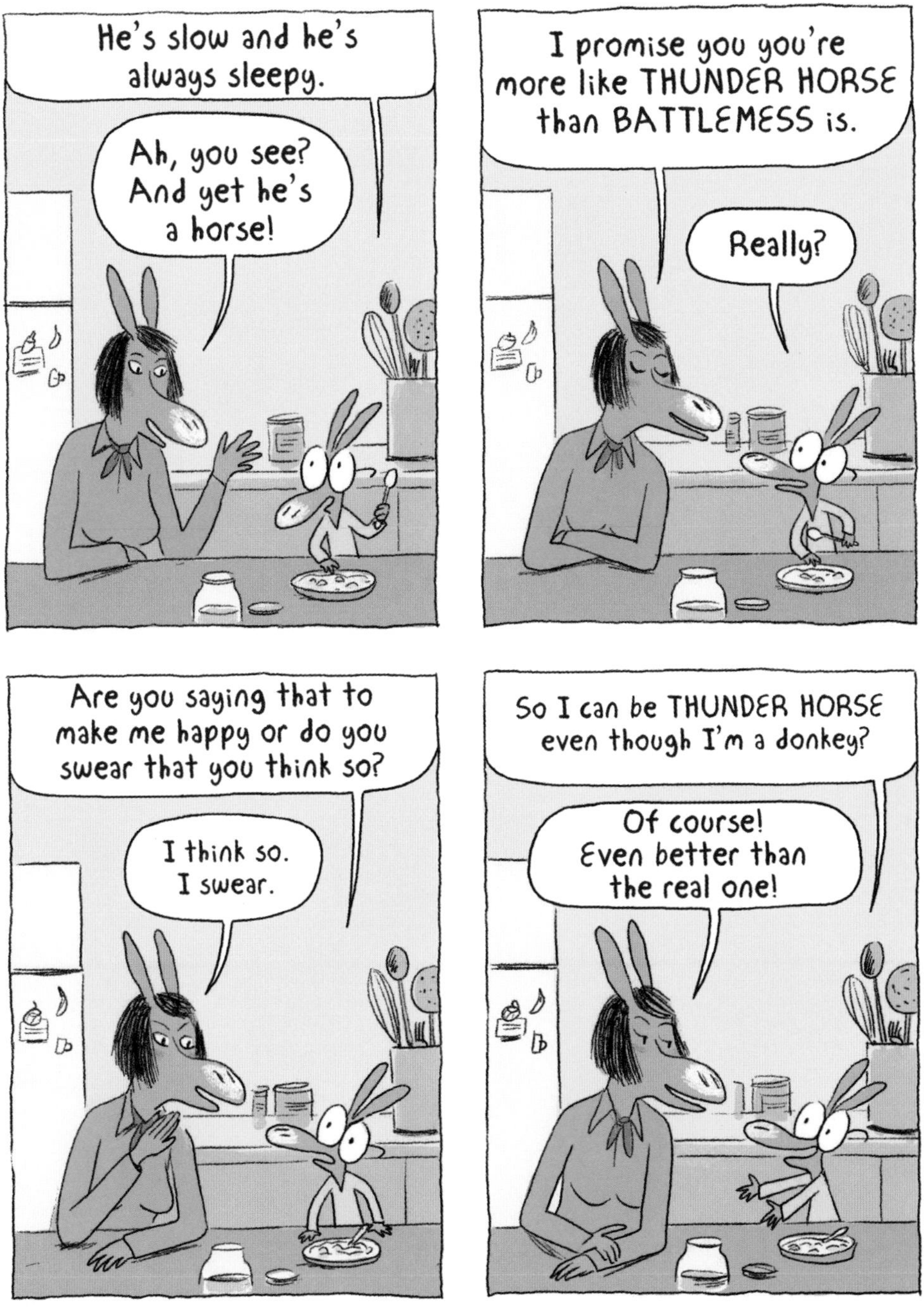
He's slow and he's always sleepy.
Ah, you see? And yet he's a horse!
I promise you you're more like THUNDER HORSE than BATTLEMESS is.
Really?
Are you saying that to make me happy or do you swear that you think so?
I think so. I swear.
So I can be THUNDER HORSE even though I'm a donkey?
Of course! Even better than the real one!

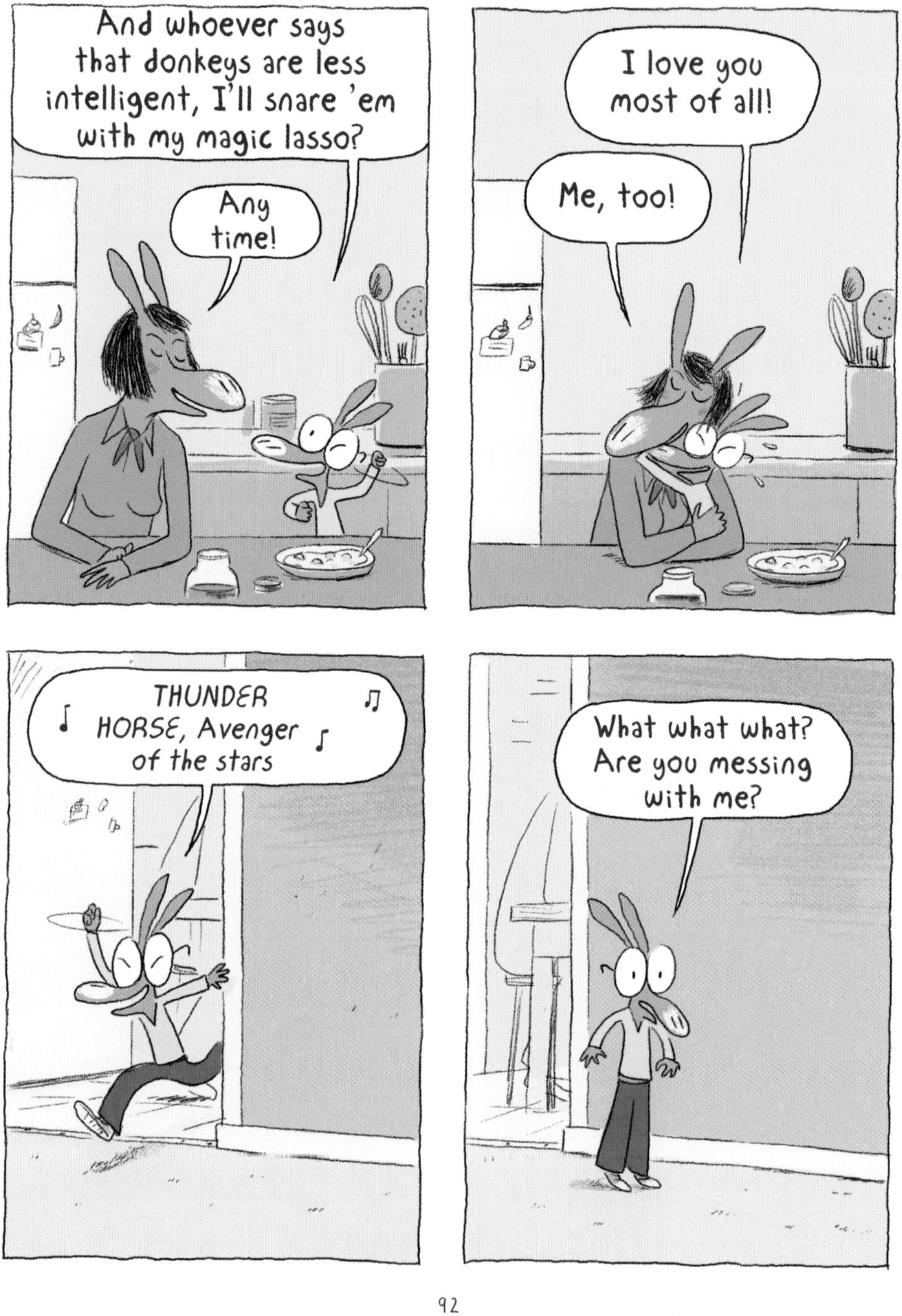
And whoever says that donkeys are less intelligent, I'll snare 'em with my magic lasso?
Any time!
I love you most of all!
Me, too!
THUNDER HORSE, Avenger of the stars
What what what? Are you messing with me?

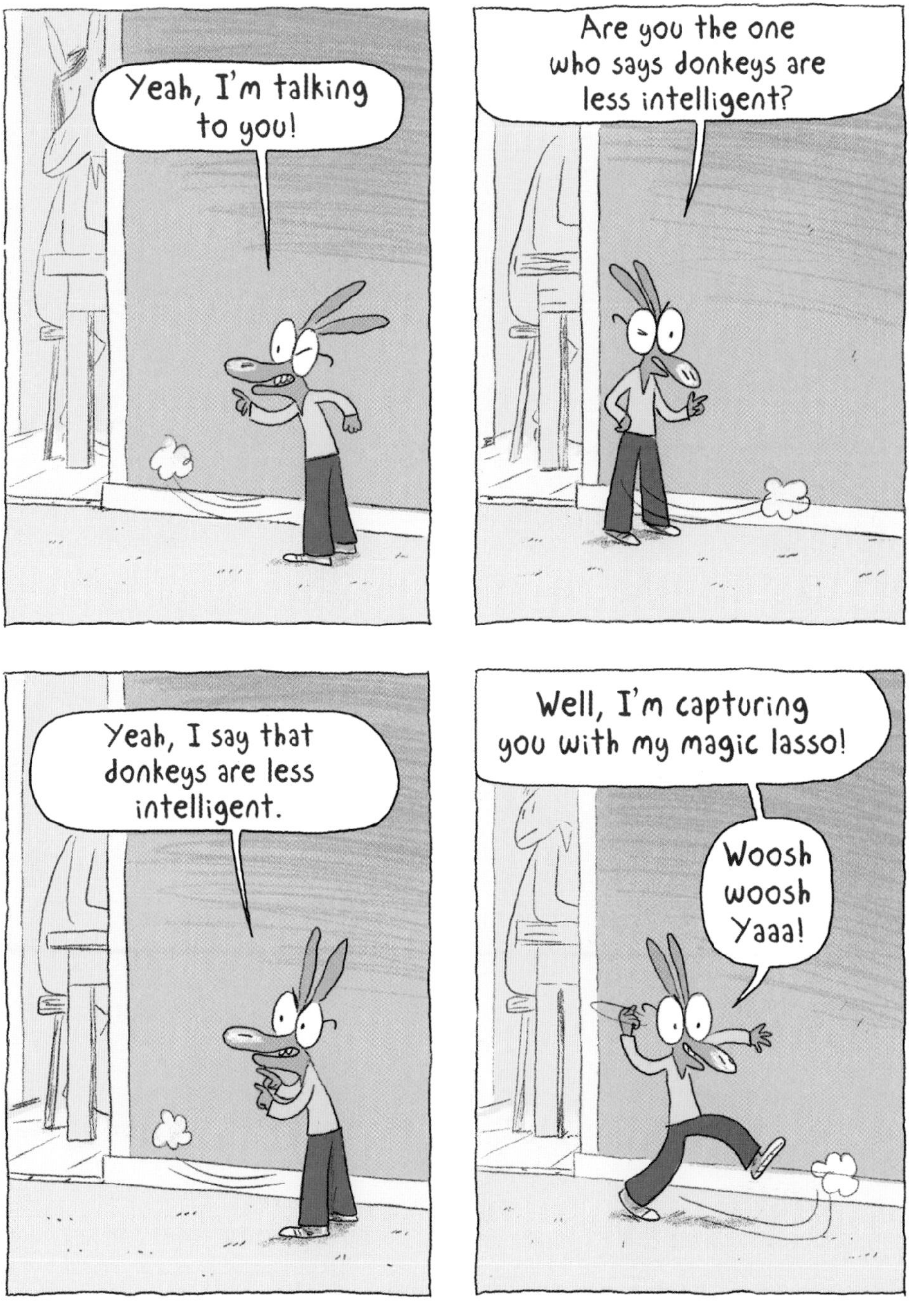
Yeah, I'm talking to you!
Are you the one who says donkeys are less intelligent?
Yeah, I say that donkeys are less intelligent.
Well, I'm capturing you with my magic lasso!
Woosh woosh Yaaa!

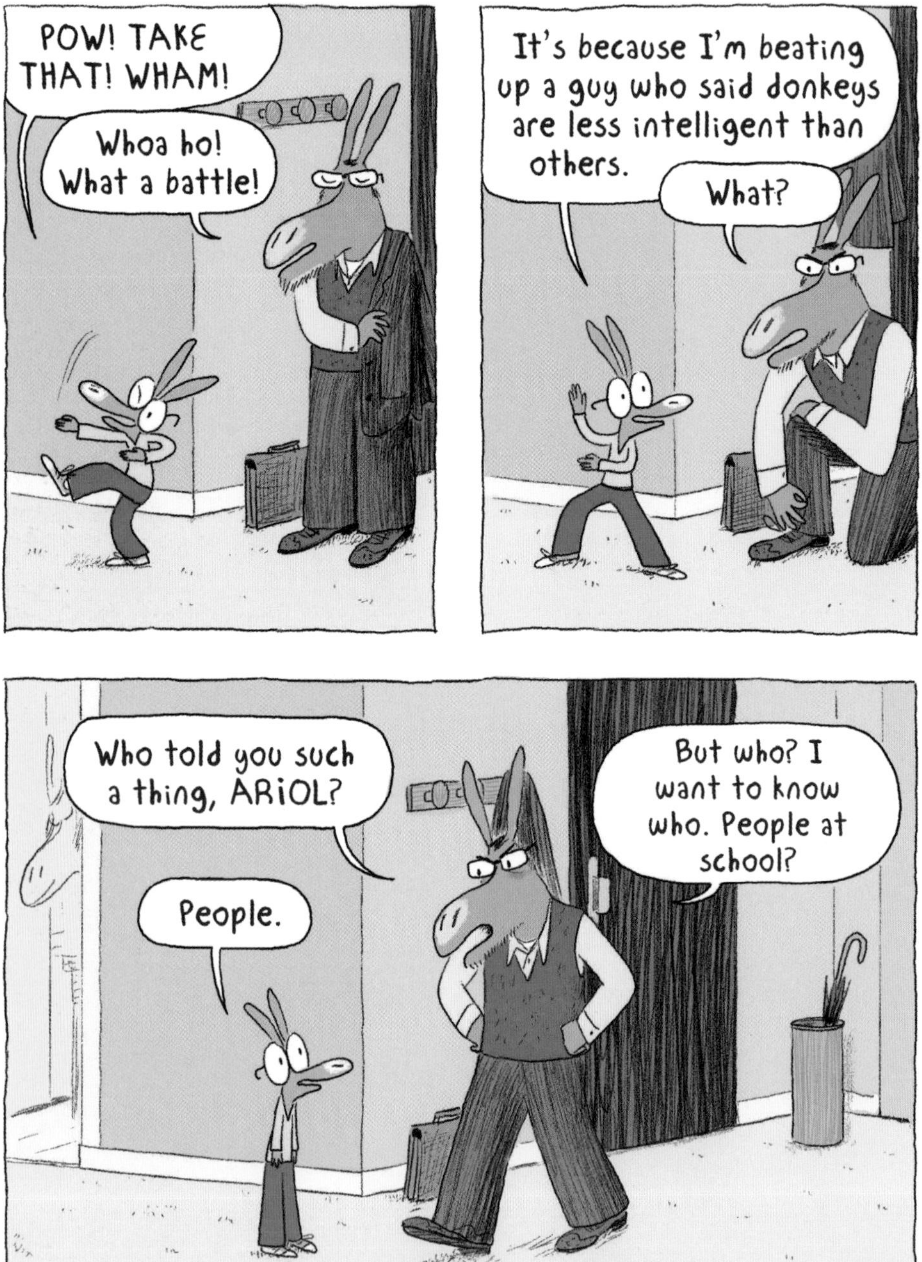
POW! TAKE THAT! WHAM!
Whoa ho! What a battle!
It's because I'm beating up a guy who said donkeys are less intelligent than others.
What?
Who told you such a thing, ARIOL?
People.
But who? I want to know who. People at school?
END

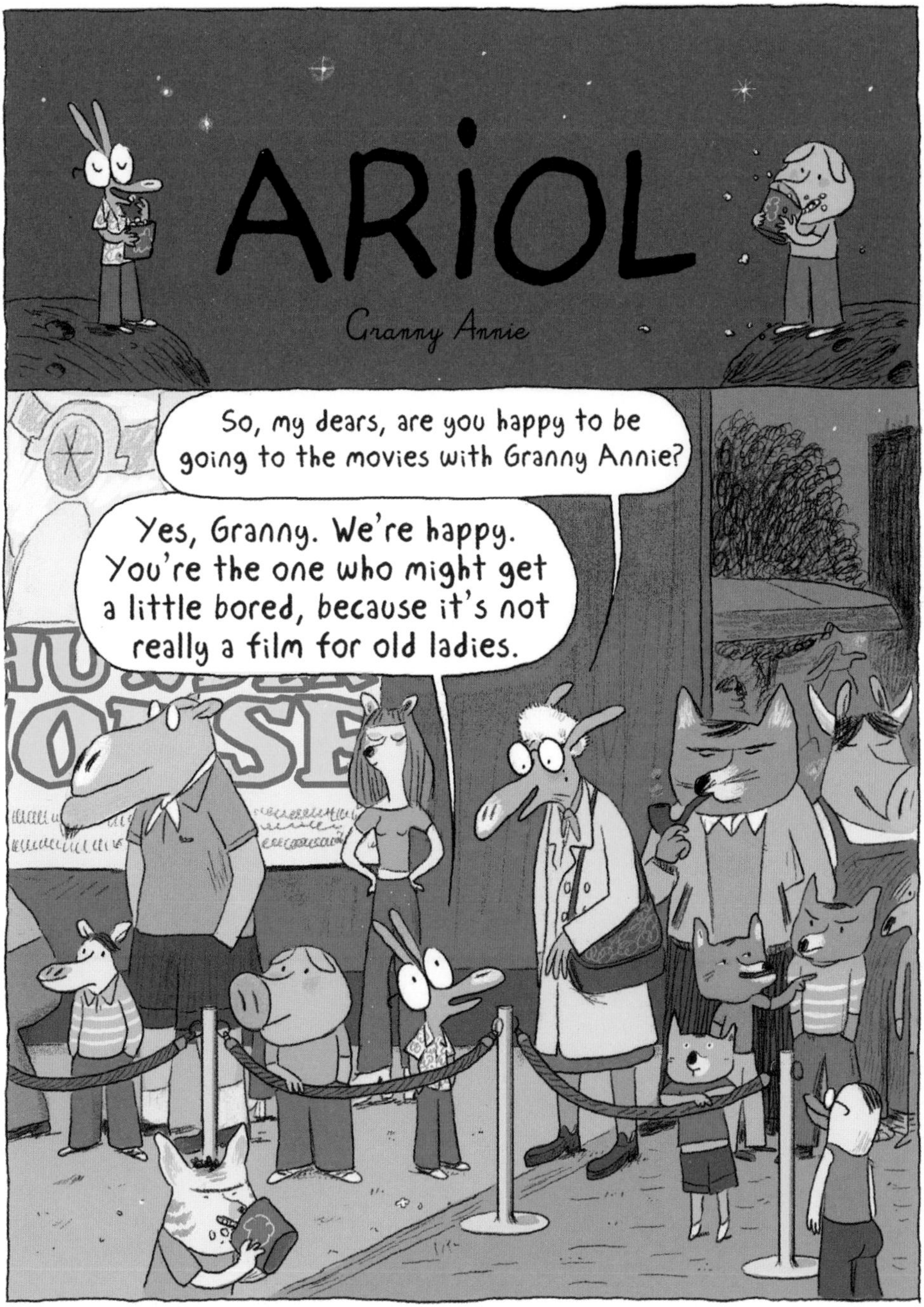
ARIOL
Granny Annie
So, my dears, are you happy to be going to the movies with Granny Annie?
Yes, Granny. We're happy. You're the one who might get a little bored, because it's not really a film for old ladies.

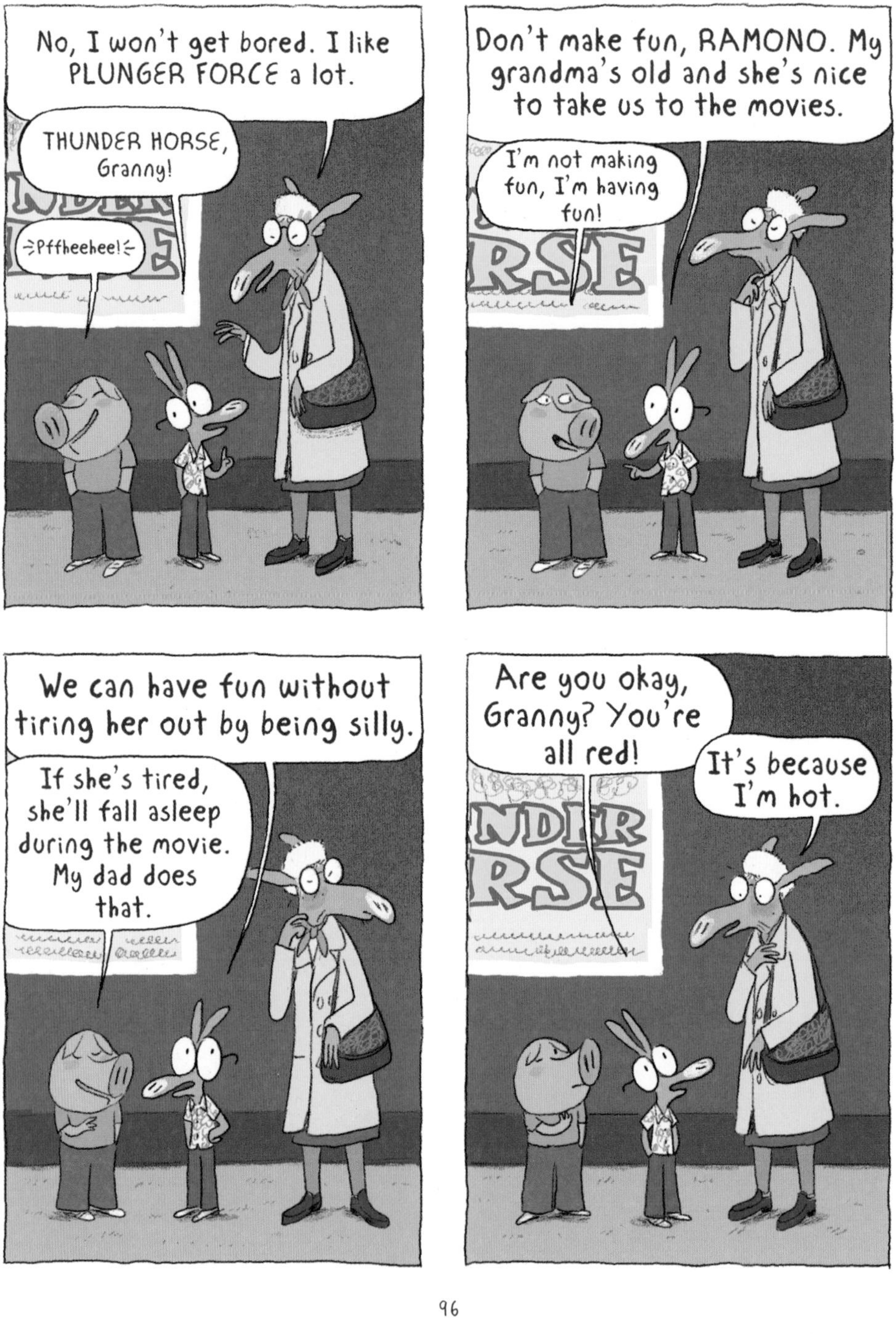
No, I won't get bored. I like PLUNGER FORCE a lot.
THUNDER HORSE, Granny!
Pffheehee!
Don't make fun, RAMONO. My grandma's old and she's nice to take us to the movies.
I'm not making fun, I'm having fun!
We can have fun without tiring her out by being silly.
If she's tired, she'll fall asleep during the movie. My dad does that.
Are you okay, Granny? You're all red!
It's because I'm hot.

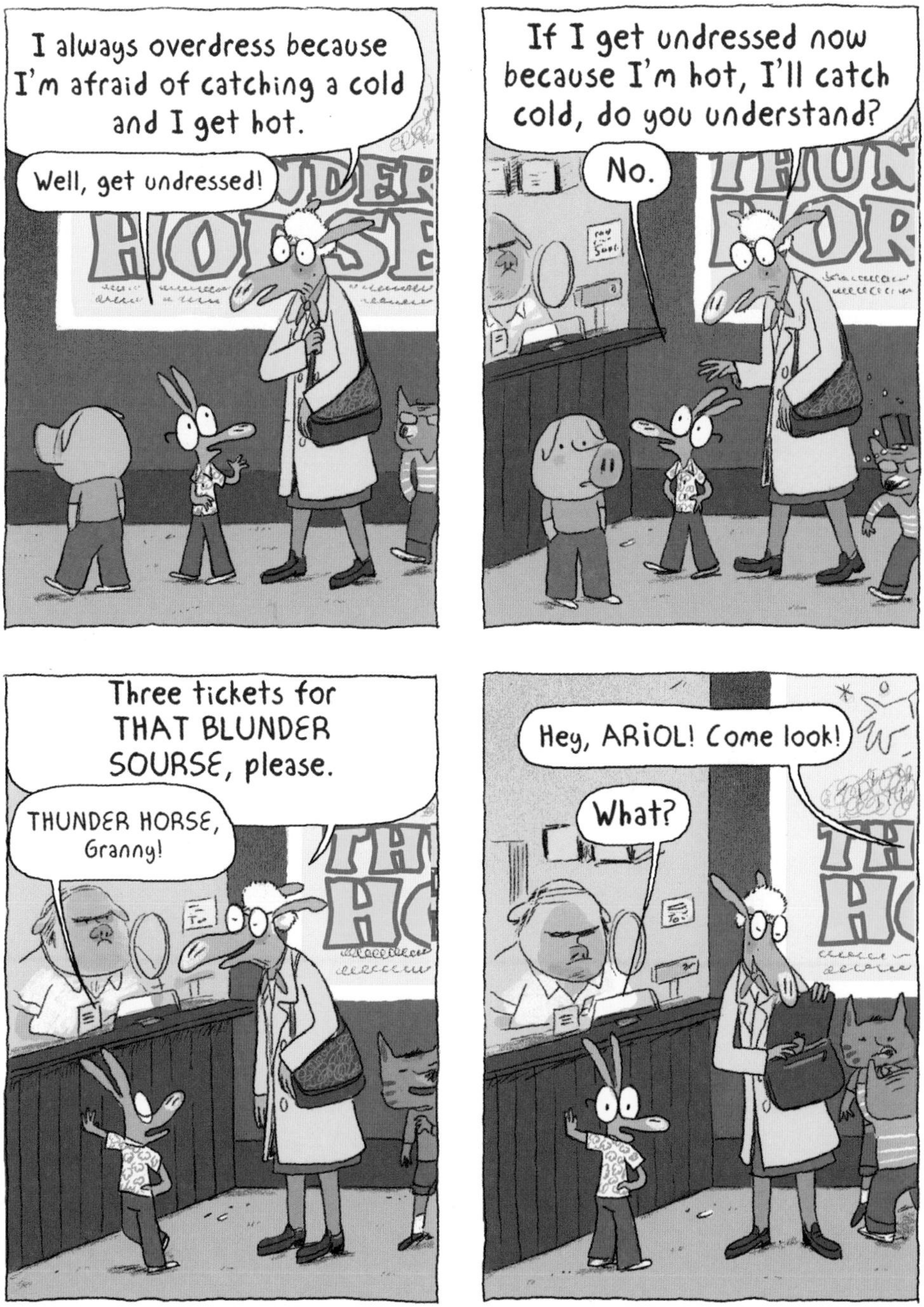
I always overdress because I'm afraid of catching a cold and I get hot.
Well, get undressed!
If I get undressed now because I'm hot, I'll catch cold, do you understand?
No.
Three tickets for THAT BLUNDER SOURSE, please.
THUNDER HORSE, Granny!
Hey, ARIOL! Come look!
What?

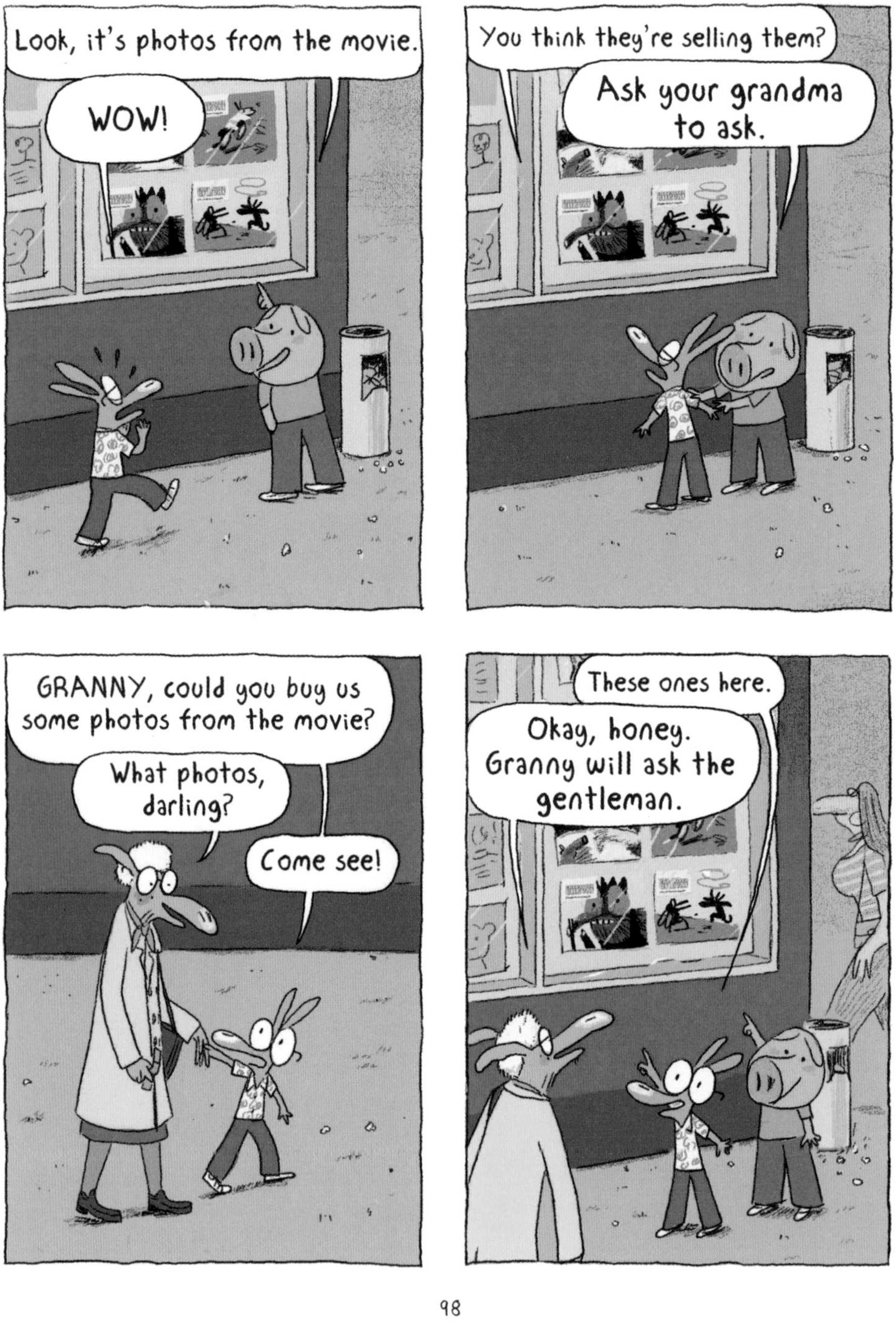

Look, it's photos from the movie.
WOW!
You think they're selling them?
Ask your grandma to ask.
GRANNY, could you buy us some photos from the movie?
What photos, darling?
Come see!
These ones here.
Okay, honey. Granny will ask the gentleman.

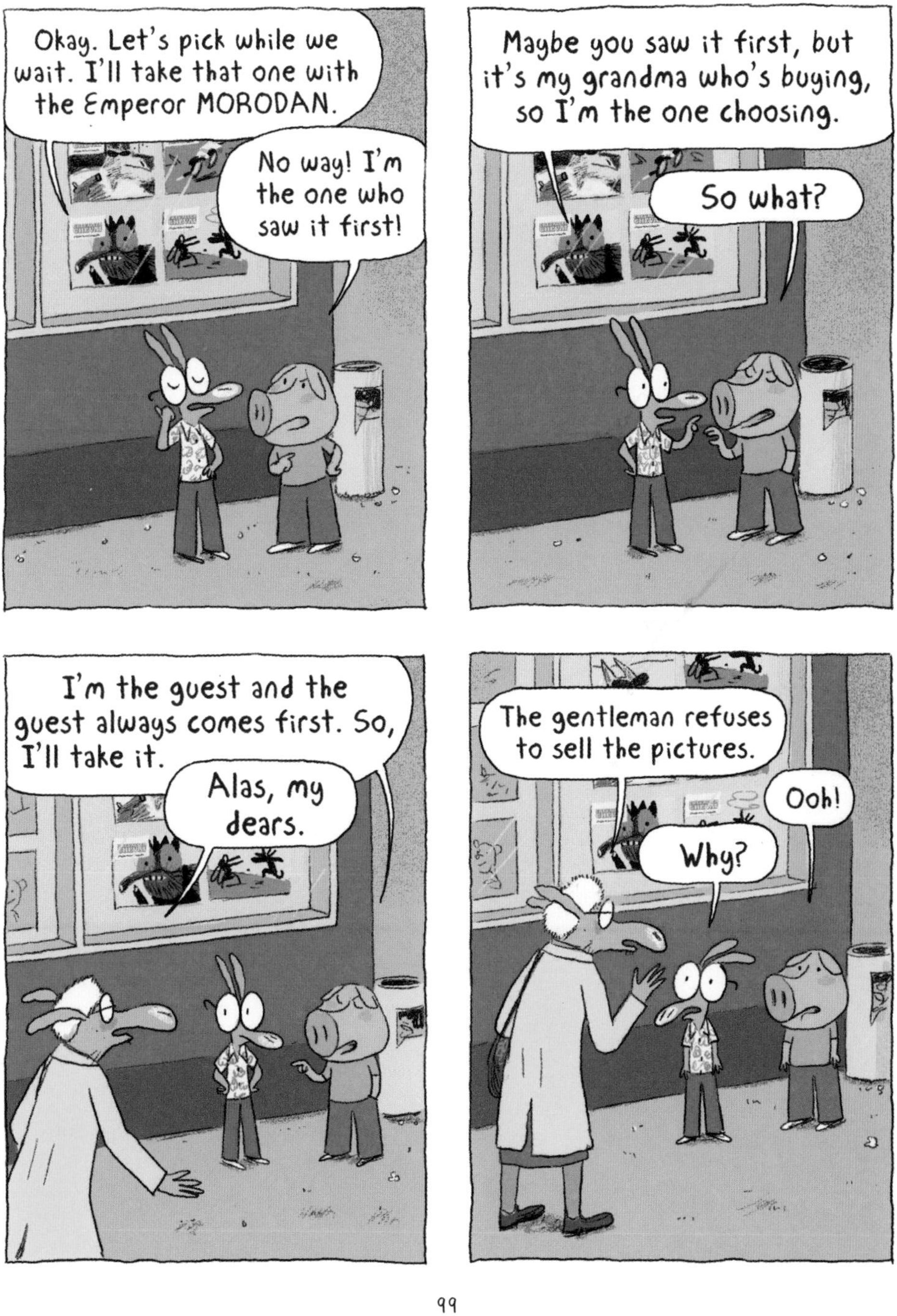
Okay. Let's pick while we wait. I'll take that one with the Emperor MORODAN.
No way! I'm the one who saw it first!
Maybe you saw it first, but it's my grandma who's buying, so I'm the one choosing.
So what?
I'm the guest and the guest always comes first. So, I'll take it.
Alas, my dears.
The gentleman refuses to sell the pictures.
Ooh!
Why?

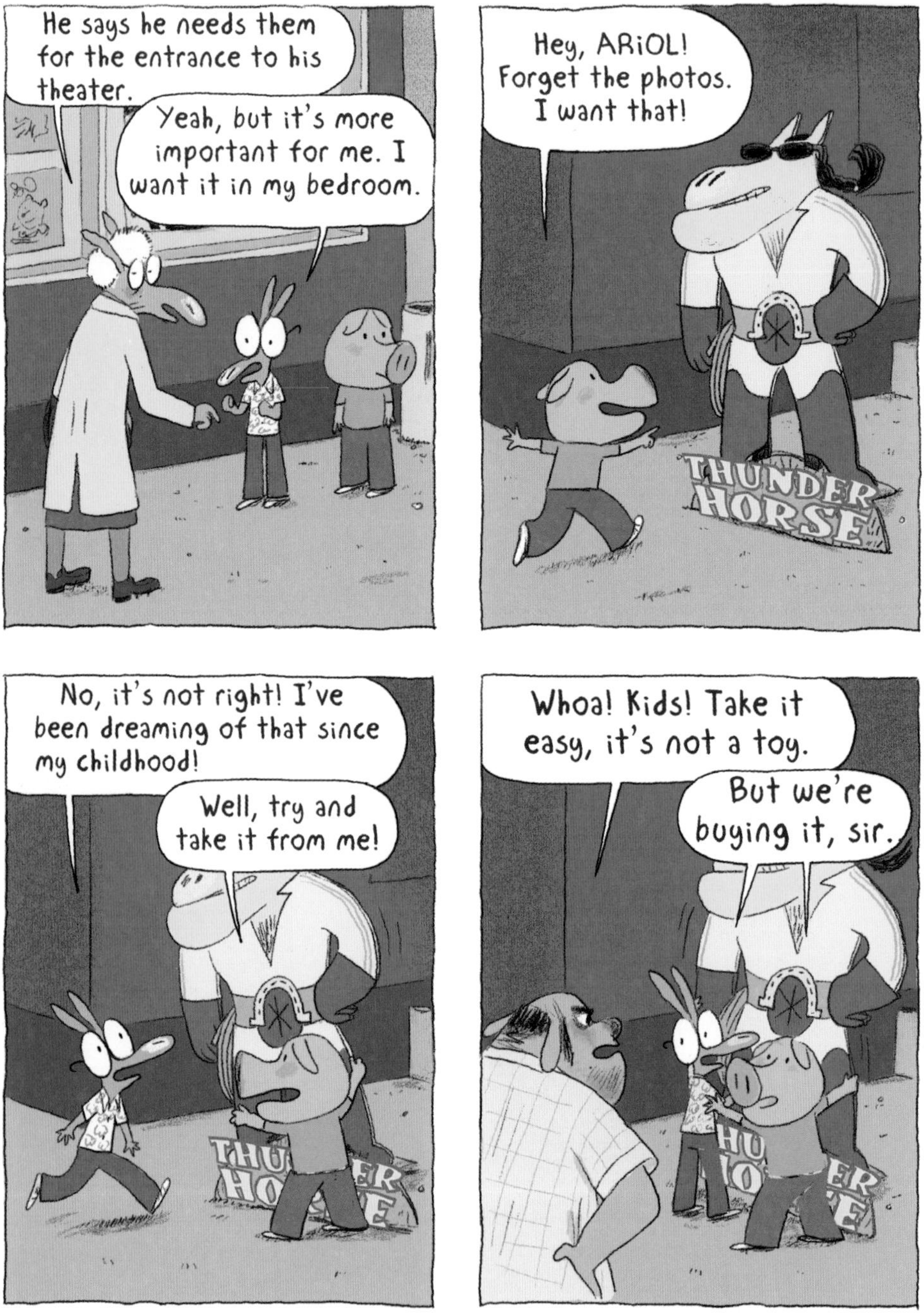
He says he needs them for the entrance to his theater.
Yeah, but it's more important for me. I want it in my bedroom.
Hey, ARiOL! Forget the photos. I want that!
THUNDER HORSE
No, it's not right! I've been dreaming of that since my childhood!
Well, try and take it from me!
Whoa! Kids! Take it easy, it's not a toy.
But we're buying it, sir.

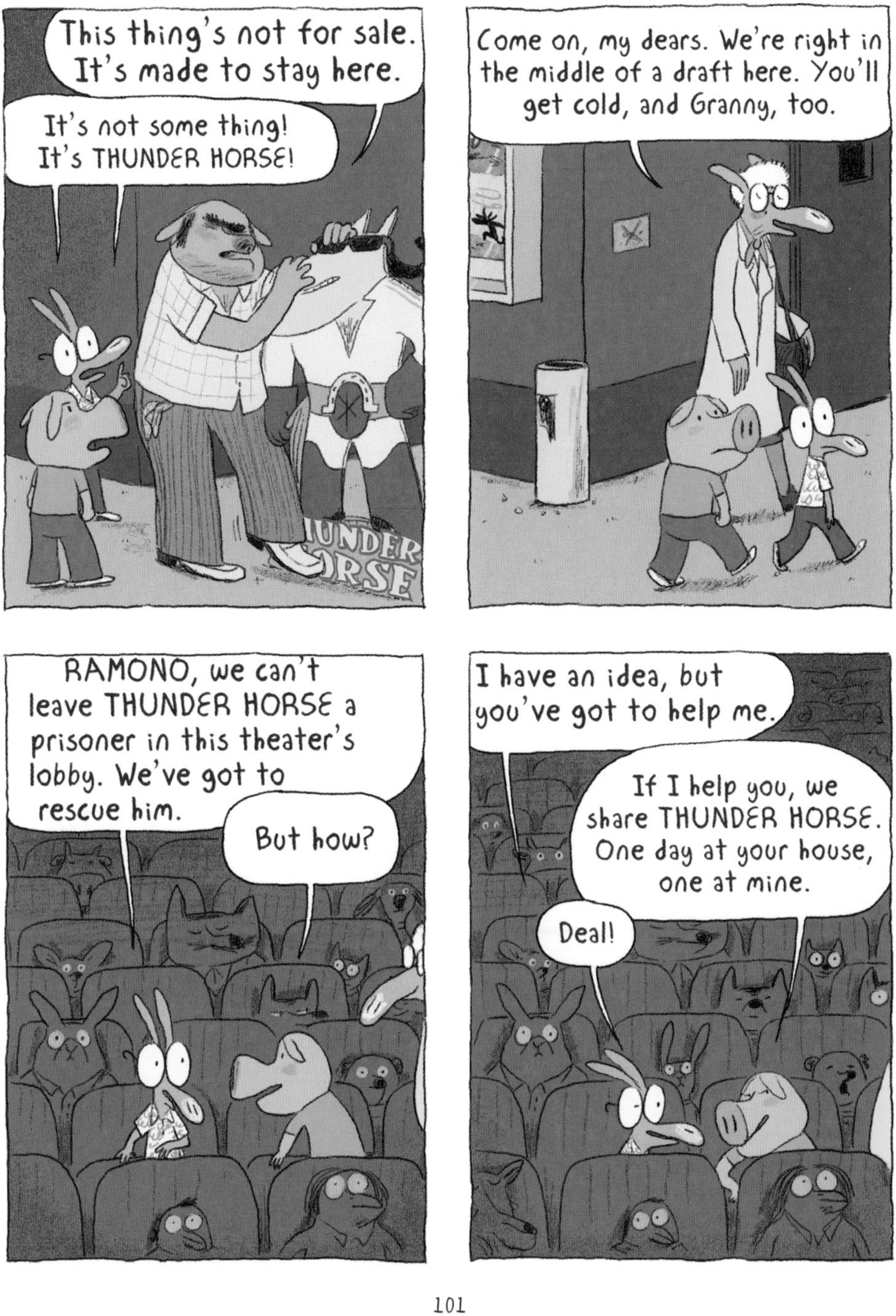
This thing's not for sale. It's made to stay here.
It's not some thing! It's THUNDER HORSE!
THUNDER HORSE
Come on, my dears. We're right in the middle of a draft here. You'll get cold, and Granny, too.
RAMONO, we can't leave THUNDER HORSE a prisoner in this theater's lobby. We've got to rescue him.
But how?
I have an idea, but you've got to help me.
If I help you, we share THUNDER HORSE. One day at your house, one at mine.
Deal!

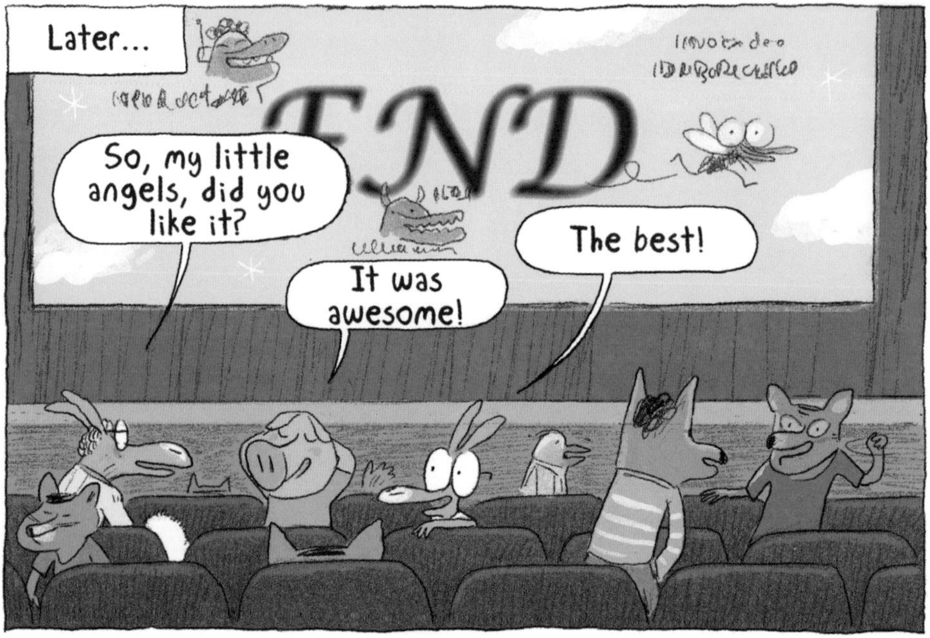
Later...
END
So, my little angels, did you like it?
It was awesome!
The best!

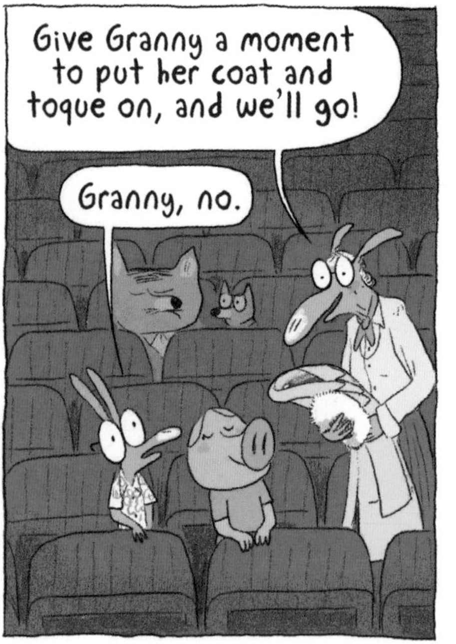
Give Granny a moment to put her coat and toque on, and we'll go!
Granny, no.

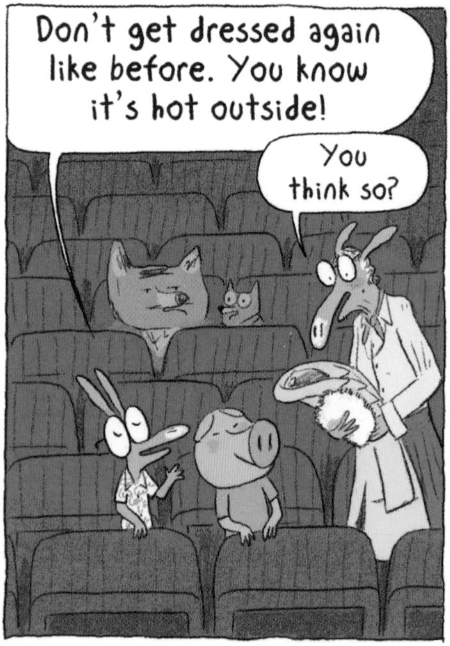
Don't get dressed again like before. You know it's hot outside!
You think so?

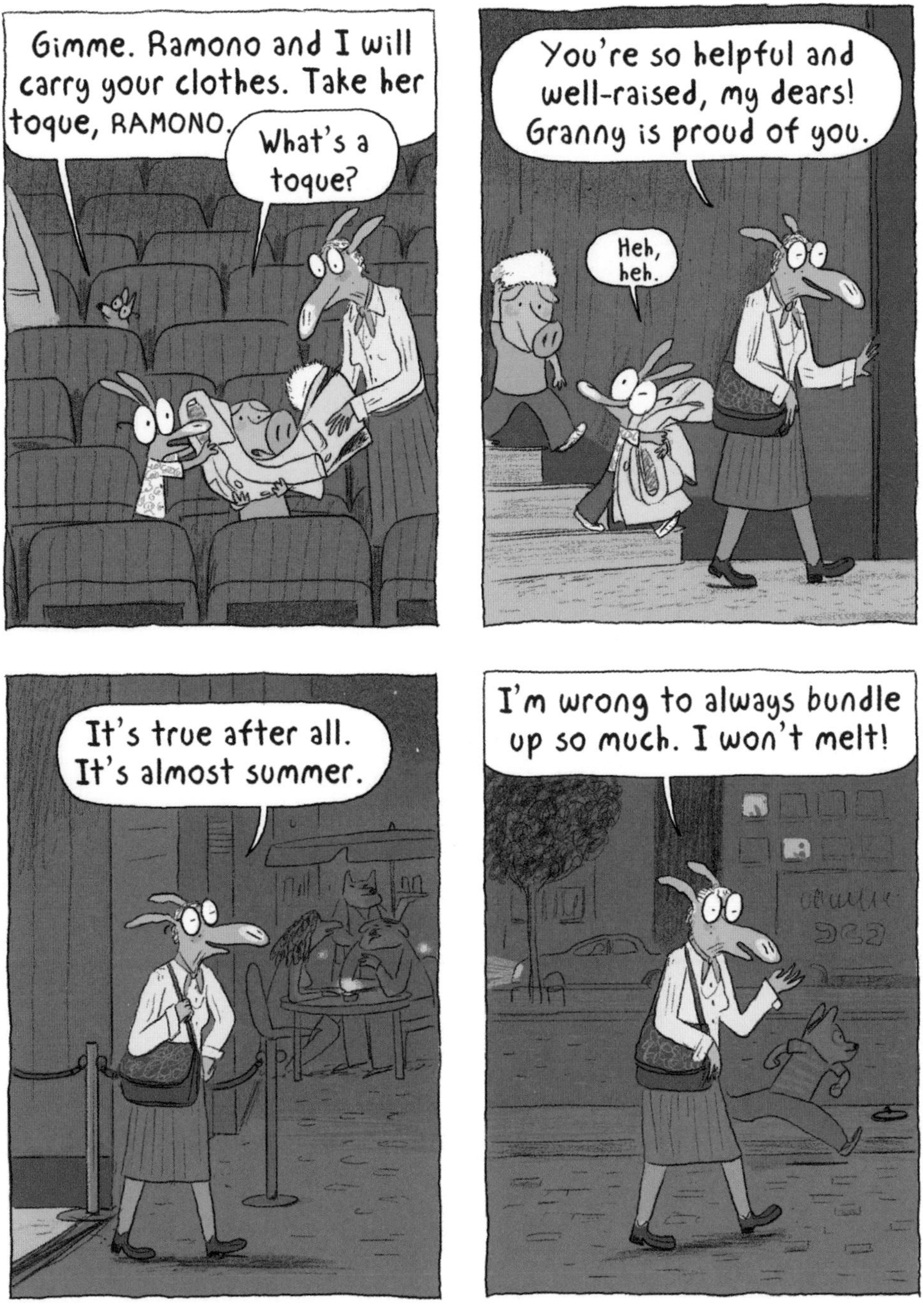
Gimme. Ramono and I will carry your clothes. Take her toque, RAMONO.
What's a toque?
You're so helpful and well-raised, my dears! Granny is proud of you.
Heh, heh.
It's true after all. It's almost summer.
I'm wrong to always bundle up so much. I won't melt!

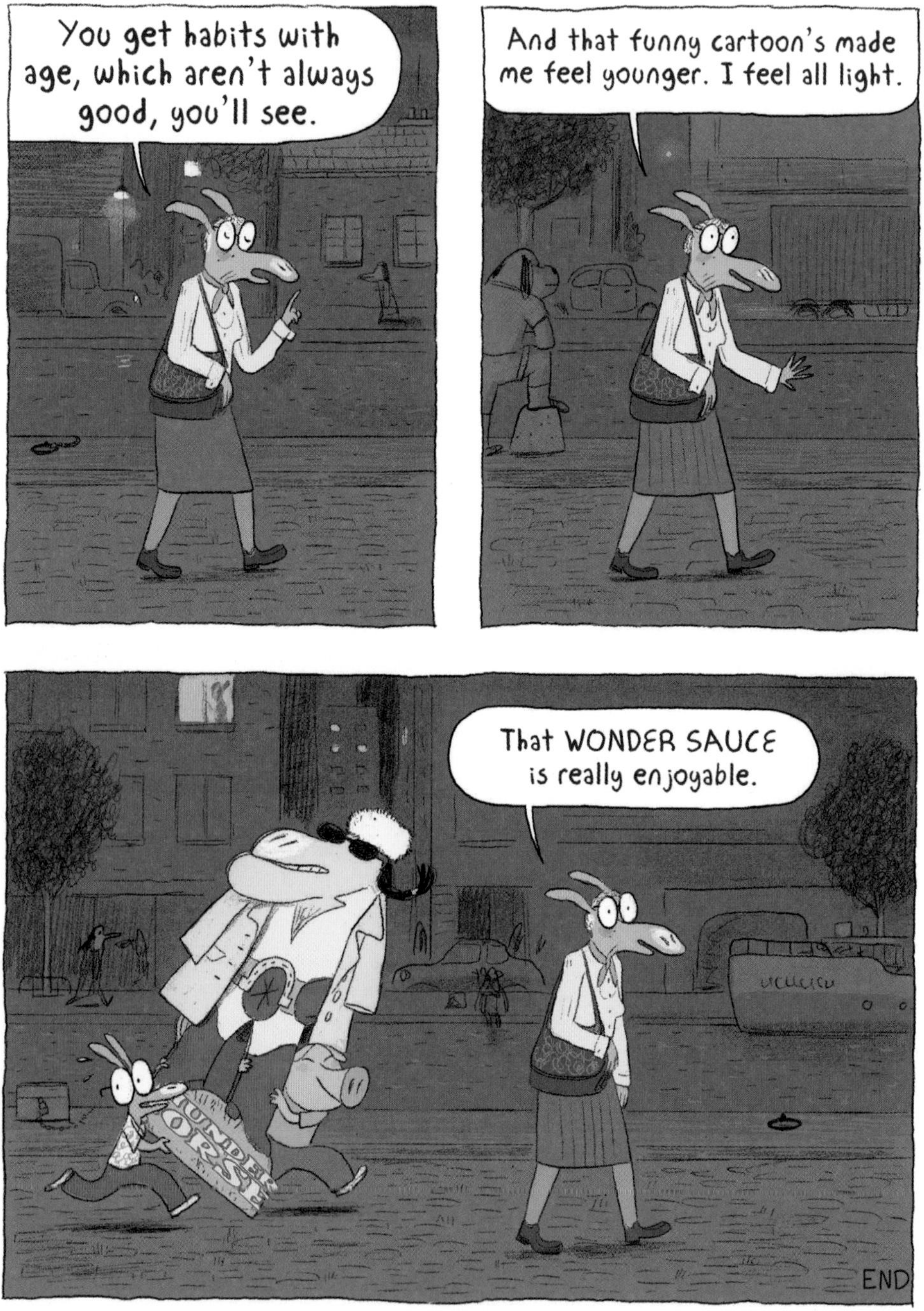
You get habits with age, which aren't always good, you'll see.
And that funny cartoon's made me feel younger. I feel all light.
That WONDER SAUCE is really enjoyable.
END

ARIOL

Vomit

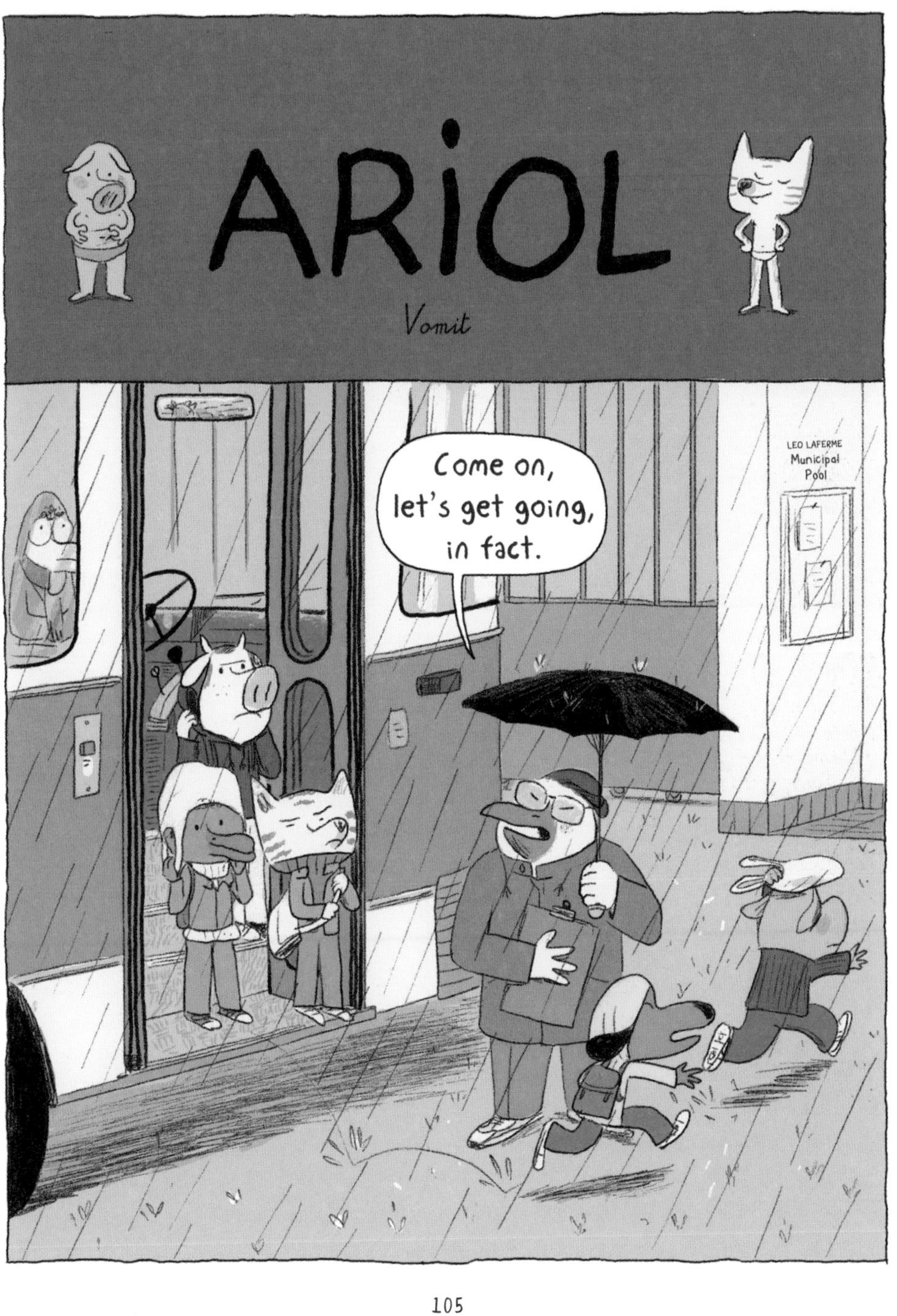
Come on, let's get going, in fact.
LEO LAFERME Municipal Pool

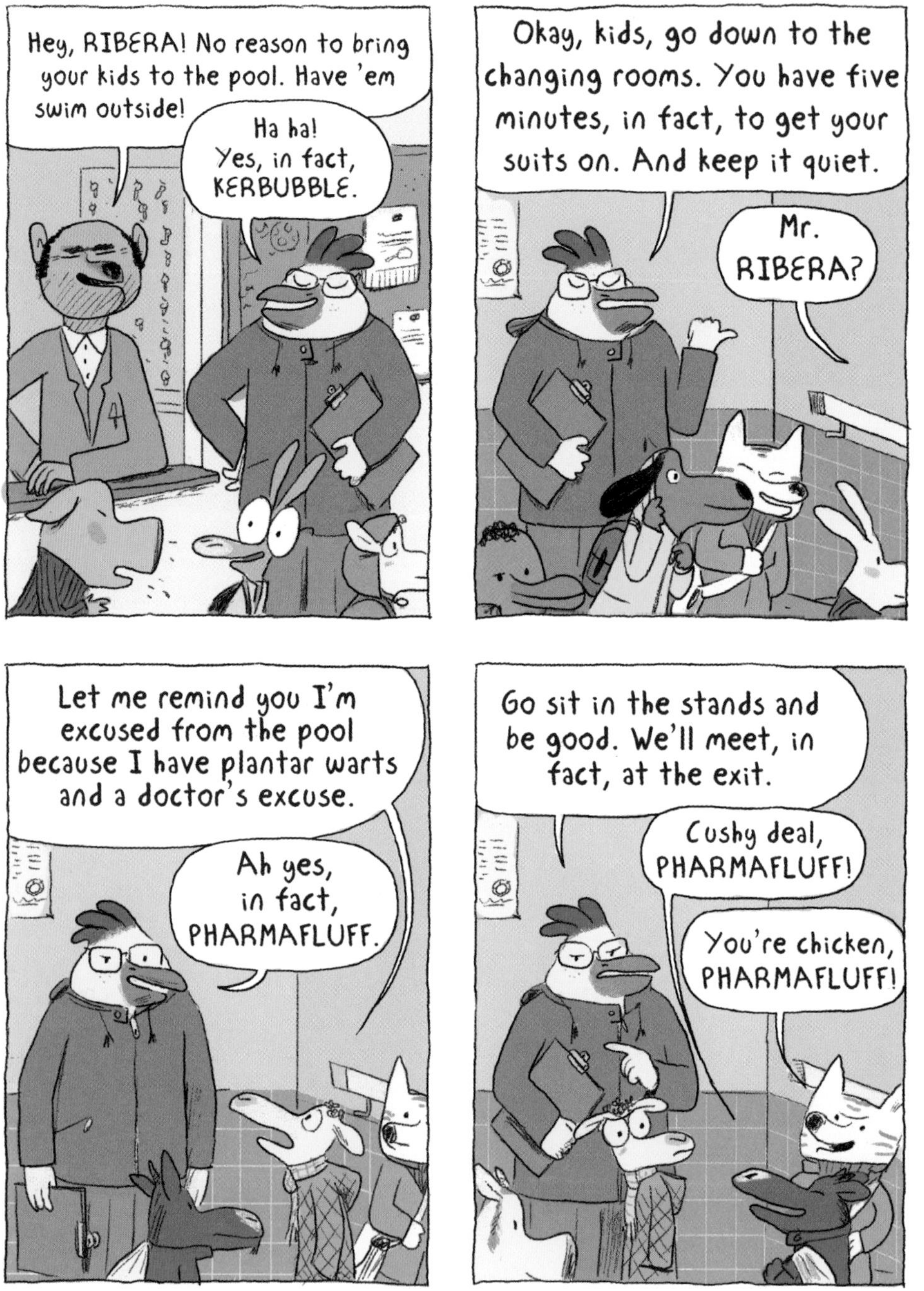
Hey, RIBERA! No reason to bring your kids to the pool. Have 'em swim outside!
Ha ha! Yes, in fact, KERBUBBLE.
Okay, kids, go down to the changing rooms. You have five minutes, in fact, to get your suits on. And keep it quiet.
Mr. RIBERA?
Let me remind you I'm excused from the pool because I have plantar warts and a doctor's excuse.
Ah yes, in fact, PHARMAFLUFF.
Go sit in the stands and be good. We'll meet, in fact, at the exit.
Cushy deal, PHARMAFLUFF!
You're chicken, PHARMAFLUFF!

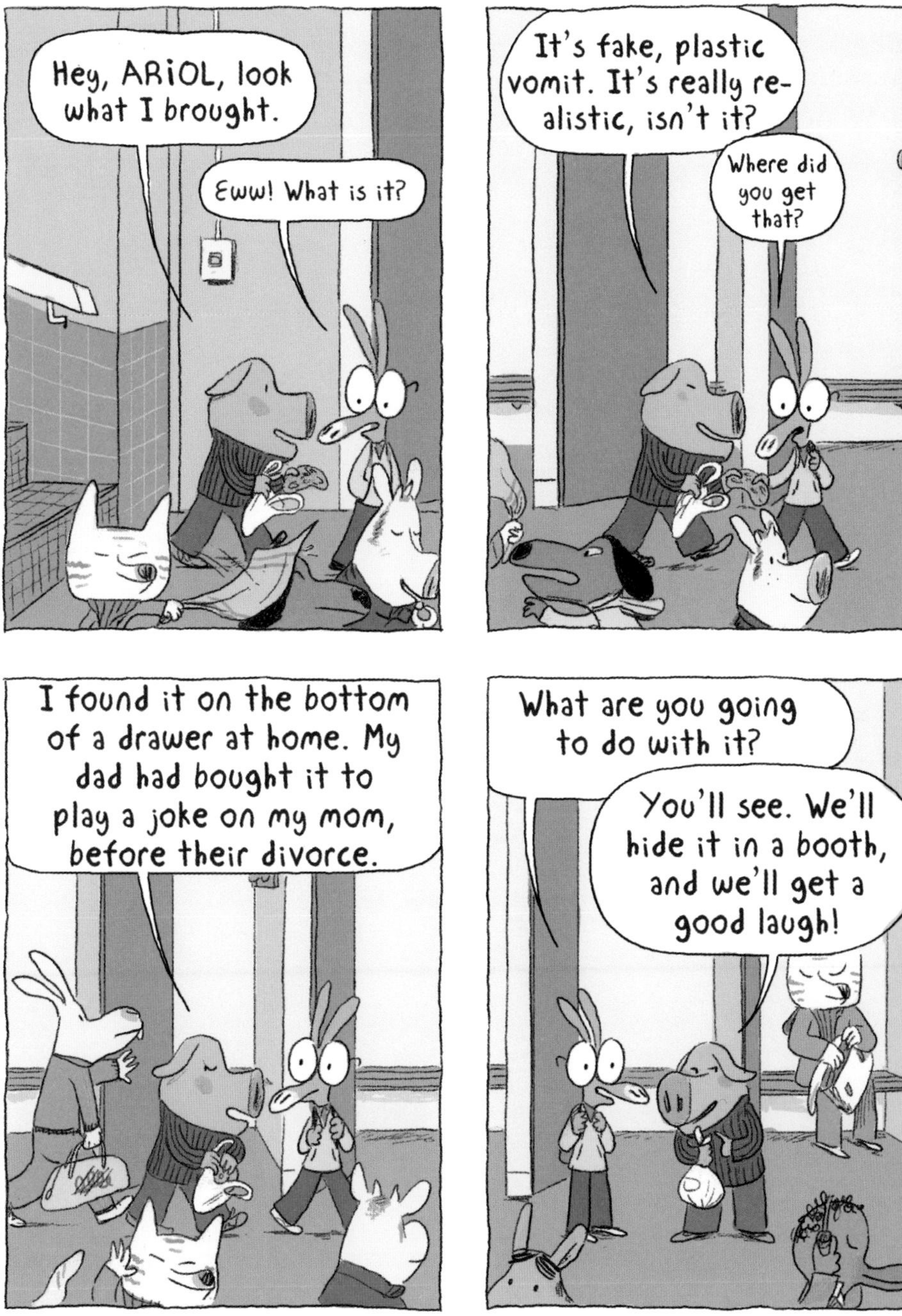
Hey, ARiOL, look what I brought.
Eww! What is it?
It's fake, plastic vomit. It's really re-alistic, isn't it?
Where did you get that?
I found it on the bottom of a drawer at home. My dad had bought it to play a joke on my mom, before their divorce.
What are you going to do with it?
You'll see. We'll hide it in a booth, and we'll get a good laugh!

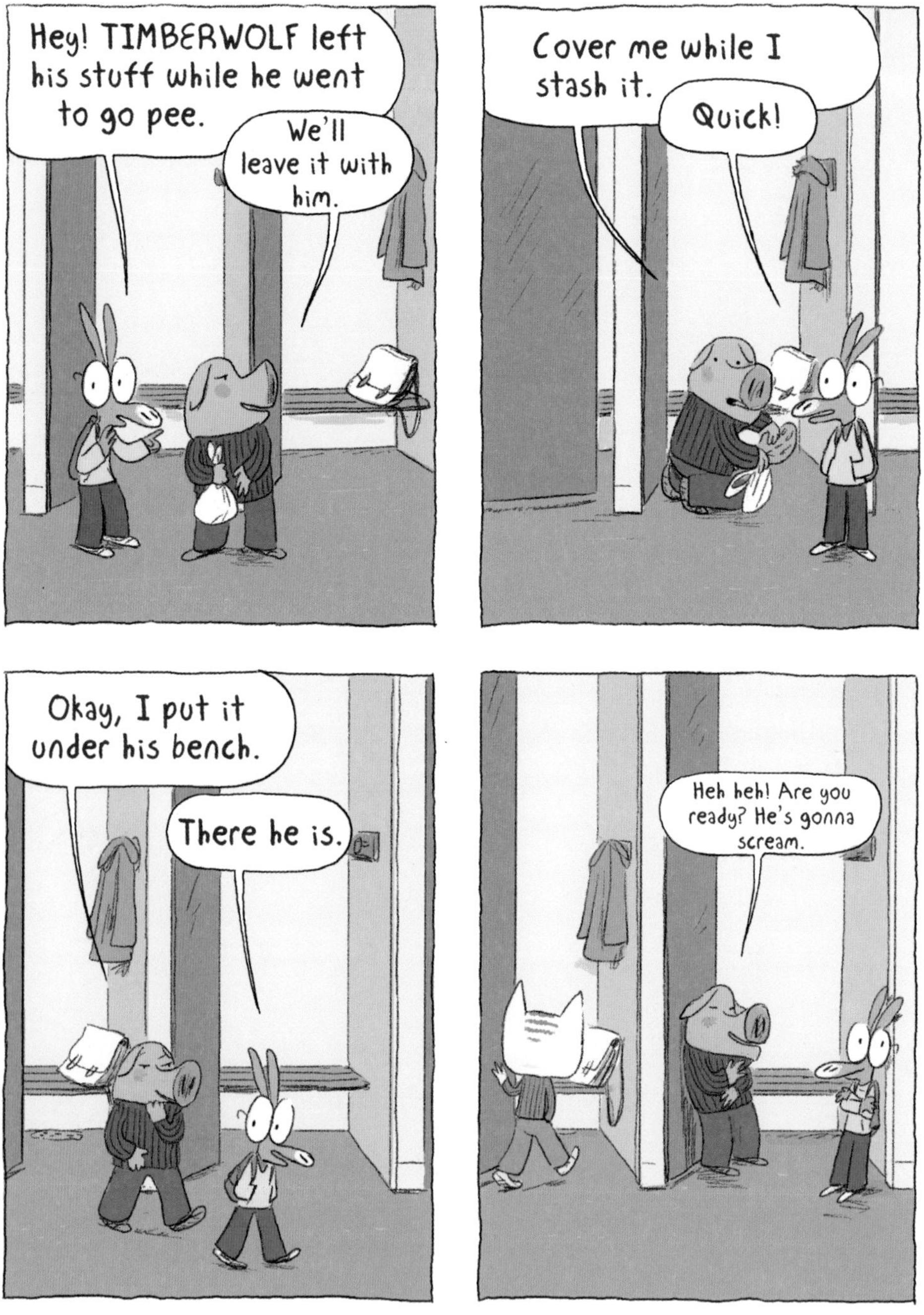
Hey! TIMBERWOLF left his stuff while he went to go pee.
We'll leave it with him.
Cover me while I stash it.
Quick!
Okay, I put it under his bench.
There he is.
Heh heh! Are you ready? He's gonna scream.

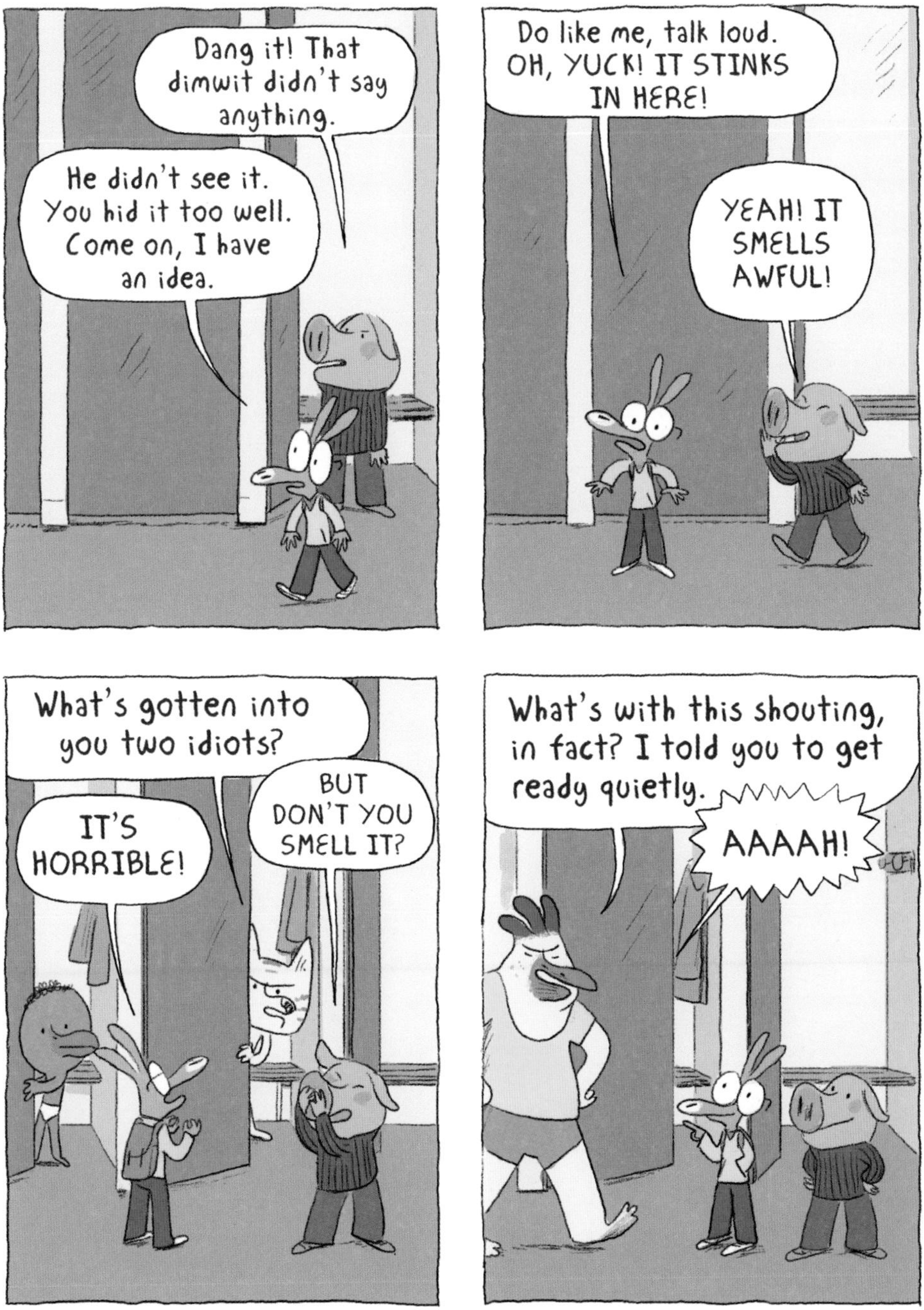
Dang it! That dimwit didn't say anything.
He didn't see it. You hid it too well. Come on, I have an idea.
Do like me, talk loud. OH, YUCK! IT STINKS IN HERE!
YEAH! IT SMELLS AWFUL!
What's gotten into you two idiots?
IT'S HORRIBLE!
BUT DON'T YOU SMELL IT?
What's with this shouting, in fact? I told you to get ready quietly.
AAAAH!

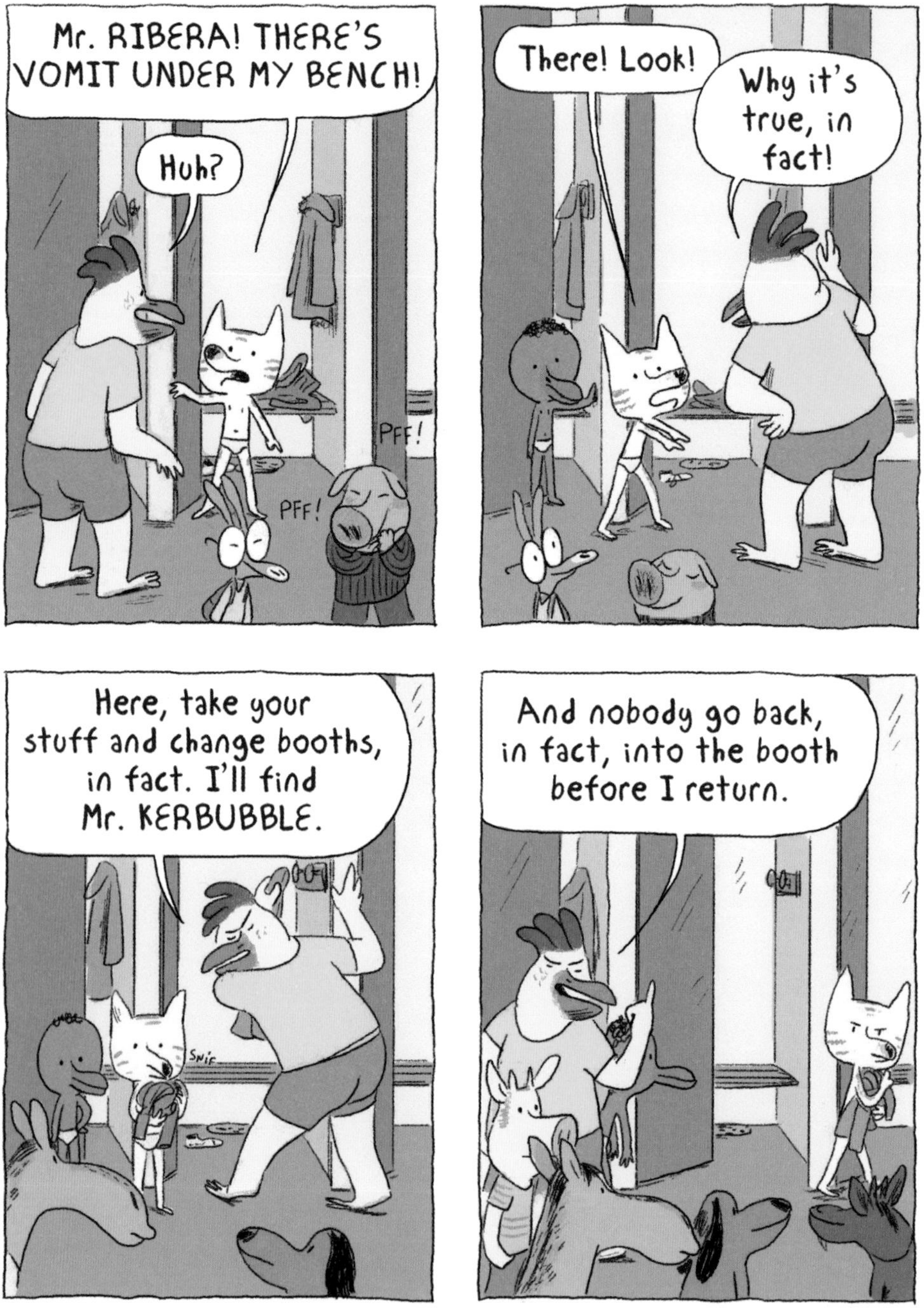
Mr. RIBERA! THERE'S VOMIT UNDER MY BENCH!
Huh?
PFF!
PFF!
There! Look!
Why it's true, in fact!
Here, take your stuff and change booths, in fact. I'll find Mr. KERBUBBLE.
SNIF
And nobody go back, in fact, into the booth before I return.

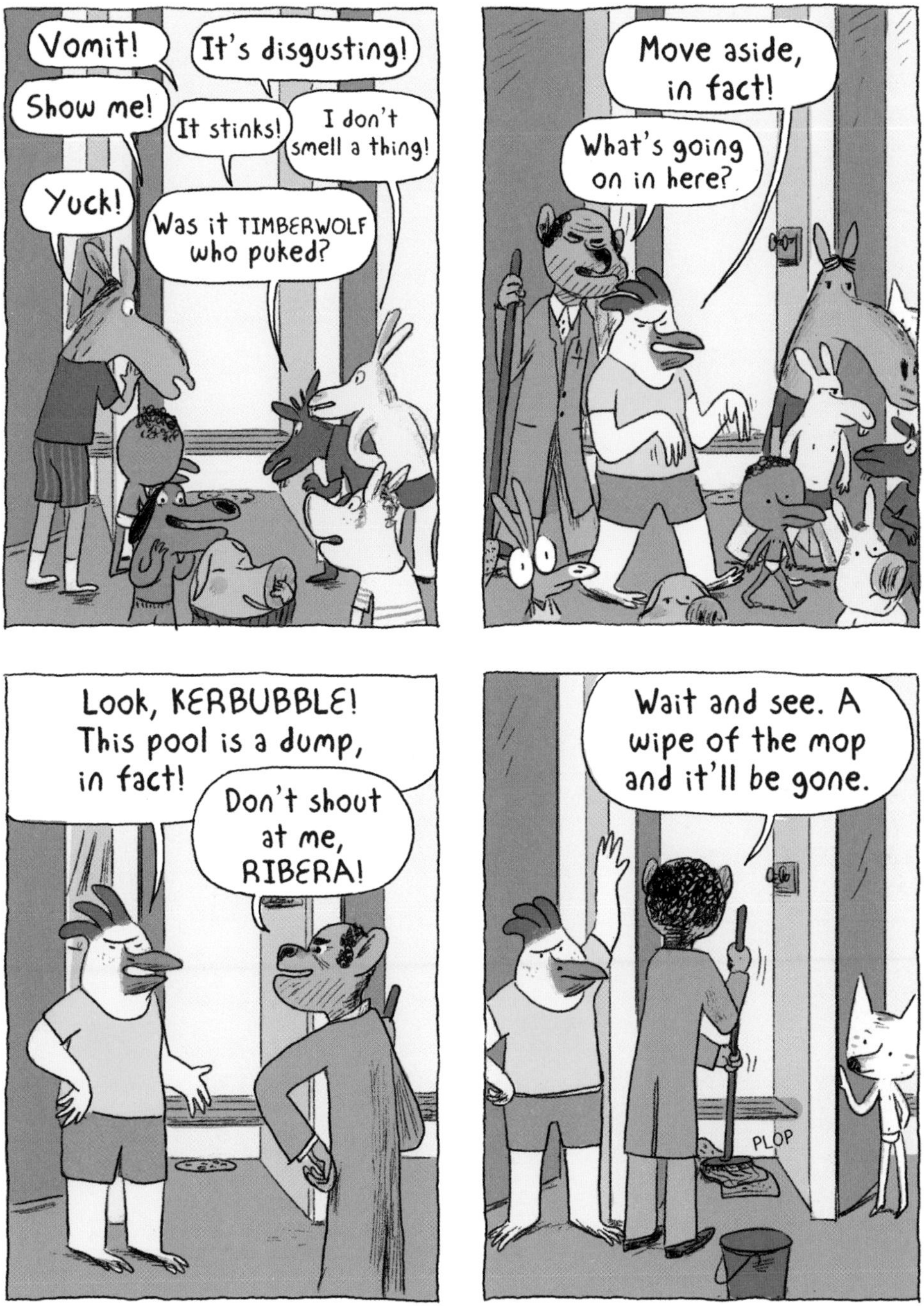
Vomit!
It's disgusting!
Show me!
It stinks!
I don't smell a thing!
Yuck!
Was it TIMBERWOLF who puked?
Move aside, in fact!
What's going on in here?
Look, KERBUBBLE! This pool is a dump, in fact!
Don't shout at me, RIBERA!
Wait and see. A wipe of the mop and it'll be gone.
PLOP

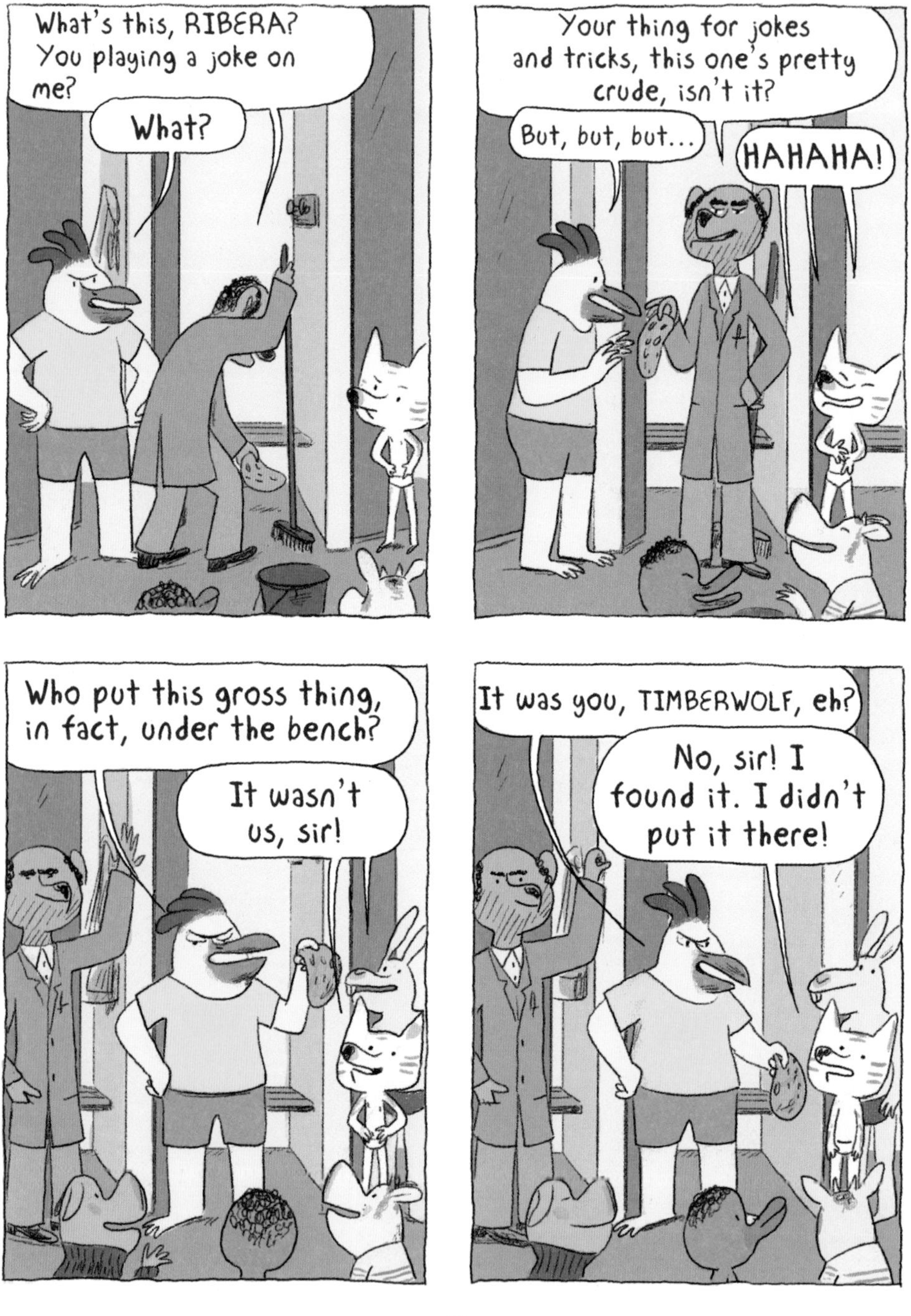
What's this, RIBERA? You playing a joke on me?
What?
Your thing for jokes and tricks, this one's pretty crude, isn't it?
But, but, but...
HAHAHA!
Who put this gross thing, in fact, under the bench?
It wasn't us, sir!
It was you, TIMBERWOLF, eh?
No, sir! I found it. I didn't put it there!

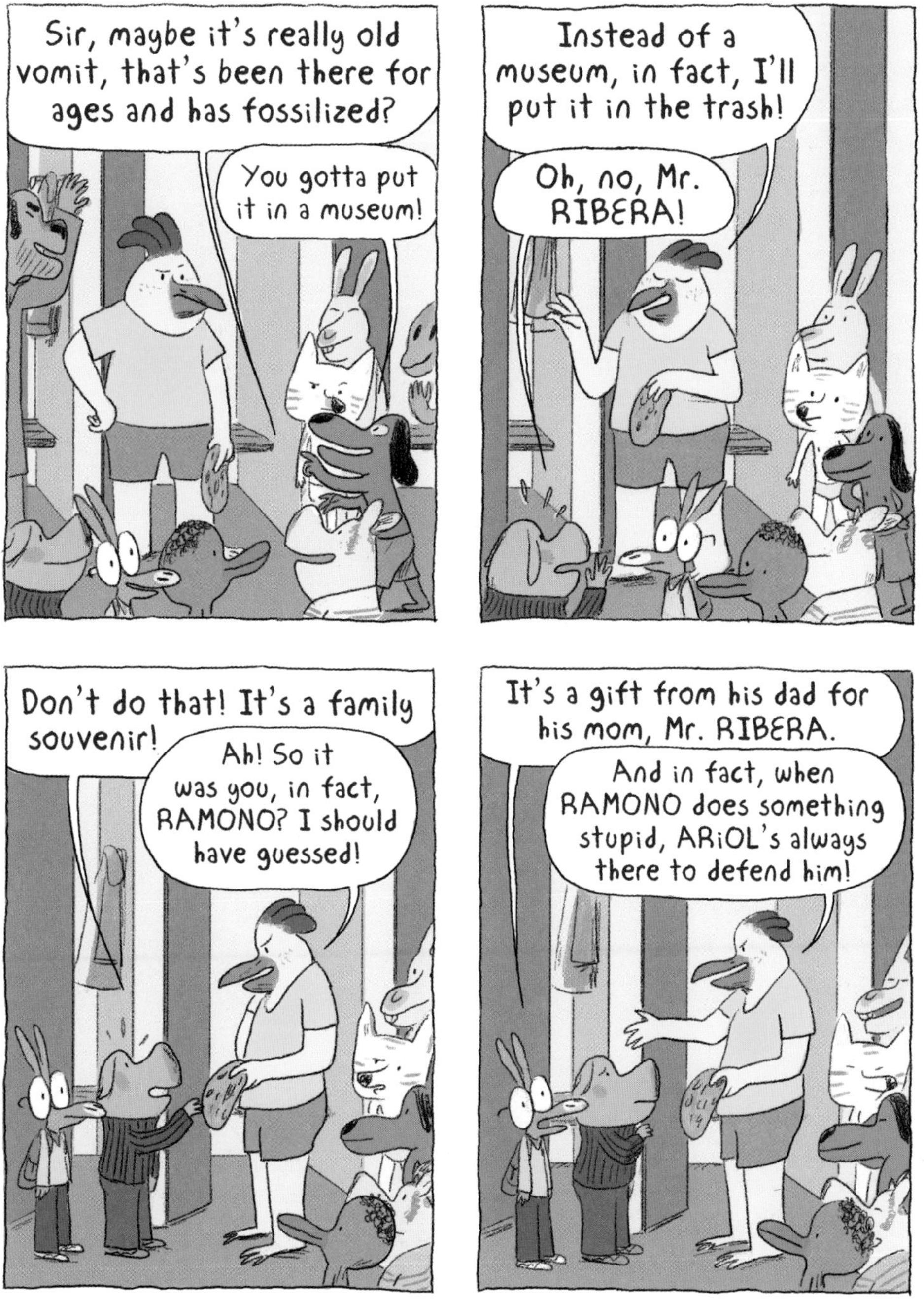
Sir, maybe it's really old vomit, that's been there for ages and has fossilized?
You gotta put it in a museum!
Instead of a museum, in fact, I'll put it in the trash!
Oh, no, Mr. RIBERA!
Don't do that! It's a family souvenir!
Ah! So it was you, in fact, RAMONO? I should have guessed!
It's a gift from his dad for his mom, Mr. RIBERA.
And in fact, when RAMONO does something stupid, ARiOL's always there to defend him!

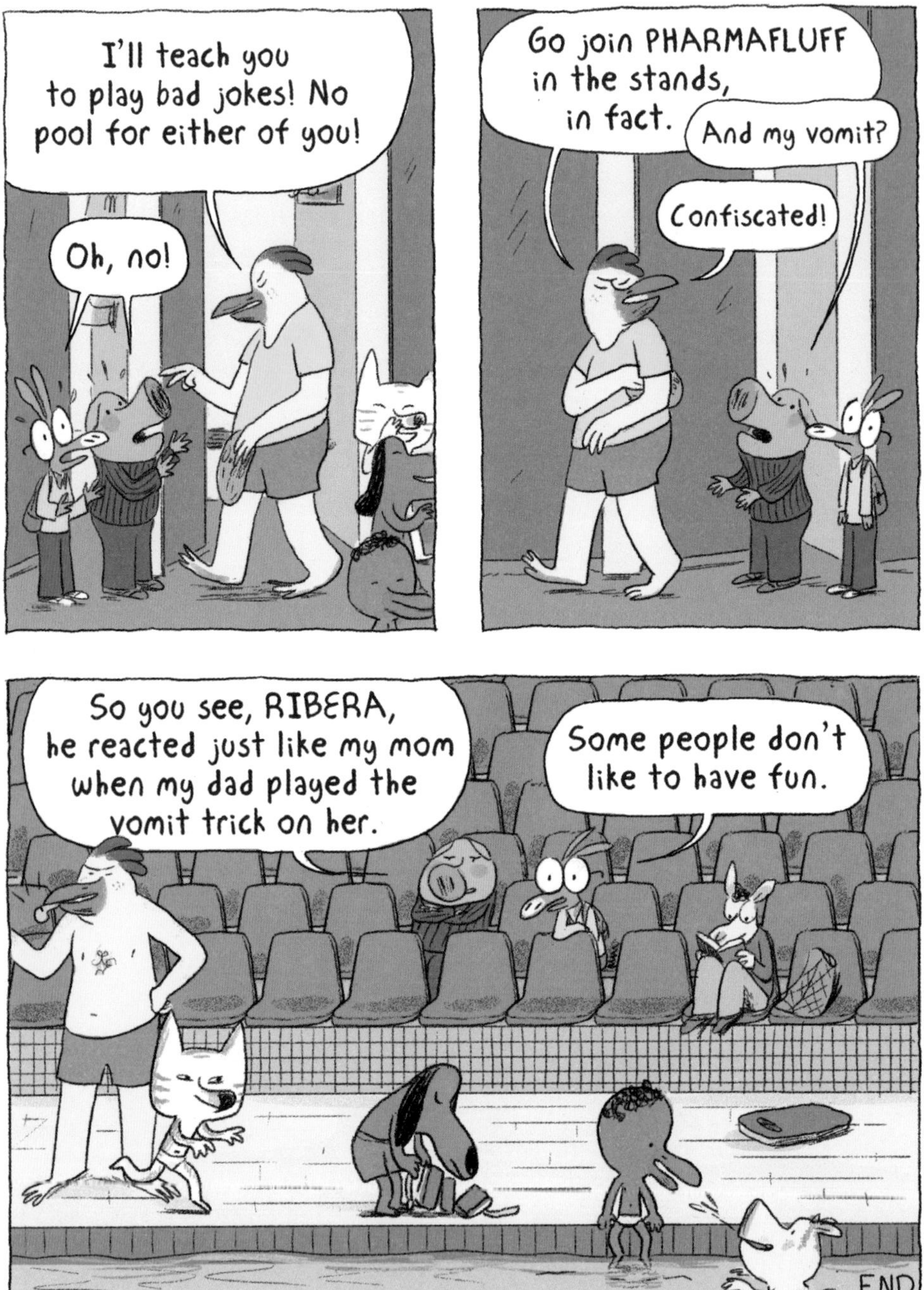
I'll teach you to play bad jokes! No pool for either of you!
Oh, no!
Go join PHARMAFLUFF in the stands, in fact.
And my vomit?
Confiscated!
So you see, RIBERA, he reacted just like my mom when my dad played the vomit trick on her.
Some people don't like to have fun.
END

ARiOL

You've Got to Choose, Ariol

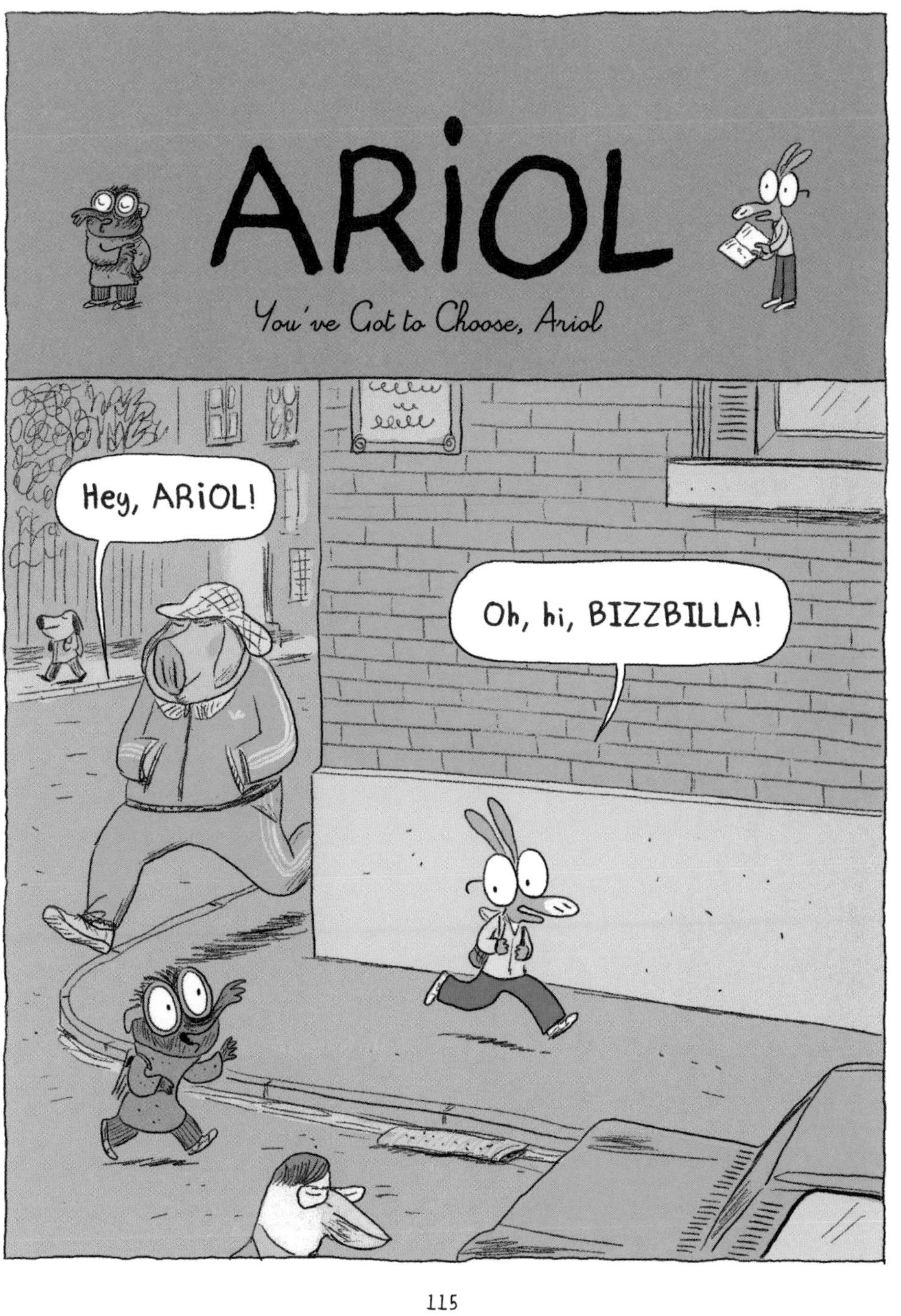

Hey, ARiOL!
Oh, hi, BIZZBILLA!

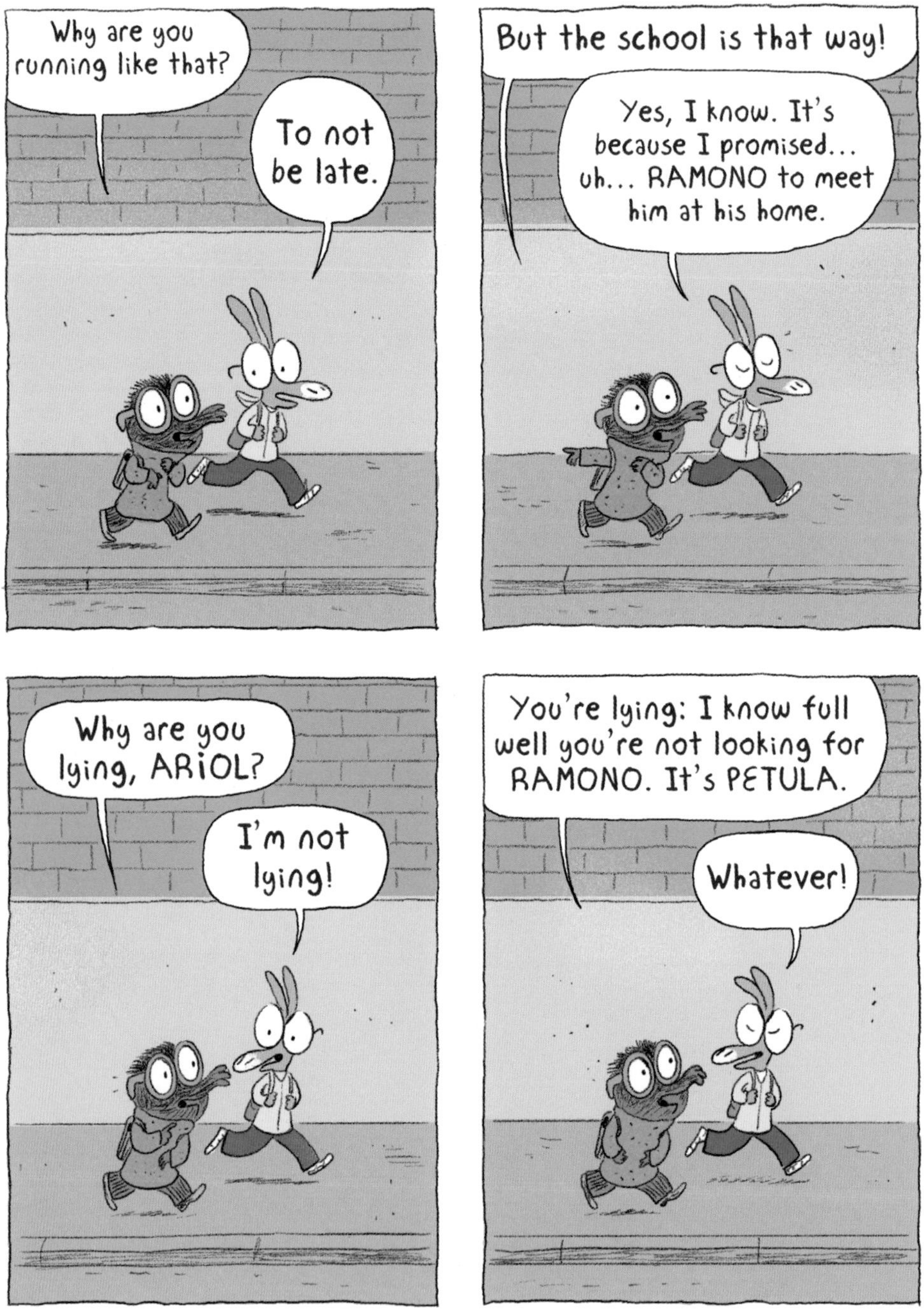

Why are you running like that?
To not be late.
But the school is that way!
Yes, I know. It's because I promised... uh... RAMONO to meet him at his home.
Why are you lying, ARiOL?
I'm not lying!
You're lying: I know full well you're not looking for RAMONO. It's PETULA.
Whatever!

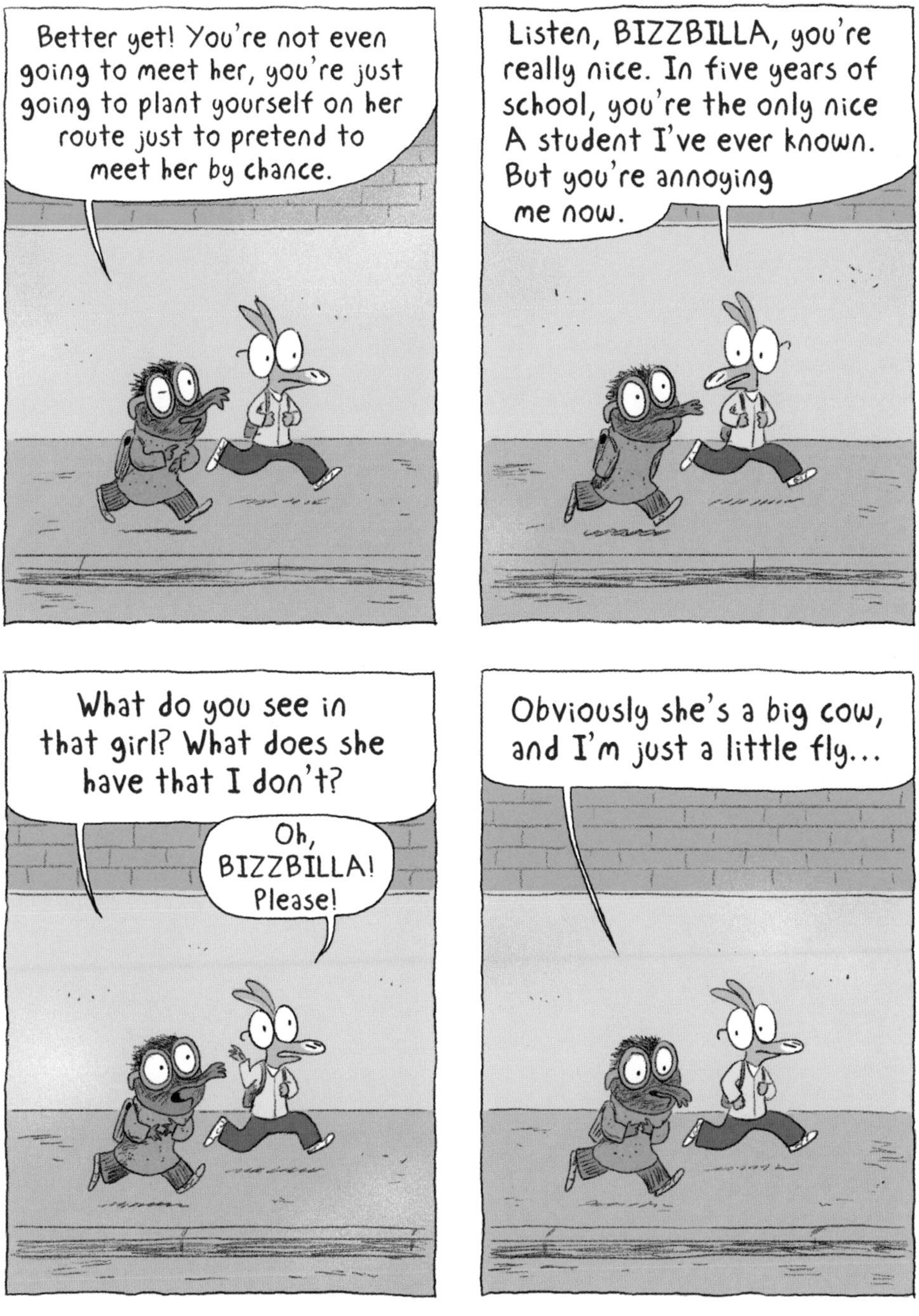
Better yet! You're not even going to meet her, you're just going to plant yourself on her route just to pretend to meet her by chance.
Listen, BIZZBILLA, you're really nice. In five years of school, you're the only nice A student I've ever known. But you're annoying me now.
What do you see in that girl? What does she have that I don't?
Oh, BIZZBILLA! Please!
Obviously she's a big cow, and I'm just a little fly...

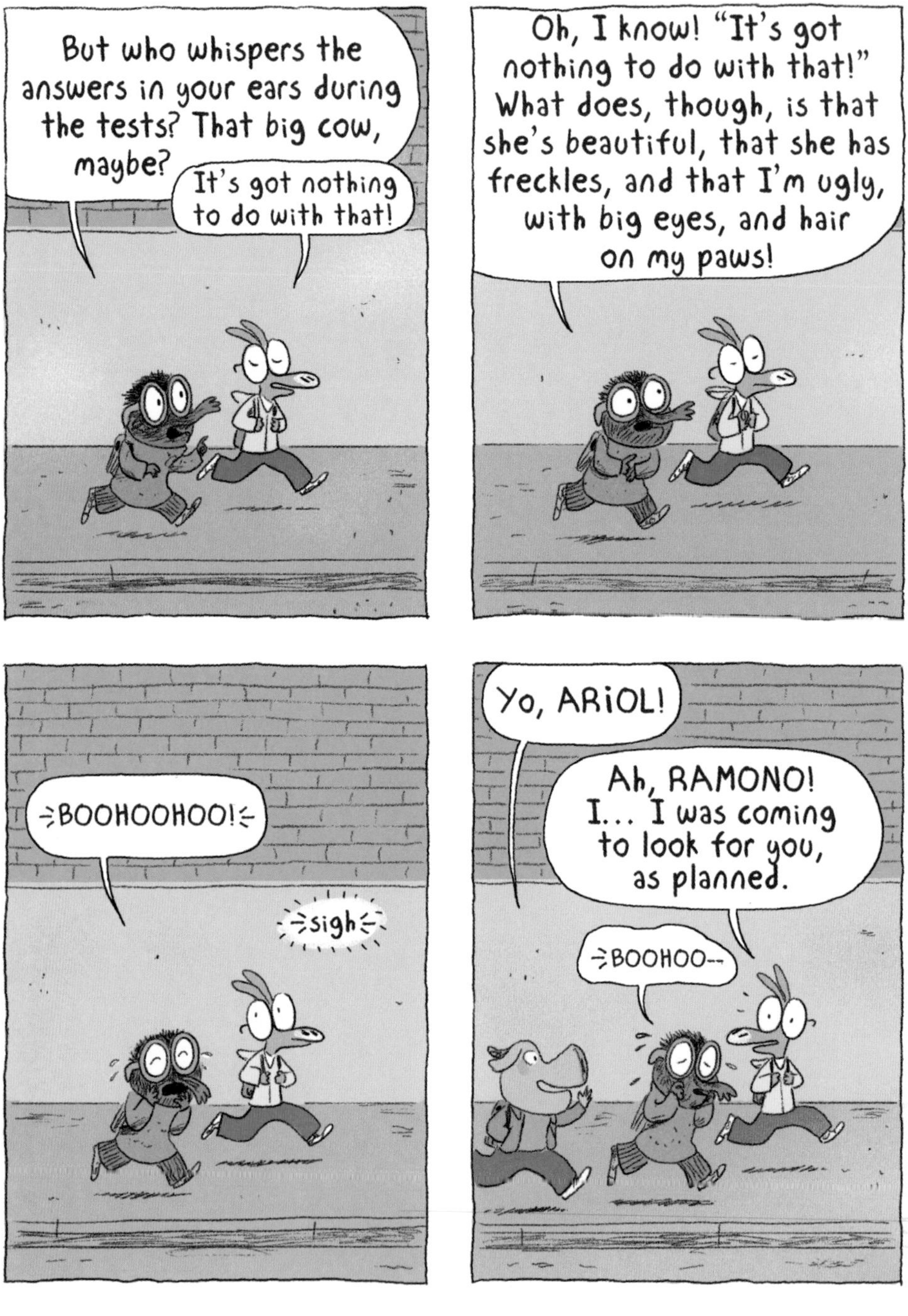

But who whispers the answers in your ears during the tests? That big cow, maybe?
It's got nothing to do with that!
Oh, I know! "It's got nothing to do with that!" What does, though, is that she's beautiful, that she has freckles, and that I'm ugly, with big eyes, and hair on my paws!
BOOHOOHOO!
sigh
Yo, ARIOL!
Ah, RAMONO! I... I was coming to look for you, as planned.
BOOHOO--

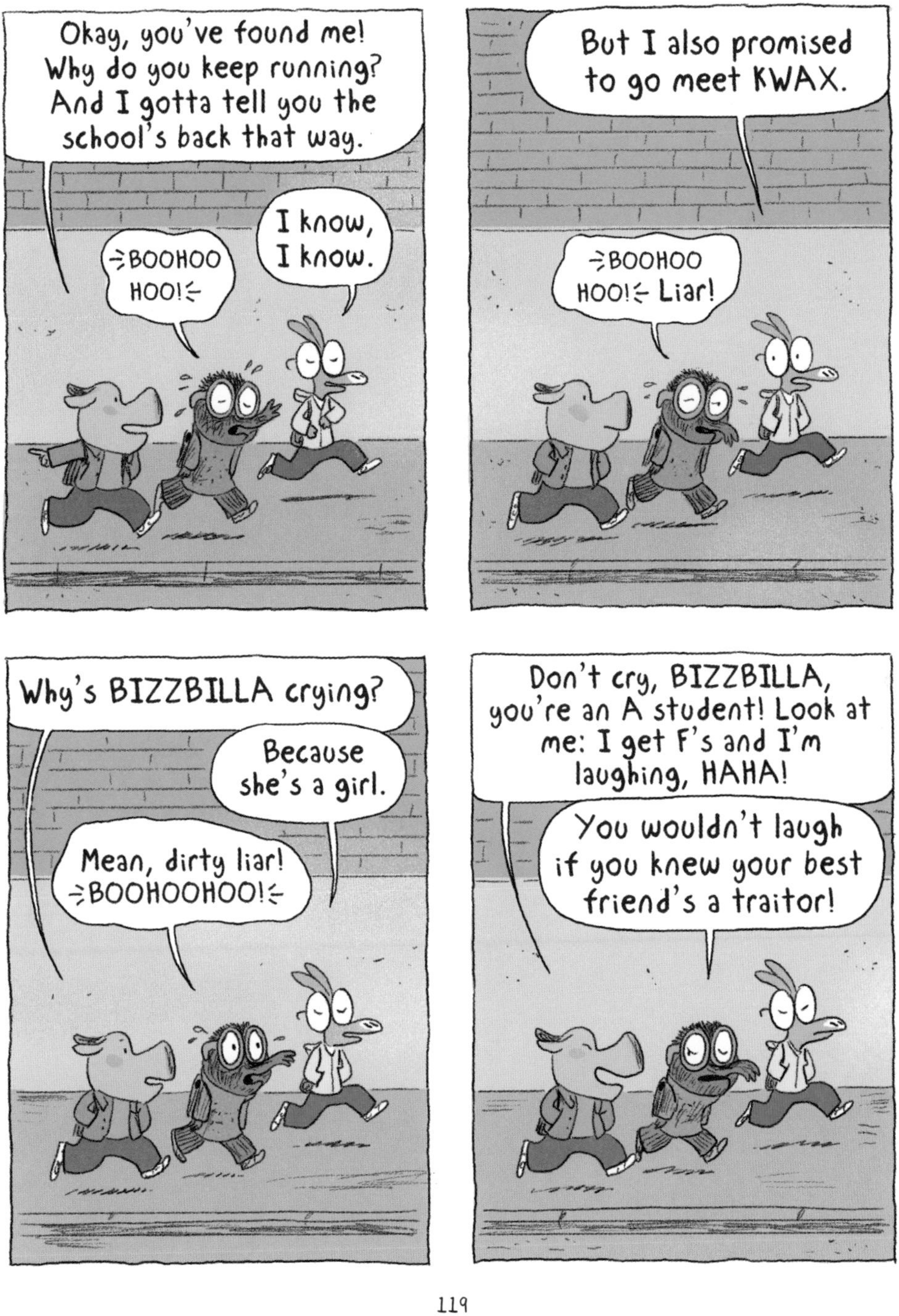
Okay, you've found me! Why do you keep running? And I gotta tell you the school's back that way.
BOOHOO HOO!
I know, I know.
But I also promised to go meet KWAX.
BOOHOO HOO! Liar!
Why's BIZZBILLA crying?
Because she's a girl.
Mean, dirty liar! BOOHOOHOO!
Don't cry, BIZZBILLA, you're an A student! Look at me: I get F's and I'm laughing, HAHA!
You wouldn't laugh if you knew your best friend's a traitor!

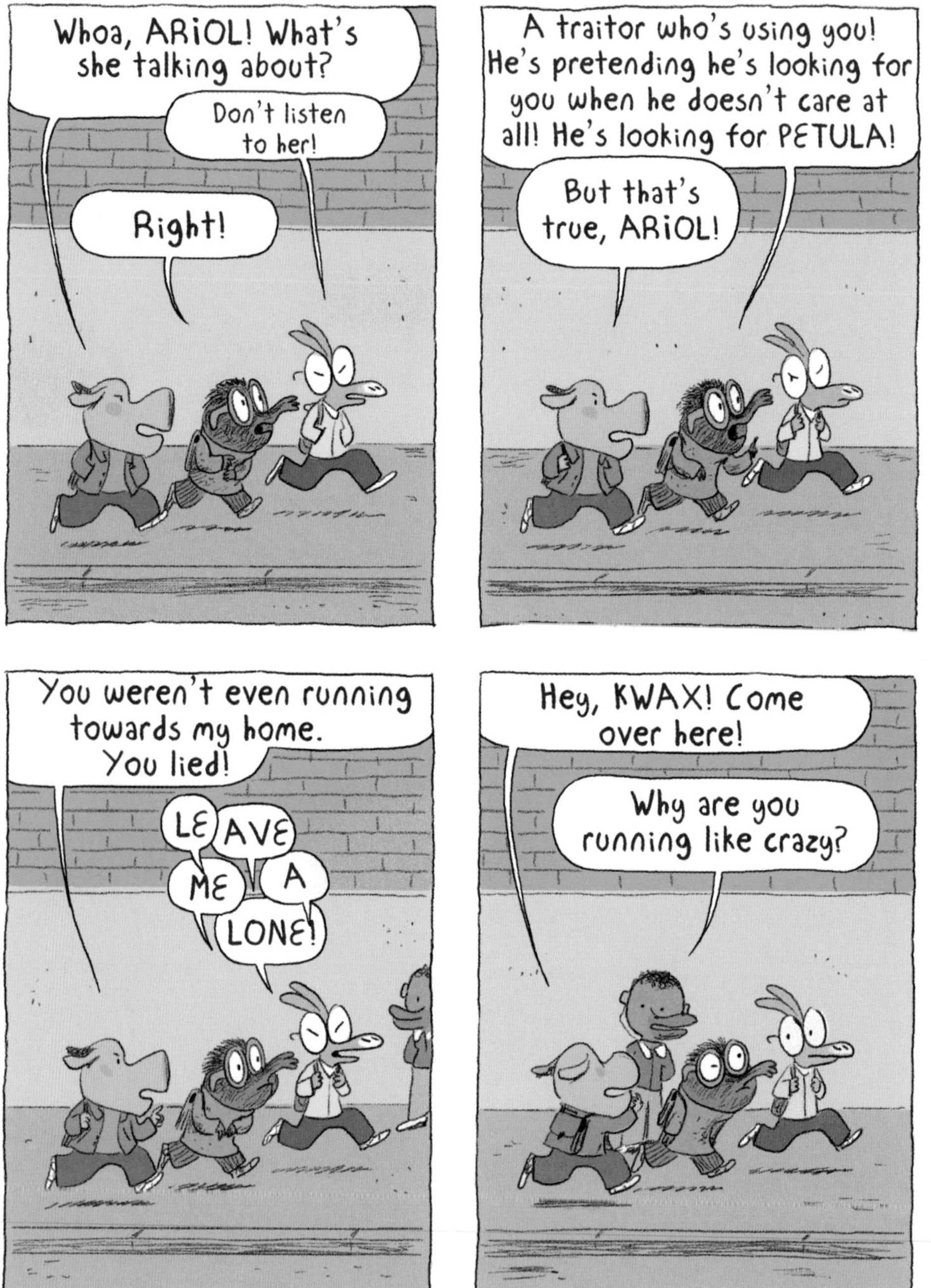

Whoa, ARIOL! What's she talking about?
Don't listen to her!
Right!
A traitor who's using you! He's pretending he's looking for you when he doesn't care at all! He's looking for PETULA!
But that's true, ARIOL!
You weren't even running towards my home. You lied!
LE AVE ME A LONE!
Hey, KWAX! Come over here!
Why are you running like crazy?

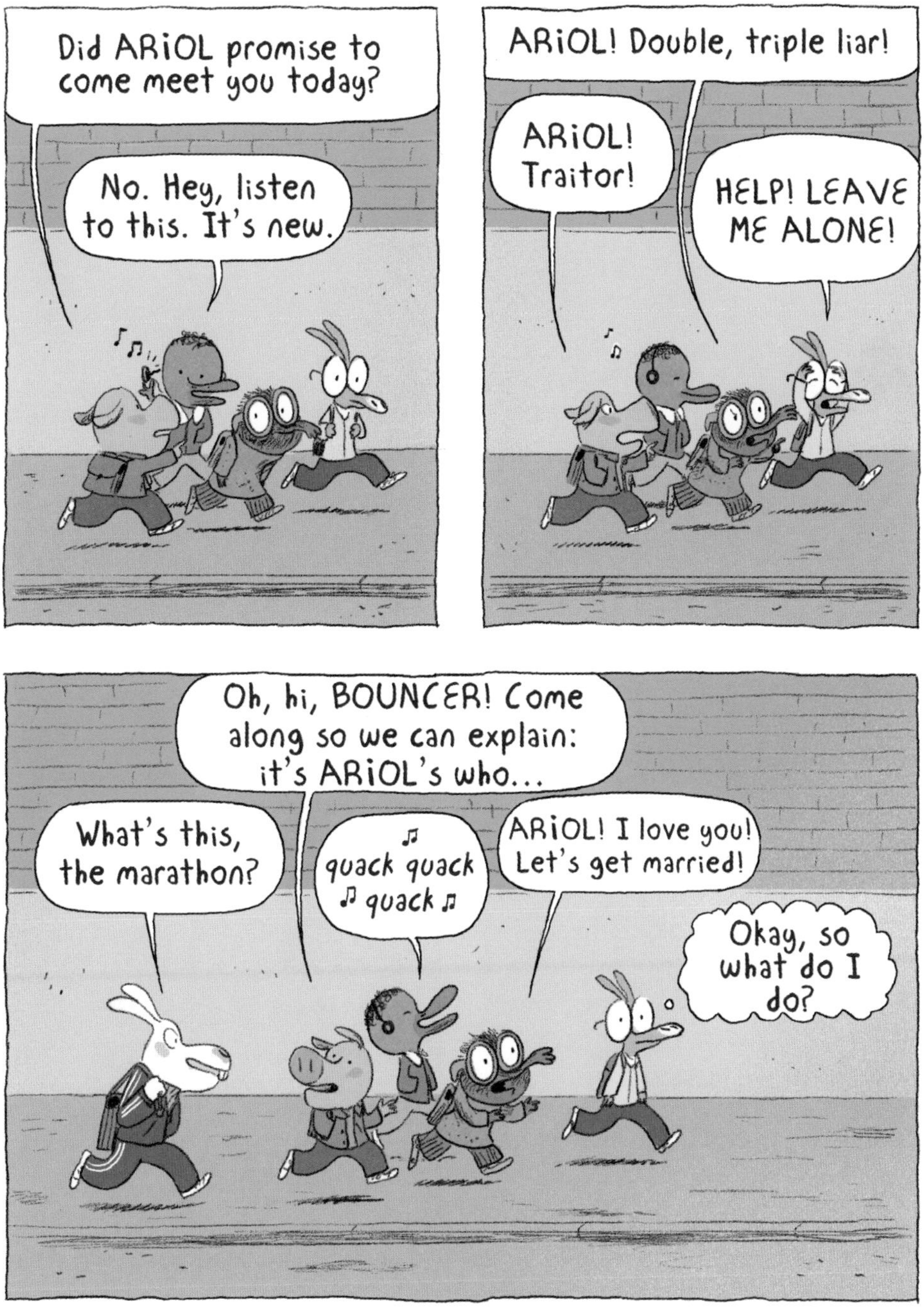
Did ARiOL promise to come meet you today?
No. Hey, listen to this. It's new.
ARiOL! Double, triple liar!
ARiOL! Traitor!
HELP! LEAVE ME ALONE!
Oh, hi, BOUNCER! Come along so we can explain: it's ARiOL's who...
What's this, the marathon?
♫ quack quack ♫ quack ♫
ARiOL! I love you! Let's get married!
Okay, so what do I do?

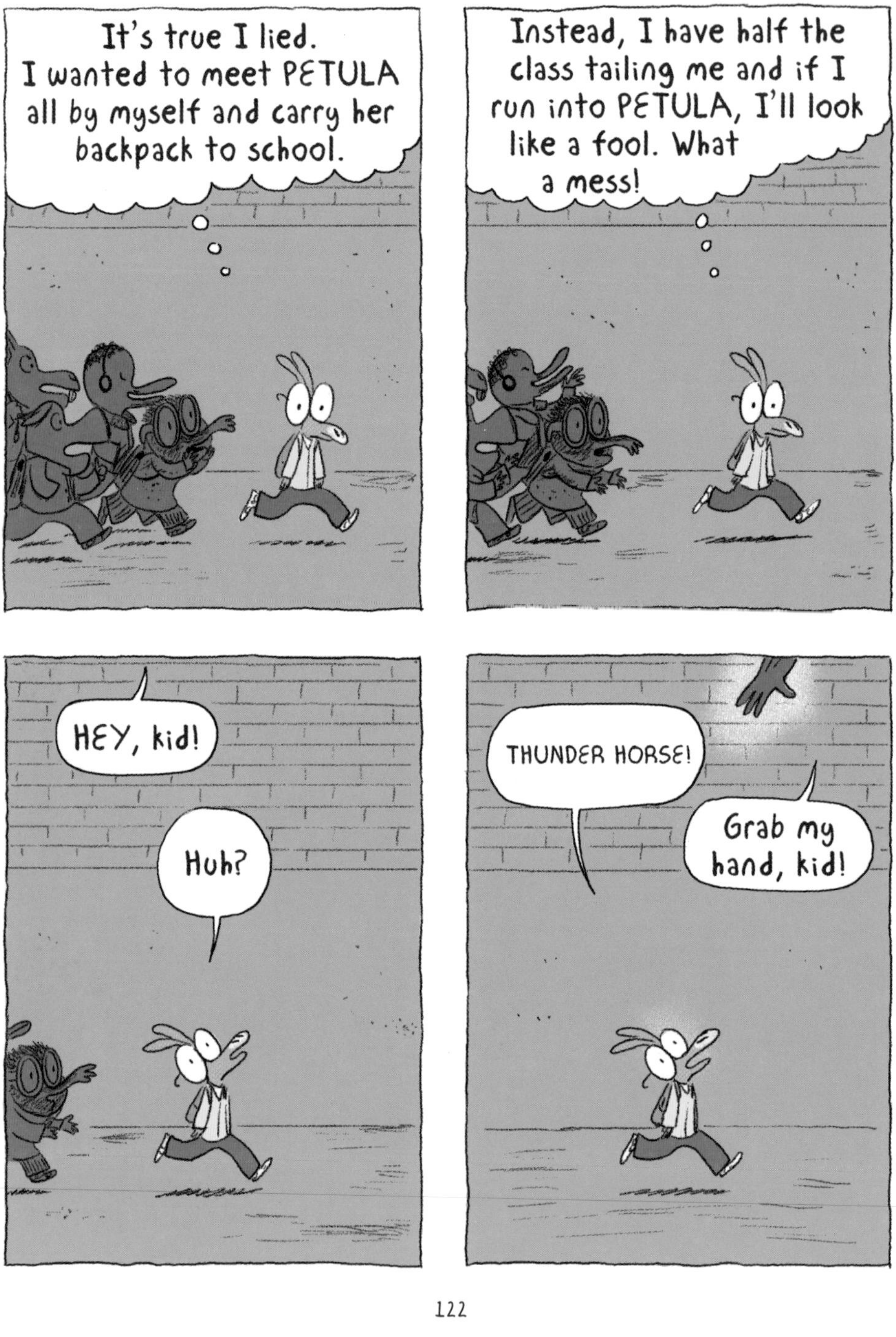

It's true I lied. I wanted to meet PETULA all by myself and carry her backpack to school.
Instead, I have half the class tailing me and if I run into PETULA, I'll look like a fool. What a mess!
HEY, kid!
Huh?
THUNDER HORSE!
Grab my hand, kid!

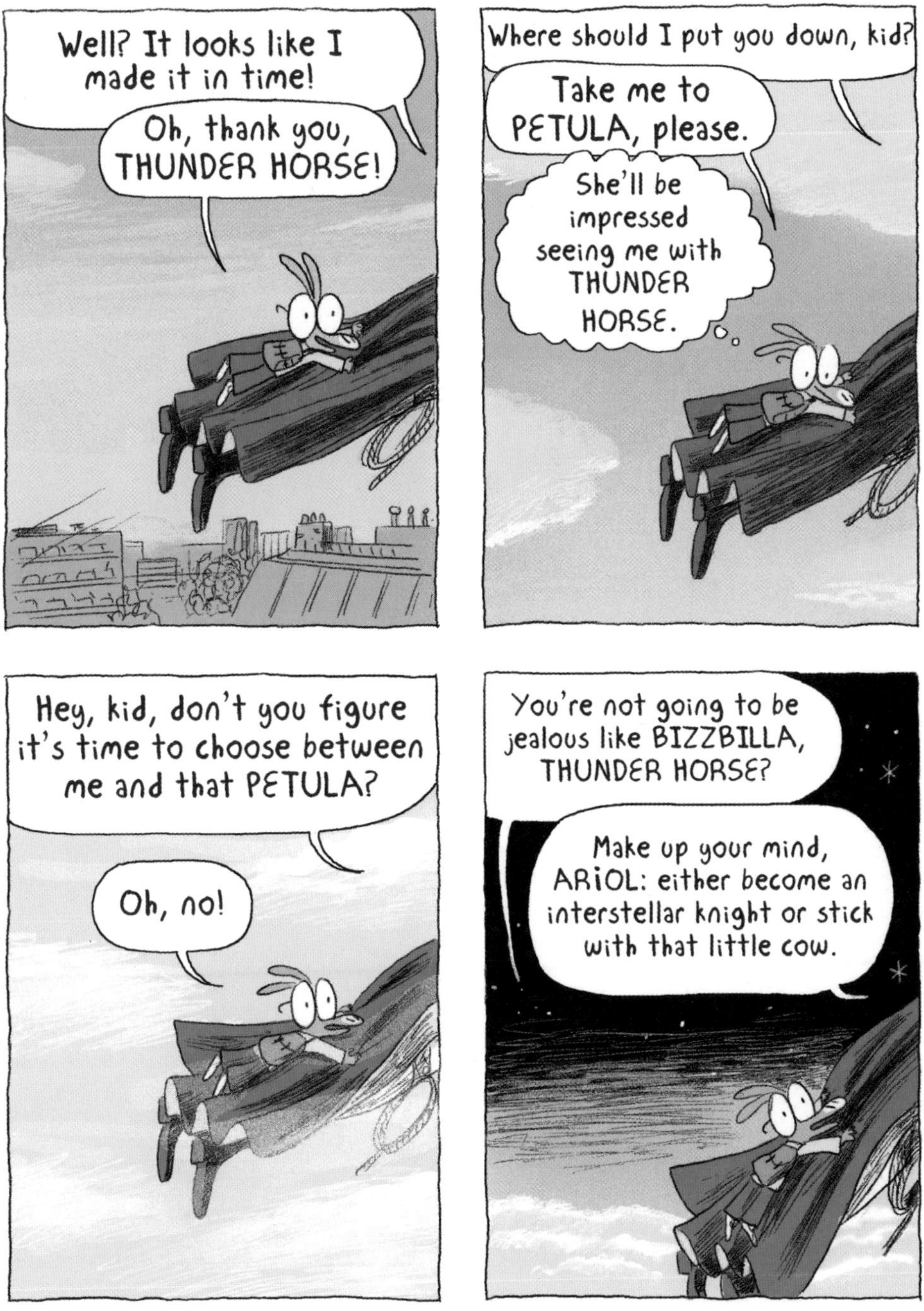

Well? It looks like I made it in time!
Oh, thank you, THUNDER HORSE!
Where should I put you down, kid?
Take me to PETULA, please.
She'll be impressed seeing me with THUNDER HORSE.
Hey, kid, don't you figure it's time to choose between me and that PETULA?
Oh, no!
You're not going to be jealous like BIZZBILLA, THUNDER HORSE?
Make up your mind, ARIOL: either become an interstellar knight or stick with that little cow.

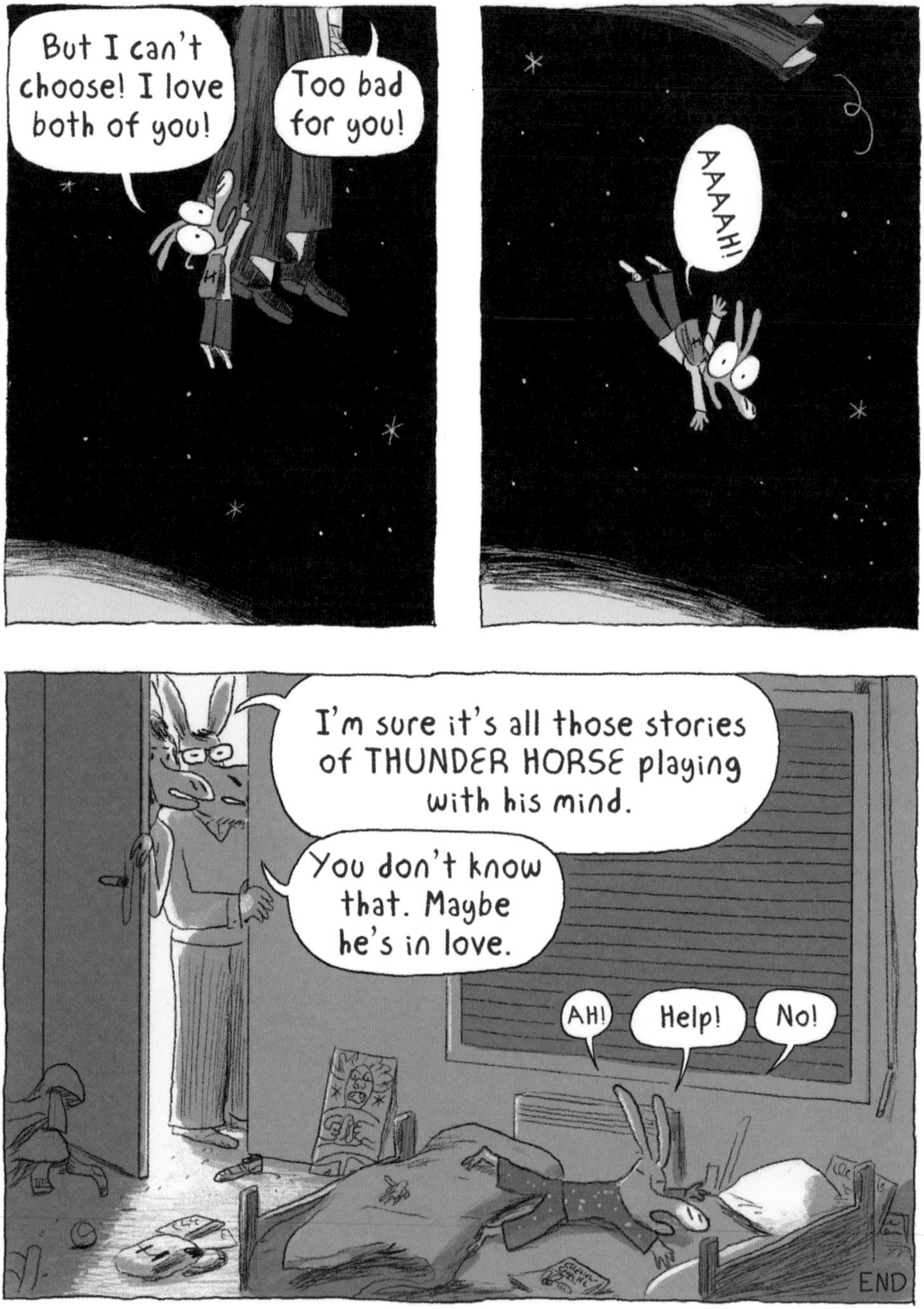
But I can't choose! I love both of you!
Too bad for you!
AAAAH!
I'm sure it's all those stories of THUNDER HORSE playing with his mind.
You don't know that. Maybe he's in love.
AH!
Help!
No!
END

WATCH OUT FOR PAPERCUTZ

Welcome to the flappable first ARiOL graphic novel by Emmanuel Guibert and Marc Boutavant from Papercutz, the folks dedicated to creating great graphic novels for all ages. I'm Jim Salicrup, Editor-in-Chief and wannabe zoologist, here to share a few behind-the-scenes secrets concerning ARiOL.

First off, we would like to thank the wonderful Janna Morishima, who was ever-so-briefly our Marketing Director (before Jesse Post), for suggesting that Papercutz publish ARiOL. Janna is someone who has done a lot to promote comics for kids, as an editor at Scholastic, and as the Director of Diamond Kids, at Diamond Comic Distributors, so when she mentioned she'd love too see the French comics series ARiOL available in America in English, we listened. And before you knew it, Papercutz publisher Terry Nantier had done the deal (He's really good at that!).

Papercutz is proud to not only create such comics as ANNOYING ORANGE, LEGO® NINJAGO, NANCY DREW AND THE CLUE CREW, POWER RANGERS, THE THREE STOOGES, STARDOLL, and others, but to be able to publish the English language editions of some of the world's greatest comics too. Papercutz titles such as DANCE CLASS, ERNEST & REBECCA, MONSTER, THE SMURFS, and SYBIL THE BACKPACK FAIRY were all originally published in French. So it's only natural that we add ARiOL-- it's exactly the kind of comic we love, featuring great characters, great stories, and great artwork.

And that's the real secret. The way we choose which titles to publish at Papercutz, is that we pick the comics we most want to see ourselves. After all, if we're not passionate and super-excited about our books, how can we possibly expect anyone else to be?

Thanks,

JiM

STAY IN TOUCH!

EMAIL: papercutz@papercutz.com
WEB: www.papercutz.com
TWITTER: @papercutzgn
FACEBOOK: PAPERCUTZGRAPHICNOVELS
REGULAR MAIL: Papercutz, 160 Broadway, Suite 700, East Wing, New York, NY 10038

Other Great Titles From PAPERCUTZ™

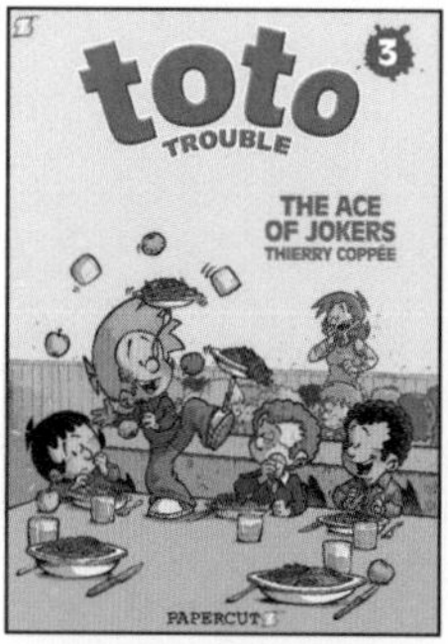
toto 3
TROUBLE
THE ACE OF JOKERS
THIERRY COPPÉE
PAPERCUTZ

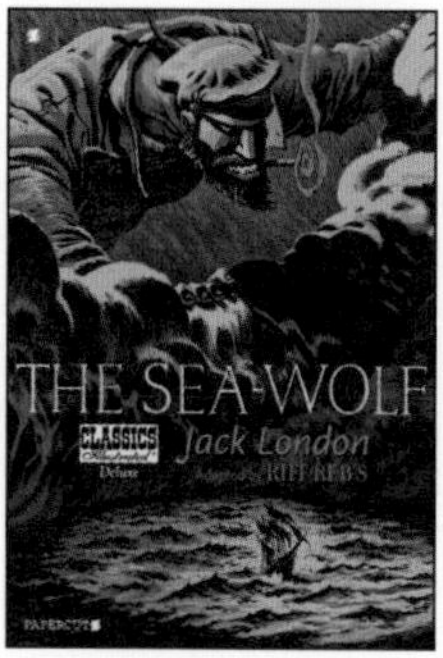
THE SEA-WOLF
CLASSICS
Jack London
PAPERCUTZ

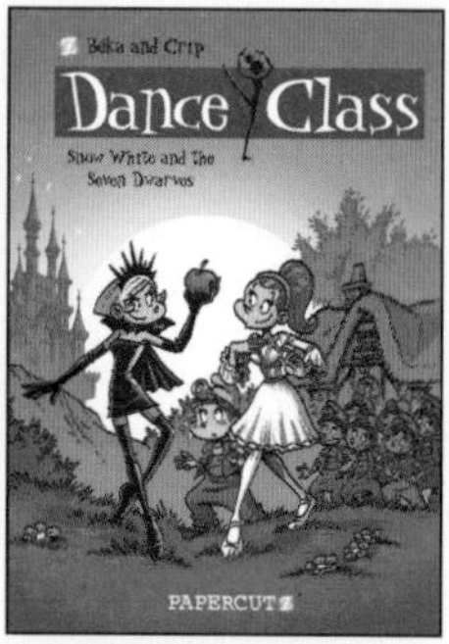
Béka and Crip
Dance Class
Snow White and The Seven Dwarves
PAPERCUTZ

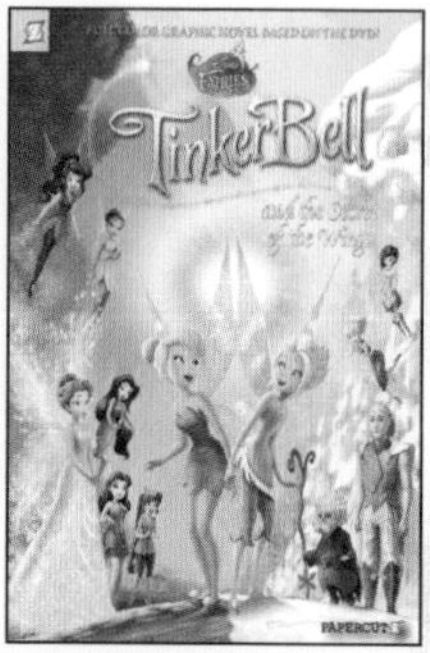
TinkerBell
PAPERCUTZ

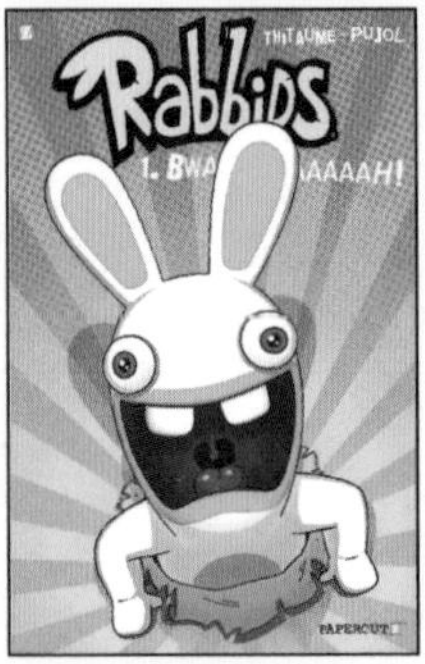
THITAUME · PUJOL
Rabbids
PAPERCUTZ

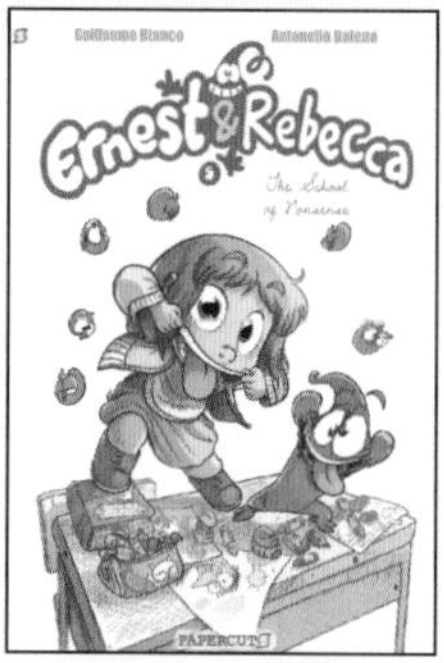
Ernest & Rebecca
PAPERCUTZ

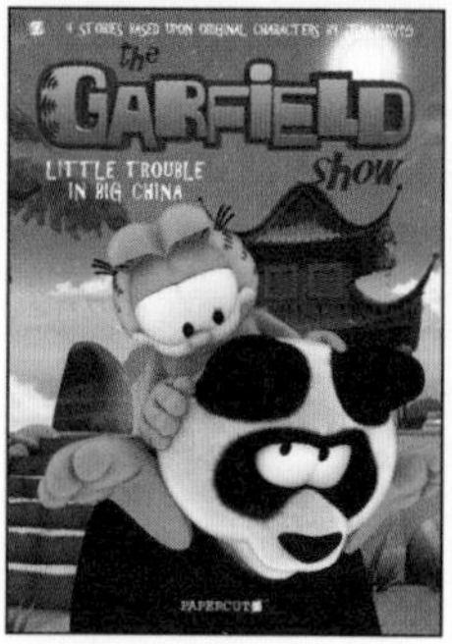
The GARFIELD Show
LITTLE TROUBLE IN BIG CHINA
PAPERCUTZ

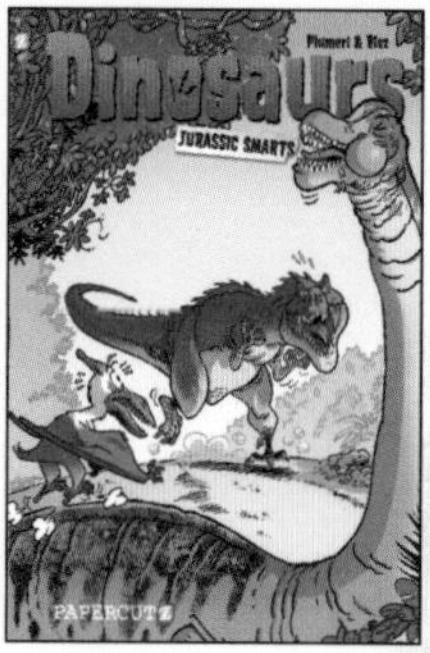
Dinosaurs
JURASSIC SMARTS
PAPERCUTZ

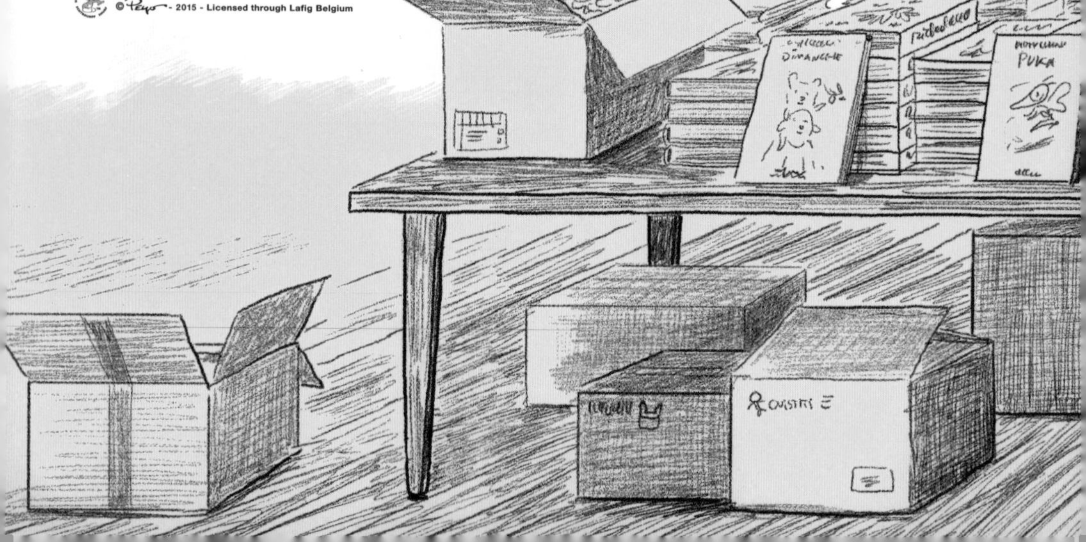

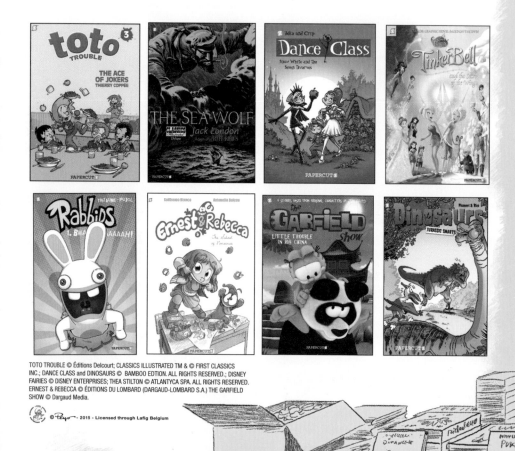

And Don't Forget . . .

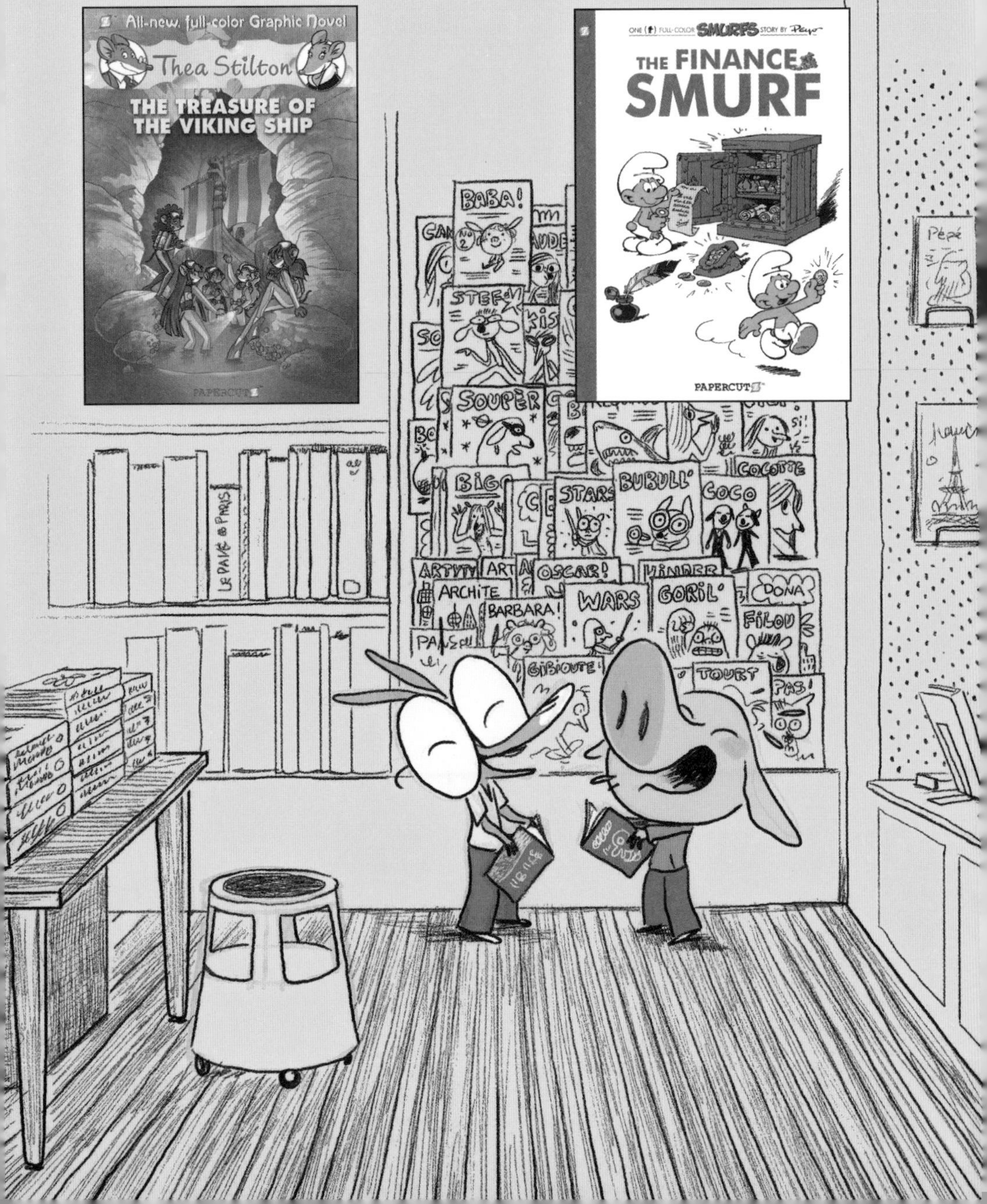
All-new, full-color Graphic Novel
Thea Stilton
THE TREASURE OF THE VIKING SHIP
PAPERCUT
ONE FULL-COLOR SMURFS STORY BY Peyo
THE FINANCE SMURF
PAPERCUT
BABA!
STEF
SOUPÈR
BIGO
STARS
BUBULL'
COCO
COCOTTE
LE PAVÉ DE PARIS
ARTYTY
OSCAR!
ARCHITE
BARBARA!
WARS
GORIL'
DONA
FILOU
GIBIOUTE!
TOURT
PAS!
Pépé